I0760958

ELIANA

KINGDOM OF FAIRYTALES
SEASON FIVE

You all know the story of your favorite fairytale, but did you ever wonder what happened after the fairytale ending? Well we know. Not all afters end up happily, sometimes the real adventure starts much later...

Following famous fairytale characters, eighteen years after their happily ever after, the Kingdom of Fairytales offers an edge of the seat thrill ride in an all new and sensational way to read.

Lighting-fast reads you won't be able to put down

Fantasy has never been so epic!

KINGDOM OF FAIRYTALES
URBIS PRISON
BADALAH
DESERT
DRACONIS
SHIPLEY
THE VALE
AZREN
KISBU
ZHORE
MOSA
ABORIA
ELDER
URBIS
AZURE
ENCHANTIA
AIRE
SKYLA
EMERALD CITY
OZ
FLORIS
TULIS
THE FORGE
ARCADIA
RENAIS
MELFALL
ATLANTICE
ANTLA
W
E
S

ISBN: 978-1-989997-27-7
Enchanted Quill Press

Contaact the author at www.enchantedquillpress.com
Cover by Enchanted Quilll Press
Interior Formatting by Enchanted Quill Press
Editing by Rose Lipscomb

QUEEN OF UNICORNS

22ND APRIL

I woke with a kick in my belly and a curse on my lips.

Rumpelstiltskin.

The oath was a childhood swear, and I wanted to say *much* worse as I bit back the jolt of pain. Turning on my side, I cradled my stomach—and the life inside of me it held. Methodically, I rubbed a hand over my stomach in slow, soothing circles. Months of experience told me this was the surest and quickest road to relief, and this time proved no different. The kicking calmed to a less insistent flutter against my hand. Like the baby was waving at me instead of pounding a drumbeat against my bladder, the little rascal. Thankful for the respite, I hummed an absent tune under my breath, all of my energy focused on getting the baby to settle.

Hush, little one, I sang, mentally willing the child to

calm down.

At last, movement abated inside of me, my unborn child soothed. I breathed a sigh of relief, thankful for a respite for my bladder as my baby rested. My lips twitched, suppressing a chuckle. His or her nap began as my own ended.

I opened my eyes to the crystal-blue sky overhead. The day was clear, with few clouds above me to spoil it. Far off in the distance, a cadre of puffy white plumes trailed over the treetops. Water from a nearby stream—one of the little inlets in the meadow that led to the ocean—bubbled merrily in a jaunty little song. Leaving one hand on my belly, I let the other drift down to run my fingers over the lush grass of the verdant meadow. Everything was perfect here. A land of eternal sunshine and beauty. Beautiful foliage. Gorgeous weather. Nature and humans coexisting in peace. This was my own paradise and, in my opinion, more beautiful than the other eleven kingdoms put together. Not one of them could hold a torch to Vale, and this part of Vale especially. The meadows that ran down the valley in front of the palace.

It would be easy for anyone to understand why this was one of the only places I felt at peace. Why I never wanted to leave. I felt protected in the meadow. Safe. Its ethereal beauty seemed as impenetrable as a magical barrier. Nothing bad could happen here.

A bitter smile twisted my lips. Nothing bad was supposed to happen in the capital, Shipley, at all. Much less in the kingdom of Vale. But my life was a perfect indicator that things don't always happen the way that they were supposed to.

My gaze drifted down to my swollen belly once again. My left hand still rested on top of the pink fabric covering it. A simple silver band encircled my ring finger. It was pointless, now that Luka was gone. Who exactly did I need to announce my fidelity to?

Despite those thoughts, I couldn't seem to take it off. No more today than any other day in the past nine months.

Nine months since Luka left me. Not that he had any choice in the matter. The illness was mercifully brief, but devastating nonetheless, leaving me with a heart torn to shreds and, as I found out just a couple of weeks after his death, a child.

Luka's baby. That and the ring were the only things I had left of him.

I heaved myself to my feet—no easy feat with the extra weight surrounding my abdomen and without a steadying hand there to help me. I managed it the same way I'd managed most of this pregnancy—alone. There hadn't been any other choice. I swayed as my center of gravity adjusted to the new position and put a hand on my spine, grimacing as I stretched out the tension in my lower back. The grass had looked like a perfectly fine mattress, but it appeared that my body begged to differ. I ran my fingers through my long, pale-blonde hair, extracting any bits of grass that had gotten caught in it.

A soft whinny sounded behind me, interrupting my thoughts of Luka. I turned, my mouth curving up into a grin. I already knew what I'd see there.

The green fields and rolling hills weren't the only reason the meadow was my favorite place in all of the kingdom. Soft, golden eyes beneath a horn of a matching hue met mine. The intelligent gaze sat atop a long white nose.

No, that wasn't quite right. Its color wasn't exactly white. The color of its snout was closer to a pearl, with a shimmering metallic sheen bordering on a pale silver, the same color as its wings.

A little thrill of pleasure shot through me, and I reached out a hand to greet the winged unicorn as it took a shy step forward to meet me. It left the shelter of the trees to nuzzle first against my palm and then butted my hip with its nose, looking for my pockets, searching for a treat.

It found the pockets, but there was nothing inside. Finding none, it huffed in disappointment and nuzzled at my cheek. This was a young one, I discerned from its wide eyes and brightly shining horn. The glimmer of a unicorn's spear dulled slightly as they aged. But she wasn't so young that I'd call her a filly, nor old enough that I'd consider her a mare. By unicorn standards, I'd call her a teenager. A newcomer at that. I knew most of the unicorns that lived in the valley and the meadows surrounding the palace, but sometimes, a new one would appear.

I put a finger to my chin playfully when it continued to nose at my dress, hoping it had just missed a treat that I'd been hiding inside. "Do you happen to know any young unicorns who may be in need of a snack? I have some treats I've been looking to offload." The unicorn's ears pricked up, standing at attention as it let out a joyful neigh. Even the unicorns that didn't know me always understood what I said when it came to snacks. Among the people of Vale, I'd become known as The Unicorn Princess. It was a silly title, but one I liked. I'd never really found my talent, so the unicorns were all I had. The unicorn renewed its search of my dress with vigor, and I laughed as I pushed it away. It was impossible to retain my morose mood in the face of her kind. They were creatures of pure joy and light. They sucked up the darkness and spat out delight.

Intending to have a picnic, I'd brought a straw basket with me to the meadow. It still rested beside my napping spot, where my imprint still showed, blades of grass squashed by my pregnant body. The unicorn followed me there as I turned to open it and peruse its contents.

"Let's see here..." I muttered as I shifted items aside in search of something she'd like. I'd brought red apples instead of the green ones that unicorns generally preferred, but...

I held out the cheery red fruit in question, and she pranced in place, jerking her head away. If she had the ability, she'd have wrinkled her nose and scrunched up her face in disgust.

"I thought not." I chuckled, eyes scanning the shadows of the basket. "All right, all right. What else do I have...?" A block of cheese... some distilled water in a flask... and...

"Aha!" I crowed in victory, emerging from the basket with my prize and unwrapping it from the brown paper I'd folded it inside. The teenage unicorn's nostrils flared as the paper crinkled. It released the nutty scent of the food inside.

She let out a horsey squeal of delight. I'd barely freed the sandwich from its wrappings when it was snatched from my hand, her lips brushing the tips of my fingers. "Watch it," I warned with a teasing tone. "Teeth nearly got me there, young one."

She gobbled down it with glee and licked her lips, searching for any hint of a taste that it had left behind. A little known fact: unicorns go crazy for peanut butter and jelly. She whickered an inquiry, craning her neck to look behind me at the open picnic basket.

I shrugged. "Sorry. That's all I've got." It had been my lunch, too, which meant I'd be returning to the palace sooner rather than later. The fruit and cheese would tide me over until I could raid the kitchens later.

The unicorn seemed to accept my apology, bumping her nose at my elbow until I raised my arm to let her underneath. I settled back down onto the ground, and she folded her knees until she lay beside me and rested her chin lightly just a little higher than my belly.

I looked down at her, raising my brow. "You realize that's my unborn child that you're using as a pillow, don't you?" I asked dryly.

The unicorn didn't move, angling her eyes up as innocently as a puppy begging for scraps.

I melted. How could I not? I swore if she had shoulders, she would have shrugged in response as if to say "*Eh. What are you gonna do*?"

According to my parents, unicorn sightings were once rare in Vale, but something changed many years ago, and their population exploded.

I wasn't sure I believed that.

It seemed impossible in a kingdom that had a combination stable-aviary that was specifically designed to cater to unicorns: the staviary. It was unbelievable in a world where there were *plenty* of unicorns. They peered at humans from safe distances, from the shadows of trees and around corners. *Everyone* who bothered to occasionally leave the city had seen a unicorn. They preferred open pastures and wide, free spaces—uncrowded by stone buildings that obscured the skies. And really, who could blame them?

My gaze ascended to the sky above me. I, for one,

understood perfectly. A person could *breathe* out here. You could think away from all of the crowds and noise. My fingers absently stroked the unicorn's coat. There was no pleasure like it in the world, the feeling like spun silk beneath my fingers. Indescribably soft. Lulled into relaxation by my ministrations, she grunted and shifted to get comfortable. Her eyes slowly closed until she fell into the soft, rhythmic breath of sleep. I smiled, watching her. Everyone had seen unicorns... but I didn't know of anyone else who was as lucky as I was. They were skittish creatures. They watched, but they did not approach. They believed in a look-but-don't-touch philosophy upon first meeting. It took most people multiple meetings with a single unicorn to coax them close enough to touch. It took time for the unicorns to trust them. That wasn't the case with me, though. I couldn't go for a walk without at least one coming to join me, hence my title. Since Luka died, they had been my only companions... well, almost only companions. I still had Jay. The young unicorn shifted in her sleep and nudged my belly with her nose. The baby in my womb softly kicked in response, ready to fight back. I was going to have fun with this little one, I mused, sleepily.

I felt a swell of affection toward the dozing unicorn in my lap. "Perhaps you'd like to come home with me," I whispered. "I could always use another friend. We could give you a name. How do you feel about Misty?"

One golden eye opened, and she sighed. I took it as a sign of acquiescence. "You'll like the staviary," I promised. We have unicorns that work at the palace. I let out a yawn. Pregnancy was incredibly tiring. As the unicorn was napping on me, I used it as an excuse to close my own eyes and continue my nap.

"Well, well, what do we have here? The beautiful princess being held hostage by a pesky unicorn. What can I do to save the lady in peril?"

I didn't open my eyes, a smirk gracing my lips. I should have known he'd find me here. "It's the baby that's holding me hostage. Misty was just keeping me company."

"Misty?"

"I named her. She's being a sweetheart."

"And here I thought I was being a knight in shining armor." The soft sound of grass crushed beneath feet reached my ears as the speaker drew closer. The air cooled above me as his shadow caressed my form. The warmth gone from my face, I opened my eyes to see my friend Jay smiling down at me.

The sun haloed his head, casting him in a golden light as I looked up at him. Already a tall man, when I lay down on the ground like this, he appeared as tall as a tree, stretching to the sky. His skin was painted by years of working outdoors, and his eyes were as green as the meadow I slept in. He wore a cap over a head of soft, brown hair. Sweat beaded his forehead, and the sun colored his cheeks rosy. A bit of scruff edged his face. It appeared he hadn't taken the time to pull a razor along his face.

He grinned, a crooked, little half-smile. A smile that made half the women in the kingdom melt and the other half wish they weren't already married. It made me wonder what mischief he had in mind. Jay was the one thing that had kept me sane in the weeks following Luka's death. Where my mother had fretted and fussed, Jay had sat and listened to me as I cried. He'd talked to me for hours about Luka, and he'd been the one to hold me close when the whole world felt like it was closing in around me.

His eyes twinkled with good humor as he sat down beside me. When he accidentally nudged the unicorn's hindquarters while settling in, she bolted upright, whinnying in indignation. Her magnificent wings stretched out, and she took flight. Airborne above us, she chittered at him angrily. I had no doubt that if we could understand her, she'd be reading him the riot act. But thankfully, she didn't leave. Only grumbled, keeping her distance in the air above.

Meanwhile, his gaze skimmed my body, lingering on my swollen belly. "How are you feeling today?"

The unicorn's gaze flicked down to me, waiting for my response. Her distance made it easier to feel all of the negative emotions that her light had swallowed up. Because the truth was: I felt the same as I did every day. Scared, alone, exhausted. And gods bless it... I missed my husband.

I swallowed down all of those responses and forced a smile. "I'm fine," I said.

Jay didn't buy it. He never did. Unfortunately, one consequence of us spending so much time together in the wake of Luka's death was that he could read me like a book. "I could help, you know."

I got to my feet and brushed away the grass that clung to my skirt. "With the wild unicorns?" I asked, being deliberately obtuse as I bent down to retrieve my basket. "Don't be silly, Jay. You know how long it takes for most people to forge a bond with one. Days, weeks, months..." I looked away from him and stretched a hand toward the sky. The unicorn flew lower and nuzzled against my hand. "I know you're used to working with the unicorns that chose a life in the staviary, but I've been looking after the unicorns in the meadows for years. I've got this."

Jay rose until he stood tall above me once more and looked down at me sternly. "That wasn't what I meant, and you know it, Eliana."

My fingers, which had been gently scratching the unicorn's snout, stilled. I sighed. He never called me by my full name. He usually went with Lia. "I knew what you meant," I said softly.

"So why pretend you didn't?"

That was the funny thing. I knew what he meant when he said he could help, and he knew why I pretended I didn't. It was a heartbreaking game we'd been playing for months, and as my belly grew, so did the frequency in which we played. It was a simple game. He offered help, I pushed him away.

His hand hovered in the air before my stomach, and his eyes met mine, seeking permission. "Can I...?" he asked, trailing off.

I nodded. He placed a hand over my stomach and pushed out a breath from between his lips. "Wow," he breathed. "Peanut's gotten so *big*."

I couldn't help but grin as he used my favorite nickname for my little boy or girl . The tension I'd been feeling drifted away. My hand joined his on my belly, touching the tips of my fingers to his. "I know."

"I'm surprised your parents let you out of the palace when you're this close to your due date," Jay said.

I bit my lip and looked to the side. "I may have snuck out," I confessed. My mother was incredibly protective, and, as Jay had said, would probably not have let me leave the palace alone. She hated me going anywhere without the guards, but the unicorns were generally scared of the palace guards, preferring to keep a safe distance from them.

He raised an eyebrow at me and snorted. “Yeah. I’m sure you’re extremely stealthy in your condition.”

“Hey! You’d be surprised how sneakily I can waddle. Besides, Mother and Father were away for a couple of nights on a royal trip.”

He laughed, shaking his head. “So. Nine months, huh?”

Here we go again. “Nine months,” I agreed with a tight-lipped smile.

“I could help,” he repeated. I‘d hoped the conversation was over, but it was never over.

“Jay... Not this again....” I turned from him and began to pack up the few bits that had escaped the basket.

“You’re *nine months pregnant*, Lia. I worry about you.”

I turned back to him and ran my hand through my hair, weaving my fingers through the ends. “I’ve had people worrying about me my entire life, Jay,” I snapped. “My parents have the worry quotient all taken care of. The job’s already taken.”

He splayed his arms in a wide shrug. “And yet... here I am.”

I looked to the side, carefully studying the trek of a ladybug as it made its way over a blade of grass. “Why do you worry about me, Jay?”

One of his hands left my belly to tilt my chin forward so that I met his eyes. His gaze on mine was steady and sure.

“You know the answer to that, too.”

I did. He’d told me the answer since we were children racing hither and dither over the meadows of Vale.

I love you.

He’d told me as a teenager, as we’d left the palace

stables to go spy on wild unicorns.

I love you, Lia.

He'd told me when Luka and I had announced our engagement, folding me into a hug and giving me his blessing even as his eyes brimmed with unshed tears.

He makes you happy. That's all I want. I love you.

And in case there was any doubt on whether his feelings had ever wavered, he told me now, grasping my hand in his.

"I love you. I've loved you forever. Marry me and let me raise this child with you. Let me *help* for once."

My heart thumped painfully in my chest. It would have been so easy to say yes. I loved Jay and cared for him deeply.

But as a brother. I wasn't over Luka, and I doubted I ever would be. And yet, I knew there was only one way this could go. One inevitable conclusion. If I didn't marry Jay, I would eventually lose him to someone that would, and I'd lose the only friend I had that didn't have four legs and wings.

"Why do you want me? I'm pregnant with another man's baby, my body is the size of a whale, and my hair is full of grass."

"This is just a situation, it isn't who you are. You've always been beautiful, and you'll always be beautiful. But that's not the reason I want you. I want you because of who you are. I love you."

"The child isn't yours," I said lamely, wishing things were different. I'd had men falling in love with me my whole life. It was part and parcel of being in the spotlight as the daughter of the king and queen, but of all the men, Jay was the only one I cared about. The only one for whom I wished my feelings were more than they were.

He shook his head angrily. "You can't honestly believe I care about that. It's a part of you. I'd love the baby whether or not I share blood with it."

"I'm sorry, Jay." I shrugged, feeling helpless. "I do love you. But not in the way that you deserve from a wife. You deserve to love and to *be* loved in return. We both do."

And there wasn't room for romance in my heart right now. There were still days I thought Luka might come walking through the door once again, his big arms open wide for me to rush into.

Jay's shoulders sagged, defeated.

"I want to be there for you."

My heart twisted at his earnest words. "I know you do," I replied quietly. "But you'll have to be there for me another way."

He sighed and struggled to smile. When his eyes lifted toward the unicorn, still hovering and watching us intently, his smile became just the tiniest bit genuine. "I suppose you won't have much need of me anyway. Not when you have such help as your unicorn brood to look after you."

"Don't forget my parents and the palace full of staff," I reminded him gently. "Plus..." I lifted my arms. "I've got two fairly capable hands myself."

He laughed softly, chuckling to himself and shaking his head ruefully. "You're not likely to let me forget it."

"You wouldn't like me any other way. But Jay..." I reached a hand up to grab his and gave it a squeeze. "None of that means there isn't room in my life for you." I glanced down at my belly and placed my other hand on top of it. "In *our* lives. I do need you. the baby needs an uncle. I need a friend." I held my breath, hoping he wouldn't point out that the baby needed a father more than an uncle.

"As long as I can be there, I don't care what position I hold," he swore fervently. He squeezed my hand back. "Thank you."

"Thank *you*," I returned. My heart twisted with pity--and fondness at the same time. I was lucky to have Jay in my life. I just wished there was more that I could give to him.

"Now..." Jay gave a jaunty little hop and swished a hand forward as he bowed. I giggled, more out of relief of the change of topic than anything else. He stood up straight and offered me his arm. "Milady, may I escort you back to the palace?"

I took his arm with aplomb, assuming a snooty air that I'd seen from some of the other nobles at court. "You may, good sir." I dropped the attitude and my voice to a whisper. "But let's hurry if we could. The baby's sitting on my bladder, and I *desperately* need to pee."

Caught by surprise, Jay let out a bark of laughter and coughed to clear his throat. "Why yes, I think we can accommodate madam's request. We'll set out post-haste."

The unicorn followed above us at a distance as we set off to the palace and home, the sun setting behind us. Jay kept up a determinedly merry stream of conversation, and I laughed, caught up in the pretense that we could remain friends. It was something I would hold onto as long as I could until in doing so, I would hurt Jay.

Whenever we lapsed into comfortable silence, I snuck looks at him. His brow furrowed in concentration as he guided me over some of the trickier rocks and ditches in the valleys, eyes on my hands and feet as he pointed out where it was safe to step. I tried picturing him by my side as more than a friend. He was an exceptionally good looking man with just enough cuteness in the brawn to get any girl's heart racing, but the hand in mine was just a hand to steady me, to help me in my current state. And while his hands were warm and steady, the buzz of electricity I'd felt while holding Luka's hand was absent.

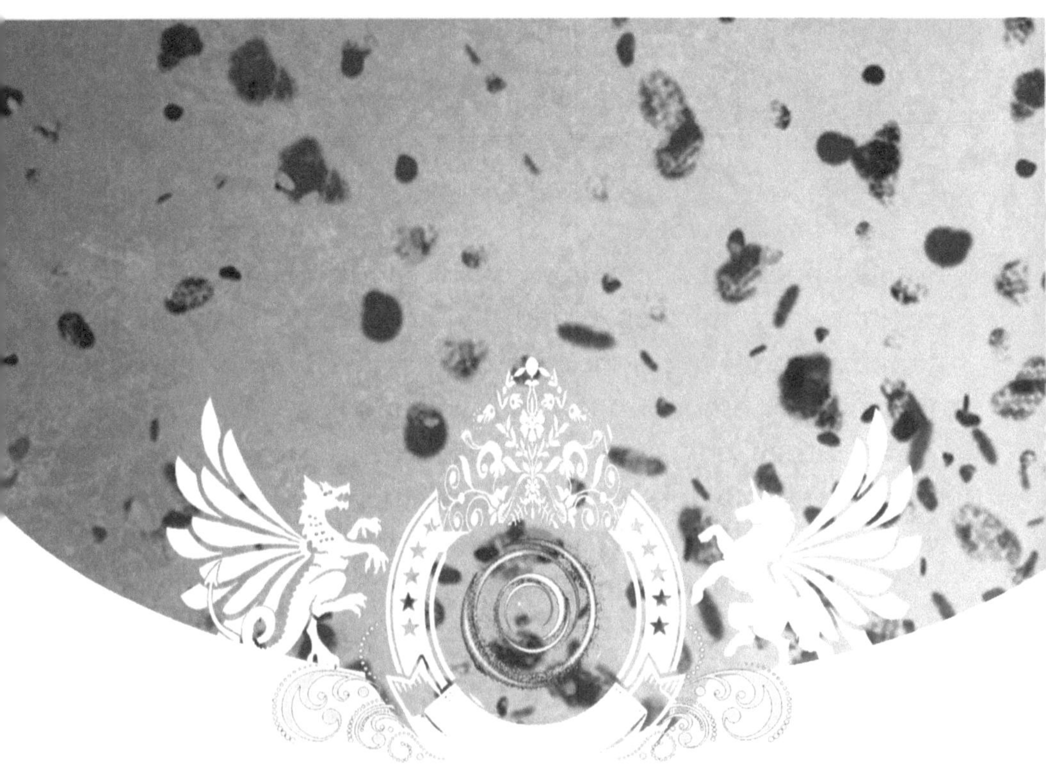

23RD APRIL

After spending a morning reading in my room, I got the word that my parents were back from their trip. They'd been gone a week, which had given me a full seven days of blissful freedom. The second the guard told me they were back, I hurried to the parlor to meet them.

"You were out yesterday," my mother started before I'd even had a chance to close the door behind me.

"I was in the meadow, yes," I said with a curtsey. It wasn't mandatory to curtsey to her, and yet, I always found myself doing so when she was on the verge of telling me off.

"You went *where?*" Queen Renee of the Kingdom of Vale set her teacup down on her saucer with so much force that the cup's base cracked. The tea spilled over her hands, and servants rushed forward with cloth napkins.

"*Mother!*" My voice twined exasperation and concern, but it appeared the temperature of the drink wasn't extreme. My mother gratefully accepted the offered napkins and waved the servants away. I took a seat opposite her on one of the rich velvet sofas.

My father looked up from his reports over his wire-rimmed spectacles with mild-mannered alarm, half-rising from his chair. "Are you all right, dear?"

"Yes, Bennett, darling."

"You just spilled hot tea all over yourself," I said dryly as my father resumed his seat after her assurance.

"Oh, don't fuss so, darling. It's tepid at best." She patted the spots on her chest dry. The smile she flashed my way was bright white. "I've had worse. Besides, I'd *much* rather talk about what made me spill the tea in the first place."

Don't fuss? That was rich, coming from her. But if she wanted to play that game, I could play too. I had, after all, learned from the best.

"All right." I folded my hands in my lap and looked at her placidly. "It's the same meadow I've gone to hundreds—if not *thousands* of times."

Her lips twisted. "You won't get off that easy with *me,* Eliana Rhiann. None of those hundreds or thousands of times had you been alone and in... the condition you're in now." The nervous glance she gave my abdomen indicated she thought it was equally as likely there was a bomb in there as a baby. "You know, I didn't want to go on this trip so close to the birth."

"My condition?" I gave a wry glance down at my belly. *Do you believe this, little one?* "Mother, I'm pregnant," I said aloud. "I don't have the plague. I was totally fine out there."

From his spot across the table, my father snorted.

Mother glared at him, and he held his hands up in surrender. "You have to admit, she's got a point, Renee."

"Don't *you* turn against me too. You know *exactly* why I worry." She pinned him with a pointed glance, and he looked away, cowed. My mother had always been this way with me. She doted on me, but she smothered me too. It was only a year or so ago that she finally let me leave the palace alone, and I'd repaid her by getting pregnant. Even though she was angry with me, she really did have every reason to be.

Taking pity on the man bobbing in the waters of my mother's disapproval, I threw my father a lifeline. "I wasn't alone, Mother. Jay was with me. Come on, you trust Jay, right?" I coaxed with a wheedling tone.

The question was rhetorical. My parents *loved* Jay. They'd love nothing more than for me be married off anew to him. I think my mother thought that if I was married, somehow I'd be safe. That's why, despite her overprotectiveness, she'd been more than happy for me to marry Luka when I was only seventeen.

At the mention of Jay, she sniffed, slightly mollified... but not completely swayed. "It would be different if you'd gone out there with him, but you didn't. You went alone, and he found you there."

"How did you know that?"

She gave me her first genuine smile of the morning. "I'm your mother, dear. I know everything."

After dinner, I walked back to my chambers, rubbing my aching lower back as I mulled over what I'd do with the rest of my day. I had half a mind to grab a book and return to the meadow just to teach my mother a lesson—that I would not be corralled like a child but then decided to head to the staviary to see the new unicorn.

I quickened my step as I left the palace proper and followed the winding paths over the palace grounds to the staviary. I wasn't two steps away from the entrance when I heard a familiar voice.

"Testing your mother again so soon?"

I turned to see Jay with a wry smile on his lips as he tossed a pitchfork aside into a waiting pile of hay. He left the wagon he'd been heaving the hay into leaning beside the side of the stables' outside walls.

"You've got a bit of dirt on your cheeks," I informed him, ignoring his accusation about my mother—whether or not it was true. I licked my thumb as though I intended to wipe it away.

Laughing, Jay dodged my outstretched hand. "Careful, Princess. I might decide that my dirty face needs wiping on those clean skirts of yours." He made a grabbing motion toward me, but I swatted his hands away, unable to keep from grinning.

"You'd never!"

He dropped his hands and shrugged. "You're right. I wouldn't." He raised an arm and leaned against the building. "So." He quirked a brow. "Your mother? I heard she was back. I also heard that she'd called you into a meeting."

"Nothing gets past you, does it?" Jay had worked at the palace for years as a stablehand and knew more of the staff than I did. He had eyes and ears everywhere.

"Not much," he agreed.

I shrugged nonchalantly, a mirror of him just a

moment ago. "She just read me the riot act for going to the meadow yesterday, but she'll get over it. She always does."

"You're going to send that poor woman to an early grave."

I stretched my arms to the sky and leaned from side to side to stretch my back out. "She's got you right where she wants you, doesn't she? That's just what she'd have you all believe, but don't let her fool you. She's made of sterner stuff than that."

"I won't say I told you so when she has to take to her bed from the shock of what you've made her endure."

I rolled my eyes at him. "Don't you worry. She'll outlive us all. *She's* the one who's going to send my child into this world with an extreme case of anxiety."

Jay stepped closer and gently took me by the shoulders, smiling down at me. He turned me back toward the palace, bending over so that his chin rested on my shoulder, and his lips brushed my ear. Gooseflesh pimpled my arm.

"Listen," he said quietly. "I get it. But—and call me crazy here—I'm just saying maybe you could give her a full twenty-four hours before you test her again."

His warm breath on my neck sent a ripple of excitement down my spine, making me suck in a breath, and I found myself leaning into him.

He nudged me back toward the palace, breaking the moment.

So I went.

Because I had a feeling that if I stayed, I'd regret it and that regret would have nothing to do with my mother.

Confusion over what had just happened followed me all the way to my room. Jay had done nothing out of the ordinary, and yet, my body had responded to his touch. Not wanting to analyze why, I fell into my bed and picked up the book I'd been reading earlier. I only left my room for meals, and in the early evening, I picked up my book again, determined to finish it before the end of the day. It was only later, when the sound of frenzied knocking pounding at my door pried me from a dream of tangling lips and entwined bodies, that I realized I'd fallen asleep. Sweat coated my body, and my hair stuck to my face as I woke up with a start. My sheets were wound around my legs—I'd been tossing and turning in my sleep, and my heart beat fast in a way that wasn't due to the visitor at my door. The dream hadn't been about Luka, it had been about Jay.

Apparently, even if I still wasn't ready to consider anything happening between me and Jay, my body and my subconscious had different ideas.

"I'm coming!" I grunted. A quick look out of the window told me it was late. The knocking paused, and I could hear the murmur of heated conversation outside as I heaved myself from the four-poster bed—no small feat with the additional girth around my middle.

I waddled slowly to the door, but it appeared I was taking too long for my visitors in the hall for the pounding resumed with vigor.

"Lia, please!" The voice was muffled by the thick wooden door, but it wasn't enough to stifle it, and my eyebrows flew up.

It was Jay.

And for Jay to come wake me in the middle of the night, it had to mean something was wrong. Something that involved the unicorns. Because there was only one reason Jay would seek me out before anyone else, and it had nothing to do with the fact that I was the heir to the kingdom.

"Just a moment!" I called, throwing a robe on and hurriedly knotting it over my nightdress. I threw the door open to reveal Jay, his expression grim. A palace groom stood beside him, red-faced and wringing his hands.

"Your Highness." The groom bowed quickly and then rushed into an explanation. "I'm so sorry to disturb you at such a late hour, but—"

I waved away his apologies, eager to get to the point. My eyes were on Jay and only Jay. There was so much distress in his eyes, and he had a tethered sort of energy to him—like it took him a great deal of restraint to remain standing in that spot to have this conversation with me.

A stone of pure dread sank in my stomach.

"What's wrong with the unicorns?" I demanded.

The groom's eyes widened with my perception, but Jay didn't look the least bit surprised. His leashed restraint vanished as he lurched forward to seize my hand. "Come with me. It'll be faster if we show you."

Uncaring about my state of undress, I walked as quickly as I could to keep pace with Jay so that he didn't have to tug me along. I didn't care how I looked as I followed him out of the palace. As we crossed the courtyard, it became apparent that we weren't heading to the staviary.

"Where are we going?" I asked, hoping that my mother didn't pick this particular time to look out of her window. If she saw me racing out of the palace grounds in only a nightdress, robe, and slippers, she'd probably murder me herself.

"You'll see," Jay replied in a whisper.

In the distance, the twinkling lights of Shipley, The

Vale's capital city, shone brightly.

The guards on the gates raised their eyebrows as we passed, but they didn't try to stop us. Their job wasn't to stop me coming and going from the palace. I was in no doubt that my mother would find out from them later and roast me alive for it.

"Jay." I tugged on his hand to draw his attention to me.

Momentarily, his eyes pulled from their locked position forward on our trek as he looked back at me.

"You still haven't told me what's wrong with the unicorns. I know it'll be faster if we just *get* there, but... I'm worried." My fingers tightened around his. "How worried should I be?"

Jay stopped momentarily. He ran his hands through his hair as he gathered his thoughts. "No one's dead," he started with.

I laughed nervously. "That's not the comfort you think it is."

"A pair of palace guards were patrolling the edge of the meadow, just outside of Shipley. Closer to the city than you were yesterday. They came across a unicorn foal—and it was in a trap. One of them stayed behind in case the hunter returned, while the other came to get us."

I balked. "But... hunting isn't allowed in those parts of the meadow. Hunters are supposed to keep to the designated areas."

He nodded grimly. "We don't think it was a rabbit they were after."

They were hunting unicorns.

The realization was like a slap, nailing me between my shoulder blades and spurring me back to action.

"Lia?" Jay asked anxiously, falling back into step

with me. "Are you all right?"

"Take me there." I'd never demanded anything from anyone, but if a baby foal was hurt, now was the time to start.

I followed Jay over the meadow as he marched quickly along a path that cut through it, worn away by footfall over the years. I waddled quickly to keep up with his fast pace, my jutting belly paining me as I ran. The sight of the unicorn brought me up short. The poor creature I saw before me knocked the breath from my body. Gods, it was even younger than the filly I'd brought home yesterday. Just a baby. Not even old enough to fly.

And some vile person had rigged a bear trap to clamp around its leg.

The unicorn whinnied in fright when it saw us, trying to fly away, but only succeeding in digging the trap's teeth deeper into its mangled leg. Its hair was stained with red, and its flesh ripped and torn.

Its eyes rolled with fear as it tried to scramble backwards, whimpering.

Next to it, another guard held a lantern so we could see. "I've tried to get near it, but every time I do, it moves, making its leg worse," the guard explained.

I splayed my hand in a gesture of peace and crept closer to the baby unicorn. "Shhh," I soothed. "Shhh."

It stilled, hearing my voice, and eyed me warily.

Jay stepped up behind me slowly, his chest a comforting presence at my back. "What do you need?" he whispered into my ear.

I didn't break my gaze from the injured animal in front of me. My mind raced, my vision narrowed to a single point of focus: the maimed unicorn.

"Space, for now. I need to calm it down before it

injures itself any more than it already has."

Jay nodded and stepped back, but I caught his arm before he moved away. "Jay?" I searched his eyes. "Don't go far."

He lifted my hand from his arm and dropped a kiss onto my knuckles. "Never," he swore. He went to have a quiet word with the groom, who had arrived, panting, behind us. They retreated several yards backward to where the guard stood with his lantern

"Hey there," I said as I cautiously approached the trapped unicorn.

It didn't move but held my gaze. The hue of its golden eyes was so close to the color of the ring that surrounded my own irises. That was part of the reason I loved the unicorns; I felt like I belonged with them.

There was no chance the trap had been set for any other creatures. The unicorns were the biggest animals in the meadows. There weren't any bears here, no wild boar. It's why, despite Mother's concerns, I felt safe roaming the hills and meadows as pregnant as I was.

"Shhh," I hushed the unicorn again through vocal cords tight with empathy over its plight. My vision blurred so badly that I could barely see through my tears. My hands shook as they hovered over the trap's release. Metal teeth cut into the foal's leg right down to the bone. I tried pulling the trap, then pressing down the levers on either side, but the small movement made the unicorn whinny in pain. It fell to its side, whimpering. The movement caused the trap to cut more. My heart nearly broke with pain of its own. I couldn't bear watching something so small and so innocent get hurt so badly.

"Eliana... Lia?" Jay called.

I blinked back the tears as I fought with the trap. "I

could use a hand now!"

I heard rustling in the bushes and turned to see a pair of golden eyes peering out at me. These were different from the young eyes before me. Older. Wiser. But just as terrified. The baby unicorn's mother.

I dropped my voice, hoping that the soothing tone would be enough to keep the unicorn and her offspring calm. "I know you can't understand me, but my friends are going to come help us. We need to get the trap from your baby's leg."

The mother blinked her eyes, sweeping her eyelashes down as if in understanding of my words. The baby didn't struggle away as Jay, the guard, and the groom came closer.

I motioned to the trap with its vicious teeth and the levers on each side that would free the unicorn. "I'm not strong enough to do this alone. If two of you press down there, I'll pull her free."

They nodded and moved into position.

The unicorn looked up at me and... it could have been my imagination, but I could have sworn that she nodded too.

"Okay," Jay breathed. "One, two..."

He locked eyes with me, and I caught my breath. "Three!"

The teeth of the bear trap sprang open, and I hugged the unicorn to my body, rolling backwards with her. She whimpered in my arms, burrowing her head into my neck, but I clasped her tightly. "It's all right," I breathed into her mane. "You're safe. We've got you."

The guard grimly collected the sprung trap and placed it into his satchel for later examination.

Jay leaned forward, hands on his knees, and squinted worriedly at us. "How is she?"

She peeked up at him. Anxiety was threaded through her body and swam in her eyes. I looked down at her mangled leg. It was bloody and limp. Now that she was free, there was nothing to stanch the flow of blood, nothing to keep it from gushing forth from the wounds the bear trap had left behind.

"I need to get this bleeding under control. We can use my robe's sash." I began to undo the robe, forgetting that we'd brought the groom with us. Jay's fingers on mine stilled me.

"Not necessary, Your Highness," the groom said, crouching down next to me and flipping his bag open. "I came prepared." With a smile, he offered me gauze and ointment. I returned his smile and accepted his offering, wrapping it around her leg to stanch the blood flow.

"We'll have to take her back to the palace. She can recover in the staviary. We'll release her once her injury is healed."

I wanted to carry the baby unicorn back myself, keep her close to me, but with my belly the size it was, doing so wouldn't be possible. I let the guard pick her up, and as he did, the mother came out of the bushes.

The fear in her eyes was palpable. I could feel it radiating from her as though I was somehow connected to her.

"We are taking her someplace to get better. You can come too."

The mother unicorn nuzzled at me before following the guard who had started the trek back with the baby. I turned to the groom. "Please go and call for the vet and tell him to go immediately to the palace staviary and notify him of the unicorn's condition."

The groom nodded and took off into the city where

the vet lived.

Now that the rush of adrenaline had faded, I was exhausted. I yawned. An unbelievable cramp spasmed across my stomach, making me gasp at the sudden pain.

"Lia? What is it?" Jay tightened his grip on my arm, his voice full of alarm.

I looked up at him wide-eyed as the unmistakable sensation of liquid poured down my legs. In the distance, the Shipley town clock struck midnight.

"I think my water just broke," I said faintly.

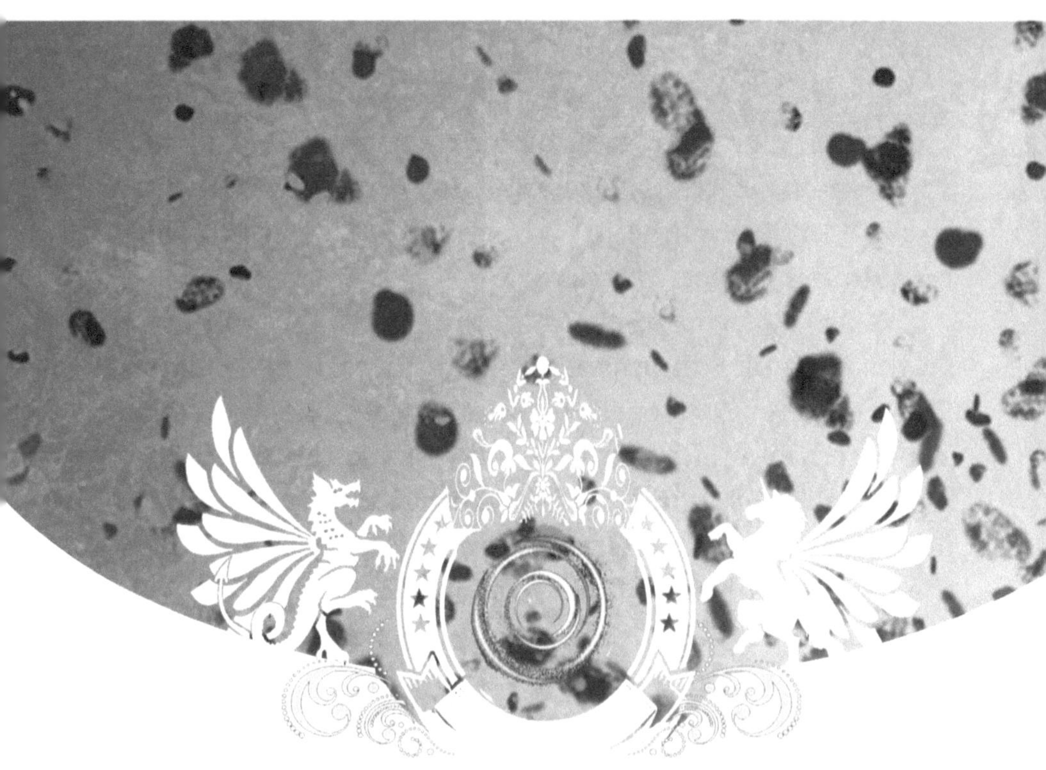

24TH APRIL

Jay's face paled. "Shit," he swore, frantically looking around as though a doctor would pop out of the bushes brandishing a stethoscope and popping latex gloves on. The groom had rushed off at such a pace he was nowhere to be seen, and in the other direction, the guard had disappeared into the darkness along with both unicorns.

Dread clenched at my insides. The meadow was my favorite place in the world... but I didn't want to give birth here. I wanted a clean bed, a doctor, and nurses to watch over me. I wanted my mother.

A contraction made me suck in my breath and groan as I curled in on myself, clutching my stomach and trying to breathe through the pain.

Most importantly, I wanted drugs. Lots and *lots* of

medicinal, gloriously numbing drugs.

"It's going to be okay, Eliana," Jay promised, reverting back to my full name in his panic. "We'll have to walk back to the palace, that's all."

"Walk? Are you freaking kidding me?" I let out a cry as the pain of a thousand daggers pierced my insides. Wasn't labor supposed to take time? The pain was supposed to build gradually, not suck the life out of me in full force with my first contraction. As the pain finally ebbed away, something nudged my arm. It was the mother unicorn. She'd come back.

Hope lit in Jay's eyes. "Get on," he said, jerking his head at the unicorn's back.

As though the unicorn understood him, she pranced forward and stood in front of me, bending at the knees as though encouraging me to mount her.

My eyes widened as I realized what he was asking me to do.

"I can't get on the unicorn's back," I said, my voice trembling.

"Why not?"

"Unicorn are wild animals. You can't just ride them."

"We ride them all the time at the palace."

I narrowed my eyes at him. "The tame ones that we trained. This is a wild unicorn."

Jay ran his hands through his hair, panic plastered onto his features. "Are you serious? She came back for you. She voluntarily left her own baby so that you could ride her back to the palace and have yours."

I shook my head. My senses were scrambled with fear, and my body was already gearing up for another contraction.

"Will you get on the damned unicorn before I lose my mind?" Jay said, his voice cracking.

“I’m scared. What if I fall?” I loved unicorns. Heights, not so much.

Jay didn’t answer me. Instead, he hauled me onto the unicorn’s back and jumped up behind me. “I won’t let you fall, Lia.” And with that, the unicorn spread her wings, and we took off into the night sky.

The flight from the meadow back to the palace was a blur of pain and delirium, and, I was pretty sure, vomit.

If I wasn’t nominated for sainthood after this, I thought, I never would be.

After what felt like hours, but in reality couldn’t have been more than ten minutes, we began the descent to the palace.

A guard shielded his eyes against the moonlight and pointed up at us. From the way his arms were moving as he gesticulated wildly, it was clear that he was addressing other guards nearby, but I couldn’t hear his words. Judging by the way the other three guards flocked to his side, he’d called them to make sure he wasn’t hallucinating.

One slowly started to raise his bow to aim an arrow towards us.

Oh, no no no, I thought with dismay, my spine tightening with dread, but the man behind him shoved his arm toward the ground.

“Are you mad?” he demanded of the archer.

We were close enough now that I could hear his words, floating up to us on a breeze as we got closer. “You *never* harm a unicorn. The worst kind of luck follows unicorn hunters.”

“There are people riding it!” the first guard complained.

The other man shook his head. “*Never* harm a unicorn,” he repeated. “You never know what kind of karma will come back to bite you in the ass if you do."

Good to know they cared about the unicorn. Now, if only I could get them to care about the princess giving birth on top of it.

I was breathless as the unicorn's hooves clattered onto the tower ramparts. The sudden impact of the unicorn's landing walloped the air from my lungs and sent another jolt of pain ricocheting through my body.

The guards stared at me, jaws agape.

The one who had been speaking elbowed his compatriot in the side. "And you can never be sure which unicorns are carrying pregnant heirs to the kingdom," he said faintly. "Apparently."

"Good morning, gentlemen," I said, smiling at them through gritted teeth. "Pleasant night, isn't it?" I tried not to think about what I must look like. Nine months pregnant, eyes red from crying, hair a mess from my midnight rescue mission, and sweating in my nightclothes.

"Could I trouble you to—" The contraction worsened, and I doubled over, at last releasing my hold on the unicorn's neck to clutch my stomach. She lowered in a sort of bow to allow me an easier route to dismount.

The guards rushed forward to help me from the unicorn's back, easing me down as I held myself in a position that was the closest I could get to folding into a ball.

"Your Highness, may we be of some assistance?" the guard with the bow said.

"Yes, absolutely," I gasped, squeezing his forearm and giving him a look filled with venom. "Or we could stand around here on this rooftop until the baby falls out of me. My voice climbed the octaves as pain ripped through me, and I yowled like a keening cat. "Get me to a doctor, you imbecile," I roared. "*Now!*"

"Impossible," I said later to the words the doctor had just uttered and wondering if she was indeed qualified to bring a child into the world.

The doctor's lips twitched as she fought to suppress a grin from between my feet up in stirrups. She stood, and her gloves made a snapping sound as she removed them and then disposed of them in the trash. "I'm afraid it's not only possible, Your Highness, but it's a fact. You're in labor—" She smiled apologetically. "You're just not in *enough* labor to push. Not yet, anyway."

I pressed the heels of my palms against my eyes and resisted the urge to scream. It seemed like contractions were taking hold of me every minute, despite what the doctor and her watch said. I'd been contracting for hours. Why didn't my baby want to come out?

I barely had time to get my breath back when another tidal force of pain washed over me.

Mother rushed in as the doctor left. She caught the door before it swung closed .

"I brought you some ice chips," she said, carrying a bucket and passing me an ice chip from it. "What did the doctor say? Are you well? Is the baby all right?"

She'd been gone from the room for less than ten minutes!

I chewed on the ice chip and let the cold liquid soothe my throat.

"Yes. No... I don't know," I moaned and turned my face into the pillow. "All I want to do is have a baby. Isn't that a nice thing to do? Why does the baby want to hurt me?" My voice was muffled, and when I peeked out to see my mother, the worry wrinkles had vanished from her face.

"You're fine," she said in a sigh of relief. "Thank the gods."

I resisted the urge to pound my fists into the sheets as Mother took a seat beside me in the well-worn rocking chair she had used to rock me in as a baby. The minute we'd found out that I was pregnant, she'd had the chair dragged into the palace's hospital suite that awaited me and my future offspring.

Hours went by, marked by the ticking of the clock on the wall and the contractions that seemed to come quicker and quicker, not letting up in their voracity and indeed getting worse. I found myself wishing they were only as bad as I'd thought they had been when they first started.

"I can't do this!" I screamed as another squeezed me, terrorizing me with its grip. My body tensed as the wave washed over me, crushing me. "I can't do this anymore." I whimpered, my head dripping with sweat.

"I'll find the doctor," my mother said as I found myself on another downhill slide that would take me into my next contraction. "Your contractions are coming thick and fast now."

"No shit!"

I'd never let a swear word leave my mouth before, but now seemed like an appropriate time to start.

The doctor bustled in and took a look, dipping her head out of my line of sight behind a sheet covering my legs to my knees.

"There'd better be a baby there," I mustered.

She let out a peal of laughter and popped up above the sheet. "Not yet, but we'll have one soon. You are ready to push."

I felt for my mother's hand as a contraction started. This time, instead of letting it take hold of me, I took hold of it, harnessing its power as I bore down.

I was vaguely aware of my mother screaming *push* beside me.

"Good, good," the doctor said as I gasped for breath. "If you feel up to it, push again."

I closed my eyes and pushed with every ounce of energy I had.

Then on the next contraction, I pushed again and then again and again until my body was spent with exhaustion.

"All right, Princess Eliana, you're almost there." The doctor sounded bright and cheery, and I ground my teeth, my cheeks feeling hot.

"You said that the last time," I grumbled.

My mother smoothed my wet hair back from my sweaty forehead and kissed my cheek. I leaned gratefully into the cool cloth that she pressed onto my skin. "You're doing splendidly, darling," she breathed. "Just another few pushes, and you'll hold that baby in your arms."

"Get ready," the doctor coached. "Just one more *big* push, and that's it. Just one tiny push, you can do that, can't you?"

"Depends," I grunted. I shifted among the sweaty bed sheets and pillows to a sitting position. "Which is it, big or tiny?"

The doctor blinked and looked uncertainly at my mother, who shook her head and hitched up her dress, underskirts and all. She kicked off her heels and, barefoot, climbed into the bed with me. She got into a position of support behind me. Her legs pillowed mine. She grasped my hands tightly.

"When you entered my life,"—she breathed into my ear as she squeezed my fingers—"I had your father to rely upon. And I never had to do this, so I can only imagine the kind of pain you're in right now," she said. "But I never want you to forget that you are not alone."

A sob tore out of my throat. "I *am* alone," I said despondently. "I want Luka." For all my big strong talk about not needing a man by my side, I was afraid. And I didn't want to do this without Luka. But I knew that I had to. My baby would depend on me.

She shook me. "You are *not,"* she said emphatically. "You are not now, nor will you *ever* be alone, Eliana Rhiann. You have your father. You have me. You have Jay and the entire kingdom behind you."

"It's not the same," I choked out. I didn't bother to blink back the tears coursing over my cheeks, unchecked.

"Of course, it's not." She threaded her fingers through mine and whispered into my ear. "But it's not nothing either."

I wept and shook my head, dismissing the idea. "I can't do this."

I felt Mother's chin tilt as she looked over my head to meet the doctor's eyes. "You can and you will, darling. It's time."

"*Push!"* the doctor shouted. Her brow furrowed in concentration as she crouched below me.

There was no other option. My body begged to push. The baby demanded it. And whether or not I was bolstered by my mother's encouragement, I screamed and did as she and the doctor and biology bade me, focusing all of my energy on pushing my baby out into the world. I could hardly think as I bore down with all of my might.

The strain stopped and the pressure eased as the doctor pulled my baby free.

A wail split the air. A beautiful, magnificent, glorious cry.

I also heard little hiccuping sounds, and I realized that my eyes were streaming tears. Hurriedly, I wiped them away. Not because I was in any way, shape, or form ashamed of the emotions that were swarming through me. No, I wiped the tears away because I wanted to *see.* And I wanted to see clearly what Luka and I had made. What my body had strained and transformed to produce and protect.

The doctor leaned over, inspecting my child held in her practiced hands as my mother scrambled free of the bed to get a closer look. And me? I was frozen there, held spellbound by the baby in the doctor's arms. A perfect, messy, gorgeous, wailing baby. *My* baby, here at last.

And as I watched my child wriggling in the doctor's arms, a surreal feeling overcame me.

The feeling that my life as I knew it had ended. And a new life—a better life—was just beginning.

"Would Grandma like to do the honors?" The doctor smiled at my mother, holding out a pair of shiny silver scissors that glinted in the light. "Your Majesty?" She waved them toward my mother, handles first, with a confident little flourish.

Grandma, my mother mouthed, beaming at me with undisguised glee.

"Go ahead, Mother," I said, smiling back as a bolt of euphoria enveloped me.

Looking awestruck by her new title of "Grandma" as she accepted the scissors, my mother turned toward the umbilical cord, the line that still tethered my baby's body to mine. Carefully, she snipped at the point that a nurse indicated to her. And then, the baby was free.

Wails still filled the room. The baby's little hand curled into an angry, indignant little fist, and its face turned an angry red.

"Is it okay?" I hiccuped, a sudden rush of fear bolting through my mind.

My mother looked up at me, her face radiant. Her eyes twinkled with pure, undiluted joy, and a grin threatened to split her face in two. "She's more than okay, darling," she said, brimming with happiness. "She's perfect."

"She?" I repeated, my cheeks splitting into a wide grin of my own in a mirror of my mother's.

"She," she affirmed, with emphasis this time and warmth in her voice. "You have a daughter, Eliana. Congratulations."

She took a few strides around the medical professionals that still crowded the room and made it to my bedside to hand me my baby—my daughter. "Now you know how I felt when you came into our lives," she said. She smoothed my sweaty hair back from the crown of my head. "However much you love this baby, know that I love you the same."

"She's the most beautiful ugly thing I've ever seen," I said on the breath of a sob.

Chuckles danced around the room as I continued to memorize the features of my new daughter.

A tiny, pert nose, tiny mouth that crinkled. I held my index finger up to her little palm, and five tiny fingers grabbed hold. Her hair looked dark. Her skin had an olive-toned complexion.

My heart twisted. She looked just like Luka.

Once, that would have seemed like torture. Today, it

seemed like the most generous gift that the gods could have bestowed upon me. Luka was gone, yes, but he would live on through our daughter.

Do you see her, my love? I asked silently, hoping he could somehow hear me, wherever he was. *Look what we made.*

"Do we have a name?" The doctor asked quietly, as though reluctant to disturb my bonding time with my child.

A name? Panic stabbed through me. Gods and goddesses above, I didn't have one. Would I let my daughter down that quickly, that easily? "I just figured the baby would be a boy. I was going to name him after Luka, but now that it's a girl..."

I looked up at my mother for guidance, and she squeezed my shoulder. "You can name her whatever you like, sweet girl. I'm sure Luka would approve, wherever he is now."

Somehow, that was exactly what I needed to hear. Calm washed over me, and confidence took hold.

"Her name is Fae," I decided.

"A fine name for a fine girl," the doctor said with a gentle smile.

My mother gazed at me, with a far-off look in her eyes. "I can't believe my baby has a baby," she said. The awe in her voice—the *pride* and excitement—was still there, but something in her words pricked my ears. Something in her tone penetrated the haze of wonder that surrounded me and my newborn daughter. She sounded almost... afraid. But why would she have any reason to be?

"Time flies," I said.

She exhaled heavily. "Oh, my dear, you have no idea. Time passes, but does it really? How much do things ever really change?"

Her hand was still stroking my hair, but she no longer seemed present, no longer here in the moment with me and rejoicing over her new grandchild. I caught her hand and stilled it with my own, finally able to break my gaze from Fae.

"Mother," I said, trying to sound calm. "What do you mean?"

"You're grown. You have a daughter of your own. But it doesn't change anything. I'm still your mother. I must still protect you. The only thing that's changed for me now is that I must find a way to protect you both."

"Protect us from *what?"* I asked, bewildered.

I didn't get an answer. She only nodded to herself and dropped my hand. "You both must be protected," she repeated, sounding like she'd come to a resolution. She strode to the door.

"You're leaving?" I struggled to sit up straighter, clutching Fae tighter to my body and pushing against the bed with one hand. The doctor and nurses exchanged nervous glances.

She spared me a single glance back before delivering her parting words. "To speak with the captain of the guard. I'm going to increase the guard duty and bring in more staff. From now on, you'll have a personal guard, and there will be one for Fae too. I'm not leaving anything to chance." And with that, she waltzed from the room, leaving me wondering what was going on. She'd always been protective, but with Fae's arrival, she'd gone completely off the edge.

25TH APRIL

The sound of my doctor's voice drifted through the door to the room, waking me from some much-needed sleep. Beside me in her bassinet, Fae snuffled in her sleep.

"Credentials?" The doctor squawked at some unknown person. "Fetch the queen. Better yet, open the door and let the princess identify me herself. I should think she'd have no trouble remembering the woman who pulled her child from her not half a day ago."

Her speech was answered only with silence, but I heard the click of the lock turning. We'd been locked in?

"For the love of the gods," the doctor muttered as she entered the room with a couple of guards following behind her. "I have a patient to see. I don't have time for this."

Hurriedly, I waved the guards off when I saw them start after her, hands on the hilts of their weapons, expressions startled by the fact that anyone dared to defy them. They'd probably not encountered many in our kingdom who required more than a stern word from someone testing their boundaries.

"How are you feeling?" the doctor asked while checking my temperature.

"Like I've been hit by a truck," I replied lazily. My body ached, but my heart was full of love. It made the aching more bearable. I leaned over and checked Fae. Her little chest rose and fell soundly.

"She's a good sleeper." The doctor worked around me, checking me out as I contented myself with watching Fae. She'd fed really well on her first try and fallen straight asleep.

"Hmmm."

"You are perfectly fine. I prescribe rest and bonding with your baby. How do you feel about being moved back to your bedroom?"

I nodded, eager to return to normality. The doctor summoned the guards and asked them to carry the bed with me in it to my room. She picked up Fae, who gave a little squawk at being so rudely awoken, and passed her to me.

The journey from the hospital wing to my room was short but strange. Everywhere I looked, there were guards. My mother had really outdone herself this time.

I was thankful when I got to my room away from prying eyes. The doctor placed the empty bassinet that she'd carried by the bed next to me.

"Give her a feed while she's awake, and then you can both settle down for the rest of the night. Do you want me to stay?"

I shook my head. I'd only ever been with Fae alone while she was sleeping. I wanted to get to know her without people watching.

"I'll be nearby. If you need me, just call one of the guards outside your room. They'll come get me."

I thanked her and waited until she left. Once again, I heard the lock click. Normally, something like this would have me running straight to my mother in anger, but if I was locked in, it meant that everyone else was locked out, which was exactly how I wanted it.

After an easy feed, Fae fell asleep in my arms. She didn't stir when I placed her back in her bassinet, and I used the chance to grab some sleep myself.

I woke hours later to early morning light pouring into my room. I sat up slowly, taking care not to jar anything down below and checked Fae. She began to fuss, making little grunting noises. From my spot in my bed, I could see her tiny fists waving in the air.

"I bet you're hungry," I murmured.

As if in answer, her cries grew louder and more insistent.

"All right, all right," I said. Wincing, I eased my feet down onto the blush-colored carpet. Fae wailed. In response, my own stomach growled, and I grinned ruefully. "I know; you're starving. I can't blame you. Let's get you taken care of first, and then we'll see if we can find something for Mama besides ice chips."

I lifted her into my arms, adjusting my clothes in the front. Fae latched on to my breast immediately after I guided her mouth there, suckling greedily. It was the strangest, most amazing feeling. I traced her tiny, delicate features with a finger while she ate. "I can't believe I made you," I whispered.

My gaze wandered back to the room surrounding us. As a child, this room had been both a comfort and a prison of sorts. My mother, so strong in some ways, always seemed to be afraid that something would happen to me. I grew up sheltered and overprotected—but always loved. Flowers covered the walls of the room with one picture adorning it. Not a painting, but the careful calligraphic script of one word.

My eyes rested on the framed art, and I mouthed the word out loud. "Rumpelstiltskin."

I'd asked Mother what it meant once. I remembered the occasion vividly. She'd been brushing my hair, a soft, gentle hand following the brush through my silvery tresses, and when I'd voiced the question, she'd stilled.

She swallowed. All she brought herself to say was "You must always remember that word, promise me, Eliana."

Try as I might, asking question after question, I could get no more out of her. And so this strange word that no one else had ever heard had evolved into a sort of curse word for me.

Mother always smiled when she heard me saying the swear word—a reaction I would never have gotten away with when it came to any other swear. But with every utterance of that word, something dark and fearful lingered in her eyes.

It was a shadow that was always there. Mother's constant companion. Always lurking beneath the depths.

And I knew that shadow was why I rarely left the palace in my early years. It had a tether on Mother—a hold that I could never, ever break.

As a pre-teen, I'd had to fight and scrap for every inch of freedom I was allotted. I never saw the city in those days—not unless it was from a balcony or from the seat of a palanquin. And even then, a sheer curtain was always drawn over my window to obscure my face. No one would know at a glance whether it was me inside or another member of the nobility. I used to bitterly joke that the people probably wondered whether there even *was* a Princess Eliana. If they didn't live or work in the palace, how would they even know I truly existed?

Those days with my mother had been... bad. Pain twinged when I thought of them. I'd screamed at her, told her I hated her, threatened to run away multiple times.

"I don't care if I get hurt," I'd spat while leaving the chambers she shared with my father one night. "Anything is better than being trapped in this prison cell with only you for company."

I'd struck a chord with that. I still remembered the hurt whisper that had followed me out of the room after that declaration.

"Trapped?"

I regretted hurting my mother... but it was a means to an end. I did not regret the result. She'd finally softened her grip. *Finally*, I was allowed to see the meadows that Vale was famous for. Guards still accompanied me... I *was* still a princess, after all. But now it was just two men or women who lingered at the edge of the meadow. I'd had the illusion of freedom.

And it was in the meadow, under that illusion, that I'd met Luka.

The crunch of his boot on the grass had been my alert that I was less alone than I'd thought. I'd been lounging on a blanket on the hillside, eyes closed, with the guards at the meadow's edge. I shaded my hands with my eyes and sat up, squinting into the sunlight as a shadowy figure brushed aside branches in his path.

The first sight of him had struck me with awe. He'd seemed as big as a tree, towering over me as he emerged from the woods with a satchel slung over one shoulder. Outfitted in a brown leather jerkin and a cream-colored doublet that looked just a hair too small and too worn for him.

My mouth dried up. He was a *big* man. Three—no, *four* heads above me and shoulders as broad as a wagon.

"Halt!" The guards had hurried toward me and stood in front of me, blocking the man from view. I'd stood on my tiptoes, trying to get a look at him. The guards had leveled their weapons threateningly and glowered at the stranger. "State your business, sir."

He stopped short upon the order and held up his satchel as evidence. It looked tiny in his enormous hands. "I'm an apprentice healer?" Nervousness made his statement a question. I couldn't have blamed him. I wasn't sure either of these guards had ever used their weapons outside of training with them, but they were polished and sharpened to nice, intimidating points. And they didn't lower when the man told them of his occupation.

"They need to know what you were doing in the woods," I stage whispered to him.

His gaze flicked down to me, and I swallowed when his eyes met mine.

My heart leaped. I hadn't known brown eyes could have so many fathomless depths to them. As dark as they were, Luka's eyes did not hold shadows. They held light. Like the sun dancing and dappling a pile of fallen leaves in winter.

"Oh!" He scrambled to undo the clasp of his satchel

and flip open the bag. I leaned forward to look inside. Greenery spilled out of its pouch. All manner of leaves, berries, and flowers were stuffed inside. "As I said, I'm an apprentice healer in the village. I was gathering herbs and medicinal plants for my master."

The weapons lowered as my guards relaxed and nodded. "Be about your business then, good sir."

Thank you, the big man had mouthed at me.

You're welcome, I had returned, a smile tugging at my lips.

He turned to leave, and I panicked. He was the first person I'd met outside the confines of the palace walls. I wasn't ready to lose this new connection I'd made. "Wait!" I blurted.

Luka paused as I turned to my picnic basket and frantically searched through it for something to offer him. My hands closed around a sandwich, and I held it out beseechingly. "You look hungry. Please, take this as an apology for the trouble."

A slow smile unfurled over his face. "A good meal is always more pleasant with good company," he said. He tilted his head toward my picnic arrangement. "Might I...?"

Yes, my heart breathed. But I played it cool. Kept it casual. "By all means, stay and enjoy yourself."

He unlooped his satchel from around his neck and settled it beside my blanket. He bit into the sandwich, and the smile turned into a full-fledged grin. "Peanut butter and jelly. My favorite."

I didn't know it then, but he was just like a unicorn. Like *my* unicorn. Hiding in plain sight. Rare and special.

I swallowed. "I'm Eliana," I said. Blurted, really. It came out like I was trying to dislodge a frog in my throat.

By contrast, his voice was warm and comforting. A

low timbre. "Nice to meet you, Your Highness."

So he recognized the name. I supposed the guards *were* a bit of a dead giveaway that I wasn't just some random girl in a meadow.

But it wasn't enough to scare him off. He just kept right on smiling at me and said, "I'm Luka."

It happened that fast. Just like that. I didn't know him, and then suddenly, we were right in the thick of it. Luka and Me. Me and Luka. Us. *We.* I began brushing aside time with Jay to go into the city and visit Luka's master's shop in the hopes that I would run into him there.

Luka seemed receptive to my tentative flirting, but nervous. More aware than I would have liked of the fact that I was a princess, someone technically of a higher social standing than he was. But still... I thought he liked the interest I showed in his work. I *knew* that I liked the way I felt around him. I'd always chafed against the idea that I needed protection, but with Luka, I felt both dainty and safe. At once protected... and like I was free. *Truly* free for what was probably the first time in my life.

Once I made my intentions clear to him—that was the best way that I could describe the way I'd bullied the guards outside and boldly asked Luka if he wanted to kiss me as badly as I wanted to kiss him—that had been it. I brought him home to meet Mom and Dad, although he'd wrung his hands the whole way there, worrying about meeting "the *King* and the *Queen*, Eliana!"

He'd been so nervous the first time I had introduced him to my parents, but I was lucky: they were no snobs. My mother, despite her desire to have me protected at all costs, had immediately folded Luka into a hug and thanked him for making me feel safe.

In the meadow where we'd met, I'd sucked in a nervous breath. I knew I wanted Luka. I was sure about Luka. But was he sure about me?

He had watched me curiously. "Are you feeling all right?"

"Yes." I gulped. "In fact, I've been... feeling all right for a while now. I've been feeling amazing ever since I met you."

That slow smile of his took over his face. "The feeling is mutual, Lia."

A warmth spread through me. I loved it when he called me Lia. Lia and Luka. We sounded like such an ordinary couple. Not princess and pauper, not child of royalty and orphaned apprentice. Just two people, together. Ordinary people sharing something extraordinary.

I'd cherished it. If I'd known how short-lived that pocket of happiness we'd found would be, I'd have cherished it that much more.

But standing in front of Luka in that moment, all that I'd thought was that I was standing before my future, staring into its eyes. And it was smiling back at me.

So, I took my heart and took a leap, lowering myself to my knees before him.

His eyes widened. "Lia, what are you doing?" He dropped his satchel at his side and hurried to kneel with me.

I had rehearsed what I was going to say before now, of course. I couldn't have imagined going in unprepared. But those words vanished when Luka joined me, kneeling in the meadow, taking my hands like we were about to utter prayers to the gods together. Suddenly, it didn't matter what I had been planning to say at all.

I knew the words that were written in my heart. Knew what I had to say.

"Luka," I said. "All my life, people have knelt before me, for all kinds of reasons. I have never knelt before anyone, but I'm kneeling before you now because you've become the most important person in my life—and I wanted to honor that feeling." I swallowed. "But you didn't let me do it alone."

He released one of my hands to run his fingers down the side of my cheek, eyes tender. "I never want you to be alone, Lia."

I gulped and met his eyes from beneath lowered lashes. "Would you maybe want to not be alone forever with me? Do you think—would you maybe want to marry me?"

I didn't have a ring. I wasn't sure if Luka would like one or what size his finger was, and I didn't want to get something like this wrong. It was too important. *He* was too important.

His eyes had glowed like a vat of melted chocolate when I'd asked. My heart had been in my throat, beating furiously like it was trying to hammer its way out as I waited for his answer.

"Yes."

Relief flooded through me. Relief and joy.

But Luka wasn't done. He reached into his pocket and pulled out a small velvet box.

I let out a little cry, my hands flying to cover my mouth. Gently, he reached up and removed my left hand, using his other hand to open the box. A ring sparkled up at me. I had practiced and practiced. But he had actually come prepared.

"As long as *you'll* marry me." Our eyes locked, and his glowing eyes closed as he leaned in for a kiss.

"Yes," I breathed in an echo of his earlier response. "Yes, yes, yes."

I couldn't believe how lucky I was that he picked me. That we picked each other.

Jay had been resentful of Luka in those early days, but over the course of the two years I'd had with Luka, Jay had ended up liking him. Luka was just like that; everyone warmed to him. When Luka died, it hit Jay almost as much as it hit me.

I looked down at our baby daughter in my arms. Fae's eyes weren't the usual gray-blue of an infant. They were the same warm brown her father's had been, positively radiating love and warmth up at me. I traced her little mouth with my finger. She had his mouth too. It would grow into a wide grin that, just like her father's, would be infectious. People couldn't help but smile back at Luka when he was happy.

The door creaked as my mother stepped inside the room. "Good morning," she said in a whisper, seeing Fae in my arms.

"Morning," I returned at a normal volume.

"She's awake, then?" Mother's skirts swished as she crossed the blue carpet and put her arms around me, looking down at the baby I'd brought into this world. Mother gave my forearm a little squeeze of pure joy and leaned her head against mine. "Hello, little one," she murmured. She sighed happily. "I just can't get enough of looking at her."

"Me either," I said.

She gave me another affectionate squeeze. "That part never goes away, you know. A mother's love for her children. Even in your most frustrating moments, there was a part of me that was just awestruck by the love I had for you." She looked down at my daughter again.

"She reminds me of you at that age."

I was eager to hear how. I saw so much of Luka in her, but so very little of myself. Perhaps it was her nose...?

But no. My mother continued, "She's so very tiny. So defenseless."

The reminder zinged into me. She saw only danger. Danger everywhere. "About that..." I started, hesitant. Things had been good between us for so long. I didn't want to get into an argument, especially not in front of Fae. I remembered vividly how we could start off reasonably and both devolve into shouting.

I decided to start with a light question. "What's up with that? The increased guard, I mean?" I asked. I tried to act as though I wasn't overly invested in the answer, adjusting Fae's blanket under her chin as I spoke.

My mother wasn't fooled. She stiffened against me, tension threading its way through her tendons. Her hands dropped from my body, and the space where she'd dropped her hand from my arm was cold now.

"What *about* the increased guard?" she snapped.

"Well... it's only that I thought we were past that." Gently, I lowered Fae into her bassinet and motioned my mother into my sitting room. I could already tell that this conversation wasn't going to go the way that I would have liked for it to go. Mother followed me, shoulder blades drawn in tight. She held her nose at an angle and regarded me warily, as though she was sizing up an opponent for battle. The door between the bedroom and sitting room clicked shut behind me.

"I..." I trailed off and splayed my hands apart pleadingly. "I am so lucky that I had you and Father growing up. But I want different things for my child. I want Fae to have a bit more freedom growing up than

I did."

My mother's eyebrows slammed together, and she swatted a hand through the air as if she could bat my ideas away like a fly. "Impossible. Completely out of the question."

I blinked, taken off guard. In the past, she'd always at least *pretended* to hear me out for a minute first. That easily, I felt my ire start to rise, but I tried my best to stamp it down and remain reasonable. "Mother," I said in a chastising tone. *Stay calm, Eliana. Stay rational. It's the only way to make her see reason.* "Has there been some threat against us?"

"No." She rolled her eyes. "But I don't see what that would have to do with anything. Safety and security must never, ever rest. Never take a breather."

"So, no threat," I summarized. "I didn't think so. So unless that becomes the case, there is no need for all of this," I said firmly. "Fae and I are going to continue to live our lives freely, the way we would have if Luka was still here." A lump grew in my throat, and I tried to swallow down the way my throat warbled when I said his name. Damn post-labor hormones.

My mother softened. Her posture relaxed, and I did too as she walked toward me to gently clasp my hands in hers. "Oh, my darling," she breathed. "I wish that it could be that way. But Luka is gone. The two of you have no husband to protect you. And despite what you would like, I am still your mother—and more importantly, I am still the queen."

She patted my hands briskly and stepped away. "The guard stays. You go nowhere without them. They will remain stationed outside of your room when you leave, or when the nursemaid is left alone with Fae."

"But—" I protested, and she held up a hand to stop

me.

"It is not up for discussion. I'm sorry, darling. But Mother knows best."

With that, she strode away, not even giving me the chance to utter a squeak of protest.

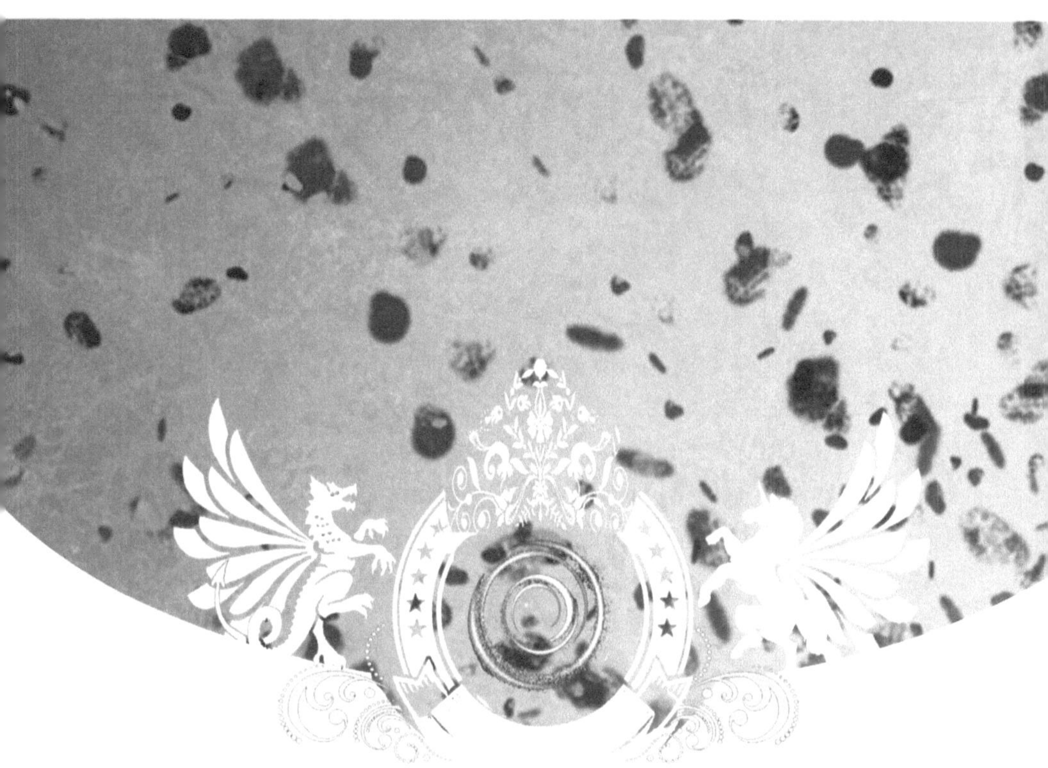

26TH APRIL

I cracked open the door of my suite and peered out into the dark hall, where the light of the torches glimmered off of the guard's weapons. Mother's men had followed her orders. Two of them had remained stationed outside of my rooms, with at least one of them remaining there at all times. But one was easy. One, I could deal with. So I waited, with my ear pressed against the door until I heard one of the guards leave for his bathroom break. Then, I made my move. The door was unlocked, which was something. The lone guard started when he saw me squinting out at him, and I smiled sweetly.

"Remind me of your name," I requested.

The guard's gaze flickered over the homely terrycloth bathrobe knotted at my waist and he straightened with my attention. "Williamson, ma'am." His eyes widened, horrified with his slip in etiquette. "That is—I'm sorry, I *meant* to say, Your Highness." With haste, he bowed awkwardly.

I waved a hand dismissively. "Oh, there's no need for all of that pomp and circumstance," I assured him. "After all, by the sounds of things, from what my mother says, you and I are going to be spending a *loooot* of time around each other." I tried not to let bitterness change my tone. You catch more flies with honey and all of that. And my quarrel wasn't with this man, who was just doing his job.

His job that I needed him to neglect for just... *one* minute.

Williamson straightened. "Is there something I can do for you, Your High— ma'am?"

"Eliana," I corrected with an easy smile.

He coughed into his hand, looking discomfited. "Eliana," he said gruffly.

I fluttered my hand around my midsection and grimaced. "I hate to be a bother, but would you mind terribly running down to the kitchen and fetching me a glass of ginger ale? I've had the most terrible upset stomach tonight."

This, I knew he would believe. I'd made my excuses of feeling sick with my parents and left dinner early, declining my mother's offer to come with me and ignoring the way they had both frowned after me.

I looked back at Williamson and tried to project the image of illness. He leaned close, keeping his voice low should anyone else hear. "I'm not supposed to leave you alone."

"Oh, you won't be," I assured him hastily. "I'm never *really* alone, am I?" I winked. "The palace is well protected. I think I'll be fine in here in my rooms within it, don't you?" *What with my mother doubling the guards,* I finished silently. Possibly even tripling them by now.

Williamson relented, sending an almost rueful smile my way, his shoulders slumping. "I s'pose you're right. My partner Benton will be back any minute now anyway, and it's not as though you're going anywhere."

Who, innocent little me, who was being held against her will by the people who loved her? Never. I widened my eyes to project an image of unimpeachable virtue.

And the thing was, people see what they want to see. I was the Unicorn Princess in their eyes, for crying out loud! Virtuous, kind, perfect. They'd never see the bottled rage flaming behind my lavender and gold eyes. Never search for the spine of steel within my flowing and ethereal gowns. They saw guileless intent.

Because that's what they always saw when they looked at me. They didn't want to see anything else.

"One ginger ale, coming right up," Williamson said. He aimed his pointer finger and thumb at me in a finger gun. "*Eliana.*"

That's right, we're buddies now.

I clasped my hands together. "Oh, thank you *so* much," I simpered.

My eyes followed him as he trotted down the hall. The poor man. I'd have to make sure that he still had a job after this, once Mother found out he'd abandoned his post.

I slammed the door shut and wriggled out of my robe. Williamson was right. His partner would be back any minute now, and I had no time to waste. I just needed a *little* bit of time away from these rooms. I needed to breathe. And I couldn't *breathe* anymore inside this gods-damned palace. I needed the open air. To feel the wind.

To see the unicorns.

With all of the guards swarming the palace, I wouldn't make it out to the meadow right now, but I didn't need to. The baby unicorn weighed heavily on my mind. Even in the haze of joy over welcoming Fae into the world, I hadn't been able to banish the image of the poor thing's mangled leg, the way that the teeth of the trap had pierced her skin and sliced deep into her tendons. I couldn't forget the way she had looked up at me, helpless, her eyes frantic and glazed with pain, begging me to do something.

I needed to see with my own two eyes that she was healing all right.

Fae gurgled from her bassinet. I picked her up, and she gave a little mewl.

"Shhh." I bounced her in my arms. "Come on, little one. No time to waste. We're on a stealth mission."

I bundled her into my arms to hustle down the hall. A little thrill shot through me. Besides wanting to check on the unicorn, this was going to be a moment for me. I'd get to introduce my daughter to the unicorns. Even as young as she was, I knew there would be awe and wonder in her eyes. One couldn't see the unicorns for the first time without showing those emotions. And I couldn't wait to see them in my sweet baby daughter for myself.

I moved quickly and efficiently through the halls of the palace, nodding with respect to anyone I passed. They eyed me curiously, probably wondering at my haste, but they wouldn't stop me. *They* didn't know of my mother's decrees. They had no reason to suspect that there was any reason why I shouldn't be able to simply come and go as freely as I pleased. I dodged corridors and corners where I thought guards might be stationed and burst from the palace toward the path that led to the staviary.

The stable aviary was a building with high rafters and beautiful glass ceilings. It was partitioned off into different sections, accommodating land horses and the creatures that I was here to see, unicorns. There were few walls to the structure, allowing for the natural meadow breezes to flow freely in and out of the staviary. The thought was that it comforted the animals to have the healing air of their homes.

I lifted my nose to the sky and breathed deeply before heading to the entrance to the building.

The stable half-door creaked as I eased it open and stepped inside. A few curious adult unicorns lifted their heads over their stall doors to peer at us, their horns glimmering in the moonlight.

"Good evening," I greeted them in a soft whisper.

I petted the heads of the different flying steeds as I passed them. These unicorns were the tame ones, the ones that worked at the palace. They were the only unicorns in the kingdom that were in service. We used them as transport—well, the palace staff did. Apart from my insane journey the other night, I'd not used them to fly. Most people thought they stayed because of me and my way with them, but I thought they stayed because of the endless supply of peanut butter and jelly sandwiches we fed them.

Aside from the working steeds, the other unicorns who were sheltered inside the staviary were injured creatures who needed time to recover from their injuries. Like the baby unicorn that I was here to visit.

One of the unicorns I passed whickered curiously, tilting its head at the bundle in my arms. They knew that I usually visited with treats for them.

I shook my head ruefully. "Not today, I'm afraid," I whispered, rubbing its long face. "Next time, I promise."

The unicorn nodded then retreated inside its stall to take a nap, grunting as it folded its legs beneath it on top of a pile of hay.

Fae made an inquisitive little noise, and I looked down at her, fiddling with her blanket. I inclined my head down toward her and eased my nose against hers gently. I breathed in deeply, inhaling her sweet baby smell. It was amazing how much holding her calmed me. Between her and the air outside of the palace, I may yet manage not to throttle my overprotective mother.

"Just wait until you see what I'm going to show you next," I promised her.

I peered over the doors of the stalls until, at last, we found the baby unicorn, sleeping peacefully on a bale of hay, its little wings outstretched. They still had the downy baby fluff that would one day transform into long silvery-white feathers.

Relief unfurled inside my chest as I flicked open the catch of the lock and stepped inside the stall with Fae.

She was here. Jay had kept his word, as I'd known he would.

The baby unicorn started awake when it heard us enter. When its eyes landed on me, she struggled to get to her feet to greet us. I hurried forward, not wanting her to hurt herself by getting up too soon.

"Oh, no, shhh, shh, that's all right." I crouched down to examine her wound. Another wave of relief washed through me. She had been well cared for. She looked freshly cleaned, her coat shining bright and silvery-white. Clean gauze was wrapped around her leg where the trap had bitten into her, tied neatly in a bow. It wasn't her first bandage; it had been recently changed. I shifted Fae to one arm and gestured to it with my free hand. "May I?" I asked the unicorn.

She didn't move, but something in her eyes looked like permission. My fingers tugged at the end of the bow until the edges of the gauze gaped open and revealed the injury. It was a clean injury. It had made some progress since I'd gone into sudden labor in the meadow while tending to her, but I hadn't expected it to be this far along. Perhaps unicorns had magical healing powers we weren't aware of. We knew so little about them, really. Only what they allowed us to know.

"That's healing nicely," I complimented her.

"Thank you," a deep male voice said with some amusement.

I bolted upright and whirled to see Jay leaning over the stall door, eyes gleaming with laughter. "I knew I'd find you here," he said. "I'm sure it comes as a complete and utter shock to you to hear that the palace is in a state of uproar looking for you. I hear tables are being overturned in case you're hiding beneath them."

Guilt twinged at me, but I tamped it down with a self-righteous flare. If my mother hadn't kept me prisoner, there would have been no need for any uproar.

"And did you tell them you were looking here?" I asked.

Jay snorted. "And risk your wrath when I led them here before you were ready? Please, give me some credit. I'm not an idiot. I like to think that all these years of friendship have taught me better than that." His eyes were soft and sympathetic as he looked at me. "Besides, I figured you wouldn't have done it without good reason. I guessed that you needed a minute or two."

"Thank you," I said gratefully.

He waved a hand, brushing that aside. "It's nothing." He grinned. "And I mean that literally. I did… absolutely nothing."

He stepped inside, and the stall suddenly felt warmer. The heat pressed in upon my cheeks. Jay wasn't *as* big a man as Luka had been… but he wasn't a small man, either. I gazed up at him, but his eyes weren't on me anymore. They were on the baby in my arms.

"Gods, Eliana," he breathed. "Is this her?" He couldn't take his eyes off Fae. And who could blame him? Luka and I had made one cute baby.

"No," I said flatly, but with an undercurrent of mirth lacing my voice. "I left my newborn daughter in the palace, and swung by the palace nursery to give some *other* baby her first glimpse of a unicorn instead."

The dry look he leveled my way let me know that he didn't much appreciate my cutting sense of humor.

He gestured in the open space between us. "Can I…" he trailed off, awkwardly forming his arms into the shape of a cradle.

"Of course." I shifted Fae into his arms and adjusted the position of his hands so that he cradled her correctly. "Support her neck," I instructed and stepped back.

Jay and Fae stared at each other with wide eyes, and it was as though I no longer existed, so spellbound were they by each other.

Jay was utterly entranced by my baby daughter in his arms. I expected him to tell me how sweet she was, how much she looked like me, that she was the spitting image of her mother. That wasn't what he said.

"She looks nothing like you," he said. I blinked. That… hadn't been what I had been expecting.

"I mean…don't get me wrong," he said hastily. "She's

beautiful. And you're beautiful, but they're different kinds of beauty. She has something that's all hers."

Then, as if I wasn't even in the room anymore, he stared down at her and began to sing. He had a lovely singing voice, and I floated away on the sound of his melody as he wove a blanket from a tune, singing of the stars and the gods who watched over us.

Fae blinked sleepily up at Jay as he continued singing his song to her.

And I melted. There was no other way to put it. The sight of the two of them together, my daughter safe in Jay's arms. It did something to me inside. Twisted the reality of what I thought I knew. Maybe I was wrong to keep Jay at arm's length. Maybe it would be good for Fae to have a father figure in her life.

I winced, wishing I could take the thought back the instant it inserted itself into my consciousness. I wanted to banish it because it felt like a betrayal of Luka.

What was more, it was unfair to Jay. I knew what he wanted from me. Pure as his intentions were, if I let him be a father to Fae, in any way, there would always be a part of him that wanted more.

Jay looked up at me and smiled. "I think she's asleep," he said in a whisper.

I moved to take Fae from him but hesitated. His eyes met mine, and my breath caught in my throat.

"It's a nice night," he said, lifting his chin up toward the glass ceiling where a blanket of stars glittered down at us from the blue-black sky above. "There's no need for the two of you to rush off. Why don't you stick around for a little stargazing?"

His gaze was expectant. Hopeful. And that scared me more even than the possibility of being locked in my room for the rest of my days. I swallowed hard and held out my arms.

"I'd better get back to my rooms. Mother may not have any hair left from stress at this point."

"Right," Jay said. He shifted Fae into my arms, unable to hide the dejected look in his eyes.

My heart twisted. *I'm sorry,* I thought desperately. I wished that I could make it better for him. But I didn't know how to do that in a way that stayed true to what I was feeling. I wasn't ready to think of being with another man besides Luka.

But as I looked at his face, I knew I didn't want to leave. I should leave, but there was something holding me back. Maybe I could stay a little longer... as a friend.

It was a thought that would never see fruition, as the cry of "Princess!" rang into the staviary like a bell clanging through the air.

I closed my eyes. Well, I'd known it would have to end sometime. They'd found me.

The guards were hardly rough with me, but it was humiliating to be escorted back to the palace like a criminal—or worse! Like a child caught doing something wrong, like sneaking a hand into the cookie jar before I'd had dinner. At least they let me walk into my chambers alone. My only companions were my daughter and the white-hot rage in my heart. I was able to hold my head high, my posture stiff with the anger that was my sidekick far too often these days. I found my mother inside, pacing a tread into the carpet and wringing her hands over a kerchief. A sob escaped her throat when she saw me, and she rushed toward me to enfold me into her arms. My body stiffened as I held Fae like a barrier between us.

"Eliana," she said into my shoulder. "They found you. Thank the gods. I—"

I broke away and headed toward the bassinet to put Fae down.

There was uncertainty in my mother's voice when she spoke again, a trembling, "Eliana?"

I speared her with a look. "Not now," I said. My whisper was quiet but steely. She and I would have it out—but not in the same room as my sleeping daughter. My mother wrung her hands together as I placed Fae into her bassinet and quietly walked to the sitting room where my mother had retreated, shutting the bedroom door behind me.

The words burst out of my mother like a dam had broken. "Thank the gods you're all right," she babbled, dabbing at her eyes as tears streamed from them. "Why did you leave? Where did you *go?* Please, *please* don't ever do that to me again. I don't know if I could take it."

"Don't ever do that to *you* again?!" I couldn't believe she'd just said those words to me. She had some nerve. "I should be asking you not to do what you just did to *me* again. It's like I'm reliving my childhood all over again, and I thought those days were behind me. In the past, where they belong. Where they should have *stayed,*" I added pointedly, glaring at her.

"I understand how you might feel that way, but I—"

I ignored her, cutting her off, my voice rising. "As for where I *went,* I didn't even leave the palace grounds. You're being strangely overprotective, and while I don't understand it, I didn't flout your commands by hopping on to a unicorn and flying off to the next kingdom over. Which we both know I could have easily done."

She looked at me helplessly. "I'm just trying to keep

you close," she said quietly. "To keep you safe. You don't understand. You're not a—" Her teeth clamped down onto her tongue, and her eyes darted to the bedroom door.

Not a mother, she'd been about to say.

It had been her excuse constantly as I'd grown up: *You couldn't understand. You're not a mother.*

But now, I *was* a mother. And I *did* understand. Love for Fae had grabbed me in its hold the second I held her in my arms and her eyes looked up at me. I knew I'd do anything to protect her.

But not at the cost of her living her life.

"Not what?" I asked. "Not a mother? But I am now."

"It's not the same," she said.

"You're right. It's not. I'll keep Fae safe, but I won't pull her in so close that she's desperate to get away from me. The way that I am with you."

My mother reared back as if I'd slapped her, but I wasn't sorry for it.

"My daughter is going to live her life," I said quietly. "And so am I."

I jerked my chin toward the door. "You should go. Rest easy tonight. I won't be going anywhere. But you should know that this isn't over. I'm tired of guards dogging my every footstep. I won't let you keep me here forever."

Shockingly, she didn't argue, only shot me a wounded look. The barest tinge of guilt wavered in my heart, but I stood firm and pointed toward the door. "I think you should go."

When she didn't move, I did instead, going into the bedroom with Fae and firmly shutting the door behind me.

She didn't follow.

27TH APRIL

I squinted into the light of day as sunlight pried its way through a crack in the curtains. It was quite an unwelcome guest. I wasn't ready to get up yet, not by a long shot. I'd slept last night, though fitfully, between late-night feedings and diaper changes. I struggled to remember the dreams that had woken me constantly, but the thoughts slipped through my fingers like smoke. I only managed to grasp the impression that Luka had been with me last night. The memory of his face fluttered like a cloud passing over the sun. Ephemeral. Fleeting.

Our daughter gurgled in her crib, but I knew that it would turn to a full-fledged wail of hunger soon. Blearily, I pried myself out of bed and over to Fae's bassinet, lifting her into my arms and cradling her against my chest. A piece of hay that had fallen from my clothes the day before caught my eye on the otherwise clean rug. It must have come from the staviary, somehow trapped on my clothes since I saw Jay yesterday, only falling off when I changed into my nightwear the night before.

With that thought, the events of yesterday came flooding back. My fingers trailed the edge of my sleeve.

Confused feelings tumbled through me when I thought of Jay. A warmth and a quickening of my heart that wasn't entirely unpleasant. I'd always fought any hints of attraction to Jay. Attraction was not the same as love—as a romantic and chemical connection. And if that was changing... well, was that *right?* It still felt like a betrayal to feel *anything* for another man, even one I'd known as long as I'd known Jay. Luka was barely cold in the ground; he hadn't even been dead a year.

And then... there was the not so small matter of my mother.

Not so small... I scoffed at myself. That was the understatement of the century. Mother was damn near *insurmountable.* This wasn't just the quarrel of an adult daughter with her mother. There were layers to my struggle. The familial relationship was one, to be sure, but it was not the only one. There were our political positions, too. She was the queen, and I was but a princess. She held all the power, and so she held all the cards.

I heaved an aggrieved sigh. She had a way of getting under my skin like no one else, a way of making me act like a prepubescent teenager rebelling against her parents. I was hardly going to pierce my nose and stay out all night drinking and imbibing illegal substances, but she reacted as if I was. As though I was stepping out onto an active racetrack with my eyes closed. I was not so reckless as she made me out to be.

But despite all of her frustrating actions, I *did* love my mother. And I regretted telling her that I was desperate to get away from her, especially blurting it out in a heated moment the way I had. Saying that I wanted to flee from her wasn't quite the truth either. What I was desperate to escape were her ever-watchful eye and her stifling protection, but that didn't mean that I didn't want to spend time with her or never see her again. Maybe it would be easier if that *was* the case. Then I could have snuck away in the night to kingdoms and lands unknown, and I would be troubled no longer. I'd have my freedom.

But I loved her. I loved *both* my parents dearly. And Vale. And that was part of what made all of this so hard. My mother almost loved me *too* much.

Fae started grunting, and I absently undid my blouse so that she could feed. I brought her to my breast, and she made cute little noises as she suckled. I stared at the ceiling in thought, my eyes tracing the spirals and whorls of the elaborate golden chandelier over my bed.

We couldn't go on like this. The constant irritation and anger that clutched at my heart was no way to live. I didn't want my daughter to grow up in a cage, but living under a cloud of negativity wasn't what I wanted for her either.

I couldn't see a way out of this situation without hurting someone that I loved.

My bedroom door creaked open, and my mother's head cautiously protruded in. "Knock, knock," she said quietly when she saw us sitting up and awake. "May I come in?"

At the sight of her, a lump rose in my throat. I didn't trust my voice, so I motioned her inside.

She hadn't slept well either, that much was evident. The dark circles under her eyes tattled on her and revealed all. Her hair wasn't up to its usual standards either. Usually, her golden hair was smoothed back, curled, and held in place by an assortment of hairpins. Today, while she'd taken the time to comb it, it was loose, falling to her navel, and frizzy; she hadn't had her handmaidens apply the typical amount of product required to tame it. *And* her skin looked duller, somehow. Like she hadn't bothered with her ordinary skincare regimen. I'd never known her to neglect her self-care. My mother wasn't vain, but she did believe that appearances mattered.

As a child, she had brushed my hair and told me sternly that while we "mustn't truss ourselves up like dolls, we must take pride in ourselves as well, for the people need to have pride in their monarchs. And how can we expect them to if we do not lead by example?"

So to see her like this now, I knew that our fight had affected her just as badly as it had affected me.

In her hands was a small box, wrapped with care. Pink and silver paper was folded around it, and purple ribbon crisscrossed over its surface, winding itself into a bow that decorated its top.

"I have a gift for Fae," she said. Her voice was soft and hesitant. Like a foot testing the ground beneath it, unsure whether or not the surface was stable.

Fae's feeding had stopped, so I turned, covering myself for the sake of modesty, and repositioned her while I buttoned my top and turned back to my mother.

"A gift? What for?"

"Does a grandmother really need an excuse to spoil her grandchild?" Her attempt at levity trembled. "Especially a brand new one like our little Fae here."

"No... I suppose she doesn't." This was weird, but I guessed it was her attempt at a peace offering. An olive branch. I was willing to meet her halfway. But that didn't mean I was going to act like all of this was super-de-duper normal when it was anything but. Shooting her a questioning look, I used one hand to tug on the end of the bow until it came loose. I set the ribbon aside, tore the paper open, and pulled the box's top off.

Inside the box was a worn, stuffed doll. Patches lined with sloppy stitches adorned its cheeks where the thread had gone bare. It had probably once had a head full of yarn hair, I thought, but now it was half-bald. And the hair that it *did* have left was dingy. I thought it had once been yellow. But it was gray with dirt now.

In short, it was the ugliest toy I'd ever seen. I bit my lip, about to ask why Mother had given this... possibly disease-carrying toy... to Fae. But I stopped short when I saw her expression. She was staring at the doll with the softest look on her face. My mother looked at it with such love in her eyes. Reverently, she lifted it out of the box and held it gently in her hands.

"This was mine when I a girl," she said softly. "Her name was Eliana."

I started, and she laughed. "Yes, in a way, you're named after this doll. I thought it was such an elegant name. No one *I* knew had a name like that."

She stared at the doll, eyes distant now, like she was seeing something past it. It was as though she was seeing the life she'd had before.

I didn't know much about my mother's life before she was the queen. Often, she refused to speak of it. I had gathered it hadn't been a happy upbringing. But somehow she'd met my father and they'd fallen in love. She'd put the past behind her.

Or so I thought.

“You never met my father, did you?” she asked, stroking her hand down the doll’s threadbare hair.

I blinked. It wasn’t a question I’d been expecting. She’d never talked about her father, my grandfather. And I’d be damned if it hadn’t piqued my interest. Wordlessly, I shook my head.

“He was a hard man. A miller.” Her mouth twisted, and she spat out her next words. “And a lazy, good-for-nothing drunk most days. It wasn’t so terrible for me while my mother was alive. She ran interference, came between the two of us during his fits of anger. Completed his jobs for him when he spent his time drinking instead of at the mill. When the coin was scarce, it was my mother who halved her meals so that we could both eat that night.” The first unblemished smile she’d worn that day spread over her face as she remembered her mother. “And she loved to spin. She’s the one who taught me how to do the same. I took great joy and pride in that for a time.” She nodded at doll-Eliana. “She’s the one who gave me that doll.”

The smile vanished from her face, and she looked... drained... and so, *so* much older, somehow.

“She died when I was fourteen. And then it was just me... and dear old dad. And when he was too drunk to do his work, the miller’s daughter went to work in the miller’s stead.”

Her focus drifted as she remembered her history.

“And that’s how I came to be known around the people of the city. As the miller’s daughter. Never as an actual person. Never with a name of my own. The miller’s daughter, not Renee.”

Known to many, but never with a name of her own... A moniker of my own echoed in my mind: *The Unicorn*

Princess. "I can relate to that," I said softly.

She eyed me, and the wisp of a smile graced her lips once again. "I suppose you can, can't you?"

"So how did you go from that to... meeting Father?"

Her smile split. "The one good thing my father ever did for me started off as the worst. Somehow, in his drunken stupor, he bragged about his daughter's spinning talents. He bragged about my work ethic. He said that I could spin straw into gold. I think the bastard meant it to be a poetic metaphor for both of those things."

"Mother!" I said, aghast. She had never sworn in my presence before.

She batted my exclamation away and continued telling her story.

"Someone listening took him literally, and when the rumors reached the king, that is, Bennet's father and your grandfather—he took them literally too. And *my* father, well..." She scoffed. "He was too embarrassed and prideful to take one word of it back and say that it was a joke."

"Spinning gold from straw is impossible, though," I said. "How did you get out of that?"

Her whole face shuttered, and I couldn't glean anything from the wooden expression she wore. "I got lucky that your father is who he is."

I bit my lip. There was more to this story, I felt certain of that, but I didn't want to press my luck. She'd already given me so much more than she'd given me before.

Gently, she deposited the doll back into the box she'd so carefully wrapped her in to gift to her baby granddaughter. And now, knowing where the doll came from and the comfort she'd probably provided to my mother when she was a young, scared girl, I saw the doll through new eyes. She may not have looked it, but the threadbare doll was an heirloom. Precious and irreplaceable, with important memories that only her eyes had seen.

My mother hadn't just given Fae a gift today. She'd given me one, too.

She replaced the lid of the box gently, tucking her past away where it was easier for her to deal with. And when she turned to me again, her smile was hesitant and a little afraid.

I'd made my mother afraid to even talk to me. And something in my heart shriveled with shame over that realization.

"I know," she said. "I know that I'm hard on you. That I don't exactly make it easy for you to live your life the way that you want to. And I'm sorry for it. But I just..." she trailed off and began to sniffle. She tried to smile, but it wobbled on her face. "I hope you know, Eliana, that you're the best thing that ever happened to me. I would move heaven and earth to protect you. And now that you have a daughter of your own, I know that you understand how I feel, but you must also understand that I have even more to lose now. You and Fae... you're just both so precious to me. If, gods forbid, anything were to happen to either of you, I just couldn't bear that. The thought of losing you..."

She couldn't bring herself to finish the sentence. Her voice choked up, and with that, she burst into tears. I looked down at my daughter in my arms. Her eyes seemed to look as bewildered as I felt. I set her in her bassinet and walked out of the bedroom, motioning for my mother to follow, and when we were both in the sitting room, I stood in front of her. We locked eyes, and her watery eyes looked at mine, searchingly as she clutched a gray handkerchief to her breast, breath shuddering in little, gasping sobs. I brought my arms forward, and I pulled my mother into an embrace.

She buried her face in my neck and clutched tightly at my shoulders with desperate hands, sobbing into me. "I love you so much, Eliana," she cried. "I can't lose you."

"You're not going to lose either of us," I soothed, rubbing my hand over her back in soft, comforting circles. "Not me. Not Fae. I don't understand why you think you would."

She pulled back, sniffling, and wiped at her eyes with the handkerchief, widening her eyes and blinking rapidly so that more tears wouldn't fall. "There's no real reason. Just a mother's fear. My fear. I'm overdramatic, right? I always have been. I'm just a silly, scared old woman, I suppose."

She wouldn't meet my eyes, so I knew that she didn't truly believe that. Suspicion stabbed me deep in the gut, an instinct that I couldn't shake off. There was more to this than simple dramatics. There had to be.

"I would never describe you as 'silly,'" I said. I took the handkerchief she was wringing from her hands and gently swiped it over her cheeks to catch a few more trailing tears. I swiped it over her nose in a playful manner. "I mean, paranoid and dramatic, sure. Absolutely. But silly?" I pursed my lips, pretending to think. "Nah."

She let out a watery burst of laughter.

"Paranoid," she repeated. The tone of her voice was strange. Mirth, with a strange coating of bitterness. "I suppose you're right. Nothing has happened in all these years. Why would it start now?"

I tilted my head to the side, catching that strange

tone. "Mother, are you sure that's all it is? Paranoia? Or is there something else that you're not telling me? Is there a reason that I should be afraid?"

She opened and closed her mouth like there was something more she wanted to say. More that she wanted to tell me. I waited with bated breath.

"I—" Her mouth settled closed, and she smiled, tight-lipped, but trying to act like everything was fine. "Enough of this sadness," she said firmly, changing the subject and leaving me with a nagging feeling in the pit of my stomach. The things she'd spoken about today were obviously hard for her to talk about, but I couldn't quite put the story of her childhood together with why she was so afraid now. Her father was a horrible man, but he was long dead and couldn't hurt us. Besides, he'd shown no interest in me when I was a young child. I doubted he'd have cared about Fae even if he was alive.

"I came here to apologize to you for the fight last night, and that's what I'm going to do. I am sorry for the way I behaved and how I reacted. Do you forgive me?"

"Of course," I said. "Thank you for apologizing. But after what I said to you, I should be asking you if *you* forgive *me.*"

Her smile turned into something real. "Oh, darling." She trailed a gentle hand down my cheek and stared lovingly into my eyes. "I'm your mother." The smile transformed into a grin. "I'll always forgive you." Her hand dropped from my cheek as she clapped them both together. "But, enough of these sad tidings and dwelling upon the past. You forgive me, and I, you, so the nasty business is taken care of." She seized my hands in hers and gave them a squeeze. "Let's turn to happier things. I want to throw a party."

The change of subject was so quick that it could have given me whiplash. I blinked in surprise. “A party?” I repeated, dumbfounded.

Glee lit up in her red-rimmed eyes. “Yes, a party!” she said, mirth and teasing lacing her voice now. “Something to celebrate you and the new baby. The new *Princess* of Vale. What do you think?” She looked nervous to hear my opinion. “You always loved a party when you were younger.”

She was right. I had. I loved the fun, food, and jovial atmosphere, and I had loved twirling about, dancing to upbeat music, and getting a flush in my cheeks from the movement.

A frisson of excitement raced through me. It had been so long since I'd attended a proper party, let alone organized one. I had barely had that big of a role in my own wedding. I'd wanted to be married so quickly that we did it simply, and I'd let Mother and Father and their staff see to most of the details. Throwing one in Fae's name felt right. A night to focus on joy, rather than all that I'd lost. All that Mother still feared we could lose. I envisioned floral centerpieces, twinkling candlelight, and a festive masquerade. I looked at my mother and returned her grin. “Yeah. Yeah, let's do it.”

She pulled me in close in order to embrace me. “We shall have such fun organizing this. It's exactly what everyone needs! And then I can really make it up to you.”

I knew in my heart that this was her way of keeping me busy so I wouldn't feel the need to leave the palace. She needed me near her at all times, and this was the best way to do it. It would work. I loved the idea of planning a party, but after that? After that, we'd fall into the same old argument, and nothing really would change.

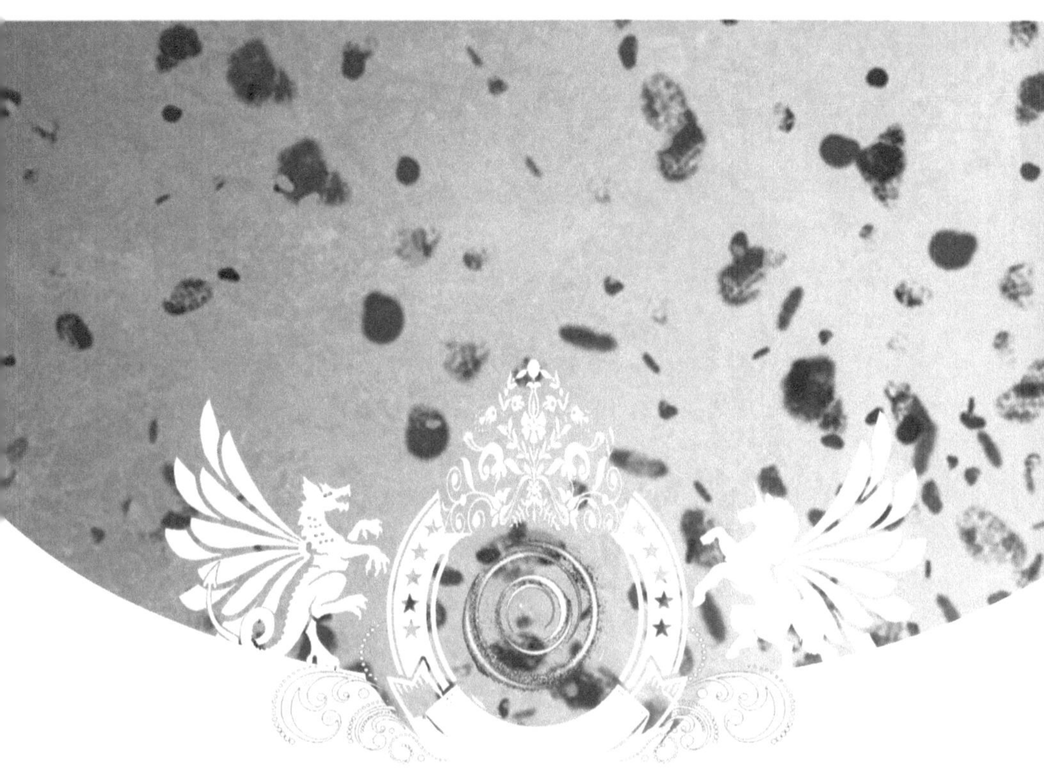

28TH APRIL

"What do you think about daisies and ranunculus from Floris, and wild garden roses and baby's breath from our own gardens?" My mother asked, poised with a pen to take notes.

We'd been at it all morning, and I'd be damned if I wasn't starting to get pretty excited about the party.

"I'd prefer the wild flowers from the meadow. So much easier and no cost." I held my breath waiting for her answer, knowing any talk of the meadow might sour the fragile truce between us. As I thought, she pursed her lips, ready to remind me that cost wasn't an object. I didn't wait for her dismissal of my idea.

"The servants can pick them fresh on the morning of the party."

As soon as I mentioned servants going out to the meadow and not me, her face brightened.

"I think that's a lovely idea." She crossed something out and wrote something else before setting the book to one side.

She stood up and stretched her arms above her head. "This has been so much fun, but I have a dance lesson with Pierre." She knelt toward Fae's bassinet. "I'll see you later, my darling girl," she cooed.

"Dance lesson?" I queried, bending to scoop Fae up as she began to fuss.

Mother clapped her hands together and beamed. "I booked them so I can look like I know what I'm doing at the party. I say, why don't you join me? It could be fun."

I narrowed my eyes at her. This was another attempt to keep my attention anywhere but the calling of the outdoors and the meadow. Not that I could really blame her. I had threatened to run away, taking Fae with me.

"What about Fae?" I asked. I'd not been separated from my daughter since she was born. I was surprised my mother wanted to do something where Fae was out of both of our sights.

"I thought Judith could take her for an hour. The weather is so glorious, I thought that maybe we could practice in the courtyard and Judith could watch while Fae naps."

I had to hand it to her. She had all the angles covered. She knew I was itching to be in the sun, and she didn't want to go too far away from Fae. This way, we'd both be safe within her eyesight while still giving me the illusion of freedom. Judith was the nanny we'd hired a couple of months ago after a long search of the best nannies in The Vale. So far, since Fae was born, she'd done nothing but twiddle her thumbs. It was about time she worked for the exorbitant amount we were paying her.

A servant was sent to summon Judith and Pierre while my mother and I walked out into the courtyard with Fae in my arms and my mother carrying the bassinet.

I got Fae comfortable and placed the bassinet in the shade. She looked up, and I followed her gaze at the fluffy clouds that dotted the perfectly blue sky. I'd heard that newborns couldn't see much further than a foot away from their nose, but Fae looked rapt as she stared skyward, so I wasn't sure that was true.

"Your Highness."

I turned to find Judith waiting patiently. She gave me a curtsey, then a warm grin at the baby. She was an extraordinarily beautiful woman, though her basic makeup, nanny costume, and severe bun hid a lot of that beauty. What it didn't hide was the joy she radiated at spending time with the baby. We'd made a good choice with her.

"I'll be just over there," I said, pointing to my mother, who was deep in conversation with Pierre. "I'll be the one falling over my feet. Holler if she wants to be fed."

"I'm sure we'll be just fine," Judith said, settling herself down on the ground next to Fae's bassinet.

It took another ten minutes to get ready as Pierre refused to teach us without music, so we had to bring part of the Royal Guard Band out to join us. Anyone watching through the palace gates must have thought we were mad. It made me glad that our palace wasn't right in the middle of the city like the ones in Antla in Atlantice and Kisbu in Badalah.

"Ve hav one man and two vomen," Pierre said in a heavy accent I couldn't quite place. He was a wisp of a man without an excess pound of flesh on his bones.

"I'll watch while you dance," I said, taking a step back. My mother grabbed my arm.

"We'll take it in turns. I'll dance with Pierre first, then you can."

I rolled my eyes and gave her a grin. "If you have to look like an idiot, you want to make sure I do too, huh?"

"Something like that," she whispered, giving me a conspiratorial wink, before heading back to Pierre, who was waiting impatiently, tapping his toes on the cobbles beneath his feet.

For the better part of an hour, Pierre corrected our posture, teaching us the appropriate steps and repositioning our arms. I lost myself in the movement of the music, closing my eyes and finding peace within it.

That was, until an unmistakable roar interrupted us.

"Eliana!"

The musicians stopped as Jay came sprinting into the courtyard, yelling my name.

He stopped short when he saw me just finishing a twirl that I felt rather daring in even attempting.

Everything went quiet as all eyes turned to him.

Jay's chest heaved, and his cheeks were tinged pink with exertion.

I raised an eyebrow of inquiry at him. "Yes?" I prompted. "Did you need something?"

He looked sharply between my mother and me. "It's the unicorns, Eliana," he said urgently, eyes locking onto mine. "We need you. It's happening again; traps have been laid. We got lucky this time. A patrol found them before anyone—human, unicorn, or otherwise—was hurt, but make no mistake, the unicorns are in danger. We need to herd them away from the traps before they're hurt just as badly—if not worse than the baby unicorn we saved before Fae was born."

"But..." Confusion swamped me. "We have plenty of hostlers, surely. Must it be me?"

His eyes darted to my mother once again. I didn't dare even look at her. I'd not mentioned my little nighttime excursion on the night of Eliana's birth, but it must have gotten to her. There was no way all those guards would have kept quiet. She'd made no mention of it either. Fae's birth had eclipsed anything else that had happened that night. If the unicorns needed me, I was loathe not to go. I did so long to help them in any way that I could. But, more, I was loathe to disturb the so recently acquired peace between Mother and me.

Jay stepped forward and seized both of my hands in his. "No one knows them like you," he said urgently. "I've no doubt the hostlers could come too, but I don't think anyone will be nearly as effective as you will be with them. So will you come?"

"I thought you said there weren't any unicorns trapped?"

"Not yet, but there are a lot of traps. It going to take hours to get to them all. We need you if a unicorn does end up in one. You know they won't let anyone near them. You have a gift with them. It has to be you."

I dropped Jay's hands and turned toward the one person that would be able to stop me.

"Mother?" I asked. We'd only just recovered from her freakout when I'd gone to the staviary. I didn't know how she'd handle the idea of me going all the way back to the meadow and out of the watchful shadow of the palace.

The meadow.

Despite the dire reasons for needing to go, a little

thrill shot through me. It seemed like so long ago since I'd smelled its sweet scent of grass and flowers. *Too* long. With that thought in my mind, I practically bounced on the balls of my feet in anticipation.

My mother smiled—a tremulous one, but one that held nevertheless. It was sincere. She meant it. "I'll look after Fae," she said. She gestured for the guards standing inside both sides of the doorway. "These two will accompany you."

"I promise I'll keep her safe, Your Majesty," Jay offered.

I'd been so ready for her to say no that I'd not expected her to let me go. She really was trying. I hesitated for just a moment, looking beyond my mother to where Fae slept in the bassinet. I hated to leave her, but I knew I could trust my mother with her. I darted forward and snatched my mother in a quick embrace, dashing a kiss upon her cheek. "I love you," I whispered in her ear.

Surprised, her arms came up behind my back to return the hug. "And I, you, darling." She squeezed me tight to her. "Always." I didn't think I imagined that her voice was a bit watery with that last part.

After a quick kiss on Fae's cheek, I sprinted toward the palace gates, seizing Jay's hand as I went. He fell into step beside me as we ran out, the guards at our heels.

My mother's voice followed us. "But please," she called after me, "for the love of the gods and all things holy, stay with Jay!"

My skirts swished around my ankles as I clutched them in my hands while we ran. "There are definitely no unicorns trapped yet?" I clarified, panting.

Jay shook his head. "No. No one's been hurt. Not yet, anyway." His tone was grim. "This isn't like the single trap that got to the baby unicorn, Eliana," he said. "This is a solid row of traps between the meadow and the city. If the unicorns keep to the skies, they'll be fine, but they have to come down sometime to eat. If we don't get to the traps first, it's only a matter of time."

I picked up my pace, but my body wasn't ready to be pushed. My breathing became labored, and I had to stop to catch my breath.

"Are you okay?" Jay asked, his eyes filling with concern.

"I was told by the doctor to rest this week," I wheezed. "Giving birth kinda takes it out of you."

His eyes widened in horror. "Lia, I'm sorry. I should have thought."

I held my hand up to quiet him. "I'll be fine."

He shook his head. "No. I'm not having you running around if the doctor ordered you not to. Hang on, I have an idea."

He took my hand and turned me around. We started back to the palace, passing the guards who looked as confused as I felt.

"We'll fly," he said by way of an explanation as we headed around the palace to the staviary.

The thought of flying again wasn't a pleasant one, but at least I wouldn't be in labor this time. I'd done it once, I could do it again.

"We'll take Misty."

"Right-o." I followed Jay into the staviary and threw open Misty's stall door. She stood quickly and nudged my pocket.

"No peanut butter sandwiches today," I said giving her a quick stroke on her nose. "I need a ride, but I promise I'll get you as many sandwiches as you like once we are done." She seemed to understand my words, lowering her front legs to I could mount her. I hopped onto her back and motioned for Jay to do the same.

"Williamson, Avery," I barked at the guards. They stood to attention, saluting me. "You'll have to follow on horseback. Take two of the horses."

They took off at a run to saddle up, no questions asked. My mouth curved. Despite mother's protection, at least no one here was questioning my authority in times of danger.

"To the meadow, Misty," I urged. "And hurry, if you please."

Jay clutched my waist as I gently prodded Misty with my heels. She cantered out of the stables and took to the skies.

I craned my neck and looked back toward the staviary, catching sight of two chestnut stallions as they streaked from the stables below us and toward the meadow.

A wave of nausea overcame me. Gripping Misty's mane tightly, I took a few deep breaths to make sure my lunch stayed on the inside. I didn't want a repeat performance of the other night, where I was sure I had thrown up at least once.

My pulse calmed as Jay pulled me closer to him. His chin nestled upon my shoulder as his arms tightened about my waist, causing my stomach to flip far more than the height had. I leaned forward, bringing Jay's body with mine so I was snug between Misty at my front and Jay at my back. He pulled his hands from around my waist and trailed them up my arms until he laced his fingers between mine, gripping Misty's mane. Suddenly, the height didn't bother me anymore. I was safe. I was protected. I was confused. Confused about how perfectly my body fit in his and how much I enjoyed the feel of him.

"Do you know where the traps are laid?" I asked Jay, raising my voice so that he could hear me over the wind in our ears.

I felt his nod against my cheek, which sent a shiver down my spine that had nothing to do with the cold air whizzing past us.

"Where are they?" I shouted back, trying to ignore the heat in my cheeks that was rapidly making its way further south.

His voice was tight. "Down the hillside... We should try to land in the trees. They haven't found any there. I don't want Misty accidentally trapping herself as we come in to land."

I nodded and looked out for a gap in the trees big enough for Misty to get her enormous wingspan through.

"There, Misty." I leaned forward, clutching her mane in one hand, and pointed to a small clearing with the other. "Come in slowly. I want to scan the ground."

She began to descend, and as she did, I scoured the ground beneath us. When I was sure it was safe, I told her to land.

Jay scrambled off of her back and held a hand up to help me down.

This time, when my hand took his, I managed to keep the blush at bay. Whatever I'd been feeling up in the air must have been produced by fear and nothing else. That thought made me feel a little better. I didn't need to complicate my life further.

"Misty, stay here. We'll be back soon. If you sense danger, fly away."

She nodded her head in understanding.

"It's almost as if she knows what you are saying,"

Jay marveled.

"I think she does. She's a smart unicorn. Now, where are these traps?"

Jay jerked his thumb to the left. "I left a couple of men on the hillside at the edge of the woods. They can't be too far away."

I looked to where he was pointing. Sunlight flittered through the canopy of leaves and, not too far in the distance, the edge of the woods was apparent.

As we walked, a couple of unicorns came out to greet us. They watched us cautiously as we walked along a well-worn path through the trees. I stopped, holding my hand out to them. They moved toward me, and the larger of the two nuzzled my hand.

"Have you seen any injured unicorns in these woods?" I asked, giving it a scratch behind its ears.

The unicorn didn't shake its head, but I could feel its answer. It wasn't scared. It had nothing to fear.

"They haven't seen anything," I said, turning to Jay.

His eyes widened, and his eyebrows lifted. "How could you possibly know that?"

I shrugged. "I just do. You head out to the men. I'll make sure these two are safe."

"I'm not leaving you. Your mother would have my guts for garters."

I laughed at his choice of words. "Fine, I'll come with you, but I think the unicorns might like to come too."

"The more, the merrier."

We ended up on the hillside, the city of Shipley below us in the distance. When we emerged from the trees, Williamson and Avery trotted over.

"We wondered where you'd ended up, Your Highness. We found the traps."

Williamson pointed to a spot by the tree line where

a couple of men were cautiously moving up and down through the tall grass, sticks in their hands to prod at the ground in front of them.

"You should stay in the trees," I cautioned the two unicorns. Jay took my hand as we walked over to the men.

"We need to keep a look at where we are going too. Those traps could take our legs clean off if they shut hard enough."

I looked to Williamson and Avery, who jumped down from their horses and tied them to a tree.

"How many are left?" Jay asked the two men, taking their attention from their job. They nodded their heads in a quick bow.

The older of the two, a man in his early sixties with a flat cap, said. "I don't know. This tall grass is murder. The trapper knew what he or she was doing. They're bloody impossible to see before you stand right on 'em, pardon my language, Your Highness."

"How many have you found?" I asked.

"Bloody hundreds of the buggers, pardon my language." He threw a long stick to Jay, who caught it in one hand.

He glanced at the two unicorns who were peeping out of the trees behind us.

"I think it's best if you stay here and make sure the unicorns stay in the trees. I'd feel a lot safer knowing that you weren't in harm's way too."

"I'm on it." That was why I'd been brought here. To make sure there were no accidents. I settled myself on a stump and watched as the five men worked.

Every couple of minutes or so, I heard a loud snap, and one of the men would bring his stick up, metal teeth biting into it. Then they'd bring it over to me, un-spring the trap, and throw it into a rapidly growing pile. The unicorns left soon after I sat down, probably growing bored with the lack of action. My mind began to wander in the warmth of the sun and the unrelenting thwack, thwack, thwack. The man was right, there were hundreds of traps. I wished I'd brought something to entertain myself with.

An hour or so in, something nudged my elbow from behind. My eyes shot wide in startling recognition as I met a pair of golden eyes that I'd looked into before.

"It's you!"

The baby unicorn's mother. She nodded her head so I could stroke her snout. I was surprised to see her, but she was probably bored cooped up in the staviary just as I had been in the palace. "Baby's doing well," I said encouragingly. "Her wound is almost entirely healed. The hostlers just want to give her a bit more time getting used to putting weight back on it, and we'll send both of you home to the meadow in just a few weeks."

She sagged in relief and let out a soft whicker.

"Thank you."

"You're very welcome!" I cheerily said aloud—then froze.

Oh. My. Gods.

My voice was quite squeaky when I spoke again. "Did you just...?"

I'd sat out in the sun for too long. I understood the unicorns. I always had, but to actually have them speak to me in words, well, that was absurd. There was no way that the unicorn had spoken to me.

"I did."

Her voice resonated in my mind but was accompanied by all the ordinary sounds that a unicorn could make. She huffed and snorted. I heard the sounds through my ears clear as day. But in my head... she sounded just as human as I did.

I was going mad. I had finally cracked.

"Don't get too hung up on this, human child. You are very well known around these parts. The unicorns far and wide have told tales of a beautiful princess. One we can understand. I wondered how long it would take you to understand us."

"No," I said, looking round in case I was a part of some weird practical joke. Jay and the others were far down the hillside, all of them immersed in their task. "This isn't real."

"Whyever not? You've always had an affinity with us. Not many humans would risk their own baby to save a unicorn baby."

"I didn't know I was going to go into labor," I said, wondering why I was pandering to this particular delusion and talking back.

"Eliana!" Jay called from the line of traps. He threw his arms up in a question when I looked at him. "Who are you talking to?"

"No one... The unicorn!" I shouted.

He didn't need to know it was actually talking *back.*

Beside me, the mother unicorn huffed as Jay went back to work. In the distance, there was another thwack of metal upon wood.

I picked up another stick from a pile nearby, ready for when the one of the men came back. They'd gone through so many sticks that I could build a bonfire with the mangled wood sitting in a pile beside the traps. As I waited for the man to trek up the hill, a thought occurred to me. "Miss, er... mother unicorn..."

"Zacarina, please."

"Zacarina, then... did you see the people laying

traps?" If we had a witness and a description, we had a chance at catching the monsters behind this.

Her eyes grew shifty, and she looked away from me. *"Not people. A man. One man. And yet... not a man at all,"* she said with a neigh. Her entire body shuddered as she spoke.

A man and not a man at all... I'd unpack *that* loaded statement later. How did one man manage to do all this without being seen?

"What did he look like?" I asked urgently, my heart pounding with excitement. We were going to catch him, whoever he was.

The unicorn shook her head. *"I don't know. I did not see. The forest felt strange, and I stayed well away."*

I deflated. Then we had nothing.

"But that doesn't mean I didn't hear him. He sang as he set about his gruesome work. And we heard him."

I frowned. A song wasn't much to go on, but maybe it would help somehow. If it was an unusual song or something that had been sung in taverns recently, perhaps we could pinpoint his origin or a place he might frequent. It was a start, at least.

"What was the song?"

"It had only one word repeating over and over again," she said grimly.

A feeling of dark foreboding washed over me.

"Rumplestiltskin."

HEIRESS OF GOLD

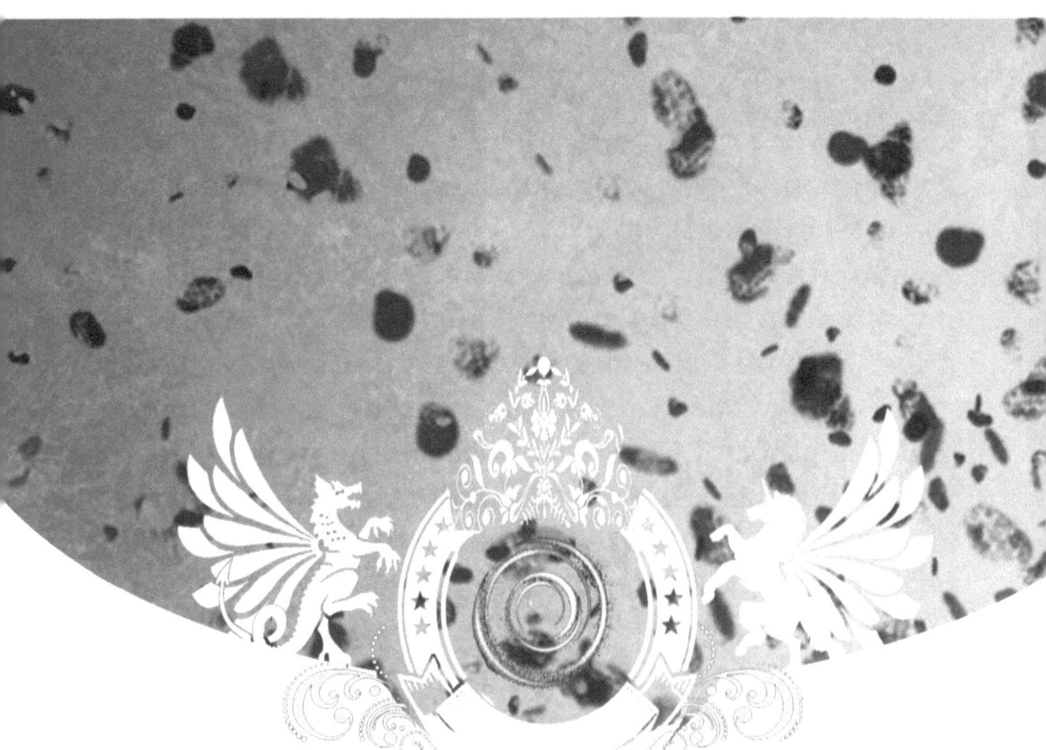

29TH APRIL

Fact: Animals don't talk.

Fact: Unicorns are a type of animal.

Ergo, unicorns don't talk.

It was a truth universally acknowledged. Not something anyone talked about it or debated because it was never even in question. Unicorns. Did not. Have the ability. To speak with humans.

I'd thought that, too, once.

But just one day ago, my world had been turned on its axis. A unicorn spoke to me. It was unthinkable. Incomprehensible. And yet... it had happened. I couldn't erase the memory if I tried. And there was no blaming it on my subconscious either. I knew that it hadn't happened in a dream or anything of the sort. The memory had the sort of sharp edges and clarity you only got from waking moments.

So either a unicorn really had spoken to me... or I'd

lost my ever-loving mind.

The sound of a little gurgle snapped me back to the present, and I blinked as I broke my gaze from the point on the wall I'd been staring at vacantly. I turned my attention instead to my daughter sleeping in my arms. She was stirring. If I didn't soothe that little gurgle away, she wouldn't be sleeping much longer, and this peaceful time rocking her in the rocking chair my mother had placed in our suite would come to an abrupt end. Already used to the movements that could be relied upon to get her to sleep, I gently bounced her and hummed a tune.

Gradually, she settled back down. And I relaxed, grateful to have a few more moments alone with my thoughts—as sleep-deprived as they were.

Fae was the most beautiful thing I'd ever created. The best thing I'd ever done. I just didn't understand why she seemed to hate for me to get any sleep. At all.

And gods above, I *needed* my sleep right now. Without it, I wasn't at all sure that the things I'd seen and done lately were much more than sleep-deprived delusions.

Like... for instance, talking unicorns. I just seemed to keep on circling right back to that point.

My tired gaze drifted outside the window.

I loved where Mother had put this rocking chair. It was right beside a big window so I could see all the hills and valleys that Vale had to offer. And there were *plenty* of them. I could see for miles. The sun beamed down over verdant green grass as winged unicorns grazed upon it and then took flight into the skies, searching for their next patch. Flowers bloomed so bold and bright that I could practically smell them, even hidden away indoors the way that I was. Trees that seemed to dwarf me when I stood before them looked small from here, stretched from the pit of the valley as though their top boughs strained to reach the peak.

I felt a slight pang at the memories of the last time I'd visited those hills and valleys. It had been tainted. I didn't even know who the culprit was. I only knew that traps had been set for unicorns the last time that I had been there. And that had changed everything.

I lived in a peaceful kingdom. A peaceful city, even. Sure, people had their good and bad days, but crime rates were, generally speaking, pretty low. And it was unthinkable that someone would harm a unicorn.

Except that these days, it was what I spent a great deal of time thinking about. Who would do it? And why?

I shook my head and shifted my attention to closer targets, hoping that they could steer my thoughts away from the mystery. I'd appreciate a distraction.

And a distraction, I got. Nearby in the palace yard, a couple picnicked. A blue and white checkered blanket was spread out with a wicker basket adorning the top of it. A young man in green trousers and a worn off-white work shirt reached inside and withdrew a bottle and two glasses. The young girl in a red dress laughed in delight when he poured, and the champagne foam overflowed over the side of the glass. From my spot here behind the window, I smiled. He handed her a dripping glass and kept one for himself. As he held her eyes, the smile faded from her lips as she gazed up at him. She blushed prettily as her beau reached forward to brush her hair from her eyes and whisper something in her ear.

My heart twinged, and I looked down at the sleeping baby in my arms. My daughter—the one who looked more like her father every day. The one whose father would never hold her in his arms, never get to know her eyes or her sweet baby smell.

Only a year ago, if you'd painted the picture just a little bit differently, that picnicking couple could have been Luka and I. Squint your eyes, and it could have been us now, only we'd be holding *Fae* in the air and laughing instead of clinking those sparkling little glasses of champagne. The fact that it wasn't... That it never could be... the fact that he was just *gone*...

I took a deep breath to center myself. The gaping maw of self-pity opened wide, but I'd spent too long already in its depths. I refused to succumb again right now.

Grief was tricky, I was finding. It waited in the wings for you. Even when it wasn't center stage, it was still *there.* One of the major players in the performance of my life. It still held me in its grasp. Probably always would. And it snuck up on me when I least expected it.

But there was no changing the fact that Luka *was* gone. And I was still here. I had to keep living. To keep breathing.

I looked outside once more, and movement from another direction diverted my eye away from the happy couple.

I smiled, shakiness dissipating and breathing easing.

A tall, well-built figure cut through the grass below, walking slowly, but with a steady and confident stride. Behind him, treading cautiously, was a small unicorn. The sun's light bounced off of her golden horn as she walked beside Jay. Next to them walked the baby's mother.

Gently, I got up from the rocking chair. Fae was sound asleep, breathing evenly. So, I deposited her into her bassinet. Her brow crinkled with the loss of my body's warmth, and she let out a little grunt. I held my breath, waiting to see if she woke up. But, thank the gods, she settled back into sleep as I watched.

I left the bassinet and crossed over to the window, pressing my fingers to the glass window pane. Baby—as I'd come to think of the baby unicorn that we'd found injured in a trap last week—limped as she gingerly put weight upon her injured leg. Her name had started as a joke at first—it was just easier to say "Baby" instead of "the baby unicorn"—but the more I used it, the more I liked it. And so far, I didn't know of any other name with which to call her.

I held my breath as I watched Baby take step after cautious step. But her leg seemed to bear her weight well. It had been bandaged well and seemed to be healing pretty beautifully. Unicorns healed much faster than humans or horses. All she had needed was for someone to set her leg properly and know how much to exercise her. At this rate, she'd be ready to return to the freedom of the meadows within a week or two.

As if feeling my gaze on him, the man with her looked up to the window and met my gaze.

Jay.

Instantly, a smile burst onto his face, and I felt the corners of my own lips turning up in return. A soft exhale left my mouth.

Jay had always been a good friend. An important friend. But now, he was an important...

An important... *Something.* But what?

The truth was, I didn't know what Jay was anymore, exactly. I'd been so sure he was just a good friend. But now... Well, he was very special to me, I knew that much. More than that, I wasn't really ready to say.

I didn't want to put a label on anything.

Pushing what was between us too fast felt like a recipe for breaking one or both of us. Like crushing the bud of a new flower between my fingers before it had time to bloom.

Seeing me smiling down at him, Jay lifted his hand in a greeting, and I pulled my hand away from the cool glass to wiggle my fingers at him in a wave, still grinning.

Until I felt eyes other than Jay's on me.

The golden-eyed mother unicorn with Baby and Jay lifted her head in a clear acknowledgment when I made eye contact with her. Her, I didn't need to invent a name for. Nor did I need to waste time calling her the mother unicorn.

Zacarina, I now knew her to be named. That's what she'd told me her name was, at any rate. Gods. My smile faded, and so did Jay's, seeing it. He tilted his head, brow crinkling. "What's up?" he mouthed.

I shook my head and rolled my eyes, clearly conveying that I had *no* idea what he was talking about.

I forced a smile onto my face so Jay wouldn't worry anymore as I looked back at Zacarina. *Had* she told me that was her name? Or... had *I* named her? And just imagined that she told me that?

I put a hand to my head and tried to play the gesture off as casual instead of the steadying movement that it was. Hopefully, Jay couldn't see my hand trembling from down below.

Gods, I was going "round the bend," wasn't I?

He gave me a salute in farewell and kept on walking with Zacarina and Baby. Likely, he'd get them their exercise and return them to the staviary where they could rest.

I'd never felt quite so shaken in the presence of

unicorns before. Normally, they had a calming effect on me. Before, being near them generally comforted me and lifted my spirits. But not lately. No, lately, my thoughts were too tumultuous for even *them* to assuage. Lately, when I was around them, I was reminded of what was going on with them. That they had spoken to me when the laws of nature decreed that should be impossible. And possibly a bigger concern was the fact that something was preying upon the unicorns. And I didn't know who or what that might be.

I left the window and began to pace, wearing a tread into the carpet.

There were clues about the unicorn trapper, but they were few and far between. They wouldn't get us very far at all in solving the case.

Most people would never attempt to capture a unicorn—the most peaceful of peaceful creatures. It was said that they were blessed by the gods—even acted as a go-between for our mortal realm and the *im*mortal realm. But now, traps had been set in the meadows not once when Baby had been caught up in their vicious jaws, but twice. Thankfully, the second time, we'd been able to intervene before anyone else had been hurt. But the culprit had grown bolder that second time. There were well over a dozen traps set when we'd found them all laid out in the meadow. I couldn't imagine who would dare to do such a thing.

Then again, maybe I could. Frankly, it was more likely that my own mind had conjured the only clue I had than it was likely to be real.

Zacarina, had seen the man laying the traps...well... she'd *heard* him, anyway. He'd sang as he worked. And his song had only one word.

Rumpelstiltskin.

I felt a chill brush over my skin as the syllables turned themselves over and over again in my mind.

Rumpelstiltskin.

It had been a childhood joke. A piece of decor. An invented swear word. A curse.

And now, a mystery.

My eyes trailed over the walls of the suite I'd grown up in. To put it more aptly, they trailed the word that festooned that wall. *Rumpelstiltskin.* One and the same. It was a fictional phrase that I'd grown up hearing, but I'd never known its true meaning. The word littered the palace, but it had always seemed a strange silliness. A weird little word that I didn't know the meaning of—because what meaning could there possibly be in something like that?

Still, it was a word that my mother wanted me to know; that she had insisted upon being a part of my vocabulary. And so artwork containing the phrase littered the walls of my childhood—and now, adulthood in my room.

I hadn't mentioned my "conversation" with Zacarina about who had set the traps to anyone. For starters, I wasn't at all sure that they'd have believed me. *I* wasn't even sure that I believed me. Secondly... there wasn't much to go on, was there?

I had a *word* to go on. A single, ridiculous word.

And then there was Mother. Mother, who had reacted to a new baby in the family by tightening her reins on me so tightly that I felt like I wasn't able to breathe. Mother, who was only now, after a somewhat cataclysmic argument, beginning to let me live my life again.

At least *now* she let me leave the palace every so often. Albeit with guards in tow, even if I'd rather not have the company. Anyone who ever said privacy was overrated had never had to live their life with someone peering interestedly over their shoulder, with someone sticking their fingers into all of their decisions. As far as I was concerned, the guards could see themselves out.

I suppose that wasn't *entirely* fair, though. My guards, Williamson and Avery, weren't bad guys. They were just... also not guys I'd choose to spend my free time with. They tried—I'd even convinced Avery to bend the rules once upon a time. But he was *so nervous* about it the whole time. There wasn't even a little part of him that could enjoy it. I guessed that I was lucky to have them, though. It was something of a miracle that Mother hadn't already had them replaced when I snuck out of the palace to visit the staviary—the time I'd convinced Avery to abandon his post outside my bedroom door. I'd made sure to intervene so that he hadn't lost his job then.

A knock came at the door.

I cringed, darting a glance toward Fae's bassinet. Thankfully, the knock hadn't woken her. But speak of the devils. That knock was sure to be Avery and Williamson, as I lived and breathed.

I stopped pacing, then turned and closed the door to the bedroom so that I wouldn't wake my sleeping daughter.

"Yes?" I raised my voice and turned toward the entrance.

Avery's voice was the one that greeted me. "Uh, we've got a visitor out here for you, ma'am. Mr. Jay? The staviary keeper," he added hastily. I couldn't help the smile the crept over my face. As though I needed to be reminded of who Jay was.

"Yes, I know who he is," I said, letting my voice reveal

my amusement. "You can go ahead and send him in!"

The lock clicked as the handle was turned, and the guards admitted Jay to the chambers. He smiled at me. It was as though I hadn't just seen that very same smile, not twenty minutes ago through the window. And there was a strange little flutter in my stomach at the sight of his sun-reddened cheeks, his wind-tousled hair and the mud on his boots standing here in front of me. For just a moment, I forgot about all of the other thoughts plaguing me, and I just saw Jay. And I smiled back, because how could I not?

"Saw you watching," he said, gesturing toward one of the windows. "I figured I should come up and say hello. Thought it would make you feel less like a creepy little spy."

Despite myself, my cheeks heated. He was teasing me. I knew that he was teasing me, but the embarrassed reaction was instantaneous and instinctive anyway. I blustered. "I... You... Oh, just shut it," I said, swatting at him.

Playfully, he leaped out of reach of my arms and danced away. My lips twitched. I should be annoyed, but really, he was so cute when he was pleased with himself that way.

"How's Baby?" I asked once he settled down and stopped laughing.

He took a seat on the couch in my sitting room and started to put his feet up on my coffee table, but stopped, grimacing when he saw all of the dirt caked on to his shoes. Gingerly, he placed them back down on the floor and looked up at me. "Do you have a rag I could use? I don't want to mess your rug all up."

"The damage has already been done, I'm afraid," I reported with feigned solemnity. Jay looked back at his path into the room and blanched at the clear track he'd left. Mud caked the carpet in the shape of the footprints.

"I'm sorry," he said, pulling his boots off and carrying them to the door in his socked feet before heading back to the couch.

I waved a hand, dismissing him. "Stop. It's fine. I'll sort it out later. Now... Baby?" I prompted again.

"Right." He relaxed, his hands falling back to his sides and grasping the edge of the couch so that he perched there, as little of his soiled clothes touching the fabric as possible. His eyes lit up, thinking of the baby unicorn. "I can hardly believe how well Baby's doing. I mean, you saw her. She's doing *great*," he enthused. "That's the great thing about her being, well... a baby. Unicorns already heal *super* fast, but at that age?" He whistled low. "It's lightning-quick when they're that young. Their bodies are already changing so fast that the healing time just sort of gets sucked up into that. She'll be ready to go back to the meadows in no time."

Back to the meadows... the hairs on the back of my neck stood on end as I remembered my earlier musings. I wasn't so sure returning Baby to the meadows where she'd been trapped was such a great idea. But I supposed it didn't matter all that much what I thought.

"Also..." he raised an eyebrow. "Baby? I see we haven't come up with any better names yet?"

"I've gotten attached to Baby," I defended my choice. "It's unique. And a hell of a lot faster than continuing to call her 'the baby unicorn' over and over again." *Plus, Zacarina seems to like it too. Or at least, she hasn't told me she* didn't *like it.*

He held up his hands. "That's a fair point, I guess. Speaking of babies..." He raised an eyebrow and gestured toward the bedroom where Fae slept. "Can

I...?"

I bit my lip, indecisive. "Ordinarily, you know I'd be only too happy to let you see her," I said. That was the truth, too. I loved that Jay seemed to honestly adore Fae. And it wasn't just the fact that she was my daughter. He just loved *her*. He was easy like that.

"Okay, so why is today different from an ordinary day, then?" he asked.

"It *is* an ordinary day," I said. "It's just not an ordinary hour. It's just that it took me an age to get her down. Catch me when she's actually awake, and you can have all the Fae time you can handle. But right now, she's sleeping." I yawned, feeling envious of my infant daughter in that moment. Sleep sounded so, *so* nice.

As if sensing that she was the topic of our conversation, a cry split the air.

I deflated. I swore, when I looked back on Fae's infancy, I was sure I'd have pleasant memories of her cute little face and her baby noises while I fed her. I'd marvel over how sweet she'd looked as she slept. But right now, I'd kill for a bit of alone time and a couple of hours of decent sleep.

But Jay, not having had *his* sleep deprived because of the sound, brightened.

"Solo...?" He trailed off questioningly, widening his eyes in a prompt for an answer.

Gods bless him. He did try *so* hard not to look too eager.

"Go," I said, sighing a little bit. "I guess it's better you than me. I just fed the little tyrant before she slept, so she shouldn't be hungry. And if you can get her back to sleep, I'll give you—"

"Your firstborn?" His lips quirked to one side, and

his eyes danced.

"No, I won't go that far. But maybe an IOU for a cookie from the castle kitchens."

He licked his lips. "A freshly baked cookie?"

"As fresh as I can manage."

He stuck out his hand to seal the bargain. "If you make it a peanut butter cookie, you've got yourself a bargain."

"Done." I shook his hand and my head, laughing. "I swear, you and the unicorns make quite the team with your peanut butter obsession."

But Jay wasn't listening. He'd already opened the door to the bedroom and was lifting Fae into his arms. My daughter's cries quieted to small fussing sounds as he cradled her against his chest, and she nestled into the warmth of his body.

I leaned against the door frame, watching the two of them, heart melting.

Part of me longed to know what that felt like—to be cradled against Jay's chest like that. I imagined it had to feel so warm, so safe. But for now, I was content just to watch him with my daughter. A soft smile played about my lips as he sang to her.

But I couldn't help but think of the lyrics to another song. A song that plagued me.

Rumpelstiltskin.

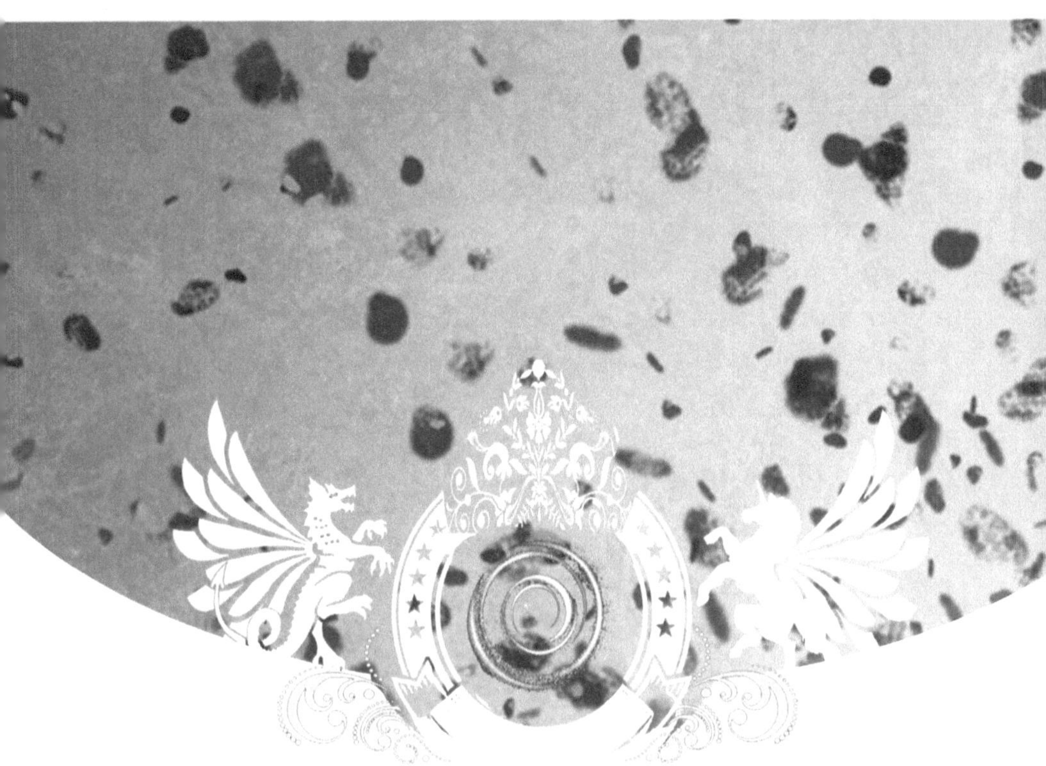

30TH APRIL

"Hand me that, would you?" I held out a hand for one of the little burp cloths I used for Fae. I'd tossed it on to her dresser in a rolled-up ball, and it needed to be put in with the dirty laundry.

Mother passed me the cloth but wasn't distracted from saying her piece. "He'd be so good for you," she said.

I sighed. I'd made the mistake of telling her how sweet Jay and Fae had looked together yesterday when he'd held her after she'd woken up from her all-too-brief nap. "I know he would, Mother."

"And it would be so wonderful for the baby, too." She clasped her hands together and gazed fondly in the direction of Fae's bassinet.

"I *know*, Mother."

"Don't you want her to have a father?"

I bristled and whipped my head around to look at her in disbelief. I couldn't believe she had the audacity to say that to me. Not just because it hadn't even been a year since Luka had passed. Fae could be twenty, and I still wouldn't think she should say that.

"She has a father," I snapped. "You might remember him. Big guy... married to me... went by the name of Luka?"

She winced. "I'm sorry. I spoke poorly. Of course, no one could ever replace Luka. We miss him too. And no one will ever be exactly what he was to you or what he would have been for Fae." She shrugged, speaking more carefully this time. "But perhaps it would be possible for you to have something equally wonderful... just different."

I bit my lip. I was willing to forgive her for misstepping. I knew she hadn't meant it the way that it had sounded. But I didn't know that I was willing to entertain the idea of moving on just yet. The best I could give her was a "Maybe."

One thing I could say about my mother: Give her an inch, and she'd take a mile. "Your father and I *really* like him," she singsonged.

The funniest thing about this conversation was that she probably thought she was just dropping subtle little hints about moving on when, in reality, she might as well have been slinging them with the force of a slingshot anvil.

I sighed and folded one corner of one of Fae's blankets up so that it made a neat little square. With the dirty laundry safely in the hamper, I was focusing on putting Fae's clean things away. For such a tiny thing, she had more laundry than a barrack full of soldiers. I could have asked the palace staff to do it for me, but I wanted to do things for Fae myself.

"Perhaps you and Father should consider marrying Jay, then," I said dismissively.

Distancing myself from the conversation was the easiest way to keep it from getting heated.

There was no bite in my tone, but when I caught a glimpse of my mother's expression, I could see that I had hurt her feelings.

"Sorry." I winced. "I didn't mean that the way that it sounded."

Round and round we went. Hurting each other and then forgiving each other. But I supposed forgiveness was the most important part of all of it. Choosing to forgive would always be something I did for the people I loved.

And most things were easy to forgive. Mother tilted her head to the side, hurt vanishing after my apology to give way to curiosity. "What *did* you mean, then? Is it so very platonic between the two of you? Do you really not have *any* feelings for Jay?"

I balked, something in me immediately denying the question. "I wouldn't say that," I said.

"He loves you, you know."

I sighed again. *That* I knew. When I knew nothing else, when my bones had turned to dust and settled into the earth, when my body had vanished, and only my soul remained, I would still know that he loved me.

When I didn't speak—couldn't really bring myself to if I was being honest—my mother laid one of her hands over mine, which was still holding the folded blanket. "And he certainly loves the baby." She tilted my chin up so that I met her eyes. "I believe you love him too," she said softly. "Am I wrong?"

Wordless, I shook my head.

"Then what's the problem? Why deny yourself this happiness?"

Why? There were so very many reasons, I didn't even know if I could list them all. For starters, I still felt married. Like it would be a betrayal to Luka. I had to constantly remind myself that it wasn't the case. And then, there was the fact that...

"I don't know if I can love him the right *way*," I confessed. "What if I do only love him as an... attractive friend?"

Mother had the good grace to hide a laugh when I admitted that I found Jay attractive.

I forged on, pretending I hadn't seen her amusement. "And if I'm *not* sure... wouldn't that be doing wrong by him? I don't want to hurt him."

"Oh, darling..." Mother smiled and squeezed my hands. She looked into my eyes and said, "All that you can do is try. All we can do is love everyone we can as well as we can in the time we've been given. Doing less than that is the only way you would do a disservice to yourself."

I remained unconvinced. Even if I *did* feel that way about Jay, I wasn't sure that I was ready to let another person into my life in a romantic capacity.

I still missed Luka. I was still sad that I lost him. It still pained me every single day that he wouldn't get to see our daughter grow up, that he would miss her first words, her first steps. He would never get to be amazed by the simple pleasures of being a parent. I still had to take a second when I woke up in the morning to remind myself that he wasn't here with me anymore.

And when I *did* become ready to move on... wouldn't it be weird for me to do so with Jay, of all people? I'd known him forever. We'd grown up together. And what if it didn't work out? If I broke his heart or if he broke mine... I didn't think I could stand to lose him from my life. He'd leave a big gaping hole in it much the same way Luka had. But losing Luka hadn't been a choice. And I didn't know if I could forgive myself if I made a choice that cost me Jay.

"Do you have plans today, dear?" my mother inquired, changing the subject.

Thank the gods. She seemed to be taking pity on me. Or maybe she was just satisfied enough that I was seriously considering what she'd asked me. Making me think was enough for her right now, I guessed. With her question about my plans, she broke me from my musings about a future romantic relationship—or perhaps a permanently platonic one; I wasn't sure which one it was yet. I considered my answer just as carefully as I had her questions about pursuing a new relationship.

The truth was, I wanted to find some answers. I couldn't just keep idly wondering about the unicorn trapper. I had to try and find some sign of the only clue I had. And if I operated under the assumption that I really *could* talk to the unicorns and that I *wasn't*... well... for lack of a better word... *crazy*... then my only lead for who was after the unicorns was the song. The *word*. Rumpelstiltskin. I knew the word, but not as a song. It wasn't a tune I'd ever heard someone sing—certainly not one that was popular in Vale. But that didn't mean it didn't exist. And if it *did* exist, I had to believe there was some mention of it that was likely to be found in the palace library.

"I thought I might visit the library with Fae," I said carefully. "It'll be nice and calm in there. A perfect napping place for her."

That was, provided my beautiful monster of a daughter didn't wake up and start screaming to the high heavens. And well, if she did… it wasn't as though Vale was the most scholarly of all the kingdoms anyway. It was a thorough collection—mother had seen to that. She didn't want anyone to be able to criticize our holdings. But when it came to afternoon occupants in there, it would most likely just be the old librarian, Mr. Swink. And I happened to know that, like my good friend Jay, he had a soft spot for the palace kitchen's cookies. Unlike Jay, though, his treat of choice wasn't a peanut butter cookie but a good old-fashioned chocolate chip. I'd bet that if I brought him a bribe—no, not a bribe, I corrected myself—a *gift* of a delicious, freshly-baked treat when I got there, he'd give me just about anything. Including a deaf ear if my baby started wailing away in his sacred space of a library.

My mother lit up. She loved it when someone actually appreciated the collection that she'd taken the time to build. "You hardly ever go to the library. Why the change of heart?"

"I thought it might be a nice compromise if I *occasionally* kept my wanderings within the palace walls rather than meandering around the city and wilderness." I winked at my mother. "From time to time at any rate."

She softened and even managed to smile. "Look at us, joking about it and everything."

I slung an arm around her shoulders. "Maybe there's hope for us after all."

~

After finishing tidying up within my suite, I headed down to the kitchens to charm my way into a cookie.

"Afternoon, Mrs. Bellon!" I hollered when I let myself into the kitchens. The wizened palace cook poked her head around the corner. Her hair was a faded ginger color and her eyes, a dusty blue. Flour dusted her cheeks, and her well-worn apron had scorch marks decorating its front.

She squinted her eyes at me, suspiciously. "I'll not be letting you dip your fingers into tonight's dessert just yet, Your Highness. You'll have to wait until after dinner like everyone else."

That momentarily distracted me from my quest. "What *is* tonight's dessert, Mrs. Bellon?"

"Caramel butter bars topped with ice cream."

My mouth watered. I could hardly wait.

"No, that's not why I'm here. Although you did guess right—I'm craving something sweet. Do you think you could help me?" I smiled winningly.

These kitchens had been an expectant mother's dream when I'd been pregnant with Fae. Anytime I'd had a craving, they'd done their best to accommodate me.

"The freshly baked cookies are in the pantry. I did a batch of chocolate chip and peanut butter this morning."

I let myself into the large food storage pantry and found a clear glass jars with a tiny chalkboard attached that read *PB.* Next to it, stood one labeled *Choc. Chip.,* which I quickly pulled from the shelf.

I gazed down at Fae, swaddled carefully in a baby sling, and idly stroked the soft hair on the crown of her head. I wondered what kind of cookies would be her favorite when she was old enough to try them. Would she like a classic chocolate chip? Or peanut butter, like Jay? Luka's favorite had always been snickerdoodles.

I smiled, thinking about it. He'd been a sucker for them too. If I greeted him at the door in the evening with a plate of snickerdoodles, he'd do anything I asked.

He'd never denied me much anyway. He'd always done his best to make me happy. As I had, him. And we'd succeeded too. I just wished we'd been able to keep making each other happy for much, much longer.

Armed with a perfectly soft and freshly baked cookie, I headed to the library.

"Your Highness!" The librarian, Mr. Swink, jumped up from his position behind the library desk. His elbow thumped a stack of books and sent them tumbling to the floor with a loud series of thumps. He winced with each one as though their falls were inflicting bruises upon him. A pink tinge rose from his cheeks all the way to his bald cap between little tufts of white hair, and I smiled, amused.

"The poor books." If I teased, it was gently and with good humor. "Do you need to rescue them?"

"No!" But, betraying him, he couldn't seem to help that his eyes darted down to the books. And they *did* look a sight. Practically indecent. Their covers flapped open, exposing the pages inside, which were bent and askew. Dust jackets hung on for dear life, and I swore that one author's portrait inside glared accusingly up at us. Mr. Swink sighed. "Yes, I suppose they do need a knight in shining armor, and I suppose it must be me." He pushed his glasses up the bridge of his nose and bent to retrieve the books.

Fae was still strapped to my chest in her complicated baby wrap. Maybe it had to do with the warmth or being so close to me, or the ability to feel my heartbeat in that position, but she was sleeping soundly. Feeling reasonably confident that I wouldn't wake her by doing so, I knelt down and handed poor Mr. Swink his last book.

"Thank you, Your Highness." He lifted the sizable stack back into his arms, set them on his desk, and sat back down with a great huff from the exertion.

Then he proceeded to open each one, smoothing out the new wrinkles on the pages as best he could with great care. He ran a hand over their spines affectionately, as one would the back of a beloved pet. At last, satisfied with his soothing of the books, he moved them to his left and clasped his hands before him, giving me his full attention. "What can I do for you today?" His eyes strayed to Fae, sleeping sweetly on my chest. Though he tried valiantly, he didn't quite succeed in hiding his grimace. "And... for the young princess?"

Good old Mr. Swink. So predictably didn't want the sanctity of his library violated with a baby's cry.

Good thing I had an ace up my sleeve. I slid the chocolate chip cookie across the desk, its warm and delicious aroma wafting up to us, and winked at him. "Just point the two of us to your music section if you'd be so kind."

His eyes lit up as I folded the napkin back so that he could see what was inside, and all signs of his doubt about a baby's presence in his library vanished. He whipped his hand to the left and pointed. "It's just that way. Two shelves in and make a right."

"Thank you, Mr. Swink." I nodded a good-bye, and Fae and I set off. Everything was going perfectly according to plan. At this rate, I'd find Rumpelstiltskin before the dinner bell rang.

However, once I'd followed his directions and walked

those two shelves in and make that right, I swallowed, daunted. I may have bitten off more than I could chew with this project.

The area Mr. Swink directed me to was but one *aisle* of the music section. It was *huge.* There were hundreds, if not thousands, of books here before me. They towered overhead, crept around the corner, and kept on going. For all I knew, they went to the end of the row.

I should have guessed that might be the case. Mother was a talented piano player and a great lover of music. If there was a book that the palace library hadn't already contained, she'd have made damn certain we obtained it. Nothing in Vale would be lacking on her watch. She had taken great pride in creating a magnificent library, and she would have been certain to concentrate on the music books section.

Where would I even start?

My eyes scanned the shelves. There were small books and tall books. Thin ones and thick. Their spines were every shade from pastel pink to the blackest of night. But at least there did seem to be a certain amount of organization They seemed to be sorted alphabetically by author, then by title—so I supposed that was as good a place to start as any. Rumpelstiltskin began with R. I'd start there.

The music aisle containing authors beginning with R was, of course, several aisles down from where I'd started. And when I found them, none of them were named Rumpelstiltskin.

"Nooo, of course not," I muttered quietly under my breath, reaching past Fae on my chest so that I could let my fingers dance over the spines. "That would have been just too easy, wouldn't it? Couldn't let a single mom have a break, could we?" I glared upwards, intending the gods to know I meant them in my indictment.

Seeing no other better starting point, I piled as many books as I could carry against my hip, made my way over to a table, pulled out a chair, and opened one of the books. The book's pages stared up at me in a challenge, and I sighed. "I guess I might as well get started."

Hours later, I'd only managed to make it through the grand sum of *four* out of the many more books that I'd picked up. I wasn't a slow reader by any means—but I wasn't a prodigy with inhuman abilities either. I rubbed at my eyes and yawned, looking down at Fae, who peered up at me curiously with her Luka eyes. I wasn't sure when she'd woken up, but somehow, miraculously, she hadn't begun to bawl. Maybe my lie to Mother had been right about this being a good napping spot. Or maybe something about this place full of books and words and knowledge spoke to my girl on an instinctive level. Perhaps it felt as spiritual to her as a temple.

I grinned. "Thank you for staying quiet, sweet girl," I whispered, carefully smoothing a hand over her little tuft of hair. "We'll go now. Get us both some dinner."

I piled three of the books that I hadn't been able to get to into my arms and deposited them into a bag that I'd brought with me for this exact purpose. Realistically, I thought I could maybe get through two more tonight. If I looked at it more optimistically, all three—though I wasn't sure when that would leave time for sleeping.

One thing was for sure, though: The answer to the mystery of Rumpelstiltskin wouldn't be solved quickly with me as its lone detective heading up the case. But until I thought of a way to explain how I'd come upon the name that did not involve telepathy with unicorns, I'd have to settle for working alone. I liked to think that it was going to make me stronger.

I left the library and nearly bumped straight into my mother walking inside.

"Oh!" she jumped back to avoid sending Fae crashing against my chest and laughed nervously, a hand fluttering against her chest. "I was just looking for you." Curiously, she glanced down into my bag to try to get a glimpse of the titles of the books I carried. "Have you been here all afternoon? What's grasped your attention so? What are you reading?"

"Just some music books." Although that answer wasn't a lie, I wanted to dismiss her question quickly, so I tugged at the top of the bag so that the titles were hidden and invented a reason why I was suddenly so fascinated by music. "I thought I'd get ideas for the party. You know, maybe do something a little fun and different? I mean, the dance lesson went so well last week that I was just... inspired."

Gods, I was lying through my teeth. Guilt squirmed through me as her expression lit up, and she clasped her hands together in excitement.

"That's perfect!" she exclaimed. "I wanted to see if you had any time to help me with the party tomorrow."

I bit my lip. That would take time away from my research...

Mother mistook my indecision for reluctance and withdrew. "Of course, if you're too busy... I mean, if you don't *want* to..."

"No, I do!" I assured her. Shame continued to spiral through me. *Liar,* it accused. *Bad daughter.*

Somehow, I had to figure out a way to both research and help her with Fae's welcome party. I'd be a model daughter *and* a crime solver.

I had to be.

What other choice was there?

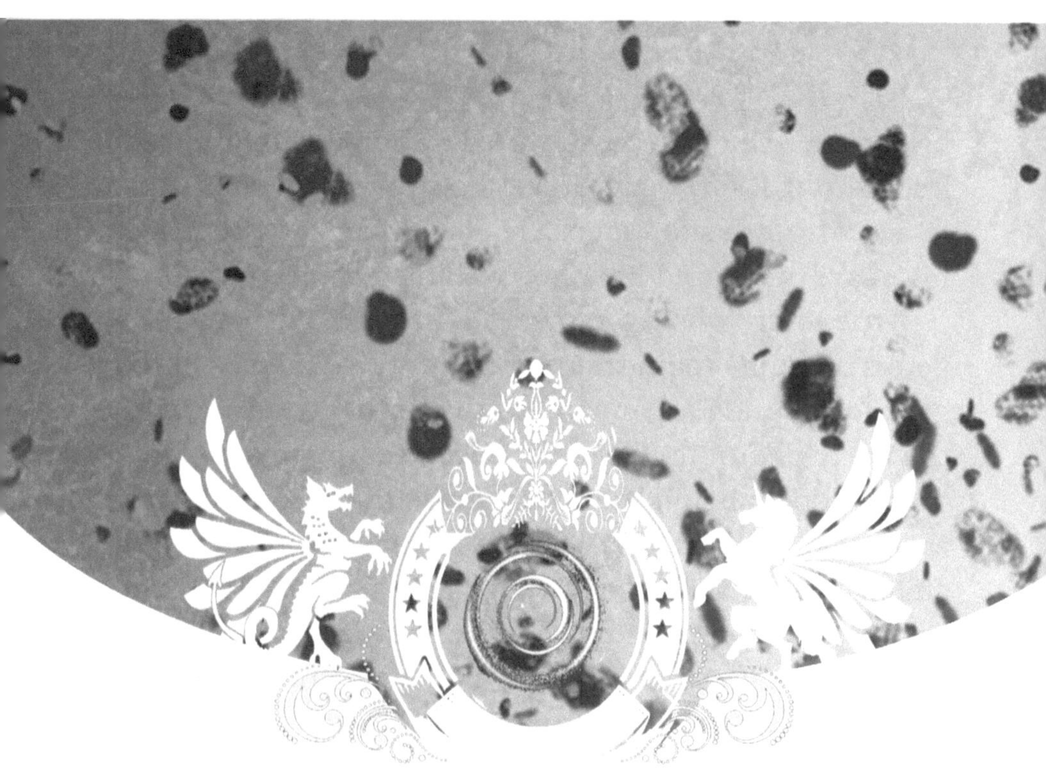

1ST MAY

The next morning, I rubbed at my tired eyes and stretched in my bed. I was loath to leave my warm and comfy sheets. In the night, the mattress had molded perfectly to my body, and it felt like the best and biggest warm hug. And, miraculously, Fae had suddenly acclimatized to sleeping when she was supposed to and only woken me for a couple of night feeds.

Sleep tugged at me like a childhood friend eager to play a game. "Come on back," it invited.

But alas, I had to leave the hug and the comfort of my bed.

Sunlight beckoned through the windows—I'd forgotten to draw the shades closed last night, or else I might *still* be asleep. So instead of a dark room, I had a bright one. The new day awaited. Much as I might wish I could put it off, I couldn't. I had things to do. People to see. Mysteries to, hopefully, solve. And a daughter to take care of. I could hear her wailing from her bassinet.

True to my word to my mother, after I'd dropped the books off in my room last night and we'd had dinner, I'd gone to her and Father's rooms to help her continue with the party planning. We'd discussed seating plans, food, decorations, and all the other things that a formal party seemed to need. I'd have been happy with something simple and elegant, but my mother, sucked in by the excitement, had insisted we go all out for Fae. Not that Fae would have cared either which way. She'd probably sleep through the whole thing.

In the end, when I started to rub at my temples, frustrated with how we were going around and around in circles, I let my mother have her way. It was easier than arguing, and I'd deprived her of a huge wedding, as she kept reminding me.

That had been about all that I could take last night.

Especially as I still fully intended on reading further in the books I'd smuggled from the palace library.

And I did, to no avail. There wasn't a single mention in any of their pages about Rumpelstiltskin or who—or what—that might be.

I fell asleep with one of the books splayed open across my chest, promising myself that I would rest my eyes for just a moment, and then I'd keep reading. When I awoke later in the night to feed Fae, the book was below me. I felt a twinge of guilt, looking at its crinkled pages. Hopefully, poor Mr. Swink wouldn't be too bent out of shape with me for the abuse they'd suffered at my hands. I made sure to be more careful with the next set.

I managed to read the last few pages of the final

book while I fed Fae and after I changed her resulting dirty diaper.

I glanced at the stately clock in the corner of my room. It had golden hands, and birds decorated its face. At the bottom of the pendulum dangled a silver shoe. It was feminine, and I'd always loved it. Mother had told me it was a gift from the royals of Arcadia when I'd been born.

It was barely 7 a.m., and I was already exhausted. Mr. Swink wouldn't be at the library for hours, so I couldn't refresh my stock of research books yet.

But I *could* go pay Jay a visit.

Mentally, I corrected the thought, feeling my whole body flush as though someone had heard the inner workings of my mind and called me out on it. No, the early hour had nothing at all to do with Jay. It simply meant that I could go down to the *meadow* and pay the *unicorns* a visit.

I had wanted to check on them after the fiasco with the traps being laid. As I understood it, we had a patrol working to keep the unicorns safe, but it was a minimal effort—a two-man job. One on the day shift. One on the night. I'd like to see with my own eyes that they were doing all right and hadn't fallen prey to any more vicious traps that had been laid.

I summoned Avery and Williamson, and by *summoned,* I mean that I walked to the door and poked my head outside my suite of rooms to tell them where I was heading. As expected, they saluted and followed me as I carried Fae from my room, strapped, once again, in her sling.

After a detour to drop Fae off with Mother, I headed outside, flanked by my trusty guards.

I found Jay in the staviary, exactly where I'd hoped

he would be. It was where he spent most of his time, even if he wasn't technically on duty. Jay didn't have the bond with the flying steeds that I did, but he certainly cared about them just as much.

Jay's face lit up when he saw me, but it fell a fraction of an inch as he scanned my empty arms and met my eyes, looking both disappointed and reproachful all at once. "No Fae?" he asked.

"She's with Mother. Not today." I shook my head.

He splayed his arms wide at his side. "But Fae wants to see Uncle Jay!"

"You're a poet," I said, grinning at him.

"That I am. A true wordsmith. You love me for it."

My heart leapt to my throat as that word—*love*. It seemed to swim through the air, etch itself into the ether, and then squirm into my insides, where it burrowed in. I wouldn't have thought much of it, not too long ago. I was more than willing to admit that I loved Jay. I still did. Only these days, I wasn't sure exactly *how* I loved him. In what way.

Jay's smile faded, his wide grin vanishing when he realized I was no longer laughing. "What is it? What's wrong?"

I shook my head and forced a smile to my lips. One that became genuine when I saw the warmth and worry in his eyes. "Nothing," I said. "It's nothing. It's a nice day to check on the unicorns, though. Do you want to take a walk down to the meadows with me and check on the traps—or I guess I should say, the hopeful lack thereof? The boys are coming too." I gestured to Avery and Williamson, who were idling by the entrance to the staviary. Avery cocked a hip to the side, and Williamson gave Jay a flippy little wave in hello.

Jay nodded back. "Hello," he said solemnly.

"Lead the way," he said to me with that damnable little head tilt of his that he did.

It made his hair fall into his eyes, casting them into the slightest shadow so that the light that did still hit them made them look as though they sparkled.

It also made my heart skip a bit.

In no particular hurry to get there, we took our time, strolling over the grass and through the flowers. The grass crunched beneath our feet and bees buzzed from flower to flower, collecting their pollen and bypassing the buds that had yet to open. Despite my resentment of the sun this morning for daring to wake before I'd really been ready to, now I relished the warmth of its rays on my skin.

The skies were clear. It was a beautiful day. And this was the perfect place to be.

And—I snuck a look at Jay—the company was about as good as it got.

The farther we walked from the palace, the more the tightness in my chest seemed to ease. I hadn't even realized it had been there.

Everything that had weighed heavily on me, pulling me down, I was leaving behind, if only for a short while. My mother and the endless arguments, the burden of motherhood, the constant worry that I was going crazy.

The only thing that wasn't weighing me down was Jay. I'd expected a walk with him to be fraught with worry about how he felt, about how I felt, but I found I was just enjoying his company.

Jay cast me a curious look. "You all right? You're quiet. Which is weird for you."

"No one knows weird better than you. You're the expert," I said playfully, sneaking another peek at him, taking in his strong profile, the shape of his jaw.

He really was a good-looking guy. How had I not noticed just how good-looking before now?

We made it to the hill where we'd found so many traps. I nodded a greeting to the guard on duty. He wiped his brow as he dropped the salute he'd assumed when he saw that I was with Jay, Avery, and Williamson. "Your Highness," he greeted. "You honor me with your visit."

"At ease," I said with a smile. The poor guy looked more nervous to be meeting me than he did to be overseeing the meadow.

He relaxed a fraction, his posture a little less rigid now. Below his helmet, a bead of sweat dripped onto his upper lip. "Phew," he said. "It's warm out today."

It was. I had broken into a light sweat myself, but I didn't mind. In fact, I relished it. "What's your name?" I asked.

"Carson, ma'am." He almost flinched at his own voice. His hand spasmed like he had to force it to stay at his side instead of flying to his head for a salute.

"Any sign of trouble, Carson?" I asked, trying to keep my tone light and friendly.

He shook his head vigorously. "Not a lick of it, Your Highness. No prowlers except for a young couple with a picnic. No traps to find anything caught in. And the unicorns themselves have been quiet too."

That twanged a string of discord within me. It didn't sound right. "Exactly how quiet are we talking?" I asked. Dread built within me.

He exchanged a look with Avery and Williamson, as if to see if they thought this line of questioning was as strange as he did. They only shrugged in response as if to say, *Beats us.* "Well..." he drew out the word. "I guess that I mean I haven't seen hide nor horn of them in my last two shifts."

Jay, however, saw exactly where I was going. He swore under his breath, but I held up a hand for quiet, heart suddenly pounding. Hope wasn't lost. "Do you consider yourself an observant man, Carson?" I asked.

I'd thought his spine looked rigid before. Now, it was like a steel rod. From his reaction, my question had obviously offended him. And I was sorry if that was the case, but I had to know.

"Yes," he said curtly, not bothering to tack on a formal address. "I'm an observant man. Soldiers in the palace guard are rarely simpletons."

I ignored that little bit of bitterness to press him further. "What about your partner? The man on the night shift. Has *he* had any unicorn sightings?"

"No, ma'am?" The end of his statement lifted it into a question. The offense had left his voice as it seemed he'd cottoned on to the fact that something was greatly amiss. "Why?"

This time, when Jay swore a blue streak, it wasn't at *all* under his breath, but loud—it would shake the leaves from the trees if he wasn't careful.

My hands shook with the revelation. I could hardly blame him for his reaction, but my turmoil stayed inside.

Why had I waited so long? Why hadn't I come sooner?

Unicorns were shy creatures, that was true. They didn't often approach many humans. But they were also innately *curious* creatures. They never could resist at least peeking at us from a safe distance. And usually, during their peeking, we'd catch a glimpse of them right back. The fact that Carson and his partner hadn't even seen light glinting off a unicorn's horn in days was... well... *Disturbing* was putting it too lightly for my tastes.

That had to mean that the unicorns weren't here at all—not in the meadow that was their home. Why would they leave it? What could make them do such a thing? Not just one of them, but all of them?

They'd either been captured... or they'd been chased away by something.

I swallowed hard and couldn't help the word that leaped into my mind. *Rumpelstiltskin.*

The singing trap-layer had to be behind this. It was too great a coincidence for those events to happen so close together. I mean, one day, traps intended to injure the unicorns of Vale were laid, something that had never been done before. And a couple of days later the unicorns just up and disappeared? I didn't believe it could be a coincidence.

I had only questions, no answers, but I thought I knew someone who might.

"We should go check on the unicorns in the staviary," I told Jay. "If the meadow unicorns are gone, they could be next."

He nodded, worry crinkling his brow. "Eliana." He caught my arm as I moved past him and lifted worry-filled eyes to mine. "Who would do this?"

I lifted his hand and twined my fingers with his, and gave them what I hoped was a comforting squeeze. I tried to smile for his benefit. "I wish I knew," I said softly.

Not officially dismissed from his post, Carson stayed in the meadow, but the rest of us raced to the staviary. Avery and Williamson checked the perimeter while Jay and I went inside.

There, we found Zacarina with her head protruding from the top of her stall as though she'd heard us coming. I let out a relieved breath when I saw her. I'd worried that whatever had gotten to the meadow unicorns had stolen her and Baby away too. At least, we could still try to keep the two of them safe.

"*There is a wild energy to you, child,*" the unicorn said. "*What has happened?*"

I stalled, not wanting to answer her in Jay's earshot. I didn't want to waste time on explanations of why I was talking to a unicorn as though she could actually understand me.

"You go check on Baby," I instructed Jay. "I'll stay here with her mother."

He nodded and set off toward Baby's stall at a sprint.

The moment he was out of earshot, I told Zacarina what we'd learned. "Do you know where they would go?"

"*Who?*"

The splinter of hope I'd been carrying fractured. She didn't know any more than we did.

"The other unicorns are *gone*," I stressed, splaying my arms apart and widening my eyes.

Zacarina made a *"tch"* sound and tossed her head disdainfully. *"You're mistaken,"* she told me. *"We do not leave the meadows. Or at least, we do not stray far from them."*

This distracted me for a moment. "You don't?"

"*We do not. There is a bond between us and this land. We can break it if we so choose, but it would be unheard of. And for it to be broken by another... that would take a dark magic indeed. And our herd would not leave me and my offspring behind.*"

A chill lanced through me. "Zacarina, you know the meadows, right?"

"*I do.*" She arched a brow over her golden eye as though to ask, "What of it?"

I continued. "So then, you know that at certain

spots, you can see all over the hills and valleys."

"Yes, that's right."

"I know those meadows as well as you do, Zacarina. And I'm telling you—I could see far from my vantage point. And I did not see a single unicorn today besides you and the others in this Staviary. They're gone."

Her eyes widened. *"Gone... where?"*

That was certainly the question, wasn't it?

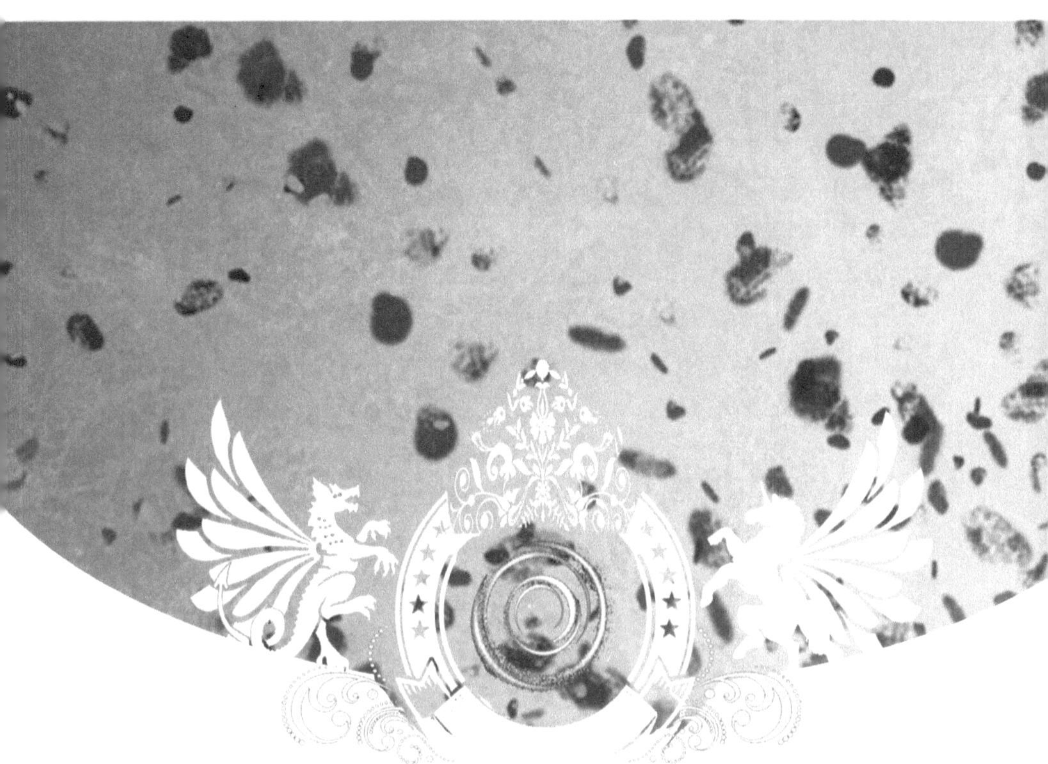

2ND MAY

"G*one... where?*"

The next day, Zacarina's words echoed in my mind like a shout bouncing around an empty room. Jay and I had gone back to the meadow and searched for any trace of them. We'd checked the woods, the valley, the hills. We'd been out all afternoon and not seen a hint of a unicorn. It was as if they had all vanished into thin air.

Despite the fact that there hadn't been evidence of any traps, I felt sure that the person or creature who laid the traps was to blame. It was too big of a coincidence to believe that they weren't.

I tugged on my boots, arranged my hair into a braid, and rang for Judith to watch Fae. I'd pumped as much milk as I could last night for bottles for my daughter. I hated to be away from her all day, but this time, I was going to use all of the resources that I had at my disposal. And Fae's nursemaid was one of them.

A knock came at the door, and I gave permission for Avery and Williamson to let Judith inside.

She curtsied as she entered the room. Surprise and confusion were written clearly across her expression. I hadn't requested a nursemaid since the day of the dance lesson, preferring to look after Fae as much as possible on my own.

"Your Highness!" she said as she stood back up. "You rang for assistance?"

"Yes," I said. "I wondered if you may be available to watch over the Princess Fae today."

Her eyes lit up, and a smile bloomed across her face. "I'd be delighted! Any way that I can assist Her Highnesses would be very much my pleasure. I've been wondering when you'd call on my services again. I've missed the princess Fae. She's such a beauty."

"She is one cute baby, that's for sure."

I took Judith about my suite of rooms and gave her a quick run-down of where she could find everything she might need. Where she could find the bottles I'd pumped, where the burp cloths, blankets, extra diapers, and other changing supplies were. I knew by the smile on Judith's lips that she thought I was being more than a little overbearing, but I still wasn't used to leaving Fae. I had to restrain myself from demonstrating Fae's different cries and telling her what they meant. The woman was a professional. She'd figure it out. There were only so many things she would need in the hours I'd be away from her. Fae would be perfectly fine in Judith's care.

I caressed Fae's cheek and bit my lip. Her little lashes rested upon her cheeks.

She'll hardly know you're gone, I told myself.

I wrenched myself away from the bassinet's side and cleared my throat. "I'll be in the library if you need me," I told Judith.

Quickly, I walked away, but I paused at the door, heartstrings tugging at me as I watched the nursemaid settle into the rocking chair, hands folded across her middle as Fae slept. I slowly closed the door to my suite behind me as I left Fae in Judith's capable hands.

When I entered the library, I hadn't brought Mr. Swink a bribe this time. His eyes eagerly searched my empty hands, and his face fell. I could see that he wanted to ask, but couldn't bring himself to. I smiled at him, anticipating the unasked question. "Go down to the kitchens later and tell Mrs. Bellon I sent you," I told him. "She promised me cookies for dessert with dinner this evening, and I told her to set a couple aside for you."

He nodded, pink overtaking his features again as he gave me an embarrassed smile. "I would never presume—but thank you. It's much appreciated. I didn't expect you back again already, Your Highness. Is there anything I could help you with?"

I paused. Perhaps, he could help me. After all, I didn't need to tell him where I'd heard of Rumpelstiltskin. I just needed to know if *he* had. He had been the palace's Master Librarian for as long as I could remember. Which meant that he'd had his hands on more of these books than anyone else.

"Actually, maybe you can," I said.

Mr. Swink set aside the books in front of him and clasped his hands. He looked at me expectantly, giving me his full undivided attention.

"Have you ever heard of a song called

'Rumpelstiltskin'?" I asked. "Actually—I'll be honest, I'm not even completely sure that that's the title of the song. But I know it's in the lyrics of the song." I tried to make the question casual, not too overeager. But despite my attempts to stay calm, my pulse beat a tattoo in my throat. This was the closest I'd come yet to telling someone what Zacarina had told me. I could hardly believe that I was telling Mr. Swink, of all people.

He hemmed and hawed, thinking it over, but finally, he shook his head. "Hmmm. I can't say that I have. Do you know anything more about it? Kingdom of origin? Composer? Anything like that? It may give you another research angle to find it."

The brief hope that had flared was extinguished. I sighed, let down. "I'm afraid that's all I know," I said glumly.

And gods, did I ever *wish* that I had anything more to go on than what I had. It would make my search a hell of a lot easier.

He smiled at me sympathetically. "Music is not my area of expertise, I'm afraid. I did help with the intake of the books in that section to a certain extent, but largely our music collection was built by..."

"My mother." I finished his sentence.

I knew that. I knew it well. I just didn't want to give her anything more to worry about when it came to me. And she *would* worry. It was in her nature. She tended to latch on to the smallest thing and blow it way out of proportion. I knew if I asked her about Rumpelstiltskin, I'd be bound to the palace until my hair turned white.

I'd just gotten to go to the meadows again. I was loath to do anything that might make her place further restrictions on me.

But between her music knowledge and the fact that

she'd used the word my entire life, she had to know *something.*

I mulled that over on my walk back to the music shelves. I'd handed the books I'd borrowed back to Mr. Swink. I knew he'd want to see them safely back to their proper places himself. I had managed to get through all three of them in the time that had passed since I'd last been in the library.

I set my things down at a table and got down to business once again.

I pulled book after book after book from the shelves and pored over their texts. Time and time again, I was only disappointed by no mention of Rumpelstiltskin in any of their pages. At one point, my heart had nearly leaped clean out of my chest when I thought I saw it once—but the book only referenced a composer named Rumpleschtein. Apparently, he had been known for his attempts in the melding of two music genres—usually, the critics said, extremely unsuccessfully.

Despondently, I shut the last book, replaced it in the stack, and glanced outside. The sun was starting to set over the valleys outside, casting them in a golden glow as it outlined the hills in light. That meant it would be dark soon, and the library would be closing. I'd save Mr. Swink the trouble of kicking me out. Neatly, I put away the books on my table and pulled some more from the shelves to take with me for evening reading.

I'd keep on with it, but this felt like a fruitless pursuit. I was beginning to fear that I would never find Rumpelstiltskin.

I looked down at the books in my bag forlornly. I'd keep on trudging along, I supposed, but unless a miracle happened, I couldn't keep on going like this. I hadn't stumbled upon Rumpelstiltskin yet, and I'd barely even made a dent in the "R" authors of the music section. How much longer would it be before I found a mention of it? Days? Weeks? Months? Years?

A chill raced through me. The unicorns might be gone for good by that point.

There had to be another way.

"There you are."

I whirled around, and my mother stood in the aisle, smiling fondly at me.

It was, I feared, a sign.

I worried what would happen if I followed where it led. But I feared what would happen if I didn't more.

"You're so dedicated to this music quest of yours for the party, aren't you, darling? Are you looking for anything in particular?" Her hair was twisted up into an elegant chignon, and her neck elongated as she tilted her head at me in question. She ran her fingers along some of the books' spines. "This is my favorite section in the whole library, so I might be able to help, you know."

"No, nothing in particular."

I lied through my teeth. I lied like a rug. I lied like Fae after a satisfying feeding. It was started to become natural, and I hated it. I hated feeling like a liar with every breath I took. And it was worse because I didn't just *feel* like one—I *was* one.

It had been a moment since I'd spoken, and my mother reached out and touched my hand gently, jarring me from my thoughts. "Are you all right, darling?" She searched my eyes. "Where did you go just now?"

I realized that my eyes were filled with tears, and I choked out a laugh. "Nowhere. I'm sorry." I pulled away and self-consciously rubbed at my eyes. But rubbing them didn't rid me of the blasted things. I waved a hand, embarrassed as the tears started to fall. “Ignore me. I don’t know what’s wrong with me. I’m sure it’s just hormones.”

Such an easy excuse. Such baloney.

Mother wouldn’t let me be self-conscious for long. She pulled me tight into her embrace. For a moment, I closed my eyes. I wished she *could* protect me from this. I had fought against her efforts for so long, but with my mother holding me, I just felt like a scared little girl—and like, somehow, my mama could make it all okay again.

Her hand stroked down my hair. “Oh my sweet girl,” she murmured. “It is perfectly natural. I think you’re missing *your* girl.” She pulled back and smiled at me with great understanding. “Am I right? It’s hard to be away from her, isn’t it?”

I sniffled and nodded, tears under control now. Fae wasn’t the primary reason that I was crying, but I couldn’t and wouldn’t tell Mother that. And she was right to an extent. Being away from Fae *was* hard. I couldn’t help but feel that seeing her at the end of this painfully long day would do me a world of good.

Mother and I left the library and swept back to my suite of rooms. I thanked Judith for her time and dismissed her.

I picked up Fae and bounced her a little in my arms. “Hello, baby girl. Did you miss me?”

“It was a pleasure, Your Highness,” Judith said. “She was an angel.”

The door clicked softly shut behind Judith, and, angel or not, she was my girl, and she was perfect exactly the way she was. I gathered Fae close to me and closed my eyes, just breathing in her scent. Already, I felt a little more calm, a little more settled after my mini-breakdown in the library.

When I opened my eyes again, my mother was smiling at me fondly. "Better?" she asked.

I returned her smile. "Much," I replied.

Mother made a sweeping motion with her arms, indicating the door. "Shall we?" she asked.

"We shall."

With Fae strapped to my front in a baby wrap, I followed my mother down to the great hall.

It was the most elegant room in the whole palace with high golden arches inlaid with carvings of flowers.

"I had the palace staff set out our different options for dinnerware for the party, so we could see what we liked best." She picked up a puce-colored plate and made a face, turning it toward me so that I could get the full, unappealing effect. "I think we can safely rule this one out."

I nodded absently, agreeing with her decision. The truth was, my mind was on other things.

I watched my mother thoughtfully as she moved down the line of plates and silverware, picking some up and moving them into the center of the table. Those were her rejects, I assumed, watching as olive green joined puce. The ones on the outer edges must still be in the running.

But though I'd allowed myself for just a moment to forget about my quest and Rumpelstiltskin, it pushed itself to the forefront of my mind once again. Maybe I *should* just ask her if she'd heard of it. Mr. Swink was right; she *was* the most likely person to know it if it was anywhere in any of the music books in the library. And then she'd shown up during my search like a sign I felt I'd have to be foolish to ignore. I could ask her the question. It didn't mean that I had to tell her its significance.

I adjusted a piece of silverware that lay crooked on the table. She hadn't gotten to this place setting yet, so it stood a better chance if it was arranged properly. "Mother," I started my lie. "I heard someone singing a tune the other day. I can't get it out of my head."

"I knew you were looking for something specific." She turned, wagging a playful finger at me. "A mother always knows."

"Yeah, you were right." I chuckled nervously. "Anyway, you offered to help, so I wondered if maybe you'd heard of it?"

"Maybe," she said, turning back to her plates and silverware. She tilted her head speculatively at the plate in front of her. "How does it go?"

I bit my lip and instantly undid the expression. If she turned around and caught me looking like that, she'd know right away that I was lying. "I can't remember exactly... but it mentioned something about Rumpelstiltskin?"

Crash.

The plate my mother had been holding fell to the floor and shattered as she whirled around to look at me. Her face was stark white.

"Who?" she demanded, voice tremulous. When I didn't answer, she marched up to me, gripped me by the shoulders and shouted, "*Who sang it, Eliana?*"

Fae woke with a start and immediately started wailing. I was speechless, gaping up at my mother. Her hands shook against me.

I pulled her hands away and started bouncing Fae, making shushing, soothing sounds until she quieted down again. But my eyes stayed on my mother, who didn't even seem to hear her granddaughter's cries.

Blood had yet to return to her face as she watched me. She swallowed and asked again, this time quieter. "Who did you hear singing that song, Eliana? Did you see them?"

Wordlessly, I shook my head. For once in the past several days, it wasn't a lie. I *hadn't* seen the mysterious singer. Wouldn't things be easier if I had?

"That word has always been important to you," I said slowly. "It's meant something to you and Father in a way it never has to me. I've asked you before what it was, and you just told me it was something I should always remember. But I'm asking you again. What does it mean?"

Her hands traveled up to cover her mouth, and she shook her head back and forth frantically. "I can't—no one should have ever—what if—"

She was nearly hyperventilating, but somehow, she seized control of herself, took several deep breaths, and forced her hands back to her sides. Fists clenched there, she looked at me. And though it was obvious something had shaken her to her core, there was a steely resolve in her gaze.

"My answer hasn't changed." She walked up to me once again and took me by the shoulders again—this time, more gently. She pressed a shaky kiss to my forehead. "Remember that word, my darling daughter." She looked down at Fae and brushed her thumb over her sweet little forehead.

"Don't you ever, ever let yourself forget it."

3RD MAY

Try as I might for the rest of the night, no matter how I pressed, my mother did not change her mind. She would not tell me what the word meant, or why it was of such importance to her that she'd been driven to decorate our home with it but would never actually clue me in on what it meant. We were equally stubborn, she and I. She'd instilled her own qualities in me. She kept determinedly trying to get me to answer her questions about place settings. She didn't realize that this wasn't a childish case of a daughter wanting to know what her mother kept from her. There were real lives at stake in her answer. Unicorn lives.

But I couldn't tell her that.

I gritted my teeth in frustration, thinking about it.

She was wound as tightly as a spring. If she'd only relinquish a little bit of that control she held on to so desperately tightly, maybe she would feel better. We could have solved the problem of the unicorn trapping together. But noooo.

So the next morning, I rang for Judith once again.

Fae was awake when she got there, making little gurgling and cooing noises in my arms. Judith grinned from ear to ear when she saw her. "Twice in two days? I must be the luckiest nursemaid in the land."

Her smile and clear joy at seeing my daughter again warmed my heart. It was definitely far easier to leave Fae with someone like her, someone who enjoyed having her in her care.

"I'll be in the staviary today, should you need me," I told Judith.

"Very good, Your Highness."

Mother was as mulish as I was, but just because she wouldn't answer my questions didn't mean I was just going to give up. I had asked both her and Mr. Swink about Rumpelstiltskin, and the world hadn't imploded. I could keep on asking questions, and maybe, eventually, I would find someone who was willing to answer them.

Mother wouldn't help me, though it certainly seemed like she had the means to. So I was turning to the other person I trusted more than anything. A person that I would do almost anything for—and, I was pretty sure, someone who would do almost anything for me as well. That was Jay in a nutshell.

I strode out of the palace with Avery and Williamson in tow, in search of Jay. I marched determinedly for the staviary, my stride businesslike and swift.

When I got there, I found Jay hard at work. His brow was furrowed in concentration as the light behind him created a halo effect. I pulled up short, taken aback by the image. Sweat from the warm day and the manual labor had soaked his shirt and made it cling to him. I could see the outline of his undershirt beneath it and beneath that, I could see the hint of his abdominal muscles, flexing each time he leaned over and stood back up. A little ribbon of sweat snaked between his eyes, running into them. From the way he blinked, I thought the salt was probably stinging his eyes, and he swiped his forearm across them to rid himself of it. He heaved a pitchfork into a pile of hay and tossed it into a stall behind him, stocking the steed there—an average horse—with straw for the day.

He still hadn't noticed me. But gods, was I noticing him.

Ogling Jay in his natural element wasn't why I'd come here today, but it surprised me that my body could react the way it did to him. A flutter of excitement ran through me, and I had to take a deep breath to push it away.

I cleared my throat to get his attention, and he looked up, a smile instantly blooming over his features when he saw me standing there. He stopped his work immediately and leaned his pitchfork against the wall. Then he leaned himself there as well, crossing his arms over his chest. "Eliana! Boys." He nodded toward the guards, laughing when Avery rolled his eyes at the address. "Sorry. Men. What brings you to my humble staviary?"

While he waited for my response, expression curious, he pushed his sleeves up to his elbows. I assumed it was to cool down a bit—his face was ruddy, and his shirt was flecked with little droplets of sweat. But I couldn't help but notice how big his hands were, how strong his forearms looked. My eyes lingered on the muscles corded through them.

Not the time or place, Eliana, I warned myself. I still had a great deal of thinking to do about the situation with Jay. Every day, it seemed, I was growing more and more attracted to Jay. I wondered what his lips felt like. How his arms might feel around me. I needed to get a grip. I'd pushed myself to wonder what it would be like to date Jay, to think of him in that way, but now it seemed those thoughts were running rampant all by themselves.

"Eliana?" Jay's voice came, amused.

I snapped back to attention and, eyes wide, whipped them up to meet Jay's gaze. His smile edged toward a smirk, but bless his heart, he did me the service of not pointing out how distracted I'd been. I colored. It was bad enough that he had noticed. My embarrassment would have been compounded tenfold if he'd said anything out loud.

"Not that I'm complaining about a royal visit," he drawled, "but is this a social visit, or did you need something? I notice Fae isn't with you again." He mock-glared at me accusingly. "Why do you deprive us of each other?"

I shook my head, my hair getting in my eyes with the movement. I pushed it out of the way with impatient hands. I'd left Fae behind because I didn't want to be distracted from my important task, but I'd allowed myself to be distracted anyway and womanhood—not motherhood—was all I could blame. It was time to get back on track for why I'd come here in the first place. "I need you—your help," I swiftly swallowed down the slip. "It's serious."

He sobered. The teasing smile on his face vanished

as he nodded seriously and motioned me inside. "Let's talk inside. I need a drink of water anyway." He nodded again to the guards. "You men are welcome to come in, as well, if you're parched. Have you got a canteen out here?"

"We do," Williamson replied.

"No need, sir," Avery replied. "We'll let you and Her Highness talk. We'll just be stationed outside in case she has need of us." The guards took their duty to me seriously, but I knew that I was lucky they didn't take it too far. Other guards might have, thirsting to prove themselves. But despite all that was going on in Vale, we still lived in a time of peace. If that should change, I knew the freedoms they let me enjoy would then be restricted considerably.

I followed behind Jay, watching his back, and his long and confident stride as his legs ate up the distance between where we were and his office. An earthy aroma filled the air—a smell that was uniquely equine. Straw, a little manure, and something else I couldn't put my finger on.

Jay was so at ease here in the stables, I thought, watching him walk around. He patted horses as he passed, sneaking a few of them sugar cubes and carrots. He straightened a crooked sign and used his sleeve to wipe the sign outside his office clean. This truly was the work that he was meant to do. I didn't mind admitting that I felt a little jealous. He had such purpose, such contentment. And he had the freedom to do the thing he loved. The closest I came to doing what I felt I was meant to do was lounging in the meadow with a unicorn.

So finding the unicorns was the best thing I could do.

Jay opened the door to his small office and gave me a little mock bow, motioning me inside. "Milady," he said, deepening his voice playfully.

I rolled my eyes, but played along, dropping him a facsimile of a curtsy and batting my eyelashes in an over the top coquettish imitation of some of the ladies I'd seen at court. "Good sir." I swept inside and balanced myself on the first seat that I saw: a little three-legged stool.

Jay didn't exactly have many seating options in here. It wasn't a room meant for meetings with others. It was a place to get work done. The work that he couldn't do out in the stalls, the work that required putting pen to paper and communicating with the outside world. Consequently, there wasn't much to the little office. There was a small table that served as his desk. Papers and order forms were strewn across it, half-completed. A haphazard stack of other papers sat in the top left corner nearest me.

It was dim in here, but Jay didn't light a lantern. Since it was daylight out, a little square window above us let in filtered, golden light that highlighted the dustiness of the window's glass. Small particles of dust and dander danced in its beam. I watched the little ballet. It was a soft light, but plenty to illuminate the small space and see by.

I turned my attention back to Jay as I heard a soft rattling sound. He was rummaging beneath his desk for something. Finally, he emerged with two tin cups and a small canteen. They pinged softly as he dropped them down on the table's surface, and he poured us each some water.

"Oh, I don't need—" I tried to protest, but he gave me a playful glare and wagged a finger at me in mock admonishment.

"None of that now. I'm playing host to the unicorn princess of Vale, heir to our fair kingdom! The least I can do is offer you what little refreshment I have available. Don't insult me by saying no."

I held my hands up and held my tongue. I thought Jay could probably use the water more than I could, but if he was sure there was enough here for the both of us, I wouldn't protest any longer. Instead, I took my cup and gripped its metal handle between my fingers. I brought it to my lips and sipped at the water. It was clean and cool. It was a warm day, and it was refreshing, so I drank the whole glass down. I hadn't realized that I actually *had* been a little thirsty. I waited with it clasped between my hands as Jay guzzled his own down and then poured another.

"Would you like anymore?" he asked.

"Oh, no, no." I waved a hand, shaking my head. "You were doing manual labor. Drink up. I'm good."

"Thanks." The sound of his cup filling was the only sound in the room for a moment but for the distant sounds of a barn.

"So." Jay's cup scraped along his desk as he brought it to his lips for another drink. "What can I do for you, Unicorn Princess?" He set his cup down and quirked a smile.

I couldn't have asked for a better segue. "Funny you should mention my hated nickname," I said. "It's actually the unicorns that I'm here about."

He sobered and straightened in his seat, moving his cup out of the way to lean closer. "What about them? Is there news? Has there been any sight of the ones who disappeared yet? Or the trapper?"

"I wish." I shook my head. And then worry streaked

through me as a new concern occurred to me. I'd checked on them before, but... "What about the ones here? Baby and Zacarina?"

"*Zacarina*?" he asked, incredulous, eyebrows shooting up to his hairline. "Boy, Fae sure got off easy with her name. Remind me not to let you name any of *my* kids, will you?"

I reddened. For a second, when he said his kids, I thought what it might be like if they were our kids.

Don't go there, Eliana. Not the time, not the place, and certainly not a path you should be walking down right now.

I was having a lot of thoughts today that would be better served at another time.

Right, back on track. I rolled my eyes at Jay. "You know exactly who I mean. The mother unicorn."

Who would probably have not-so-politely delivered a hoof into his buttocks if she'd heard him mocking her name. Unicorns were gentle creatures, but this one certainly had spunk.

And I still wasn't sure how all of that worked. I could understand them. They could understand me. But could they understand all of us? *Would* she have understood Jay's jesting about her name? Questions for another time.

Jay softened, seeing my concern. "Relax. She and Baby are still doing fine. They do seem restless, though, especially the mother. Sorry—especially Zacarina. It's like they know that their brethren are missing." He sighed, a grimace of frustration splaying over his features. "And like they also know that we haven't got a clue where to even begin looking for them."

I swallowed hard. Here went nothing...

"I do."

"You do what?" He looked at me, eyes narrowed in confusion.

"I have one," I said. I held his gaze, widening my eyes meaningfully.

He stared at me blankly. "Have one what? Wait—a clue?"

His chair screeched as he pushed back from his desk in excitement, and it clattered to the floor. He crossed around his desk and picked me up to twirl me around, laughing in disbelief. A startled laugh of my own escaped me as I held on to him for dear life, the room spinning around us. Gently, he placed me back onto my feet and ran a hand through his hair. "Eliana, that's just... I can't believe this. I mean, of course, I can believe it, *you* found it." He shook his head in awe. "This is amazing. *You're* amazing."

My breath caught in my throat. Jay was thrilled but didn't question that I'd been able to succeed with such an impossible task. He always had so much faith in me. I didn't know what I'd ever done to deserve it.

"Where did you find it?" he asked eagerly. "Do you realize what this means? We may actually be able to find the missing unicorns now!"

Whoa, there. It sounded like I had better set some expectations for my "amazing" clue, and fast.

"It's not much," I warned. "And I can't tell you how I know this, so don't ask. But if we want to find the unicorns, we've got to find the word Rumpelstiltskin and figure out what it means."

Jay's eyes widened in instant recognition. Of course, they did. He knew the word just as well as I did. After all, he had been my constant companion as a child, and Rumpelstiltskin had been our favorite of all the nonsense words we'd played around with.

It made my heart twist in the strangest way now to think of how we'd used it so cavalierly. Why hadn't we questioned its meaning before now, even if it had just been a little bit? Maybe, if we had, we'd have started the process of wearing my mother down on the subject early. Maybe, right now, we'd already know the meaning of the mysterious word. Maybe we'd have a real place to start looking for the unicorns instead of just combing endlessly through the library collection, feeling like a fool.

Oh, wait, that last one was just me.

"Did you ask your mother?" He returned to the other side of the desk, picked up his chair, and righted it to resume his seat. He'd known the source of the once-silly word as well as I did.

I sighed and tried not to let the extreme frustration I felt on the subject show. "I almost wish that I hadn't, to be honest with you. But I did. She's being stubborn and refuses to say anything."

"A woman in your family? Stubborn? Nooooo." He let the sarcasm roll off his tongue, and I glared to let him know that it wasn't at all appreciated. He ran a hand through his hair and huffed out a breath, eyes distant as he thought it over. "I haven't ever heard the word before. Have you?"

"If I had, I wouldn't be here."

"And are you sure it has something to do with the unicorns?"

"One hundred percent positive," I said, nodding resolutely.

His brow furrowed. "How can you be *that* sure? Did you find something in the meadows that you didn't show me?"

I bit my lip. I still couldn't tell him that. If he knew I

believed the unicorns were speaking to me, he'd think I was crazy. And with the best of intentions, I was sure, he'd go to my mother if he was worried about my mental health. She'd have the best of intentions too, but she'd lock me up and throw away the key.

"I can't tell you that," I said. I splayed my hands and fingers in front of me and shrugged helplessly. "Can you just... trust me on this?"

"Well, of course, I trust you. I have a lot of questions, right now, Lia, but trusting you was never in question." A corner of his lip lifted in a warm half-smile. He was still clearly preoccupied by the matter at hand, though. "Is there anything else that you *can* tell me?" he asked.

I thought about it. So far, I hadn't told him more than Mother, or Mr. Swink, really. But this was *Jay* for crying out loud. He had so much faith in me. He had earned a little faith in him in return. "I can tell you this much," I said. "Whoever it was who trapped the unicorns was singing as they laid the traps. And the song had just one word to it. It was Rumpelstiltskin."

He leaned back, clearly rocked to his core. His mouth opened and closed as what was probably a thousand and one questions leaped to his mind. But I'd told him that that was all I could tell him and he took me at my word. "I'll ask around," he finally said.

A wave of relief washed over me. It was amazing just to know that one of my burdens didn't have to be carried alone. It may not seem like a lot for Jay to start asking around about Rumpelstiltskin, but to me, it was huge. It meant a great deal.

"Thank you," I said. I felt so light suddenly. It was incredible.

"Not a problem. Anytime," he replied. A funny little smile played about his lips. "You know I'm always happy to help you however I can."

I smiled back. "I do know that," I said softly. "I can always count on you, Jay."

He held eye contact with me for a few beats longer and I started to feel my pulse beat in my throat. I cleared my throat to rid myself of the sensation and looked away.

He allowed me to let the intimate moment pass us by, without comment and without deepening the moment to something else. "So, you're helping your mom party plan," he said.

Oh, thank goodness. A safe topic. We wouldn't get into any trouble talking about Fae's party, I was sure.

"That I am," I said. "Royal Party Planner, at your service." I gave him a wink.

He raised an eyebrow. "Are you having any fun with it? I know sometimes your mom can make you a little..." He trailed off to wiggle his hand back and forth in the air, then his finger gravitated up toward his head to swirl near his ear as he made a face.

I gasped and put a hand to my chest in mock outrage. "How *dare* you insinuate that my mother drives me crazy. We have the most functional of functional relationships. And she *always* listens to the boundaries I set— Okay, I can't even pretend to say that seriously. I mean, I had to bring the guards with me just to pay you a visit today. But surprisingly, it's been okay. I keep reminding myself that she means well. Having Fae has helped me be a little more understanding of her. We have our hiccups, but overall, it's gotten a lot better on both sides, I think."

"That's great." He grinned, sincere about it. "And aside from your relationship with your mother, how goes the party planning itself?"

I brightened. It was so nice to think about something that wasn't hunted unicorns, strange abilities, my fraught relationship with my mother, my dead husband, or confusing romances for a change. Just something simple and happy. But I wouldn't explain all of that to Jay, of course. Instead, I simply said, "It's good. It's a nice distraction from the unicorns, actually."

"I can believe that." He sighed. "To be honest, I think that I could do with one of those myself, so I'm looking forward to it. It'll be a nice evening for all of us, I think. Will you save me a dance?"

"I'll save them all for you," I said without thinking.

"Does that mean..." He looked so hopeful. I cursed myself for speaking before I'd thought. I couldn't bear to see his expression fall.

Besides, if I was being honest, there was no one else I'd rather dance with.

"Yeah," I said. "Be my date?"

A smile the likes of which I'd never seen burst onto his face, and my heart did something that defied explanation. It felt amazing to have put that expression on his face. I'd do anything I could to keep it there.

"I can hardly wait."

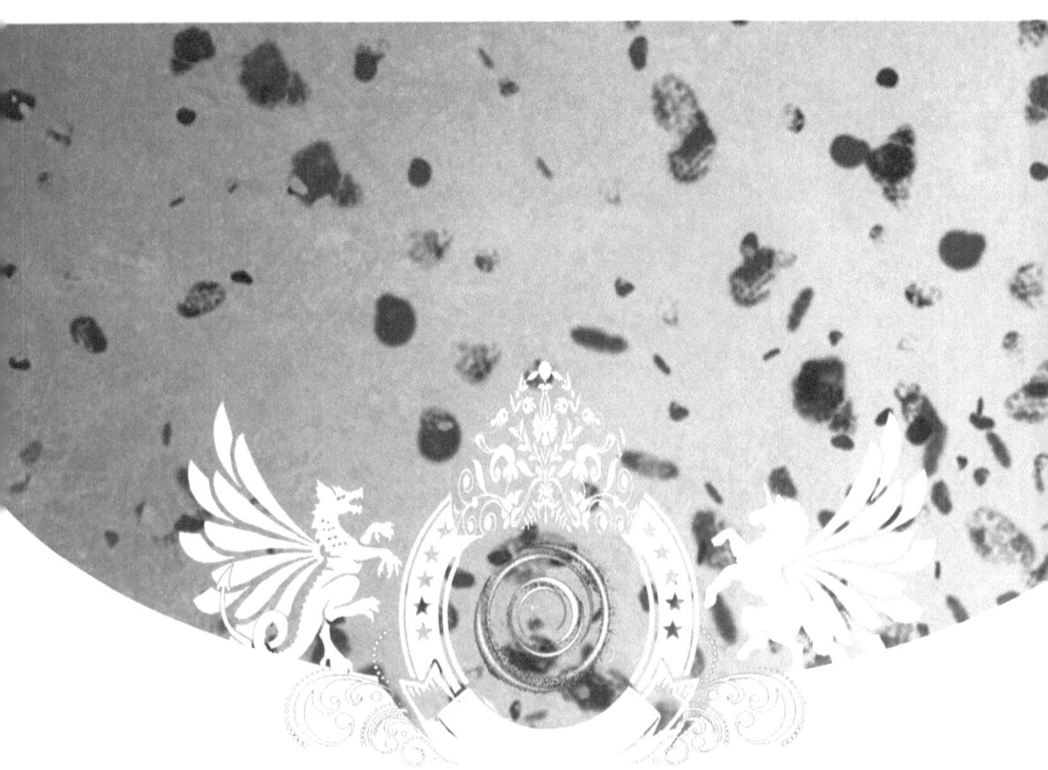

4TH MAY

"I was wondering if you'd mind if I spent a little bit of time with Fae today?" my mother asked over breakfast. I looked up from my cereal and saw the eagerness in her eyes.

"I think she would love to spend some time with her grandmother," I replied.

"And grandfather. Your father has agreed to take a little time away from his duties today."

My father was a great man, but he wasn't the type to want to spend time with a baby. My mother must have bent his ear to get him to agree.

"I was thinking of heading out to the stables anyway," I said. Almost as soon as the words had escaped my lips, a knowing smile appeared on her face.

"To see Jay?" she inquired, moving around the table

to pick Fae up from her crib.

"To see the unicorns," I said aloud. *Among other things.*

Pushing my still-full cereal bowl away, I got up from the table, eager to be away from my mother questioning me about Jay. With a kiss to both Mother and Fae, I set off for the staviary. I once again asked the guards to wait outside, and, respecting my privacy, they agreed to do so. I suspected they let me go into the staviary alone because they knew Jay would be there. It wasn't Jay, however, that I'd made this particular visit for. Well, not only Jay. I needed to speak to someone else first.

The mother unicorn poked her head over her stall's door and fixed those intimidating golden eyes on me. They looked hopeful as she waited for my news.

"Any word?" Zacarina's voice echoed in my mind, and I shook my head in response, replying out loud.

"I wish I had better news. But we haven't seen hide or horn of any of your herd since they disappeared," I reported grimly.

She sighed, a more horse-like sound than the voice that followed. *"I feared as much. Once I knew they were gone, I could feel the difference in the air. With them gone, it's—"* she trailed off, searching for the right word *"—emptier, somehow. My foal and I are alone here now."*

Alone.

The word struck me. I could understand that feeling. A sinking feeling of despair—that no one would understand her grief or what she'd lost. I'd felt so alone in the days following Luka's death. Some days, I still did. But this was different--Luka had died. I'd seen his body, his soul fled from it. The life and color drained from his cheeks. And the unicorns weren't dead. I refused to believe that was the case. All hope was not lost for them.

Besides, regardless of who we had or hadn't lost, I wasn't alone. And neither was Zacarina. There were other unicorns in the staviary, the ones that worked for the palace.

I moved in front of her to cup her long horse face between my hands and leaned my forehead toward her horn. "Now, you listen here," I demanded fiercely, meeting her gaze, golden eye to golden eye. "You are *not alone.* You may not have your flock right now, but you have me. I am fighting for you. For all of you. And I am going to do everything in my power to ensure that your brethren are returned to you. And I know it's not the same as having them back or having someone who can understand you, but there are other humans working to help as well. Jay's trying to help me find Rumpelstiltskin. We have men patrolling in the meadows in the hopes that the culprit will return to the scene of the crime. We'll find whoever did this, and we'll get your herd back."

Zacarina moved so that her chin rested upon my shoulder. A bolt of fierce pride and determination lanced through me. *"You're right, young one. And it's time I did something to help as well."*

I smiled and slipped inside the stall. "I thought you might say something like that. Why do you think I'm here?"

I twisted my hair up from its loose waves into a messy sort of bun and stripped off my overcoat--an elaborate, gaudy thing with a train that hid my choice of footwear. It had been a gift from a visiting dignitary from lands far colder than Vale. In their culture, this was a light frock. Here in Vale with our temperate climate, it had me sweating. Underneath, I wore riding breeches, boots, and a tunic.

I'd ridden a unicorn bareback before—I felt a pang in my chest when I thought of the young unicorn I'd called Misty, who had been brought to the staviary at around the same time as Zacarina and Baby. Unlike them, she'd elected not to stay very long. Misty had left and likely was wherever the rest of the unicorn flock was now.

Thank the gods Zacarina had elected to stay behind with her offspring.

I could have taken any number of the palace unicorns, the ones that delivered parcels and notes, but I didn't have the same affinity with them as I did with Zacarina. Besides, flying terrified me. At least I'd ridden Zacarina before, and she knew about my fear of heights.

She gave me her permission to fasten a saddle and stirrups over her back.

"Not too tight. And none of that bridle and reins nonsense either," she commanded sternly. *"You can hold onto my mane."*

I nodded. There wouldn't have been any sense in that anyway. Bridles and reins were used to steer a mount in the direction you wished to go. My newfound abilities were certainly strange, but they did mean that I wouldn't have any trouble telling Zacarina where we were going.

I opened the stall door and motioned her out into the hall. There, we were met with a stern-looking Jay. His arms were crossed over his chest, and one eyebrow arched wryly.

"And where, exactly, do you young ladies think you are going?" he asked.

His impression of my mother was uncanny. But

unlike with her, I didn't try to play him off. "We're going to try to find Zacarina's flock," I said, with one hand on her to keep her calm. "No one else has thought to try an aerial search before. I think it's worth a shot."

Zacarina pranced in place, a little worried. *"He'll try to stop us."*

I put the other hand on her flank as well, trying to calm her. "Shh. It's fine. Jay will help us."

She calmed under my touch.

Jay uncrossed his arms, watching us. "You have such a way with them," he said, sounding awed. "It's like they understand you."

If only you knew. My chest tightened with regret. Maybe someday, I'd be able to tell him the truth.

Jay took a deep breath and nodded once. "I think you're right," he said. "It is worth a shot. But you're not going alone."

I started to protest and he held up a hand. "Don't even try. I don't want to hear it, Lia. We have no idea who or what is after the unicorns. It could be dangerous. If they went to the trouble to take all of the unicorns and they see you astride one they missed..." He shuddered and looked away. "I don't want to think about what might happen to you. Maybe they'd take you too. Maybe they'd cast you aside. But I *don't* think they'd leave you alive and well, able to tell others of their identity. With two of us, if someone takes Zacarina down, we just might stand a fighting chance."

I saw his point, but that didn't mean that I had to like it. "Fine," I acquiesced. "You can come with us. *But—*" I thumbed myself in the chest. "—I am in charge up there. What I say, goes."

He rolled his eyes. "Yes, General Eliana."

His brow crinkled as he surveyed Zacarina. "You

forgot to dress her the rest of the way."

"Did I?" I feigned ignorance. Zacarina had expressly forbidden a bridle, so I knew that wasn't going to happen. "Oh, you mean the reins and everything? I tried. She wasn't having it. And you know we don't do anything to the unicorns they don't damn well want us to. She'll get us back safely. Her foal is here."

"Good point." Without any more arguments to make, he started toward the main staviary entrance, and I hastily rushed to stop him, putting my hands against his chest to halt him in his place.

"No, no. Let's... go out the back way."

He looked down at me and covered my hands with his. "Why, Miss Eliana... Am I to suppose that you didn't inform your guards or mother about this half-cocked plan of yours? Why, I am shocked! Shocked, I say!"

I swatted at him. "Yes," I hissed. "Okay? You got me. We're off on a secret mission, but she has Fae with her, so I'm hoping she won't notice my departure."

My stomach growled, rather undercutting my stern voice.

Jay's lip twitched, and I held up a finger. "Don't," I warned with as fierce a glare as I could muster. "Don't you dare laugh at me."

He held up his hands innocently. "Laugh? I would never. But you know, I think, dear princess, that you might be hungry. Could this mission wait just a few more minutes while I grab my lunch for us to share?" His eyes flicked to Zacarina and then back to me. "I may have an extra PB and J in there for Madam Zacarina as well."

"Lunch? I've just come from breakfast!"

"Get the sandwich."

I whipped my head around to look at Zacarina, who

only stared back at me stoically. Well, I guess that answered the question of whether or not she could understand all humans or just me.

"Yes, fine, get the food," I said, stepping to the side so he could slip past me and Zacarina. "But be quick about it!"

He winked at me, and off he went. "Back in a jiffy."

He returned with the food fairly quickly, throwing a sandwich to Zacarina and putting the rest in a saddlebag. I tried not to pay attention to the flutter that ran through me as Jay helped me up onto Zacarina's back.

My nerves soon took over whatever I'd felt at Jay's touch as we cantered out of the staviary and took to the skies.

My heart raced as we climbed higher and higher. I'd completely forgotten how truly terrifying flying was. The first time I'd been doing it, I'd also been in labor with Fae. Now I had nothing to take me away from the terror I felt as the world slipped away from us. Jay's arms wrapped around me, pulling me closer to him so my back was up against his chest. He'd done it to calm me down, but being in such close proximity to him had only made my heart beat even quicker. I inhaled deeply and focused my eyes on the ground to do what we actually came up here for.

Green, green, and more green as we sailed over the meadows and valleys that gave Vale its name.

A fierce determination enveloped me.

"Thank you," Zacarina's voice whispered through my mind. *"It means a great deal to know that this is as important to you as it is to me."*

I patted her neck, wordlessly conveying that thanks were not necessary. *"We'll find them."*

She jerked her head in a curt nod.

"Isn't it beautiful?" Jay called to me, his voice raised to make sure that I could hear him over the wind in our ears.

I exhaled shakily. "Wouldn't know. You're handling the looking part of this mission, right?"

He tightened his grip on me and whispered in my ear, tickling it with his breath. "I've got you."

My whole body trembled in a way I wasn't sure had to do with fear anymore. I leaned back, content to enjoy the feeling of his body against mine, knowing my fear of heights gave me the perfect excuse.

We passed the meadows where I usually strolled, but the hills and valleys of Vale extended far beyond the palace. After perhaps an hour, Zacarina began to descend to a valley bare of trees. From up here, it looked like a smooth green plain.

Jay's grip around my waist tightened again as we descended, and the wind in our hair picked up.

We both grunted with the impact when Zacarina's hooves struck the ground, but other than that, we were unscathed. I could finally breathe again.

He helped me to the ground, and as I was busy praising any gods that would listen that I was back on solid ground again, Jay pulled out the bag he'd packed.

"Lunch?" he asked brightly.

I'd given him a hard time about it after my stomach growled, but I sure was glad that he'd brought the food with us now. If I'd been a little hungry before, now, over an hour later, I was starving. But Jay had thought of everything. He threw Zacarina another sandwich and laid the rest of his food out on a blanket he'd packed. There was only one sandwich left, but he'd brought plenty of snacks.

"Girl."

"Hmm?" I looked up from the half sandwich Jay had given me and found Zacarina staring at me intently. *"What is it?"* I asked, using my mind to speak.

"I knew that I felt drawn to this clearing for a reason. Look." She jerked her head to a small patch of plants. *"Do you see that?"*

I did. Some branches were full, the leaves untorn, while others were ripped, branches snapped.

They almost looked as if they'd been stepped on. I got hastily to my feet and brushed my knees off.

"Eliana? What is it?" Jay got up too and looked around for the source of my investigation.

I pointed, walking quickly toward the plants. "Do you see those? They look like they've been trampled."

Jay followed me toward them, and he knelt down in the dirt when we got to them. "Unicorn tracks." He whistled lowly. "I think we just found our second clue, Eliana."

A swell of pride that came at the accomplishment quickly collapsed when I considered all that we still needed to do and all that we hadn't done. A second clue was good... but it didn't mean that we'd found them. And that was what I'd hoped to do here today.

I noticed a silvery sheen on some of the leaves, and my heart dropped. That looked an awful lot like...

"Blood," Zacarina and Jay said at the same time.

Jay looked up, and his eyes met mine. "Unicorn blood."

I swallowed. "Who would do this?"

Jay shook his head slowly. "No one that I'd like to meet in a dark alley, that's for damn sure."

Zacarina's eyes rolled. I thought that if it had been possible for a unicorn's face to pale, hers would have.

Instead those golden eyes darted about, finding it impossible to settle. *"We need to get out of here. My flock is gone, but whatever is after them would bleed me next."*

"Zacarina, it will be okay," I said.

She reared and, with no reins to seize to help her keep all of her feet on the ground, Jay ran forward to grab hold of her stirrups instead.

All four hooves fell back to the ground, but it did not calm her for long. She looked at me steely-eyed. *"We leave now, or I leave without you. I will not leave my daughter without a mother."*

A pang went straight through my heart. She was right. Baby needed Zacarina. And Fae needed me. I couldn't take the chance of something happening to us if whoever had hurt the unicorns came back this way.

"Let's go, Jay. It's getting late. The guards and Mother are bound to be looking for me soon. We have a starting point of a trail, at least. Whenever we can get back here, we can see if we can find where it leads."

He nodded and slung the saddle blanket over his shoulders. I put one foot in Zacarina's stirrups and slung the other over her back. She lowered her body so that Jay could mount as well. And no sooner had he hooked his arms around my waist again than we were off, leaving blood and a sunset behind us.

Zacarina returned us to the staviary. We dismounted, and Jay told me to meet him in his office. But I stayed behind. I wanted to console the beautiful unicorn, but I wasn't sure I'd be able to find the words. "We'll find your herd," I whispered.

She just shook her great head, her mane flipping to and fro with the movement. *"Will we? I'm not so sure."*

"We will."

Her eyes seemed sad and tired when she looked at me. *"Your mate is waiting for you. Go. I don't feel much like talking anymore anyway."*

I sputtered. "My *mate?!* Jay's not—he's—*We* are not—"

A small tinge of amusement lit her gaze. "*Humans. You protest the strangest things.*"

After that exchange with Zacarina, I only ducked my head back into Jay's office to quickly say goodbye. I could barely look him in the eye, and I was sure my face was beet red. I walked outside and found Avery and Williamson exactly where I'd left them. As neither of them said anything about the amount of time they'd been waiting for me, I could only assume they'd not looked to the sky and seen my unicorn flight.

"All set there, Your Highness?" Williamson asked.

"Yes." I adjusted my overcoat, tightening its ties. I didn't want them to notice the informal clothes beneath. Better to let them believe I was simply the unicorn princess, visiting the only known unicorns left in Vale. Let them believe I was chatting with Jay all day.

It was better than them reporting the truth to my mother. That was a headache I certainly didn't need.

They escorted me back to the palace and dropped me at my rooms. Inside, I found my mother, sound asleep in the rocking chair, with Fae dozing fitfully on her chest.

My heart swelled inside of me. These were two of the people I loved most in the whole world. And this was why I felt I *must* keep these truths to myself. My mother looked so peaceful, an expression of utter contentment written across her face. No worries wrinkled her brow. No grunts of disturbed dreams escaped her mouth. She just slept, holding on to her granddaughter.

I hated to wake her, but it had to be done. Gently, I put my hand on her shoulder and whispered a feather-soft, "Mother."

Her eyes fluttered open and met mine. "Eliana." She yawned and then blinked hard to clear the sleep from her eyes. Her eyes caught on the darkness outside of the windows. "What time is it?"

"About seven."

"*PM?*" she asked, incredulous, and started to sit up.

"Shh, shh!" I held a finger to my lips and pointed frantically at Fae.

"Oh!" She fell back to whispers and cradled Fae protectively. "I can't believe I slept in the middle of the day like that. This little one can really take it out of you."

I trailed a finger over her soft little forehead. "I told you. Did she scream bloody murder?" I asked fondly

"Like a banshee. I think she must have missed her mama."

Guilt only a mother could know squirmed within me. My child had wanted me, and I hadn't been there to hold her. But I steeled myself against falling into that trap. Just because I couldn't be present for every breath she took didn't make me any less of a mother. I had been off trying to solve a mystery that would make this a safer world for all of us.

5TH MAY

Tap. Tap. Tap.

"Your Highness?" Williamson's muffled voice came through the door after his knock as I rocked Fae beside her bassinet. It was pretty early in the morning after the stomach-curdling discovery that not only had the unicorns gone missing, but that they were being harmed. My thoughts were consumed with worry for the creatures and the uncertainty of where to go next. I didn't know that we could follow the trail—if, indeed, there would be any trail for us *to* follow. That might have been it. Plus, we'd left so hastily, I wasn't one hundred percent certain that I would be able to find my way back there.

So I was left waiting until a brilliant idea struck me to make my next move. Left wondering... and waiting

Speaking of waiting, poor Williamson was probably

still waiting for me to respond with permission to come inside before he poked his head into my suite.

"Sorry!" I called. "I was a bit distracted. What can I do for you, Williamson?" I asked.

"Mr. Jay is here to see you again, Your Highness."

I stood up curiously, Fae still cradled against my chest. I hadn't gotten her to sleep quite yet, but her eyes were at half mast. Jay? Maybe he hadn't been able to rid his thoughts of what we'd discovered either. Well, two minds were better than one. Maybe if we talked it over and brainstormed together, we'd come up with something that neither of us could on our own.

"Thank you. Send him in."

Unlike when he'd dropped in earlier that week, this time when Jay walked in, his shoes and clothing were spic and span. The leather of his boots practically gleamed under the light.

"Come to visit your favorite princess?" I asked.

His eyes flew to mine and his face colored. I felt my own cheeks heat in response.

Oh gods, bad joke. Bad joke. Undo it.

"Fae," I amended hastily. "I'm talking about Fae, of course."

I turned Fae around so he could see her. Her sleepy little eyes shot open and I bit my lip. Had I woken the beast? But they started to lower once again, and I breathed a sigh of relief.

Seeing her, his expression brightened for a moment before he sobered abruptly. "I wish this was a simple social call. I'd much rather be making silly faces at her than telling you what I'm here to say," he said. He thumbed toward my sitting room and motioned to the sofa. "Could we talk?"

My smile faded. That sounded awfully serious.

I guessed that my first instinct had been right. This wasn't about visiting with Fae. It had to have something to do with the unicorns. "Oh. Sure."

We sat down next to each other and I nervously tugged a piece of my hair behind my ear. It was strange how self-conscious I felt. His knee was barely bumping mine. Yesterday, his body had been wrapped around me and I hadn't felt half as nervous. I supposed it had something to do with the setting. We'd been with Zacarina, out in the wide, open air yesterday. But being in my suite, when my bedroom was just steps away... somehow it felt just far more intimate.

It felt more intimate than it had even a week ago.

But so much had happened in a week. The unicorns had disappeared. Now, we knew they were in more serious trouble than we'd initially thought. And through it all, Jay had been right there beside me, lending me a hand whenever I asked.

And I'd asked him on a date.

Things were changing. Was I ready to meet the future, whatever it might bring?

I wasn't sure I knew the answer.

Jay looked up to the ceiling and sighed. "I'm not sure exactly where to start. I barely slept last night."

Uh-huh. Uh-huh. *Focus on anything besides the warmth of his leg beside yours, Eliana,* I instructed myself sternly. *You're probably imagining it anyway.*

Fae started fussing and I gratefully seized the excuse to move this conversation somewhere a little less... awkward for me. Hastily, I jumped back up like someone had lit a match beneath my bottom. "Actually, would it be all right with you if we *walk* and talk?" I bounced Fae a little and explained. "Lately, she's just much better if I'm moving around with her instead of trying to hold still for too long." Not a *total* lie. Although I probably could have achieved the same effect if I'd just had Jay follow me over to her rocking chair and we'd spoken there. But I wanted to get out of here.

Jay blinked twice, startled by the request, but still, he said, "Sure," and pushed to his feet.

Once his skin wasn't touching mine, I could think clearly again. So I strapped Fae into her stroller and we set off for the palace gardens. It would take less time to reach them than the meadows and I didn't want to keep Jay waiting long. It was an ideal location because it would be quiet there so we could talk privately without any fear of being overheard and we'd be able to feel the sun on our skin—which I always seized any opportunity to do.

Jay had an anxious, tense sort of energy to him as we walked swiftly toward the gardens, but he wouldn't speak yet. Every time I prodded him, he shook his head. "Not here," he said tersely. It was all he *would* say, eyeing different ladies of the court, servants, and guards. Did he have reason to believe that an insider was at work in the palace? I worried, but I sincerely hoped not. Hopefully, he just didn't want it getting back to our mysterious culprit somehow that we were on to him.

But just before we left my living quarters, I had noticed how his eyes lingered on the word *Rumpelstiltskin* on the walls.

Now, I swore inwardly, cursing myself. I wished that I had gotten over my damn spell of self-consciousness. If he had news about Rumpelstiltskin, I wanted to hear it and I wanted to hear it quickly. It made me quicken my step, eager to hear what he had to say. The faster we got to the gardens, the faster I could find out.

The palace gardens were beautiful but not often busy, and today was no different. We walked inside where tall hedges towered over us, stretching toward the sky.

When you lived in a place like Vale, you didn't often have a need for meticulously maintained flower beds—the ones that grew wild and free in the meadows were just as beautiful and much easier to access for most people, so that was where they went. But this was where our gardeners cultivated the seeds that were gifts from other kingdoms—the ones with climates similar enough to Vale. Others went into our greenhouses. So we had native flowers here as well as rare, fragrant blooms. It was a beautiful place, if a little... overly manicured.

Though this trip had been under false pretenses, supposedly for the purpose of getting my daughter to sleep, it had served that purpose: Fae had fallen asleep during our walk from the palace to get here, lulled by the gentle motion of the stroller's wheels over carpeted floors. Even when we'd left the palace, she hadn't stirred when those soft floors transitioned into cement pathways.

I found us a stone bench to sit on and Jay and I settled down. This time, I sat at the edge of the bench. I messed with my skirts a bit so that they provided a little more cushion on the rough-hewn stone, and once comfortable, I idly pushed Fae's stroller back and forth, getting into a rhythm. I fixed my attention on Jay and whatever it was that he had to say.

"What is it that you wanted to talk about?" I asked.

Please be about the unicorns. Please be about the unicorns. Please be about the unicorns.

"After we saw the unicorn blood yesterday," he started slowly. "I couldn't get it out of my head."

“That’s right,” I said. “You said you didn’t sleep much.” Now that I knew it, I could see that there were deep, dark circles beneath both of Jay’s eyes, and that his eyes themselves were shot through with red.

He nodded. “Right. And it wasn’t just because of what we found. After you left the staviary, I went somewhere else.”

My mind went immediately to the blood splatter we’d found. I’d thought that there wasn’t much of a trail to follow, but... “You didn’t follow the trail alone, did you?” That would be irresponsible. And irresponsible was not Jay’s M.O.

He scoffed, dismissing that idea. “ No, I would never do anything like that without telling you where I was going. I wouldn’t have been able to follow a trail in the dark anyway. But I wanted to do *something.* Instead, I thought about what we’d talked about the day before. About Rumpelstiltskin.”

My heart jumped into my throat. So I’d been right. He had been eyeing the art in my rooms with renewed interest.

“What is it? What did you find?” I asked eagerly.

He got up and began to pace, raking his hands through his hair. “It was late in the afternoon but still early enough that when I went into the city, the library hadn’t closed yet. I took a page out of your book.” I cringed at the bad joke and he gave me an unabashed grin. “Ba-dum ching,” he said, miming a drum and cymbals.

“I knew they wouldn’t be open very much longer last night, so that was my first stop,” he continued. “I asked the librarians. But that got me nowhere. They have what they assured me was an incredibly thorough indexed catalog that included every subject, every title, and every author contained within that library's walls. There wasn't a single mention of a Rumpelstiltskin. After all of our years of hide and go seek, I know how it's spelled, obviously, but I even had them try alternate spellings, just in case your mother had gotten her decor wrong for all those years. We tried Ramplestiltskin, Remplestiltskin, Rimplestiltskin..." He ticked the variations off on his fingers and shook his head. "Got me nowhere. Nothing."

My heart sank. He'd come all this way and acted like it was so important just to report another dead end?

"Then we're stuck," I said, feeling hopeless. "All we have to go on is the trail of blood." And words from a talking unicorn. "The unicorns might just be the next valley over, but they could just as easily have flown to some island miles and miles away. Or gone south. Or north."

The point was, there was very little direction to be had.

Jay resumed his seat and looked at me excitedly. "Hold on. I told you that the library was only my first stop. I thought we were stuck too, at first. So my next stop was to a tavern to get myself a beer and think it over."

I arched an eyebrow. "'Think it over?'" I air-quoted skeptically.

He shrugged. "Or drown my sorrows about the matter. Whatever you'd like to call it. Anyway, I don't know if you remember John McKenna?"

I shook my head and he waved a hand. "I didn't expect you to, really. He's the older man who drives the carriage that delivers grain to the palace and sometimes straw down to the staviary. You probably only met him once or twice. But I've met him more than a few times, so he recognized me and claimed the bar stool next to me, clinked his glass, and asked what I was doing in the city. I don't get down there too often."

I nodded, following along. It wasn't like Jay to go to a bar. He wasn't the drinking type usually.

"So I was feeling a little down and looking into those smiling blue eyes in this friendly wrinkled face, I just thought—what the hell? Why not? So I told him."

My eyes shot open wide. "You *told*—"

He raised his hands to proclaim his innocence, seeing where my assumptions had leapt. "*Not* about the unicorns."

My heartbeat calmed down. Good. The last thing we needed was a citywide panic about the vanishing unicorns. Some of our citizens were a superstitious lot. They would jump to all sorts of conclusions if they knew. It would be like the gods abandoning us to an elaborate unicorn racing ring, run and covered up by the royal family. Vale and the unicorns were practically synonymous. I questioned our kingdom's identity without them.

"*But,*" Jay said, "I *did* tell him that I was in the city trying to find out about something called Rumpelstiltskin. And Eliana... he knew the name."

I sucked in a startled breath as Jay continued.

"He choked on his beer and asked me to repeat myself. And when I did, he looked at me, pale-faced. He immediately downed the rest of his drink and thumped it down on the counter, hollering for the barkeep to bring him another."

Jay put a hand to his head, eyes far away as he relived the conversation.

"And when he got it, he looked down into his glass and said, 'I had hoped to never to hear that name again.'

He gathered himself, then looked at me, and croaked, 'Rumpelstiltskin is not a some*thing.* It's a some*one.* And if you've never met him, you should count yourself as gods-blessed.'"

A *him.* My mind sang out with the realization. It wasn't just a song. It was a man. And Rumpelstiltskin was his name. My mind whirled. And a cocky enough man too, if he was singing his name while he committed a heinous crime. He had to have been confident he wouldn't be overheard. Or—a chill went through me—been certain that there was nothing anyone could do about it even if they *did* figure out who he was.

"How did he know this Rumpelstiltskin?" I asked. There were no problems with my attention span now. My eyes were locked onto Jay and there was no chance I was looking away until I heard the end of this story. He'd taken the hopelessness I'd felt about this quest and was spinning it into gold. A golden promise—at last we'd learn the true source of Rumpelstiltskin.

Jay took a shaky breath. "It was more than fifty years ago, he said."

Fifty years ago? My brow crinkled, trying to do the math. That didn't make sense to me. I knew that Jay said that this John McKenna was old, but if his Rumpelstiltskin was the same one as ours, that would have to make the culprit around seventy years old at least. And I had a hard time imagining an elderly man laying traps for unicorns. The bending alone was bound to make a senior citizen's back seize up. I knew men half that age who couldn't handle that much leaning over.

But I let Jay carry on with his story, not pointing out these inconsistencies yet. We'd figure out the "how" of it all—later.

At last, it seemed, we were finally getting closer to the "who" of it all.

"At first, he tried to keep his story simple. He wanted to just tell me that Rumpelstiltskin was a slippery character who helped him out of a sticky situation a long time ago. That was all he wanted to say. But I pressed and after a little more persuasion and—" Jay shot me a secret little smile "—after buying him a couple more beers—he gave me a bit more detail."

"Rumpelstiltskin is in the business of making bargains," Jay explained. "When my friend was a young man, he and his new wife and child had been in an impossible situation." Jay shrugged. "That, I didn't ask about. Figured that part of the story didn't matter much and I'd pried into the poor guy's private affairs enough already. But when he had nowhere else to turn, this Rumpelstiltskin was the only one who gave him a way out.

"At the time, he said, all he remembered feeling when the situation was taken care of was relief. He'd been so grateful that he babbled his thanks for Rumpelstiltskin agreeing to take his burden on. John agreed to give him whatever he asked for." Jay's eyes turned down as he shook his head.

"The poor guy. He thought it was just an expression, no more than a simple turn of phrase. He didn't know that for Rumpelstiltskin, saying that was as good as a binding, verbal contract.

"Then the task was completed. And the time came for payment."

"What did he want?" I asked, fully drawn into the story.

Jay spread his hands in a helpless shrug. "Everything. Rumpelstiltskin asked for all of their livestock in return. Every last cow, sheep, and chicken. Of course, they immediately refused and tried to clarify their initial agreement. Rumpelstiltskin could have whatever he wanted—within *reason.* But taking their livestock wasn't reasonable. It was how they earned a living. Without it, they'd land in the poorhouse. They tried to make him see reason."

Jay huffed out a breath. "And then, to hear John tell it, something *turned* then in the friendly fellow who had been so willing to help them. He flew into a rage. He demanded he be paid what he asked for, as the initial terms they'd set out guaranteed. They'd *agreed*, he'd bellowed. *Whatever* he asked for. He left their house with the intent of heading straight for their livestock. Of course, John tried to stop him and he turned on him next. He moved so swiftly that they never even saw the weapon." Jay exhaled shakily. "I'd always wondered how he'd lost that hand."

I let out a soft cry and my hands went to my mouth.

A missing hand. I did know who John McKenna was now. I could picture his face with his friendly blue eyes beneath white hair that peeked out beneath the cap he'd worn the few times our paths had crossed. I had wondered about that missing hand too, but I would never have asked him about it. I guess I had my answer now. But wished that I didn't.

"John said the pain was blinding so he didn't remember much after that. His wife rushed him to a healer, but she told him that Rumpelstiltskin just cackled and called it *interest.*" Jay's lip was curled into an expression of distaste. "He took the hand with him."

Bile rose up in my throat at Jay's story. I'd never heard anything so horrific in my whole life. What kind of sick mind must Rumpelstiltskin have to even contemplate such horrors?

"And even taking that from them didn't stop him. To this day, John isn't sure how he did it—their gates had already been padlocked shut that night. The key was still in its place on a hook. But when his wife returned home to fetch payment for the healer the next morning while John slept in the healer's bed, all of their livestock was gone.

"He destroyed their livelihood. Left them penniless. They had to sell the house and land. His wife got sick, but they had little money for doctors and she soon passed. And, while his son lived, he blamed his father for their lot in life. He left Vale and John hasn't even seen him in twenty years."

My hand went to my throat. Jay's story was getting worse and worse. A part of me wanted to cover Fae's ears so as she wouldn't hear it, but I knew how ridiculous that was. She was asleep and wouldn't understand Jay's words anyway. It didn't stop me from wanting to shield her from the horror, though. Maybe that was what my mother had been doing for me all these years. Shielding me from all the bad in the world.

"At the end of the story, he told me that if I was really set on looking for Rumpelstiltskin, if and when I find him, I must make absolutely sure not to barter, bargain, or trade with him unless I was prepared to lose everything I held dear. The price is never worth it," Jay said, his face grim.

I couldn't find the words to speak for a moment. "Poor Mr. McKenna," I said softly.

"Yeah," Jay said. "You'd never know from how nice he is what a hard time of it he's had."

"That's awful," I said slowly. My mind tried to turn over what I'd learned, but it was so much to absorb so quickly. But one thing stood out to me and failed to make sense. Rumpelstiltskin made bargains. But I didn't think that mattered in this case. I didn't think an agreement could have been struck that would get us into the situation we were in now.

"But Jay—we *haven't* made a deal. We've never even met this man. So he has to be operating on his own accord. No one would have the authority to promise him the unicorns. And I don't know of anyone who would be horrible enough to try."

"You're right," he said. "But that's not my point. Don't you get it?" He pointed back in the direction of the palace. His finger was like a knife, stabbing toward it. His eyes were fierce on mine and I couldn't look away. "The point is, we know his name. We may not have known who he was, or what he did, but we damn well know his name, Eliana."

His *name.* The images danced through my mind. Of my nursery. My rooms growing up. The word splayed across my walls, framed as art. Jay and I shrieking it during a round of hide and go seek as children, growing into teenagers and using it as a creative swear. The stupid decor, the made up word that hadn't even been made up at all, but a warning of its own.

And my mother. My mother's pale face and tight lips as she made me promise to never forget it. As she pressed upon me how important it was. The shattered plate on the floor when I'd questioned her about it the other night, her hands on my shoulders demanding to know who had sung that word where I might overhear.

It was all so clear now. She wasn't so much worried that I'd uncover her secret.

No... she was afraid of something else.

She was afraid Rumpelstiltskin was back.

And that explained why Jay was acting so odd about talking in the palace too. He was worried that our discussion would get back to her before we could see what we made of it all.

I lifted my eyes to Jay's, stunned by the revelation.

"My mother."

He nodded, his arm slowly descending from its accusatory direction toward the castle.

I swallowed, feeling sick, repeating it.

"My mother. My mother had to have made a deal with Rumpelstiltskin."

THRONE OF SACRIFICE

5TH MAY

"He told me that if I was really set on looking for Rumpelstiltskin, I must make absolutely sure not to barter, bargain, or trade with him unless I was prepared to lose everything I held dear. The price is never worth it."

The memory of Jay's voice echoed in my mind as I swept through the palace, fists clenched at my sides, anger burning a flame within my chest. Courtiers and servants bid me a good morning with cheery grins on their faces, used to being greeted with the same in return from me. But that wasn't what they got today. Oh, no, *today* they backed away hastily when I turned to them, an uncharacteristic scowl on my face.

If word spread of this, no one would be calling me

the Unicorn Princess for long. That moniker brought to mind someone serene, someone gentle and pure of heart like the unicorns themselves. I didn't exactly feel like I fit the bill right now. I felt as though I could breathe fire, like a dragon, if the wrong person looked at me the wrong way today.

They would be innocent victims if they were to step into my path. After all, it was hardly their fault. They couldn't have known the information I'd learned yesterday. How could they possibly be expected to guess how the news had shaken me to my core?

At a fast clip, blindly, I turned a corner, then another one, my feet quickly finding their way in a palace I knew as well as the back of my hand. Good thing, too. My eyes were open, but I had to admit that I wasn't really *seeing* the pathways before me. My mind's eye was too busy remembering the expression on Jay's face—pale and deeply disturbed as he told me of everything a man had lost at the hands of the man named Rumpelstiltskin.

"But Jay," I'd said when he'd explained how Rumpelstiltskin had a reputation of dire bargains where his partners in trade almost always came off worse than he did. *"We* haven't *made a deal. We've never even met this man. So he has to be operating on his accord. No one would have the authority to promise him the unicorns. And I don't know of anyone who would be horrible enough to try."*

"Don't you get it? The point is, we know his name. We may not have known who he was, or what he did, but we damn well knew his name, Eliana."

And just like that, all of the pieces had fallen into place like the simplest puzzle. I did know the word *Rumpelstiltskin.* Not its meaning or who it belonged to, but I had grown up with the word. There was one person who had made sure it was a part of my vocabulary by decorating the walls of my childhood bedroom with it.

My mother. My mother had to have made a deal with Rumpelstiltskin.

"Your Highness!" A shout echoed down the hallway after me. Not long after that, the sound of panting and clanking weapons reached my ears as my guards, Avery and Williamson, jogged to keep up with me. "Your Highness," Avery repeated in a huff, face growing red with exertion.

Williamson picked up the thread of conversation that Avery had dropped. "We thought you were still in your chambers."

"Oh?" I said, uncaring. Mechanically, my feet turned another corner, and the men kept pace with me. We were almost to my parents' rooms now. My blood thrummed with the promise of the inevitable conversation. At last, I'd have my answers, one way or another.

"Ye-es." He sounded annoyed.

I couldn't blame him. I probably would have been irritated if I were in his shoes too. But I had my own problems to deal with. Didn't we all?

"We thought that because," Williamson continued, "*you* told us you wouldn't leave until at least the normal breakfast time." He didn't specifically admonish me, but it was implicit in his tone; Williamson's voice sounded as if he was gritting his teeth. Probably regretting the day that he and his partner were saddled with the duty of babysitting the rebellious princess. Well, the two men were fine and upstanding fellows, but their job still grated against my principles. I wanted my independence, so I didn't much like it either.

"My mistake," I said. I was flippant, not even bothering to try and pretend to cover up the out-and-out lie. I knew that I wasn't fooling either of them or sparing their feelings, as they knew they couldn't trust me. Trust was a valuable currency. They were better off learning not to just give it away as I had.

But that was too bad. I was going to speak to my mother today, and I was going to do it now—or as soon as humanly possible, anyway. Jay had convinced me to wait a day. I wouldn't wait any longer.

I reached the door to my parents' bedrooms and nodded curtly at the single guard stationed outside their chambers—her favored man, Hardy. He'd grown up with my father and been with my parents since he was old enough to enter royal service.

"Princess Eliana," he said. His caterpillar eyebrows knitted together in confusion. "Is your mother expecting you? She hasn't mentioned any visitors. I don't think she expected to see you in between any occasions when you dined together today."

"Can't a daughter pay her mother an unscheduled visit?" I smiled and made it as saccharine as I could. But Hardy wasn't fooled. The fact that he'd been with my parents so long meant that he'd seen me grow up. And he could occasionally figure out when I was lying or playing at sweetness in order to get what I wanted like I was today.

Hardy slid a cautious glance behind me to my guards. I turned my head enough that, out of the corner of my eye, I could see Avery shrug helplessly and mouth "No idea."

But Hardy seemed to decide that whatever business I had with my mother, it was a matter between mother and daughter. Oh, if only he knew. It was a matter that may well have concerned the entire kingdom.

Finally, he stepped aside so that I had unbarred

access to her door.

I lifted my hand and paused for a moment, looking over at him. Just the one man outside the King and Queen of Vale's rooms.

It had never escaped my notice that my parents had perilously few personal guards. Sometimes, my mother allowed me to be unescorted—although those days seem to be over now—but whenever I had an armed escort, it was always at least two guards.

My mother wasn't half so concerned with her safety or my father's as she was with mine. I had always thought it a strange thing. Yes, I was the heir to the throne, and it made a certain amount of sense for my safety to be thought of, but they were the ruling monarchs. Surely *their* safety should take a great deal of precedence over mine. Vale would be left in a lurch without them. I was a long way away from being ready to inherit the crown and keys to the kingdom.

My mother had hand-waved away such questions, citing Vale's history of a low crime rate as the reason they didn't have a larger personal guard. I'd told her that explained absolutely nothing. If anything, it should have meant that if she just had one guard, I should have had no guards at all.

She didn't see it that way. I had always wondered why.

Now, I had more than a sneaking suspicion that it had to do with the dangerous man named Rumpelstiltskin.

My blood curdled. What had he done to her? To all of us?

I banged on the door, not bothering with the light, polite taps as I usually did. No, this knock sounded like the boom of cannon fire at her door that would blow it in if she didn't answer quickly enough. "Mother? Open up!" I hollered.

The door flew open, my mother's normally coiffed appearance not nearly as put together as usual. Her face was free of makeup, and her hair was tied up in a sleeping cap.

"Eliana? Are you all right? What on earth is going on?" Her worried eyes scanned my body from head to toe, taking me in and inspecting me for any possible injuries. Finding none, she hastily knotted the belt of her dressing gown and motioned me inside as her concerned expression gave way to bewilderment.

"What's going on?" she asked again.

"Where's Father?" I returned. Did he know too? I wondered. Who exactly was to blame for all these years of secrets? Who besides her had intentionally kept me in the dark?

She opened her arms wide, indicating the rooms, empty of all but us. "He left already. He had to meet with some advisors early this morning. But if it's important and you need him, I'm sure he'd be happy to come. Shall I ring and have him join us?" Her hand gravitated toward the bell pull and was halfway there when I shook my head.

"That won't be necessary. I may speak with him later as well, but it's really you I wanted to talk to."

Her hand stilled, something in my tone giving me away. It was grim and foreboding; not the tone of someone who just had a hankering to see her loving parents.

"All right," my mother said slowly. Her hand drifted through the air to settle in her lap. Her eyes flicked over me in a crude inspection. Before, she'd looked me over for injuries, but now she seemed to notice my furrowed brows, my stiff posture. And now, she understood this wouldn't be an altogether pleasant visit. She seemed to gather herself, squirming in the chair—wriggling left and right until she found a position comfortable to her, and she straightened like someone who was preparing to be dealt a great blow. Now that her initial concern had passed, she seemed to sense the charged air between us and gathered that something was amiss. Something that was a big enough deal to send me charging to her door, pounding on it like the palace was under attack. "What's—"

"What's going on?" I air quoted with a *great* deal of sarcasm, then crossed my arms aggressively. I could hardly believe she even had the nerve to ask me that. "That's funny. Hilarious, even. What. A. Coincidence." I punctuated each word with a rhythmic and insincere cadence, tilting my head from side to side. "You see, it's funny because I had the same question for you. But you did always teach me to respect my elders, so why don't you go first?" I gestured toward her as though I was passing the conversation her way.

She squinted in confusion, forehead wrinkling as though she'd be able to spy my meaning if she just looked at me hard enough. "I'm sorry, darling, but I just don't understand what you're getting at. What is that supposed to mean?"

I could speed this up quickly enough. So I did. I held a single finger in the air and glared at her. "One word, Mother: Rumpelstiltskin."

All of the air seemed to leave her body like I'd socked her in the stomach unexpectedly. It was that quick. That effective. Her perfect posture disappeared as she inhaled a shaky breath and sagged back into her seat. She suddenly looked old beyond her years. She rubbed at her temples. "I had hoped never to have this conversation." She looked back up at me. "What do you know?"

"I don't want you leaving anything out because you think that I don't need to know it anymore. I know enough that I'm here," I said curtly.

...Well, *that* simply wasn't true. I tried again. "Well, I know *some*," I corrected myself. "It's not nearly enough. And that's why I've come. So you could be honest with me for once in your life."

But I could see that she still wasn't ready to relinquish the truth. She was like a safe that had been shut for so many years that the lock was rusting. I needed more than just a key to open it with. She eyed me warily. "And what you know is...?"

I took a deep breath and said it again. The word. The name that would tell her all that she needed to know. "Rumpelstiltskin."

She shuddered visibly upon hearing it, but I forged on, unsympathetic. "I know he's a man. A dangerous one. I know he makes deals." Another deep breath and I went for the kill shot. "And I know that you made one with him."

She scooted forward in her seat and smiled wanly, running stressed fingers over her cheeks. She leaned forward onto her knees and looked me in the eyes. "I knew this day would come someday. But gods, I hoped to be wrong and that I'd never have to tell you. This knowledge is not kind to anyone, and I vowed that I would be a kind parent. Not like my own father. You remember me telling you about him? About how he was not a kind man? A lazy drunk?"

"Yes, of course." A frisson of pity for the girl my mother had been sparked, but I hardened my heart against it. I wouldn't let her distract me like this. I'd come here for answers, and I was damn well going to get them.

"Well, there's more to the story." She took a deep breath and began. "My story—mine and Rumpelstiltskin's—began when my father bragged in a bar one day that I could spin straw into gold."

My eyebrows shot up. "But spinning straw into gold is impossible without magic." And unicorns aside, there wasn't a whole lot of magic in Vale, so I knew my mother certainly didn't possess such a gift.

She snorted. "Impossible didn't matter to my drunk of a father. And didn't much matter to your other grandfather, the king, either. After my father made such a bold claim, and it reached the ears of the king, it was spin straw into gold or be killed. Those were my choices. And not much of a choice either, seeing as how I was just a miller's daughter. Not exactly a sorceress with magic at the tips of my fingers."

Her expression became far away. "And in the midst of the impossible... *he* appeared. Rumpelstiltskin. Though back in those days, I knew him only as 'the imp.' And he gave me a chance. I didn't have any magic, but he did. He could do what I couldn't. It was simple, at first. All he asked for was a small thing. The necklace I wore. It was just a trinket, and I couldn't get it off my neck and into his hands fast enough. He did what he promised, and the king let me live. But your royal grandfather wasn't done with me. Greedy, now that he had a room full of gold where only straw had been before, he shoved me in another room filled with straw—bigger, this time—and demanded I turn all of that into gold as well. Again, I thought that I was doomed, but again, the imp appeared, offering to do the deed so that I might live. This time, the price was a little harder to part with. The ring I wore." She smiled sadly. "It had been my mother's. But it still wasn't worth refusing when it would cost me my life. I yanked it from my finger, and he spun the straw. I hoped that would be the end of it. But it wasn't.

"The king put me in another room, even bigger than the last. I was told he'd make me a queen if I succeeded one last time. The consequences if I were to fail remained the same. I'd die. I remember thinking the life he promised wasn't much better. I'd be marrying a monster. But gods, despite knowing the life that awaited me, I wanted to live. And the imp told me he could make sure that happened. If I just promised him my firstborn child."

Her *child.*

All of my anger suddenly flew away as though my rage had been a balloon, and my mother had just neatly punctured it with a pin.

I understood now. I understood why she was always so afraid for me, that some terrible tragedy would befall me.

I may not have been borne of her body, but I had never thought that I wasn't her child. And all my life, she had had a reason to believe I was in danger.

Would I have behaved so very differently if it was Fae's life at stake? I wasn't sure that I would.

"At the time, I didn't have any children to be concerned about. And I certainly hoped that if I married the king, I'd be able to figure out a way not to conceive his children." She shuddered a little, her thoughts clearly back in that time, back with the girl she used to be. "I agreed. He did it again." Her expression brightened a little. "But it wasn't your grandfather they intended for me, but your father." For the first time in the telling of this story, a true smile graced her face. "Prince Bennet was good and kind. And even if it meant I'd be related to his father, I considered myself lucky to be marrying him. And we grew to love each other easily over that first year of marriage."

My heart swelled. My parents were quiet together, but the love between them was evident and genuine. It was nice to hear that had been the case from the beginning.

"It was only after I married your father that I regretted my bargain. I was diligent with my contraceptive potions, but both Bennet and I longed for a child. When your father examined the magical contract the imp had left behind, he found a loophole by guessing his name—I'd known him only as a devious imp, you see.

"The clause was written in as a goodwill gesture, I supposed. He'd written in a cancellation clause, but never expected anyone to actually be able to *use* it. And he'd been confident that Rumpelstiltskin was a name we'd never, *ever* guess. He was right, too. Except that he grew cocky and didn't account for the fact that we'd been combing the kingdom for him. We spied him, heard him gloating to himself that was his name. When he came the next day for our series of guesses, we were freed.

"But I was still afraid to conceive. Rumpelstiltskin had left us with a terrifying oath. *'One day, we'll play another game. And you will have only yourself to blame.'*" Her face was white. "I knew we hadn't seen the last of him.

"But then, a year later, I received the most wonderful gift." A trembling hand caressed my cheek. "You, my darling girl. Two strangers—women—knocked on our door one night. You were snuggled up in their arms, cozy in your blankets and fast asleep. They told me you were ours if we wanted you. That we'd be keeping you safe if we took you. And 'if we wanted you?'" She scoffed. "I'd never wanted anything more. And I thought perhaps that since you were my child, but not the firstborn I gave birth to, and since we had theoretically broken the agreement with Rumpelstiltskin, I said yes. I was still afraid, but based on what they said, there was other danger out there for you as well. Perhaps the protection we could offer you from that outweighed the risk from Rumpelstiltskin. Whatever the risks, you were worth it."

She swallowed hard. "But now that you have a child, borne of your body, I worry for you and Fae. I worry that my curse will somehow become yours. And I want nothing else less for you than that. I hoped it was over, but with all these questions... I know now that it's not. It can't be." She rose to her feet and extended a hand, pulling me to mine as well so she could look deeply into my eyes. "So now I've told you everything I know, and it's time for you to tell me: What brings this talk of Rumpelstiltskin to me?"

I took a deep breath and told her everything I knew of Rumpelstiltskin's involvement in the unicorns' disappearance. All the while, through the whole of my story, she grew visibly paler and groped behind her for a chair, sagging into it anew when she found it.

But she gathered herself, that spine of steel I'd always seen in her reasserting itself.

"If Rumpelstiltskin is at large, let's not waste our time here." She pulled a long rope near the credenza, and Hardy instantly entered the room, weapons drawn.

When he didn't see any danger, he lowered his sword, brow furrowed, and expression confused. "Your

Majesty, have you a need of me?"

"Yes." She took a deep breath. "I want you to go into the city and villages and root out Rumpelstiltskin."

Hardy shuddered. That alone would have made me worry. He was my mother's most trusted guard. If he knew enough of Rumpelstiltskin to be concerned, we all should be.

"He's back?" he asked.

My mother sighed. "I'm afraid so. Take whomever you need for the investigation and keep me informed. I want a status report at the end of each day. Whether progress has been made or not, I want to know each place you've checked, who you spoke to, and what they said."

Hardy bowed deeply and stood, thumping his fist against his heart. "It will be done, Your Majesty."

"Wait." I grabbed Hardy's arm as he moved past me. "Find Jay and bring him with you. He's begun some initial research already and knows a man, John Little, who bargained with Rumpelstiltskin years ago. If you hear his story yourself, you may be able to glean a clue that we wouldn't. Or maybe he'll mention something he hasn't already."

He nodded. "Yes, Your Highness. Thank you. We'll follow any lead we are lucky enough to find with a creature as elusive as Rumpelstiltskin."

I tried to fight back the growing lump in my throat. I had a feeling that I had not yet begun to understand what we were dealing with when it came to Rumpelstiltskin.

And I hoped that we could catch him before I had the chance to truly grasp it.

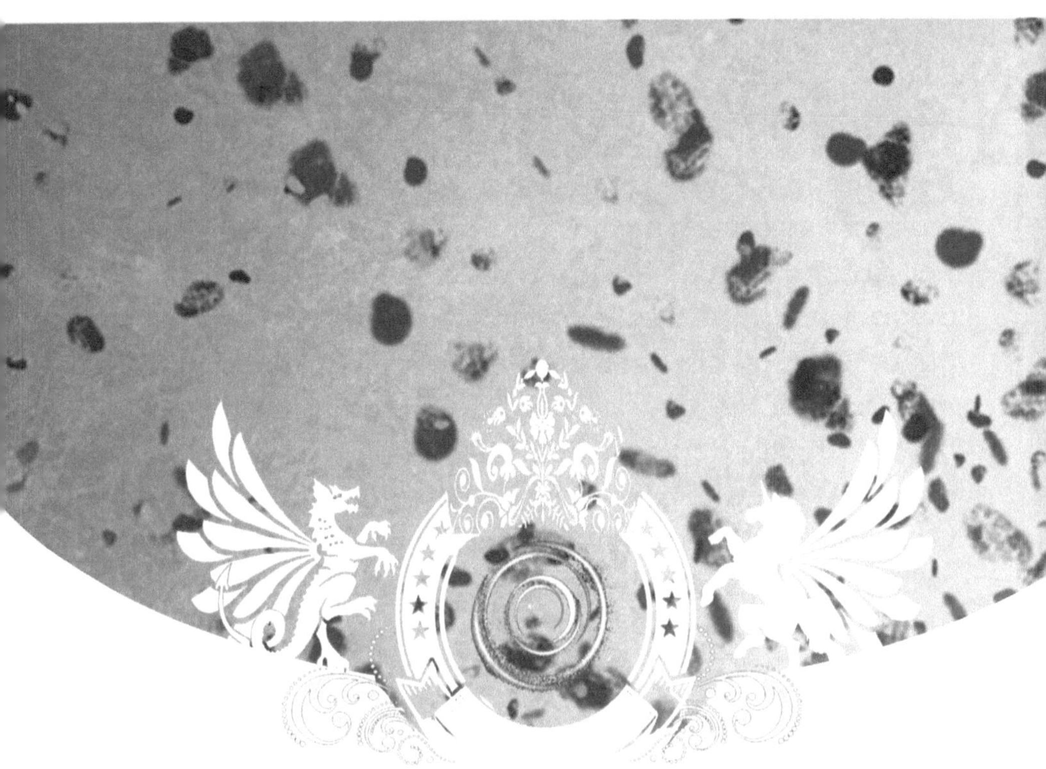

6TH MAY

I had distracted myself the rest of the day yesterday with motherly duties. Without using the nursemaid at my disposal in the palace, there was certainly plenty to do with a newborn to keep me occupied, even if they weren't the most thrilling of tasks.

During Fae's nap, I used the free time to organize the gifts that had been sent from friends and other kingdoms in celebration of her birth. I shoved a drawer shut, and the sleeve of a onesie peeked out as if it was waving at me. I was running out of places to put things. I could only imagine what I was going to do when I had to organize the gifts from the party my mother was throwing for Fae.

I put a hand to my head. That was coming up soon. Gods, I hadn't thought about that in days. Was there still stuff left to do for it? I felt as though the list was never-ending. I wondered if party planning was how my mother was occupying her time in between reports from her guards. After all, she didn't have a new baby to distract her. And she had many years' worth of worries about Rumpelstiltskin to obsess over. I was sure that the memories of her days with him were running through her mind over and over again like a play in which you couldn't leave the theatre and the actors just repeated their scenes over and over again.

Maybe I'd check on her. I couldn't take the lack of knowledge about what was going on anyway. When Fae went down for her next nap, I rang for Judith and let Avery follow me to my mother's rooms while Williamson stayed behind to stand guard over Fae.

Hardy's presence at the door had been replaced by another guard, which made sense, of course. Mother wanted her most trusted man leading the expedition to find Rumpelstiltskin.

The new guard gave me a little nod of respect when he realized who I was and allowed me access to the door to knock. This time, the knock returned to my usual: a few cheery little taps.

The door swung open—and my mother greeted me with what I could only describe as a sympathetic smile. My hopes plummeted before she even spoke and confirmed my suspicions. "They haven't come back yet, sweet."

Damn.

I made a disappointed little sound, and my mother tutted, stepping forward to envelope me in a warm embrace. "This is another reason I never told you about him," she murmured. "Better that you should be angry with me for the methods I used protecting you than having worries prey upon your mind like this. That's a mother's job, not yours."

She might have been right. I gave her a quick squeeze and stepped back, giving her a close-lipped smile of regret. "Be that as it may, I am a mother now too. And you're right. It's my job to worry."

She smiled sadly and swept her arm around the room, indicating the large, empty chambers. "Do you want to come in? Misery loves company. We could waste our hours worrying together."

"Thank you, but no." I shook my head. "I'll only feel worse that way."

"I understand. I'll see you for dinner?" she asked.

I nodded. "You can count on it."

I headed back to my rooms. Fae was probably still sleeping, so I took the long way around and tried to treat the brisk walk around the castle as exercise. Getting my heart pumping would surely take my mind off things. But that was to no avail. I couldn't stop thinking about Rumpelstiltskin, even after I returned to my rooms and relieved Judith and was back on mom duty.

When I went to dinner, Mother still had nothing new to report. I tried one last time that day, but when I went by her rooms around ten o'clock at night, it was the same message. The guards hadn't returned yet.

I clenched my fists, trying to hide my frustration. I was sure they were combing every nook, cranny, and hidey-hole that Rumpelstiltskin could be inside. Their lateness was likely only due to their thoroughness; so, doubtless, their status report would be arriving late. But I felt like a petulant child. I wanted it *now*, gods damn it.

Gently, my mother took my hands and led me back to the door. "Why don't you go to bed?" she suggested. "If there is anything to know, we'll know it in the morning."

So, without any other action left to take (*gods,* I felt useless), I took her suggestion and put both Fae and myself to bed. Between Fae's cries in the middle of the night and my own thoughts swirling about my head, I didn't sleep well, but I did at least sleep a little bit, even if it was fitfully. When I woke, I didn't feel rested, but at least the time had seemed to have gone by a bit faster. That was a small blessing, but one I was thankful for, given how the previous day had seemed to just drag on and on and on.

In the morning, I fed Fae and dressed her in a hurry, bringing her with me and my guards to my mother's rooms. My mother had said she wanted daily reports. The guards *had* to have returned to deliver their first one by now. It was the next day, for goodness' sake.

And, as luck would have it, I was right. Hardy was exiting my parents' rooms with another guard just as I was arriving. The two men conversed briefly outside their doors and then seemed to come to an agreement, nodding. The other man headed off in one direction, Hardy in the opposite.

"Hardy!" I called out, not wanting to lose him. I quickened my pace to a light jog, holding Fae's head gently against my chest so that I didn't jostle her too much with the bouncing movement.

The guard stopped when he heard his name and turned, waiting for me to catch up.

I exhaled a quick breath when I reached him, my heart pounding just from that light exercise. Man, I was out of shape. Pregnancy and labor will do that to a person.

"What news?" I asked eagerly. Finally, I'd have some answers. "What did you find?"

He shook his head, expression grim, and pushed his helmet higher on his head as he sighed, disappointed. "I wish the news was better, but we didn't find much, I'm afraid, Your Highness. I'm off to try to drum up more avenues to search while my men speak with the senior citizens in Shipley—those who were alive and living here during John's days when he dealt with Rumpelstiltskin. The thought is, we'll see if anyone else had any encounters with Rumpelstiltskin that they haven't mentioned up until now. Perhaps knowing that they weren't alone in their dealings with him will give them the courage to speak up where they never have before."

Damn. Disappointment flared in my chest, and I tried not to let the discouragement show on my face. Because truly, it had been foolish for me to hope for more results that quickly, I supposed.

In a rare gesture of kindness that broke the thin wall of decorum between royalty and subject, Hardy clapped a hand onto my shoulder and inclined his head toward me, meeting my eyes seriously. He gave my shoulder an encouraging squeeze. "Fret not, Princess. We'll get him in the end. I promise you that."

Perhaps Hardy was a fool too. But better we should be fools than pessimists. I'd much rather be an optimist.

I managed a small smile for him as I nodded, accepting his encouragement. I hoped to the gods that we two fools were right. "Thank you, Hardy. I'm sure you're right."

His hand dropped back to his side, then lifted and thumped his heart as he gave me a quick bow. "A pleasure. It's the honor and privilege of my life to serve the royal family of Vale, Your Highness. Your Mother has the rest of my report, should you require details.

For now...” He jerked his head in the direction of the castle’s exit. “I’d best be on my way. Plenty more people to investigate and interrogate. We want to catch the cretin as quickly as possible.”

Hastily, I stepped to the side, out of his path so he could get past me. “Yes, by all means. Thank you again.”

I watched him walk away for a moment, then took a deep breath and knocked on my mother’s door for the fourth time in twenty-four hours.

The door swung open. Unlike yesterday, she was far more put together. Granted, I had come a bit later this time. I hadn’t wanted to be disappointed by the lack of news again. And the circumstances were different this morning than they were yesterday morning as well. I wasn’t as fueled by rage and frustration as I had been yesterday. So it was late enough in the day that rather than Mother greeting me in her dressing gown, she was fully dressed and coiffed for the day, with her hair and makeup done. I supposed she’d made certain to be ready and able to receive her guards when they arrived to deliver their report from the day before.

She smiled when she saw me, and it wrinkled the corners of her tired eyes. She clearly hadn’t slept much better than I had. “I should have known it would be you, Eliana.”

I shrugged and grinned guiltily, my hands held in the air. “Sue me and call me predictable then, I guess.”

She motioned me inside and I stepped in gladly, leaving Avery and Williamson in the hall with her guard. “I just spoke with Hardy in the hall. He told me they hadn’t had much luck.”

“He’s right. But no one is giving up.”

“I know.” I nodded and bit my lip. “I was hoping you had a little more elaboration from him though? It’s just, he only had a few minutes to speak with me before he had to run off to continue the investigation. And I know he gave you the full debrief..." I trailed off, letting my wheedling tone do my suggesting for me.

She rolled her eyes and grabbed a note pad off of the end table, passing it over to me. My eyes scanned the scrawled words eagerly. It really *wasn't* much. Just a simple list of names of the places that they had checked and the names of the people they had spoken with. I turned the page and found a more detailed narrative of their conversation with John. But I already knew everything there as well. Jay had told me that story. I turned the page again.

And there was a list of more names. I looked up at her. The list had no title and also didn't have any indication of what it was.

"What's this?"

"The people John mentioned in his story. They're hoping one of them can remember something about Rumpelstiltskin that can turn the tide of the investigation. Sometimes, all it takes is one small detail to crack the entire case wide open."

Hardy had been right. There truly wasn't much more for my mother to tell me about the investigation. And now, I had all the information that they had in hand, but what good would it do me? They wouldn't deliver another report until tomorrow. Suddenly, that seemed very far away, an endless sea of time just stretching out before me. I couldn't think how I would manage to fill the hours until then. Yesterday had driven me crazy enough. How was I to do it again today?

"Hey." My mother laid a hand over the words on the pages and I looked up at her, feeling not a little despondent. She smiled warmly. "I know better than anyone else what fixating on the problem of Rumpelstiltskin can do to a person's mind. Why don't you and Fae—" she nodded at my daughter, asleep against my chest— "do something to take your mind off of it. Something fun, something that will cheer you up."

"Not bad advice," I said. I raised a brow. "So, what will *you* do today?"

She laughed, caught off guard. "All right, point taken." Her eyes drifted again to Fae and her expression softened. She stretched out her arms toward the baby. "Well, if you'll let me, I certainly wouldn't mind just being a grandma and getting to babysit for a while..."

I carefully loosened Fae from the complicated contraption that held her against my chest and I placed her in my mother's arms, happy to be able to do a small thing that would cheer her up. "Of course. She loves spending time with her Granny."

Mother's nose wrinkled a little. "I never thought I'd love being called something that makes me feel so old. And yet, here we are." She gathered Fae close and inhaled her sweet baby smell. She looked up at me. "What about you?"

"Me? I've been cooped up in these walls too many days in a row. I've got to get myself outside."

"Take—"

I waved a hand. "Take Williamson and Avery, yeah, yeah. Don't you think I know that by now?" Knowing was well and good of course... it didn't mean that I wasn't going to still find ways to escape the guards' constant presence in my life.

"I know that you know." She pursed her lips and narrowed her gaze playfully. "I just want you to actually *do* it."

Mothers... They know us too well.

She'd get her way for now. I beckoned Avery and Williamson to follow me down to the staviary. My mind hadn't had to wander far when Mother had suggested I find something besides Rumpelstiltskin to occupy my time and thoughts. My mind was, as was so often the case, with the unicorns.

It was my plan to find Baby, the infant unicorn who, in a way, had been there at the start of this whole mess with Rumpelstiltskin, though I hadn't known who had been behind it at the time. She had been caught in a unicorn trap and injured the day that I'd given birth to Fae. At the time, we'd wondered who would dare to go after creatures like unicorns—a protected species; protected by the gods themselves, it was said. Those who hurt or crossed them were doomed to bad luck—often fatally doomed.

Now, we had those answers. We knew exactly who would dare. A man—or imp, as my mother called him—with power all his own. A man named Rumpelstiltskin.

I found Baby's stall, in with her mother, the unicorn Zacarina. Zacarina's noble head protruded over the top of the stall door and she fixed her golden gaze, so like my own, upon me.

It was sometimes strange, seeing my own eyes reflected in the gaze of the unicorns. I thought of myself as ordinary most days, but I had never seen my peculiar eye color in another human being. At least, not one in Vale. There had been a time when I wondered if perhaps my birth parents might share it. But I supposed I would never know the answer to that. Instead, I would settle for the strange and unearthly friendship that I shared with the unicorns. Perhaps my new ability to speak with them, mind to mind, and our shared eye color meant that I shared a kinship not with humans, but with the unicorns. They, after all, were said to be the favorites of the gods—and after all that was happening to and around me, I was beginning to suspect that I was gods-touched too. I hope that meant that the deities up above were looking after both my people and Zacarina's flock. I'd happily take a little divine intervention if it meant getting the unicorns back safe and sound and securing Fae's safety from any bargains with Rumpelstiltskin that may possibly touch her.

"Good morning, young one. What preys upon your mind? You look distracted."

I smiled as Zacarina's voice entered my mind and spoke aloud to answer her. She kept insisting that I could mind-speak back, but it was a habit that was hard to break, having known no other way in my entire life. "I'm sorry. You're right, I am a bit distracted, but I'm well. And a good morning to the both of you in return." I tilted my head toward Baby, indicating it was her that I meant. "And how is the leg?"

"Good."

I froze. *That* voice in my mind was not Zacarina's. It did not have the presence that the great unicorn did. It sounded timid, shy... *new.* "Was that...?" I looked at Zacarina for confirmation, wide-eyed.

I didn't think that I imagined the tinge of pride in Zacarina's eyes. *"It was. My offspring has begun to mind-speak."*

I laughed in disbelief. I had never expected to be able to speak with unicorns in the first place, it was true. But once I had started, had I thought about it, I certainly would not have expected to speak with a unicorn—with *any* being, for that matter—who was under a month old.

But if I'd learned nothing else other the past few

weeks, I had certainly learned that life was full of surprises.

"Baby," I breathed. "You're... You can... wow."

Zacarina seemed to stand taller. *"Epiphany. We reveal our own names at the time that we begin mind-speaking. She is Baby no longer."*

"My... name is... Epiphany." Small pauses of silence pocketed the space between the words, like a speaker of a foreign language trying to wrap their tongue around the strange words.

I smiled. My mother had been right. It *was* cheering me up to visit the staviary. I could imagine no greater gift than conversing with the most innocent creature I'd ever met. A baby unicorn, talking to me. I couldn't stop marveling over it. "It's a pleasure to make your acquaintance then, Epiphany. And the leg is doing well?"

"It is." She had a sweet presence in my mind. It made me think of spun sugar and dandelions.

"Thank you for looking after her," Zacarina said. *"You may not realize it, but it's meant a great deal to me. To both of us."*

"Of course," I replied aloud, and meaning every word of it. "I'd hope that someone would do the same for Fae if she ever needed it."

Zacarina nodded solemnly. *"I will."*

I waved my hands, trying to backtrack. It had sounded like I was hinting at something, hadn't it? "Oh, I hadn't meant to imply you somehow owed me."

"It's fine. You didn't imply anything. But it doesn't change the fact that I appreciate all that you've done. I may not owe *you, but I would return the favor in a heartbeat if I could. I will always be there for you and your offspring should you have a need of me."*

A chill went over me. There was a gravitas to Zacarina's words. As though they were not spoken idly, but a binding oath. Were the gods watching us even now?

They could watch all they liked—they would whether I liked it or not. But I hoped to never need to see her words fulfilled.

"Never mind all that," I said flippantly, not pausing to allow myself to dwell over it. "I'm just sorry that I haven't been able to do any more for you. I haven't stopped looking for your flock, you know. They're out there and I'm going to find them. We have leads now."

The solemnity with which she'd uttered her oath drained from her voice, leaving behind a tone of great sadness. *"I appreciate that. Appreciate all that you're doing and have done for us. I do hope that you manage to succeed. It is—lonely without them. But it helps to have someone to talk to."*

I smiled. "Likewise. We have men in the villages searching for Rumpelstiltskin. We'll get him." I was just like Hardy, making promises when I had no clue how I'd fulfill them. I only knew that I had to do it.

"Hey," a soft voice—a *human* voice—interrupted our conversation and I whirled around to find Jay draped over the stall's door. He looked tired—haggard, with deep, dark circles under his eyes.

That was right. He had gone with the soldiers who had been conducting the investigation looking for Rumpelstiltskin last night. From the looks of him, he had to have been out all night.

"No luck, I hear," I said, with a sympathetic tilt of my head.

He shook his head, settling down onto the floor. Hay clung to his pant legs and I tried in vain to clean a spot on the floor to join him there. Whatever. I'd just get dirty.

"No. They sent me home. I stayed a bit longer than the others hoping maybe some people we spoke with would be more willing to speak with someone who wasn't an official of the palace, but no dice. Either they really know nothing, or I'd done damage just by being seen with them. But I'm not giving up."

"None of us are," I said, glad that we were having this conversation in front of Zacarina. She'd see that it wasn't just me pulling for the unicorns, but all of us, working together to find Rumpelstiltskin and bring her brethren home.

"You going out to search with them again tonight?"

He nodded.

I sighed. "Gods, I wish that I could join you. But Mother is in enough of a state about me leaving the palace walls. No way she'd happily let me skip off into the city to ask some questions."

"Yeah..." Jay ran a hand through his hair and huffed out an aggrieved breath. "I know that the guards are spreading to the further towns soon to search, but I can't help but feel Rumpelstiltskin is closer than that. Of course it would make more sense for him to take the unicorns and to run just as far as he possibly could, but I don't know... I think he's here in Shipley." He shrugged helplessly. "Can't say why."

"I thought the same." It struck me then that I had yet to fill Jay in on the bargain my mother had with the devious imp. I quickly told him the story and when I was done, he puffed out a breath, running a distressed hand through his hair as he took it all in.

"That's... a lot."

"I know. But it makes sense, like you said, that

he would be close. My mother seems to think that he would want revenge upon her. Stealing the unicorns is terrible, and I'm sure he has a sinister plot in mind for them... but it's not personal. It's not the way to hurt her. That would be my father, me, her home..."

He nodded. "All of which he'd need to be close to reach."

Groaning like his entire body ached, he pushed to his knees. "I've got to go."

"Where?"

His eyebrows ratcheted up into his hairline. "Are you kidding? You just told me this guy might be after you specifically. I'm not wasting another second."

I tried to ignore the warm fluttering of my heart in response.

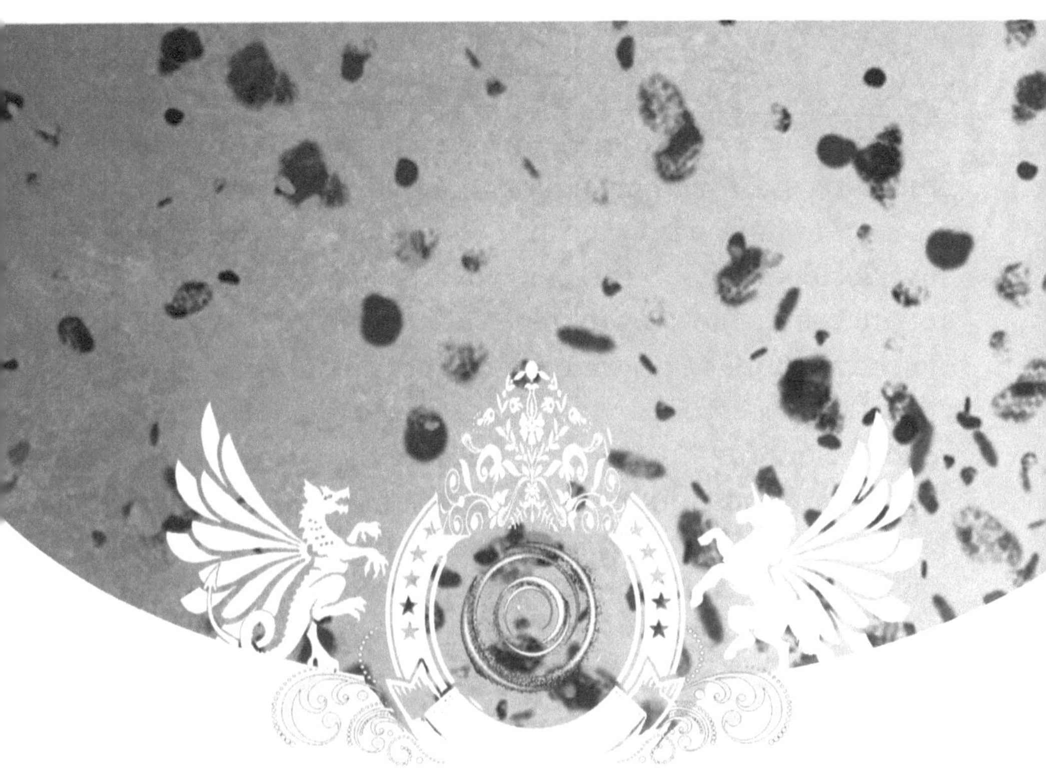

7TH MAY

I tugged on my boots the next morning, intending to visit Mother once again. We were late enough into the morning that Hardy should have delivered his report by now. I doubted that he and his men had gotten very far in the investigation since yesterday morning, but that didn't much change the fact that I wanted to know how far they *had* gotten. Whether it was an inch or a millimeter, I hoped we'd gained at least a *little* bit of ground. I'd cling onto any shred of hope that I could that we were gaining some ground on Rumpelstiltskin.

Maybe I'd go see Jay later as well. I'd like to hear it from someone who had boots on the ground.

And maybe, just maybe, I'd plain old like to see my friend as well.

My friend who was becoming something a bit... more.

I paused and exhaled, my hands on my knees as fluttering started in my stomach. I hadn't thought of my upcoming date with Jay in a few days. Last week, we had decided to go to the party my mother was throwing to celebrate Fae's birth together. Ordinarily, I might not have thought all that much about it. But the word "date" had been used. And I hadn't been on one of those since before my husband, Luka, had died.

There wasn't much room in my mind for anything beyond Fae, Rumpelstiltskin, and the unicorns these days. But the thought of Jay always seemed to find the little crevices and worm its way in, burrowing through my thoughts and finding its way into my heart.

When I exited my rooms with my guards in tow and Fae left behind with a nursemaid again, I pulled my sleeves down to cover my wrists and pushed all other thoughts but those of business from my mind. I straightened my posture, squared my shoulders, and knocked on my mother's door.

As I feared, not much progress had been made. If you could call it progress at all. All Hardy and his men had managed was to rule more and more out. Rumpelstiltskin *wasn't* in the pub. He *wasn't* in the library. He *hadn't* spoken to the innkeeper or the stable boy of the most frequented establishment in the village, which meant they'd be giving up on the city any day now in favor of pursuing more distant leads.

I left my parents' rooms, deep in thought when a hand suddenly tugged at my wrist. Jay. Williamson and Avery made a move toward him, startled by his sudden appearance, but dropped their weapons when they realized who it was and that Jay would never intend me harm.

He was red-faced and panting. "*There* you are. I went

to your rooms first, but you weren't there. I've been looking everywhere."

Clearly, this wasn't a social visit. "What's happened?"

"The mother unicorn," Jay said. "I was sleeping in my office after passing out there after the search last night and I heard her start to make a ruckus so loud that it woke me up. When I went to check on her she wouldn't let me get near her. I thought that since you always seemed to have a calming effect on her, maybe you could come?"

I was already quickening my step. Acting out that way wasn't like Zacarina. The same way that Jay thought I had a calming effect on the mother unicorn, she had always had a calming effect on me. In fact, the last time I had seen her upset and acting out, it was because we had found unicorn blood in the vicinity. This wasn't some sort of wild overreaction, I was sure of it.

When we got down to the staviary, I rushed inside and flipped the latch on Zacarina and Epiphany's stall. Zacarina pranced far from the corner where her daughter watched wide-eyed.

"Mama?" Epiphany asked. *"Maybe the mortals can help?"*

Zacarina fixed wild golden eyes on me. *"Get out of my way,"* she demanded imperiously. She tossed her mane.

"What's going on?" The watchful eyes of Jay and my guards pressed in on me, and I bit my lip. With them watching, I couldn't speak to her aloud as I usually would. I needed to mind-speak, the way that she did.

I put a hand to her nose and leaned my head toward her. *"Talk to me. Please."*

Gradually, she calmed under my touch, but when her thoughts came, they were frayed and desperate. *"I can feel them. My herd. My flock. They're close, and I need—"*

Frustrated, she whinnied and stamped a hoof on the ground. *"I* need *to be with them. Please help me."*

Her sense of urgency filled my body. I too needed to escape this stall. I too needed to find our flock. "Of course, I'll help you," I murmured. The presence of Jay and the others outside the stall reminded me to be careful what I said aloud. I had accepted this new gift of mine, being able to speak with the unicorns, but I hardly had faith that everyone else would as well. To my knowledge, no other mortal beings could communicate with any animals, much less the nigh–on-untouchable creatures that the unicorns were. *"We established yesterday: we're a team."* I spoke mind to mind. *"If you need my help, I'm there. But you're not going alone. That helps no one. If he takes you too, then Epiphany will be left all alone. The last of the unicorns. No flock. No mother. Is that what you want?"*

Her restless prancing stilled. *"Of course not."*

I smiled. *"Good. Then we'll make haste, but we will go together."*

With Zacarina temporarily calmed, I whirled around, turning to Jay and my guards, who watched from the hall of the staviary.

"That's amazing," Jay breathed. "It's like she really understands that you're here to help her."

She understood more than they could possibly know. More than even he understood about me these days.

"Send word to the castle," I ordered. "Tell my mother we've gone for a ride."

~

I may have been an optimistic fool, but one thing I was most certainly was *not* was foolhardy. A guard patrolling near the stables was dispatched to the palace to send word to my mother about where we'd gone. Williamson stayed behind in order to keep watch over Baby—over Epiphany. I was not going to leave the little unicorn unguarded. My own child was safe within the walls of the palace while I was gone. I'd make sure that Zacarina's offspring was just as safe in the staviary with someone watching over her while she was gone.

I told Jay and the guards that I had a theory: what if—I posed the question as if it was a possibility that had just leapt into my mind—what if Zacarina was as wild as she was because her herd was nearby and she had no way of reaching them? It sounded crazy, I knew, but it couldn't hurt to check... could it? I made sure to widen my eyes nice and innocently when I asked.

And it worked like a damn charm.

Zacarina allowed me to once again place a saddle on her back and reins around her neck. Jay and I would ride astride, searching for the missing unicorns as we had the other day. This time, though, I wouldn't be sneaking out or evading my guards to do it. No, *this* time, while Williamson stayed behind, Avery would be following on horseback, hopefully able to provide us with backup in the event that we did indeed meet with Rumpelstiltskin today. And *this* time, instead of flying, our feet would be staying planted firmly on the ground.

My heart pounded in my chest. Was it really possible that after all the searching and combing through towns that my mother's men were doing to locate him, we would find him first, just this easily? And finding him was one thing, but if he *did* have the unicorns with him, as Zacarina's senses suggested, would we really be able to wrest them away from him? There was only one way to find out, I supposed.

On Zacarina's back, Jay's arms clutched me tightly around the waist, knowing how scared I was of flying. I held the reins loosely in one hand and patted his hands to comfort him with the other. "I'll be all right," I assured him. "I won't ask her to fly today. We'll find the unicorns the old-fashioned way."

Still his arms tightened just a little bit more, and he pulled me back so that I could feel the rumble of his words in his chest. "That's *not* why I'm holding on to you so tightly, Eliana. Point the first: You think Zacarina is acting like this because she senses her herd nearby. Point the second: Our working theory is that the person who took the unicorns in the first place is Rumpelstiltskin. And point the third." His tone was grim now. "You told me yesterday that your mother made a bargain before you were born that could mean that Rumpelstiltskin is targeting you very personally. I'm holding you tightly because I don't intend to let that happen. Not while there's breath in my body, anyway."

Again, my damnable heart fluttered at his words and I became keenly aware of everywhere we touched. Chest to back. Thigh to thigh. Hand to hand. I was warmed from the inside out.

Clearly I needed a distraction. I cleared my throat and spoke to Zacarina silently. *"Can you still feel them?"*

"Yes." Her own voice sounded distracted as well. *"It is like a tether, pulling me to them. The connection grows stronger, the closer that we get. I think... I think we'll be there very soon now."*

We had already taken the meadows at a steady cantering pace and the unicorns had been nowhere to be found, so we moved deeper into the pockets of the hills and valleys that lined the Valean countryside. The sound of distant, rushing waters reached my ears. Rivers could be deep here; some ran through the country all the way to the coast on sinister shores.

Zacarina stilled. *"Do you hear that?"* Her voice in my mind was hushed and fearful. I strained to listen. At the edges of my senses, I heard what sounded like a chorus of cries for help.

Jay's hands spasmed on my waist. "Eliana? I think—do you hear whinnying?"

My head snapped around to look at him. His eyes were wide as if he couldn't believe what he was hearing. "I think it's coming from the river."

Zacarina lit off like a shot. We weren't cantering anymore, but in a full-fledged gallop as we raced toward the river and hopefully toward her lost brethren, Avery and his steed right behind us. I could hardly catch my breath from the anticipation. Had we really done it? Had we *actually* managed to find the missing unicorns? And with not a little fear, I wondered too: Did Rumpelstiltskin wait with them?

There was only one way to find out for sure.

I couldn't believe my eyes when the line of the river came into sight. The unicorns were there all right. And now that we were close enough to them, they were *screaming* into my mind. Sobs, shouts for help, terrified, wordless cries, assurances to each other that it would be all right. And it wasn't hard to tell why. They were *in* the river, which was bad enough. The muscle-bound equine creatures were not known for their graceful swimming abilities. But to make matters about a thousand times worse, they were tangled up in a net, thrashing together in their attempts to get to land. They were struggling just to keep their heads above water, to keep on being able to just keep *breathing.* But already, they looked exhausted from their efforts. They couldn't keep this up for long or they'd surely drown.

What sort of monster would do this?

The answer came unfortunately far too easily, and I clenched my fist. I knew *exactly* which sort of monster would do this.

He answered to the name of Rumpelstiltskin. But one day he would have to answer to more than that. He'd have to answer to *me.*

I wasn't sure whether it was fortunate or unfortunate that I saw no sign of the imp here today. Fortunate, I supposed, in that it meant that all of our efforts could go toward rescuing the unicorns. *Un*fortunate because it meant that, yet again, the imp would not be held accountable for his horrendous crimes against them.

Jay hurried down from Zacarina's back and held a hand up to me. I took it and scrambled down as well. Zacarina took flight and hovered above us.

"Have faith, my kin. The mortals will help us."

"Avery, your sword!" I shouted, hitching my skirts up as I ran. The unicorns' net wasn't far—just in the shallows of the water. If we could get to it and pull them closer and use Avery's sword to cut them free, we might yet manage to save them. I plunged into the river's edge and picked up the net. A frisson of horror went through me the instant that I touched it. *No.* It wasn't a simple string net, but a net comprised of wire, twisted and gnarled together.

Avery splashed into the river behind me and lifted his sword, hacking at the net, but it was exactly as I feared—there was no effect at all. His weapon might as well have bounced off of it for all the good it was doing.

"Young one, how is it going?" Zacarina called.

I bit my lip. *"The net is strong, but we're going to figure something out,"* I called back, evading the question. Because we *had* to figure something out, and quickly, too. I didn't know how much longer the unicorns would be able to keep at it.

Zacarina swooped down and took the net between her teeth. I held my breath, daring to hope as she shook it like a dog with its prey, grinding down on it and trying to break it with her teeth.

But to no avail. The net held strong. The unicorns were just as trapped as ever.

What were we going to do?

A cheery tune reached my ears, and the crunching of leaves and grass underfoot. Branches broke as someone drew closer.

"The game afoot,

"The lass did look,

"For a way to win it all.

"How was she supposed to know

"That she'd lose it by the ball—Oh!" The jaunty singing cut itself short as a man pulled aside a large bushy branch and emerged from the trees. My heart skipped about three beats.

Those eyes. And that stance, at the same height...

For a moment, I'd thought that it was Luka coming through the trees. Coming from the afterlife itself to help me.

But now that the stranger drew closer, I could see the differences too. His skin had a different hue from Luka's; his face was more narrow and angular.

And the most important difference: there was no warmth filling his gaze when his eyes met mine.

But I knew that I wasn't the only one who saw the similarities, which, at least, made me feel a little bit better. I could tell from the way that Jay shuffled closer and picked up my hand to give it a light squeeze that he saw it too.

"My apologies," the stranger said, oblivious to my internal strife. "I don't usually bother others with my terrible voice, but I didn't see you there. Oh my." His eyes grew to the size of saucers as he took in the sight of the unicorns' plight.

"May I be of some assistance?" Hastily, he crouched to the ground and opened the large satchel at his side, tossing out a screwdriver, a large canteen, and a small napkin that spilled open to reveal a gathering of berries as he tossed it aside in his search to find whatever he was searching for in the bag. Finally, he seemed to find what he was looking for: a large knife. Its blade was covered by a large leather sheath. He held it toward me, handle first. "I won this in a game of cards years ago. The man I won it off of said it had been blessed by the fairies—and whether that's true or not, I've cut diamonds with it; it's good and strong."

This might be our last chance. Breathless with hope, I forged through the river toward my dead husband's lookalike and put my hand on the knife. "Thank you so much," I said.

"Not at all," he said lightly. "I'm sure you'll be able to find a way to repay me." This was said with a joking wink.

Knife in hand, I rushed back to the river and tried the knife on the net. It cut true. My heart leapt. This was actually going to work. Tears of joy pricked at my eyes and I called back to the man, who stood on the shore, hands in his pockets as he watched.

"My name is Princess Eliana," I shouted, still working at the net as I spoke. The wires snapped as the man's blade cut through them like butter. "Find me at the palace. I promise I'll be able to repay you with anything you want."

I glanced back and saw him grin.

As I cut, Jay and Avery worked to move the discarded pieces of the net aside. From above, Zacarina snatched pieces between her teeth and flew them onto the ground, where they would no longer be able to do harm to anyone, spitting them out with great distaste. With all four of us working, it wasn't long before the first unicorn was freed, stepping foot from the river onto the ground—the unicorn was shuddering, soaking wet, and clearly traumatized. But the most important thing was that she was alive and would stay that way too.

And then the next unicorn was freed. And the next. And the next. Before long, that blasted net was in scraps and pieces and each and every unicorn was accounted for.

One of them stepped forward, recovered enough to speak. She sank to her haunches and bowed her head to me. *"We are in your debt, Princess Eliana."*

I recognized this unicorn. She was the one who had flown me to the castle from the meadow the day that I'd gone into labor with Fae. I'd called her Misty then and made Jay promise to get her a peanut butter and jelly sandwich—a favorite treat for unicorns. She'd disappeared from the staviary not long after that, choosing to take her leave, and she'd been with the unicorn herd when it had gone missing. I'd worried over all the unicorns, of course, but her a little more than the others. She, after all, was one that I felt I owed a debt to.

"Think nothing of it," I said. "I'm so glad you're all okay."

And we had this stranger in the woods to thank for it. I slipped the man's knife back into its sheath and turned to thank him.

But there was no one behind me except Jay and Avery.

The stranger had disappeared.

Avery wasn't about to leave me alone, and Zacarina and I weren't about to leave the unicorns. So after a quick, cursory check to make sure that none of them needed urgent medical attention, Jay took Avery's horse back to the castle with the intent of retrieving more guards and hostlers. We'd need more hands to get them safely back to the palace. And with Rumpelstiltskin still on the loose, I wasn't taking any more chances with them. I wanted guards around the unicorns at all times, and lots of them.

I knew it wasn't a permanent solution, of course. The unicorns were creatures that needed to be free. I couldn't cage them like my mother used to try to do to me. But while they recovered from their captivity and trauma, they'd stay in the staviary and convalesce. And while that happened, they'd have armed bodyguards around the clock.

Rumpelstiltskin wouldn't lay a hand on them again if I had anything to say about the matter.

I clenched a fist as I thought about the imp who had caused so much misery. I hadn't even met him and yet he'd turned my life upside down and topsy-turvy. I wasn't going to lie—I'd very much like to land a punch squarely on his cheek and turn his *face* topsy-turvy, for starters.

I wasn't going to tell my mother that, though. After all, princesses don't start fights.

But we know how to finish them.

And I certainly hadn't started *this* fight. Rumpelstiltskin had, so many years ago. It grated on me that he had used my mother's distress against her and sought personal gain from it. She'd been younger then than I was now, and all she had wanted was just to keep on living. He could have helped her just because he had the ability to. He could even have taken a physical payment from it—it was normal to be paid for your work, after all, and as a new princess and then Queen, Mother could have rewarded him with a more-than-generous sum for saving her life.

But no, he had asked for too much.

Chills danced down my spine. To ask for someone's *child*. I could never fathom someone trying to take Fae away from me.

No wonder Mother hadn't wanted to give birth.

I swiped my hand over my forehead after we escorted the unicorns to the staviary and bid Jay a good night—I was too tired for a long, drawn-out goodbye, so I settled for a quick one of his trademark bear hugs and set off to go home. Avery and I met Williamson at my suite's door.

"All well, my lady?" he asked in a whisper.

I rubbed my temple and yawned. "Not all, Williamson. But more is well than we started the day with. I can be grateful enough for that."

His lips quirked up in a smile. "True enough, Your Highness."

Avery took up his position beside Williamson outside the door, and I said good night to the two of them, going into the room quietly and waking the nursemaid, who was sound asleep in the rocking chair. She left and I peered in on Fae, sound asleep.

Warmth filled my chest as I gazed down at my sleeping daughter. Rumpelstiltskin was a blight upon this world, that was true. But there was still so very much in it that was good. She was so beautiful.

"We did a good job, Luka," I whispered to the room. Maybe it was just that I'd seen a stranger who looked so much like him today, but somehow, I couldn't help but feel as though he was with us tonight.

I changed into pajamas and pulled the covers aside to climb into bed, sliding into the cool and comfortable sheets.

When I closed my eyes, for the first time in days, I drifted off to sleep effortlessly.

And in my dreams, Luka greeted me, two champagne flutes in hand. I glided into his arms, taking my glass and toasting him. He smiled, returning the gesture. Music began to play, and he took the glass from my hand and set it aside, crooking an arm around my waist, and taking my hand to lead me around the room in a dance.

My brow crinkled. This tune was familiar. Where had I heard it before?

It clicked—the stranger's song when he'd stumbled through the woods. That was the melody that the violins played now.

"Remember," Luka breathed into my ear. His arms were strong around my body and his breath was warm upon my ear. I closed my eyes, aching, even in a dream, knowing that this wouldn't last.

"A promise," he said, "is a promise."

8TH MAY

Luka's words in my dream echoed in my mind the next morning when I woke up. My eyes fluttered open with a gasp as I stared at the ceiling, heart pounding and unable to catch my breath. It was as though I'd either had a terrible nightmare or as if I'd run for miles. *Not* as if I'd just had a gentle and comforting dream about my late husband.

The light in my rooms was dim. As I tried to regain a normal breathing rhythm, I peered toward the curtain. It was an hour of the morning where the sky still clung to the night, though the sun slowly rose, doing its best to banish its darkness. It would succeed. But it couldn't banish the memories of the dream I'd had. And was it terrible that part of me wished that I could sink right back into it? It had felt so real.

"Remember," Dream Luka had said. "A promise is a promise."

Awake now, my hand drifted up to my ear, where he'd breathed the words. Gods, I'd been able to feel his breath on my skin last night. I'd forgotten what that felt like. And now, I missed it all over again.

Dreams were confusing, though—and damn my own subconscious for making it so. "A promise is a promise." Huh? What did that mean? I turned the words over and over again in my mind. Was he referring to our marriage vows?

I searched for another meaning, racking my brain and raking through my memories for anything else that he could have meant—really, that *I* could have meant. The dream had, after all, come from my own brain. But despite as hard as I tried, I came up empty-handed, drawing a blank over other meanings.

So my thoughts turned then to our marriage vows. Luka and I had written our own vows when we'd wed. We'd foregone the traditional language at our ceremony, dismissing royal tradition. I had to give my mother credit for that; maybe it was because she hadn't grown up in the tradition of the royals, but she hadn't really fought me on those decisions. All she'd cared about when I decided to get married was that I was happy. And I most certainly had been.

Luka had made me so happy. We had made *each other* so happy. The feeling of ecstasy on my wedding day was like my heart had turned into a fluttering bird

When it came time to declare our intention to marry each other, I'd given him a deeply impassioned speech and meant every word that I said. I hadn't promised to love him until death did us part like the old vows would have had me do. That time wasn't enough for me.

If only I had known what a small amount of time we would really get together. I would have spirited him away from this place.

But instead of death parting us, I had promised to love Luka forever.

My fists clenched the sheets of my bed, remembering as my heart twisted. And I had meant every word of those vows. I wanted to love him forever. I still did.

But call it what you will—fate or destiny... the hands of the gods—it didn't really matter what you called it. Because the decision for us to be together had been ripped away when they had taken Luka from this world into the next and left me here.

I could and would love him forever, but except for in dreams, I'd never again feel his touch. Never feel the returned kiss or embrace that was him loving me forever right back.

Fae's cry tore through the peace of the early morning and I sighed as my daughter's wails interrupted my reverie. It was a rare occasion, indeed, that I woke up on my own before my little princess woke me up. I supposed I should be thankful I'd had as long alone with my thoughts as I had. But I wouldn't lie; I welcomed the distraction that tending to my motherly duties would provide. Last night's dream was taking its toll on me emotionally. My throat was tight and tears kept threatening when I dwelled upon it.

I turned the covers aside, stepping first one foot and then the other onto the warm rug. My feet slipped into the slippers that I'd left at my bedside, and I pulled on a robe that was draped over the chair next to my bed, knotting it around my waist before I shuffled over to Fae's bassinet.

She was on her back, her little face scrunched up and growing red as she wailed her dissatisfaction to the heavens above. I knew the feeling, but it would be pretty frowned upon for me to scream my dissatisfaction the same way at my age. I'd let her announce our indignation to the world for the both of us.

Her tiny fists were knotted, and from the way her knees bent slightly toward her chest, I was willing to bet that inside the onesie that hid her feet, her little toes were much the same way.

"Shhh, Little One," I hushed, reaching inside and scooping her up from where she'd slept. Her weight in my arms was a comfort after a morning of sad thoughts of loss. At least I had this precious gift from the gods.

I felt her diaper. Yes, it was as I'd thought it was: wet. It was swollen with liquid and hanging low. No wonder she was so unhappy. Who wouldn't be?

I kept humming and making little soothing noises as I placed Fae onto the changing table, swiftly removing her soiled diaper and disposing of it. I grabbed a diaper wipe, baby powder, and some cream to prevent a rash and fixed her up in a fresh, clean diaper. Her cries had quieted somewhat with this improved situation, but she hadn't stopped crying entirely yet. I wasn't altogether surprised. After being her mother for a few weeks, I was coming to know my daughter. The girl liked her food. She woke up hungry, so if she was still crying this early it was because she needed breakfast.

I settled down into the rocker, moving my robe to the side and unbuttoning my pajama top so that she could suckle at my breast—which she did eagerly.

Breastfeeding had hurt a bit at first. It was an entirely new and unexpected feeling. But now, it felt like the most natural thing in the world. And with my world falling apart at the seams around me, I was grateful for this constant. For the peace that came with it. I relished these moments bonding with my daughter where I could simply hold her in my arms, her eyes fixed on me.

Luka's eyes.

Damn it. Just like that, my thoughts circled back around to him. Thoughts swirling, I closed my eyes and inclined my neck, leaning a little closer to Fae so that I could take a deep, comforting whiff of her little baby smell: baby powder, lotion, and something different. Something that was all uniquely Fae.

But just as changing Fae's diaper hadn't been enough to stop her cries, this peaceful time with my daughter had helped to soothe me—but not enough. Try as I might, I couldn't shake the thought of Luka today. I didn't think of him as often as I used to. When he'd first passed, I couldn't take a breath without it feeling like a painful reminder that I lived while he did not. Breathing had eased as time went by; I no longer felt like my windpipe was in danger of collapsing with each passing heartbeat.

They said grief came in waves. Well they were right, and today, I was drowning. Because today, I couldn't rid myself of the specter of Luka; he was here with me, like a shadow peeking over my shoulder and watching all that I did.

And some of the things I was doing lately... the thoughts that I was having... they made me feel guilty. The idea that Luka might see them bothered me. What if he was really here? His spirit, anyway. If any form of him still wandered the earth and watched over me, I didn't like to think of what he'd seen lately when he'd looked in on me. There were times that my thoughts were written clearly upon my face, I was sure. And I didn't want Luka reading those thoughts. Because they *weren't* the thoughts of a married woman.

They were thoughts about Jay. About moving on with him, *without* Luka.

I wasn't sure that I was doing the right thing by starting something with Jay now. I gulped. And forget just the thoughts I was having... could I *be* with Jay with thoughts of Luka still filling my mind? Could I kiss Jay and hold him and let it one day turn into something more? My time to decide against it was ending. Because I knew, I *knew* that if I chose to go down this path with Jay, it would all start at Fae's ball. That was in what—a week? And if I went there with Jay at that party, there would be no turning back. No saving our friendship from that.

And if I went there with Jay at that party—what would Luka, watching over me from up above with the gods—what would he think of me then?

"Your Highness." A swift three taps came at my door and I started, shaking myself from my thoughts.

At some point during my reverie, Fae had stopped suckling at my breast, closed the eyes that looked so much like her father's, and drifted off back to sleep in my arms. Gently, I stood back up and placed her back in her bassinet. I guessed she wasn't ready to be up for the day after all.

I tiptoed out of the bedroom and gently closed the door behind me, cringing even at the sound of the lock clicking into place. I leaned against the door, sighing. With everything I'd turned over in my mind already today, I couldn't believe it wasn't later in the day already. Still, no matter what hour it truly was, I wasn't one to look a gift horse in the mouth. If Fae wanted more sleep, I was definitely happy to oblige.

The taps at the door came again and this time Avery sounded concerned that I had yet to answer them. “My lady?” he called again. “Is everything all right in there?”

“I’m coming,” I called softly. I kept my volume low, not wanting the sound to travel behind me into Fae’s room and wake her.

“Mister—”

A muffled conversation outside the door. “Just Jay, Avery.” Jay’s voice, low, nonetheless traveled through the doors to easily reach my ears.

My heart leapt from its normal spot in my chest up to my throat and then plummeted back to my stomach.

And then a corrected announcement came from Williamson, coughing. “*Jay* is here, Your Highness.”

My footsteps had already paused in their route to opening the door. Jay.

Damn. Damn, damn, damn.

I was not prepared to see him today. Not with all of these thoughts about Luka. I needed time. Time to go through them and sort them out. I couldn’t see him when I wasn’t sure I was doing the right *thing* by seeing him and starting something up with him. Our date at the party loomed closer every day and today it wasn’t like a bright light in the future; it was like a black cloud hovering over me.

But what was I supposed to do? I hadn’t gone to him. He had come to me. And now... well, I couldn’t leave him just standing out there in the hallway for the rest of the day.

Could I?

I shook my head, banishing the notion. No. No, I couldn’t do that. I was an adult, a mother. And adults did not ignore their problems. Or leave them standing in the hallway.

I took a deep breath and shook my hands out, bouncing on my heels. Okay. Okay, okay. I could do this. I could make a plan. I would let him in and I'd get him out before I ruined everything. I'd say anything—I wasn't feeling well, I was overtired. Something that would involve a brief conversation, but not last too long before he left again.

That way, whatever I decided, whatever I wanted to do, it would buy me time to actually *make* a decision.

Why *was* Luka in my thoughts so much today, anyway?

I could only assume it was because of the stranger I'd met yesterday by the river. The Good Samaritan who had looked so much like my dead husband and then disappeared.

But it wasn't Luka. There would never be another one.

Had he even actually looked like him? I rubbed my temples. I mean, Jay hadn't said anything. Maybe it had all been in my head?

But regardless of whether he had or not, the effect of his sudden appearance and disappearance was the same. And that effect was that today, I felt like I had lost Luka all over again.

And I had to wonder at that sudden disappearance.

I was grateful that the man had helped us and the unicorns under the dire circumstances that we'd been in; but if I had been in his position, I don't think you'd have been able to pull me away if you'd tried. I'd have needed to see the situation through to the end. I wouldn't have been able to pull my gaze away from the sight that I'd stumbled upon.

But not him. He had just... vanished. As if into thin

air.

Another knock, rapping on the door loudly. "Eliana?"

That was Jay's voice this time. There was no point putting this off any longer. I had to face him.

I opened the door and forced a smile onto my face. "Sorry," I apologized, tucking a stray piece of hair behind my ear. "I was just... getting Fae back down. She wasn't quite ready to get on with the day."

And neither was her mother, I finished silently.

A relaxed smile in return to my own forced one bloomed across Jay's face when he saw me, lighting up his eyes. My heart twisted in my chest in response. Gods, I *wished* I could be as happy to see him as I usually was. I wished the smile on my face felt real and genuine, instead of me feeling like I was operating my body like a puppet. I might as well have stuck my fingers into the corners of my lips and pushed them up toward my cheeks. It felt painted on.

"Hey," Jay greeted me from his position leaning against the wall. He had one leg up like a flamingo as he waited. He pushed forward off the wall and strode toward me, walking into the room. He flipped Avery and Williamson a little salute of farewell as the door shut behind him. He kept striding toward me and gathered me up into his arms in a loose embrace without hesitation.

My body went rigid at his touch. I didn't know what to do.

Yesterday, I would have returned the embrace without hesitation and would have done so fiercely. But today, I was just trying to hang on to my sanity.

"What an exhausting day," he breathed. I took a shaky breath. Just like Luka in my dreams last night, I could feel Jay's breath on my ear when he spoke. His arms tightened. "And you were the only person I wanted to see at the end of it. Well, you and Fae. But I settled for waiting until I thought you'd at least be awake."

Gingerly, I returned his embrace, patting him tentatively on his back. He released me and stood back, grinning.

"So how'd I do?" He spread his arms wide and quirked an eyebrow. "Do I get any points for restraint? I managed to wait until the sun came up and everything!"

"I'm so proud," I croaked, going for a normal response even though my throat was dry.

He ruffled the hair at the back of his head. "So, Fae's asleep, huh? I guess it is pretty early. I always feel like I just miss her." He tilted his head toward me with a smile. "And I *am* missing her, you know."

"I know," I said softly.

It would hurt him so badly if I called things off. Told him just when I'd been making steps toward him that I was no longer sure about this whole thing. Because it wasn't just me that Jay loved. I'd seen it in his eyes whenever he saw Fae. He'd fallen in love with my daughter as well.

And that was a whole other thing. I was already worried that I was betraying Luka by moving on myself. Would it be an even greater betrayal if I brought another father figure into Fae's life?

I'd been so determined to do things on my own at the beginning. Maybe that was what I still should do. Perhaps that would be the best way for me to honor Luka's memory.

"So, how are the unicorns?" I asked, changing the subject. I couldn't bear to hear any more about how Jay had missed me or my daughter.

Instead of sitting next to him on the couch, as I

usually would, where I would be able to brush my leg against his and feel a little thrill just from that slight touch, I settled down in a chair and gestured for him to sit across from me on the couch. I crossed my ankles and folded my hands in my lap. I was trying to look relaxed, but was sure that, instead, I looked like I was trying to pose for a painting. It was hard to act relaxed; I wasn't entirely sure what my body language should be because when I was *actually* relaxed, I never really had to think about it.

"Good." He shook his head in disbelief as he settled down. "*Great,* actually. I couldn't really believe it. I knew they healed quickly, but since they weren't actually physically injured, they were chomping at the bit to get free of the stalls."

"They weren't physically injured?" I thought back to that afternoon where Jay and I had gone searching for the flock with Zacarina—and spotted unicorn blood. "What about the blood we saw?"

He shook his head again. "I can only assume the wounds were days old and minor—I'm telling you, we checked them all over for injuries and we came up empty-handed; not even a scar for us to tell which of the unicorns had been hurt. By all indications, they're in perfect health. And since they had clearly grown weary of our hospitality, about breaking down the stall doors, they're back in the meadow already."

My eyebrows shot up. Well, *this* was an effective distraction from all of the dating thoughts I was worried about. I had certainly not been expecting that. "But the trauma," I started. "The toll it must have taken on them mentally and emotionally. Are you sure they're ready?"

He shrugged. "Well, it's not like I can actually talk to them, but I'm pretty sure, yeah."

He couldn't talk to them, but I sure could. I made a mental note for myself to speak with the unicorns when I could and see for myself if I really thought that they were ready.

It was too bad a therapist couldn't talk to them instead, but I would have to do in their stead.

"If you think about it," Jay continued, "it makes sense. After all, they've been in captivity for what... a week or more? Makes sense that they would want to just be free after that. If it was me, I know that I would. So they're all back there now. In the meadows and the woods."

His phrasing caught my attention. "Wait, *all* of them?" That couldn't mean...

But yes, Jay was nodding, so apparently it *did* mean what I was afraid of. "Yeah, Zacarina went back with them. Baby, too."

Epiphany, I mentally corrected. But Jay didn't know that Zacarina's daughter had revealed her name to me. "But was Epiph—I mean, Baby, she can't have been healed enough for that, could she?"

"She is." Jay gestured to the window where I'd watched him walking with Epiphany a little over a week ago. "I mean, you saw her yourself. They heal quickly, like I said. And she was doing really, really well."

"Huh." I sagged back in the seat, reeling. And feeling a little bit... well, bereft, I guessed. I had come to expect that I could rely on finding Zacarina and Epiphany waiting for me in the stable. I'd come to expect that I'd be able to find someone to talk to who really knew what was going on with me. They knew what no one else did—that I could talk to unicorns now.

That secret would be mine alone to keep now.

"On another note," Jay drawled. A small smile

crawled across his cheeks. "The party's pretty soon," he said, his voice soft and eyes sparkling. "I've got my snazzy duds all ready to go."

Gods, my stomach was rollicking. This was exactly what I was afraid of. I couldn't do this with Jay.

Luka's face flew into my mind and my gut clenched.

I had to tell him.

"About that..." I drew out the words awkwardly "I'm sorry. I've thought about it a lot, and I think it may have been a mistake to make that date so quickly."

Jay couldn't have looked more shocked than if I'd slapped him in the face. He blinked rapidly; it was like the flipping pages of a book whose pages were being rifled through. Water shone at the corners of his eyes. "I don't understand. What changed?" he asked.

I splayed my fingers over my knees and turned my hands over helplessly. "I'm just not ready."

He stood up quickly. "I better go."

"Jay, wait." I stood up fast, not sure what I was going to say.

He held a hand up. "Save it, Eliana." He shot me a disappointed look. "I don't want you to do anything you don't want to do." His voice was choked up, and a hint of bitterness spiked it.

He opened the door and walked away from me as a pit in my stomach appeared and threatened to swallow me whole.

Gods above, what had I done?

9TH MAY

The next day, I dwelled within a fog of sickness and regret.

I couldn't believe what I had done to Jay. I had dreamt of Luka two nights ago, but now I wished that my conversation with Jay had been the dream—or nightmare, more aptly.

I tried to distract myself, but this wasn't like my worries about the unicorns and Rumpelstiltskin. I'd been worried and very concerned then. But how could I distract myself when my heart felt as though I had ripped it out of my chest and then tried to mash it back in. It was like... like trying to unpack a new duvet from its packaging—it would never fit back inside the same way again.

Low on things that could distract me when Fae fell

asleep, I put her in her baby carrier and went by my mother's room to receive the updated report on the search for Rumpelstiltskin. When I entered the room, Mother greedily took Fae from her carrier and gathered her into her arms while she talked to me and gave me the updated report.

But try as I might have for a solid distraction, it did me no good. The idea had been for her to distract me, but *I'd* been too distracted even to hear what she said. So this was really nothing more than a gigantic waste of time for everyone.

With the unicorns safely returned to the meadows, albeit with guards patrolling out there far more frequently than they used to before all of this, a great deal of the urgency I'd felt to find the imp that my mother had dealt with so long ago had vanished. And with the loss of that urgency, came a lack of attention, unfortunately.

Logically, I knew that he could be and likely still was a danger to us all. My mother seemed certain that he was not the sort to forgive and forget. He felt she'd violated their agreement. He was going to have his revenge. And I felt sure that seizing the unicorns and then them being returned to us did not count as revenge for a second.

I still wondered about that. I hadn't had the chance to ask them yesterday. Had they escaped? Or had Rumpelstiltskin let them go?

Regardless of the answer, with no one in active peril, the impetus to keep moving, keep hunting for the culprit who had kidnapped them, had faded—for me, at least.

But Mother had been worried he'd return my entire life. She wasn't going to give up now that he had shown himself once more.

"So I guess that's it—we just keep on looking." Mother's voice finally penetrated the thick fog in my mind and I shook my head, blinking hard and trying to come back to attention.

I could have tried to pretend I had listened to everything she'd said, but what was the point? "Huh?" I asked.

She smiled at me sympathetically. "You're distracted today. Is everything all right?"

"Yes," I said quickly. *Liar*, my mind accused.

"Hmmm." Her mouth twisted, unconvinced. "Are you sure?"

"Yes."

Her lips stayed pursed. She still wasn't buying it. "Jay hasn't come by the palace today."

I stiffened at the sound of his name. It was uncanny, her ability to just zero in on the problem I was having. It could have been the guards reporting on me, but I knew better. This was just my mother. How did mothers always, *always* know when something was bothering us, no matter how hard we tried to pretend that we were feeling just fine and dandy?

Maybe it started in infancy. I was probably in training for the same set of motherly skills for Fae right now and didn't even know it. One day, my ability to decipher her hungry cries from her wet diaper cries would translate into an ability to be able to tell when something was a little off about her, even if she was acting like everything was okay.

Seeing that she was on the right track, thanks to the betrayal of my body language, my mother continued. "In *fact*," she said, emphasizing the T at the end of fact, "word was sent up from the stables. He isn't working today. They said that he'd made an excuse of being sick and taken the day away from the staviary."

"He's sick?" My brow furrowed in concern, thinking back. He'd looked fine when I'd seen him yesterday. Full color in his cheeks, alert eyes, steady stance. Well, he *had* looked fine... but that was right up until I had delivered the equivalent of a verbal gut punch and told him I thought it was wrong for the two of us to be together after all. Dismay and shame spiraled through me at the memory.

Now that the dream of Luka had faded a bit, I couldn't shake the feeling that I had made a terrible mistake by ending things with Jay.

"Eliana." Mother's voice was sharp and I snapped to attention. "I feel reasonably confident that Jay is in good health. That boy once came to work with a one hundred and two degree fever and tried to still pitch hay into the stalls. So he's either dying, or he's got other problems that he's focusing on."

Other problems. She'd hit the nail on the head with that one. Jay *did* have other problems and I was the cause of all of them.

This was exactly what my hesitation had been in starting things up with Jay in the first place. I'd been worried that I would hurt him and cause irrevocable damage to our friendship, which had been a constant in my life for as long as I could remember.

At this point, honestly, I thought Jay was probably better off without me. All I did was cause him pain. Our whole lives, he'd loved me, and I had kept him back at arms' length, turning my attention to others and then falling in love with Luka. And Jay had never begrudged me that. All he wanted was for me to be happy, and if he wasn't the source of it, he'd never try to force me or convince me that we should be together.

And then, finally, just when it seemed as though things had changed, when I'd finally thought that there could be something more between us—when I *felt* something more for him, something beyond mere friendship—I'd thrown it away like it was nothing. And all for what? A dream? The appearance of a stranger?

Gods, I'd been a fool. I'd let superstition and guilt take me over and run my life. I hadn't been strong enough to make the decisions that *I* really wanted in the face of those suffocating emotions.

Now, I didn't know what I could do about it, though. Apologizing didn't seem like it would be enough. I didn't know if Jay would ever be able to forgive me. I didn't know that I would be that kind if I were in his shoes.

He wasn't ordinarily one to hold a grudge—but it wasn't like I had eaten a sandwich of his without asking or something. This was no small and minor infraction we were talking about here. I had broken his heart. I had ripped it from his chest and stomped upon it with high-heeled shoes—stiletto ones. His heart had taken a beating; it was no wonder he had reported that he was sick.

He *was* sick. But it wasn't a physical ailment that he suffered from. There were no germs that he needed to eradicate to make himself better. He was heartsick.

And gods help me, so was I. But unfortunately, I had no one to blame for that but myself.

"Eliana?" Mother's voice came again; gentler, this time. "Did something happen between the two of you?"

I covered my face and shook my head, unable to look at her. "Yes, but I..." I trailed off, my voice cracking with emotion. I swallowed it back down again, just enough to speak and get the words out around my rapidly tightening throat. Behind my hands, tears welled in my eyes. "I can't talk about it yet. I've been an idiot." The sentences warbled unsteadily, like a piano out of tune, but I managed to get them out, which was an accomplishment given how I was feeling. It was a miracle that I hadn't started sobbing in my mother's arms already.

"All right," she said softly. "Well, whenever you're ready to talk, just know that I'm always here for you."

I peeked through my fingers and looked at her. Her smile was as understanding as her voice. "Thank you," I said. My own voice was tiny in response.

My hands fell from my cheeks as I looked at Mother sitting there again, cradling Fae. I'd brought my daughter with me for the report this morning, knowing that my mother would have absolutely no protests. She seized upon any chance she could to see her granddaughter. The minute I'd walked into her rooms, she'd greedily gathered Fae from my arms into hers and sat down, holding her against her chest. Fae hadn't protested once.

"Do you think...?" I gestured to the two of them. "Would you mind watching her for a little while? I think I need to think."

A peal of laughter erupted from my mother's lips as if what I'd said was the most hilarious thing she'd ever heard. "Do I *mind?* Mind being a grandmother? Never. Never, ever."

She met my eyes and inclined her head toward me, the diamond tiara that she'd put on to confer with her guards sparkling as it caught the light. "Take all the time to think that you need, darling. I'll watch over your daughter for you. We'll be here when you return.

"And if you need to speak with anyone while you're out... well, you can take that time too."

~

Leaving my mother's rooms, my walk through the palace was not altogether that different from the one that I'd taken only a few days ago, when I'd determinedly ripped through the halls on a course to find my mother. My fists then had been clenched with coiled tension, with anger that I had been trying desperately to keep a tight hold on, lest I inadvertently release it on some innocent bystander. This time, it was my heart that was coiled tightly, shrinking with shame over how I'd treated Jay. I knew I needed to make amends somehow. I just didn't know what that "somehow" method was.

And I might not have been scowling this time when I tore through the castle's hallways and corridors at an unusual pace, but I sure wasn't smiling. I made no effort to paste a false one on for the people who might see me. I didn't really care.

But the results weren't all that different. Nobles and courtiers started to greet me, but then quickly stopped talking, withdrawing and not attempting to hold me there for a conversation. I didn't think that my expression looked as forbidding as it had a few days ago, but maybe they simply couldn't stand to look at someone in the eyes who looked as despondent as I did. Maybe my dismay was as plain to see as my anger had been.

I might have been grateful for the quick reprieve, for the bit of distraction—I could maybe convince strangers that I was paying attention if I tried—but to be honest, I didn't even have the energy or focus to feign that amount of attention.

Mother had seen it in an instant, and I'd actually

been *trying* to listen to her. What *she* was saying was important. What these people, however well-meaning, would have amounted to nothing more than chitchat. *The weather was lovely today. They'd seen me in the gardens with Princess Fae. She must be the cutest baby they'd ever seen. Had I heard that the kitchens were making lemon cakes for dessert this evening?* They knew they were my favorites.

Not even compliments about my daughter or the news that my favorite sweet treats were on the menu tonight would cheer me up today, though. In response to whatever the conversationalist was saying to me, all I could bring myself to do was to nod politely, distantly, and at the first pause, the first silence in the conversation—even if the speaker had only stopped for long enough to take a breath, I excused myself and continued on.

Avery and Williamson, as they always did, followed behind me. They were silent, but even their presence distracted me. It was like the humming of their thoughts, indecipherable though they were, followed behind me like a swam of buzzing bees. I was no mindreader, but I could imagine what they were thinking. Wondering what was going on with me. And I didn't have space in my head for their thoughts. I needed the extra room to sort out my own thoughts and wonderings.

I needed the peace that came with being alone to sort out my own thoughts without feeling like theirs were with me.

It didn't seem like very long before we were outside the castle and at the edge of the meadow, but it must have been. The castle was not a tiny building and it took a fair amount of time for one to make their way through it and its grounds, especially with the multiple interruptions we'd encountered.

All the while, Avery and Williamson said not a word, just following behind me like shadows stitched to the back of my feet. At the meadow's edge, finally, I could take it no longer. I whirled around and put my hands out toward them, signaling for them to stop. I'd caught them by surprise with the movement, and they came up short, startled.

"Please," I begged. "Can you stop here? I need to be alone."

They exchanged a glance. "Your Highness knows that Her Majesty the Queen has given her express orders that the princess should *not* be left alone, except with guards posted outside. Perhaps if that is Your Highness's wish, then we should return to the castle and you may be alone in your rooms."

Williamson's tone was not unsympathetic, but also firm. So was the resolve in his eyes. After all, this request was not as simple as it seemed. I was asking him to violate orders he'd been given from his lieges. Orders he had sworn an oath to uphold. And he wasn't the type to flout that sort of thing.

But without realizing it, he'd given me a loophole. And one that I fully intended to exploit.

"Those were your orders?" I confirmed. "That was how my mother worded it, right? Those exact words? 'With guards posted outside?'"

His brows knitted, not sure where I was going with this. "Ye-essss?" he drew out the word into a question. But his tone said that he wasn't sure that he wanted to receive the answer.

"Great, then!" I clapped my hands together and threw my arms open wide, indicating the great outdoors around us. "The two of you are guards. We are outside.

Ergo, there are guards posted outside and you will not have violated an order at all if you let me have a little time to myself to think." I rocked back on my heels and crossed my arms, a little smug and pleased with myself.

"Your Highness, please," Williamson protested, shaking his head and frowning. "We both know that that wasn't... I feel very sure that that was not the *spirit* of what the queen intended."

"Please," I begged. I clasped my hands together like I was praying. In a way, I was. If the gods were so hell-bent on making me gods-touched as I suspected, I thought it was only fair that they do me this teeny, tiny favor and intervene so that I could have a little bit of time alone.

"Williamson, you're right, I know. And I know that what I am asking of you is a very big favor." I pointed emphatically back toward the castle. "But I can't *think* in there. It's like a cage." I huffed out an aggrieved breath. "Just... put yourself in my shoes for a minute. Imagine never having a minute to yourself. You guys, at least, get to trade shifts with other guards at night and go back to your own room in the barracks. I am *always* watched. Always. Can you imagine how that makes me feel?"

The two guards exchanged glances, communicating silently.

"Williamson," Avery clasped a hand on the older guard's shoulder. "I think we should do as the princess asks. She's right. We'll have followed orders. Our oath holds true. And we're not the only guards out here anymore, especially not since all the trouble started with the unicorns and the hunt for Rumpelstiltskin has been on. There are patrols constantly. We can make them aware that they need to be especially vigilant while Her Highness is in there. Nothing will come after the princess."

My heart leapt, not having expected to find myself an ally in either of the guards. But I would happily accept the help Avery was providing without complaint. My eyes turned back to Williamson. I knew, as the senior guard, the decision was ultimately his. So I held my breath, waiting for his verdict.

Williamson sighed, knowing when he was beaten. Between myself and Avery, his motivation to agree far outweighed his inclination to say no. "Fine," he grumbled. Just because he'd agreed didn't necessarily mean he was happy about it.

I squealed and darted forward to give him a hug. This was the happiest I'd felt in two days. Finally, I'd get some open air. Finally, it would just be me, my thoughts, and the sky up above.

I squeezed the disgruntled old guard around the middle, rocking from side to side in my glee. "Oh, thank you, Williamson. Thank you so much."

He stiffened at my touch, not used to open shows of affection from royalty. Pretty sure he'd always thought of us as untouchable up until now. In response to my embrace, all he could bring himself to do was to give me a few awkward pats on the back in return. "You're um... You are very welcome, Your Highness." I pulled back and he coughed, awkward for a moment longer before he regained his composure and he gave me a grim smile. "Please do not make me regret the decision."

"You won't," I said quickly, waving an arm hastily and shaking my head. "I just need a little bit of time to sort out some thoughts. I won't be long."

I hoped not, anyway.

Leaving my guards behind with their full knowledge

and consent for a change, for the first time in weeks, I set off into the meadows by myself and just walked, allowing my thoughts to wander. But though I walked in a straight line for the most part, my thoughts did not. They went around and around in circles with each step that I took, essentially arguing with myself.

I'd made a mistake with Jay.

Or had the mistake been getting involved with him in the first place?

I needed to apologize.

But had I done the wrong thing?

I hoped that Jay would take me back.

But should he? Would us being together be right?

That was really the question, wasn't it? My heart clenched. I stopped, closing my eyes and concentrating. Luka was gone and, yesterday's strange doubts aside, I did believe that he'd want me to be happy. I didn't believe, as kind of a man as he had been while he'd been alive, that he would change so much in death that he'd wish for me to go the rest of my days unloved by any other man.

And if I was going to be with anyone, I thought he'd approve of my choice in Jay.

Jay had always been very respectful of my choice in marrying Luka and never made things uncomfortable by making Luka feel like he had designs on his wife. When Luka had been alive, the two of them had gotten along well when they'd met.

Luka had liked Jay. And known that he was a good man.

A warm breeze washed over my face, and I tilted my chin up into it, feeling like it was Luka's blessing.

I was going to be with Jay. And my past love would not be forgotten. I'd make sure that, as loved by Jay and myself as Fae was, that she knew her father. I would tell her stories about him and keep his memory alive.

I stopped, suddenly realizing that I was out of breath. I'd only given birth a couple of weeks ago and my fitness level wasn't where it had been before I'd had Fae.

When I looked up, at last at peace with my decision, my surroundings had changed. I was no longer in the wide-open air of the meadows. At some point in my wanderings, I'd crossed into the thicker woods. Deeper in the forest than I had ever gone before.

And it was getting darker, too.

I shielded my eyes as I looked up toward the sun. It was far lower in the sky than it had been when I began my trek. And the sky was a burnt orange color that could only mean that the sun was setting. The trees obscured my vision, though, and I wasn't sure exactly how low it was.

Damn. My insides squirmed with guilt. I had *promised* Williamson that I wouldn't be long. It had to have been hours by now and the older guard was probably in a tizzy. I needed to head back.

I turned on my heel. The sun set in the west—the castle was back east in the exact opposite direction. And that was where I needed to go now.

With my head a bit clearer, I started the trek once more. It was amazing how much longer the journey felt now that I wasn't distracted. I noticed every time my ankle almost turned on a small rock, every little branch that snatched at my clothing.

Another breeze blew past and I shivered, clutching my arms and looking around. As it got darker, the temperatures began to dip. I really needed to get back home.

I kept walking forward, trying to aim for a straight

line back, but now the sun was down, and with it had gone any sense of direction that I had.

I took another step and felt something tighten around my ankle. Looking down, I saw the culprit.

My leg was caught in a trap.

Bending down to examine it, for the first time, a spike of fear shot through me. This wasn't like the traps we'd found Epiphany in a couple of weeks ago. My leg wasn't maimed from being caught. But that didn't make me feel that much better. I might not have been harmed physically, but I tugged at the trap experimentally and then a little bit more insistently, and I couldn't see how I would get out of this either.

"Help," I croaked. My throat was dry from hours of disuse and not speaking to anyone. I cleared it and tried again, shouting this time. "Help!" I said loudly, calling into the darkness. "I'm trapped!"

But there was no one nearby. I kept on shouting—I knew Williamson and his vigilance. A search party would be coming soon, and I needed them to find me. They'd have dogs involved in the search, but shouting was sure to be a help to them in locating their missing princess.

I heard a rustling and turned. They'd found me already. That was nothing short of a miracle.

But the moon's light caught on golden eyes and a golden horn protruding through the bushes.

Zacarina.

"We heard your cries of distress and came." She walked closer, Epiphany trailing behind her.

"Wait!" I cried. I threw my hand out. Her hooves paused in their steps. My eyes flicked uneasily over the forest floor.

"Be careful," I warned. "I don't know if there are

other traps here. I'd hate for either of you to get stuck the way that I am."

Zacarina nodded, inspecting the ground beneath her with each step carefully. *"Follow exactly where I step, young one,"* she instructed her daughter.

I held my breath, and at last they reached me.

The great equine creature leaned forward to take a look at the trap that I'd gotten myself caught in.

She looked up at me, somber. *"I do not think we can free you. But you will not be alone tonight."*

Somehow sensing her call, unicorns began to descend from the heavens, landing beside me. Zacarina and Epiphany stood behind me and the others came up along my sides. They were so warm. My muscles, tense from the cold, began to relax.

"It's all right, young one. I told you I would be there when you had need of me. We will watch over you tonight."

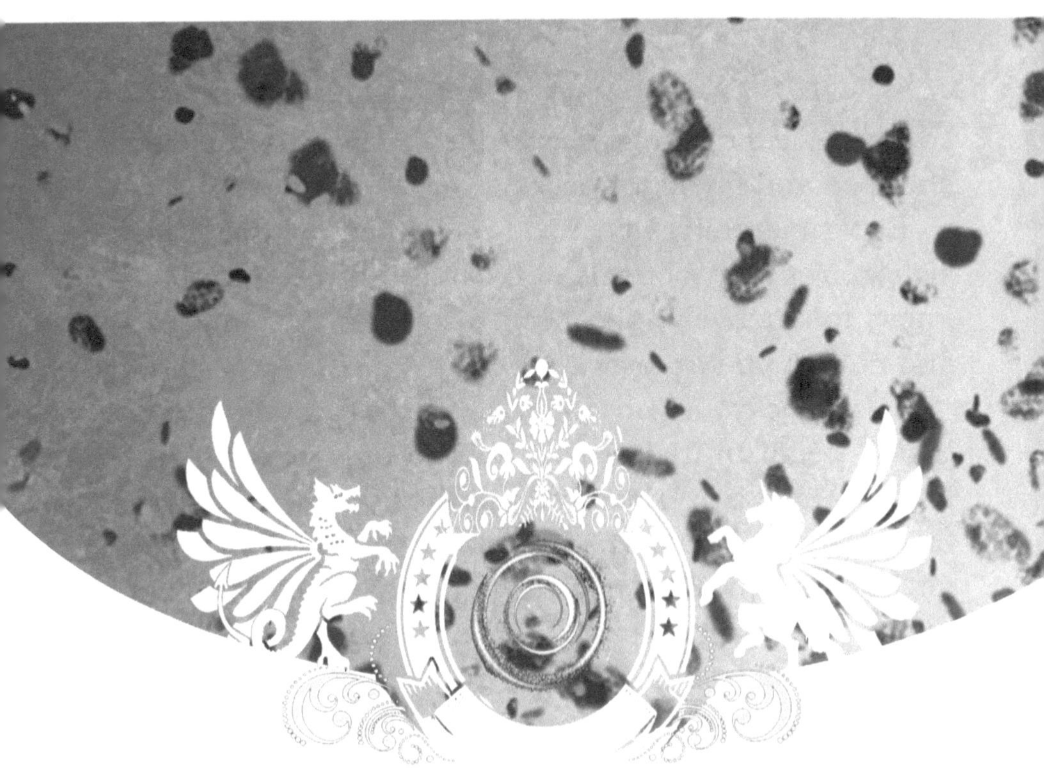

10TH MAY

"Eliana? Eliana!"

I snapped awake, hearing voices shouting my name. I rubbed at my eyes. It was still dark outside.

I listened closer, straining my ears. But maybe I had only imagined that I'd heard those voices. Maybe they had been a dream that lingered into my waking. Because now all I heard were the sounds of the forest around me. The rustling leaves, the wind through the trees, and crickets chirping in the distance. The heartbeat of the unicorn at my back.

I could barely see my hand in front of my face. But I could still feel the warmth of the unicorns' bodies surrounding mine. They were warm against me, keeping the cold from me, but it didn't change that the way

I'd been sleeping was hardly ideal. My muscles were cramped and my foot was...

Experimentally, I twisted and turned my ankle and sighed. Yep. My foot was still caught in the trap that I knew, instinctively, had been meant for the unicorns, and not for human prey.

I was lucky, if you could call it that. Lucky that I hadn't been injured seriously. The only injury I was likely to have sustained was, at most, a turned ankle. Lucky that the unicorns had come to answer my cries for help—even if I hadn't realized that I'd been calling them. I'd continued calling for help aloud for a while, but eventually, exhausted, I'd drifted off.

It had to be after midnight at this point.

Poor Williamson. I rubbed my tired eyes and leaned my head back against the unicorn, sighing, looking up toward the sky. I really had meant to keep my promise to him. But someone—and I suspected one monstrous imp in particular—had intervened in those well-laid plans that I had made with the best of intentions and purest of will.

And Williamson was nothing—*nothing*—compared with my mother. I was sure that Fae was safe with her, but knowing that I was missing, just out in the wilds somewhere, and hadn't returned home? It had to be driving her mad, especially knowing that I wasn't just missing. I was missing while Rumpelstiltskin was at large. While Rumpelstiltskin was not only at large, but acting in the kingdom with malicious intent.

I sighed again and looked down at my captive ankle. And here was the evidence of that malicious intent right before my very eyes, with the moonlight shining down upon it.

"Eliana!"

My head turned toward the cry. All right, that was not the sounds of the forest and it *definitely* wasn't a dream. I'd know that voice anywhere, no matter how much distance I had ever tried and failed to put between us. That voice was Jay.

"Your Highness! Are you near?"

"Are you out there?"

And *that* was Williamson and Avery. Bless those unrelenting guards' hearts.

"I'm here!" I shouted.

The unicorn at my back started at the cry and scrambled to its feet. Not Zacarina. Nor was it Epiphany. A steady number of unicorns had been rotating in and out throughout the night as it seemed like they'd decided, through a conversation I was not privy to, that they would take turns keeping me warm and then taking to the skies for... well, whatever it was unicorns did when they flew around. Who was I to keep them from that?

It *was* interesting, the way that they communicated, though. It seemed different from human speech. For humans to have privacy, we had to sequester ourselves behind closed doors and make sure that there was no one within hearing distance in order to have that privacy. Unicorns, it seemed, could communicate mind to mind with only those of their choosing, or they could broadcast a wider net—say, to cry for help the way that the unicorns trapped in the river had done.

I eased onto the side of my hip and winced, hissing through my teeth. It had gone numb from the weight being on it throughout the night, but I stood anyway. It hurt as feeling assaulted the previously numb limb and blood began flowing throughout my extremities again.

"Eliana?"

I turned to the left. His voice was more distant than it had been the last time, but I was *sure* that was where it was coming from. "Jay?" I called back, voice hopeful.

I didn't think my voice was loud enough for Jay to hear me. It was as though the forest was a carpet-coated room. It seemed to swallow up the sound of my voice like spilled water soaking into cloth.

But despite that, as though disturbed by my voice, the unicorns all suddenly jolted to their feet, joining the one that I'd been leaning against in standing. I eyed them all carefully and spoke aloud, taking no chances that any of them would not be able to hear me if I didn't project my mind speech in exactly the right way.

"Are all of you... all right?" I asked cautiously.

That was it. That was all I said. "Are all of you all right?" But as though I'd mortally offended them, every single, solitary unicorn took flight toward the trees, raining leaves down upon me and lighting a path toward the sky and the moon that hung in it without ever looking back at me.

And leaving me alone, trapped and with no clue as to what I had done wrong.

I sank back down to my knees, overwhelmed. The unicorns had left me. My guards were close, but couldn't hear my cries for help. And Jay was with them. Jay. Whom I had pushed away. Maybe I was destined to be alone. Maybe I *deserved* to be trapped in this forest. I'd just sink into the ground and over time I'd dissolve into the earth. At least, I'd make myself useful that way. I would make myself into fertilizer and give something back to someone.

Aaaaand that was probably enough self-pity for the night. Yup, I'd filled my quota up, all right.

I shivered and rubbed my arms, trying to create

some friction. Without the unicorns surrounding me, it was *awfully* cold out here.

There had to be a way out of this. I just wasn't seeing it yet.

I stood back up. Okay, the first and easiest option was that help was near. I'd heard the voices, and even if they did seem to be getting further away rather than closer, they were out there. That was the plan. And if I couldn't make enough noise to guide them to me, well, I would cross that bridge when I got to it and make a new plan after that.

So I started shouting. And shouting and shouting and shouting. Sometimes I thought that I heard their voices shouting in reply. Sometimes I thought that only silence answered me. But I kept on yelling. I kept on trying.

But I wasn't inhuman. My voice was hoarse from the stressful night and the more I used it, the more I shouted, the softer it seemed to get.

Just when I thought my voice was gone—it was no more than a whisper by now—just when I was about to give up hope, I saw what I thought was the most glorious sight that I'd ever seen in my entire life:

It was Zacarina, gliding through the air between the trees.

And on her back, with his face as white as a sheet, gripping fistfuls of her mane between his hands... was Jay.

My heart leaped.

In their wake was the rest of the unicorn flock. Most did not have riders on their backs, but I spotted two men on the backs of one of them: Williamson and Avery. There had to be a larger search party out there, but this was all I needed. The men who guarded me so fiercely and the unicorns that I connected with on such a deep level.

I closed my eyes and offered a prayer up to the heavens, thanking whatever gods were listening. I didn't know if I deserved to be rescued. But regardless of that, I was thankful that they'd decided to do it.

I wanted to go home. Home to my mother and father. Home to my daughter.

And if I hadn't already made up my mind about where I stood on the Jay situation, this would have been the most telling detail of all: I ached to be in his arms. I wanted to be home, and I wanted his arms around me. That was where I wanted to be.

"Eliana," Jay called.

Zacarina landed gracefully and Jay scrambled off of her back and over to me. Williamson and Avery followed suit, but they kept their distance while Jay checked me over with anxious hands, searching for any injury.

"Are you all right?" he asked.

"A little banged up, but no worse for wear," I said, smiling tremulously. There was a suspicious little lump of emotion clogging my throat. "Jay, are you—"

Jay interrupted my question when he caught sight of the trap around my ankle. "Damn. No *wonder* you were late." He crouched to get a better look at it, then looked up at me. "You're sure you're okay?"

"I mean, I'm not *comfortable,* but... you're here now," I said, dazed with relief. Overjoyed that he was here—it was like a dream. Who needed knights in shining armor or battle-ready princes when there was Jay coming to the rescue? Jay, who would never let me down. "I'm great." That was the gods'-honest truth, too.

He blinked, then shook his head as if he was trying to shake water out of his ear because he couldn't believe, based on the last time we'd spoken, that he'd actually heard me correctly. So I guessed that was why he chose not to respond to it.

"We're gonna get you out of this, Lia. I just... thank the gods that you're all right."

He walked away for a moment to confer with Avery and Williamson. The elder guard slipped a satchel over his shoulder and they all headed my way. Jay hovered awkwardly in the background, watching as the guards got to work. It was tough to tear my eyes away from him, but I tore them, nonetheless, and focused my attention on the guards who planned to free me.

"I never thought I'd be so glad to see you," I told the guards.

"The feeling is mutual, Your Highness," Avery responded.

Williamson was tightlipped as he bent to my ankle and opened the satchel to reveal the tools that were inside and set to work. The tools made little clinking sounds as he set at them.

Clink. Clink.

"Williamson?"

A pause. Then, his work resumed, but he kept a stubborn silence, not saying anything. *Clink. Clink.*

"I am sorry, Williamson. I really wanted to be on time, I promise you."

He sighed. "I know you did, Your Highness. And I promise you that I forgive you. But I'm not sure that the queen will forgive me and Avery."

"I'll speak with her," I swore.

"Don't concern yourself with that. There are more important things to worry about. For starters—" He grunted and turned the tool in his hand decisively, then grinned up at me. The feeling magically rushed back into my ankle as the metal fell away from it. It felt like a tiny miracle.

I breathed deeply and massaged the stiff joint. "Thank you," I said.

Then, I turned my attention to Jay. I took two tentative steps toward him. "How did you find me?" I asked.

He hesitantly walked the same distance toward me. "We didn't, really. It was the unicorns. They found us. We'd thought to follow them, but then Zacarina knelt in front of me." His lips quirked up in a smile. "It seemed a pretty clear message that I had better climb on to her back if I knew what was good for me."

The unicorns had found them. It all made sense now. The unicorns hadn't really left me at all. They'd heard the cries of the search party, just the same as I had. I hadn't *disturbed* them when I'd risen to my feet; I'd alerted them to my distress. Just as Jay and I had worked to free them, they'd gone to find him so that he could do the same thing for me. They didn't abandon me; just the opposite. They were just as responsible for my rescue as Jay, Avery, and Williamson were.

I turned back to the divine equines, who watched us with their inscrutable golden gazes. I could have spoken aloud to thank them, but it felt more proper to do it their way. So I concentrated and cast a wide net out with my mind so that all of the unicorns in the small area surrounding us would be able to hear me. "*Thank you,*" I mind-spoke. "*I could never have gotten out of this without your help.*"

Holding my gaze, Zacarina slowly sank down onto her forequarters, landing in what was an unmistakable bow. Behind her, the rest of the unicorns slowly followed suit, until the floor was blanketed with a sea of folded-over unicorns.

"It was our pleasure," Zacarina spoke for the rest of the herd. *"You may not have the form of a unicorn—but you have the spirit of one. That makes you kin. We never abandon our kin. We will always be there when you need us."*

There was a silence from behind me, where Avery, Williamson, and Jay stood. A sense of quiet awe filled the air around us.

I was glad that the rest of the search party hadn't arrived yet. If word got out about this, I would truly never shake that nickname that I so abhorred of the "unicorn princess." It wasn't that I hated being associated with the unicorns, either. No, I was honored and touched to be thought of being the unicorn's *kin.* It was the insinuation and assumption that I was somehow in a position of power over them that I loathed. I was not their princess. I was not their queen. The gods had chosen them and they had chosen me. In a way, that meant Zacarina was right. They were my brethren as much as I was theirs.

I walked toward her as she and the rest of her herd rose to their feet. I put my hand on her long face and eased my head against hers. "Thank you," I said, this time aloud, for the benefit of Jay and the guards. "Kin or not. You didn't have to help me. It means the world that you did."

"I told you I would always return the favor when I could," she said. *"Just because we have left your shelter does not change that. It does not end here for us. It never does."*

I stepped back and nodded, stepping away from her and giving her the space to turn. The unicorns turned and walked away into the night, leaving me with only the humans to explain to.

I swallowed a lump in my throat, looking at Jay. He looked so handsome, standing there, silhouetted in the moonlight coming in through the trees. So handsome... and so undeniably awkward. As we stared at each other, his eyes flicked around as he tried to look at anything but me. His hands went into his pockets and he rocked back on his heels, trying to ease some of the tension.

"Have you seen Fae?" I asked, thinking of my daughter spending her first night without me with a pang. "Is she all right?"

He nodded. "Yeah, I poked my head in on her and your mom before I joined the search party. She's fine. They bottle-fed her at dinner, so she's eaten. I'm sure she's missing you, but she's okay."

"And my mother?" I asked, almost dreading the answer.

He shook his head, laughing a bit in spite of himself. "Yeah... your mother is probably who you should be worried about. At least, that's who I would be worried about if I were you. She's going mad up there. I thought she was going to come into the woods and search herself, but the guards insisted that she stay in the palace, especially with you missing."

He swallowed visibly, no longer looking amused. "They were afraid it was a plot, you see. And if you had been kidnapped, they didn't want to give your captor a chance to also get their hands on the queen."

The expression on his face... I could see the ghost of the fear that must have been eating him alive for all of the hours that I had been missing. Guilt assaulted me. "I've made a mess of things, haven't I? And all because I needed to be alone so that I could think about..."

I trailed off and Jay looked up at me, his expression

arrested. "Think about what?"

I shook my head. We could have this reunion now, sure. But I was filthy and exhausted. I wanted it to be a real and productive conversation, not delirious words spoken in the forest. I wanted it to be coherent. Because it *mattered*; this conversation was important. And I didn't want to mess it up, not again.

"Later," I told him. I slipped my hand into his, and, hand in hand, we walked toward Williamson and Avery. "Promise me we'll talk later. For now, I need a bath—and I need to see my mother and daughter."

We made it back to the castle as the sun was rising, casting hues of orange and pink over the castle. It looked like a painting that my mother would have commissioned. I had been right when I'd awoken to shouts of my name and guessed that it was after midnight; it was *well* after midnight. In fact, it was the early hours of the morning, so early that the sun had not yet awoken.

The search party had caught up with us shortly after we began our trek through the forest to get back to the castle. We made quite the picture. All of us were bedraggled, sleep-deprived, and exhausted. But none more so than me.

After the initial adrenaline of being rescued had faded, I'd slumped with exhaustion onto the back of one of the party's horses. We pulled up in front of the castle entrance and I eased off. Jay took the reins.

"I'll take him to the staviary. I'll come find you in the afternoon so you can get some rest. We can talk then." He nodded behind me to where the castle gate was.

"You've got other concerns right now."

As I turned, a small train slammed into me, and I let out an oomph, my arms automatically coming around the figure with its arms around me. "Mother."

"Don't you ever do that again." Her words were muffled from speaking into my shoulder. "I thought Rumpelstiltskin had finally come to collect on our bargain. I thought I had lost you."

Oh, the guilt. I closed my eyes, battling the waves of it washing over me. Before, whenever my mother had seemed to overreact to me going missing for a few hours, I'd only been frustrated, angry, or annoyed. This was different. Now, I had been in actual danger. And now, I understood the reasons behind her fears. She wasn't paranoid that something random would happen to me. There was legitimately someone out to get me. Out to get *her.* Rumpelstiltskin wanted revenge. And I hoped beyond anything that he wouldn't get to have it. But I'd been a fruit on the vine, ripe for the picking tonight. No protection. No way to defend myself. I shuddered, thinking of how close he'd come to getting his hands on me.

"I'm sorry," I said. "I really didn't think anything would happen."

She pulled back, expression stern. "And that was foolish. I could understand before, but you know the dangers now. And you don't just have yourself to think of anymore. You have a child. You can't afford to go running off willy-nilly. I assigned you guards for a reason. I do things for a *reason.*"

She sighed and ran an aggrieved hand through her mussed hair. Dark circles ringed her eyes; I doubted if she'd slept any more than I had tonight, probably less. I'd had the comfort of the unicorns, at the very least.

She'd only had the fear of the unknown over what was happening to me.

"I know. I'm sorry." I quirked a smile at her. "If it's any consolation, the night definitely provided me with the clarity that I was looking for."

"I bet." She laughed, but it was a watery sounding laugh. She massaged her eyes. "We can talk about this more later. I'd imagine you're exhausted and to be quite frank, so am I. Let's get some sleep."

I nodded. "And Fae?"

"She's fine. Still asleep; she was in and out all night; even she seemed to sense that you weren't where you should be last night. You know what they say; let sleeping babes lie. Come by and get her after you've gotten some sleep."

"I will."

I slept forty winks. And then, maybe forty more.

And finally, I woke to knocking at my door.

Yawning, I pulled on a robe and schlepped over to the door, poking my head out to the two guards who were *not* Williamson and Avery. Well, they deserved to get some rest too. And if that wasn't the reason they weren't there, I'd deal with that tomorrow.

Jay was the reason they were knocking.

I blinked, stunned from my sleepy haze into alertness, and hurriedly ran a hand through my mussed hair.

"You said we should talk," Jay said softly, looking at me through hooded eyes.

That quickly, my heart started doing double time.

"I did, didn't I?" I replied. Time to show Jay I was ready to get him back. "Come in."

I gestured to the couch and Jay chuckled, shaking his head ruefully. “Deja vu,” he commented, taking his seat. He ran his palms down his pant legs.

Deja vu, huh? I wasn’t going to give him a reason to relive the day where I’d made a mistake that had almost cost me one of the most important people in my life. My mouth firmed, and I resolutely took a seat next to him, so close that our thighs were touching.

Jay’s gaze drifted down to where our legs met, and he stared there for a long moment. “Lia, wha—”

I wasted no more time in pressing my lips to his, cutting off his words.

Kissing Jay was... it was everything. It was understanding, passion, desperation. The peck I’d initiated opened the floodgates. My mouth opened to him and his to mine. His hands tangled in my hair and he pressed me close like he was afraid this was a dream and that if he held me tightly enough, he’d be able to stay asleep in it.

Eventually, reluctantly, we withdrew from each other, breathing hard. Jay leaned his forehead against mine.

“I made a mistake the other day,” I whispered. “A big one. You’re the best thing that’s happened to me in a long while and I won’t make the same mistake again. Can you forgive me?”

He grinned, the light dancing in his eyes, and he leaned in close. Eagerly, I met him halfway.

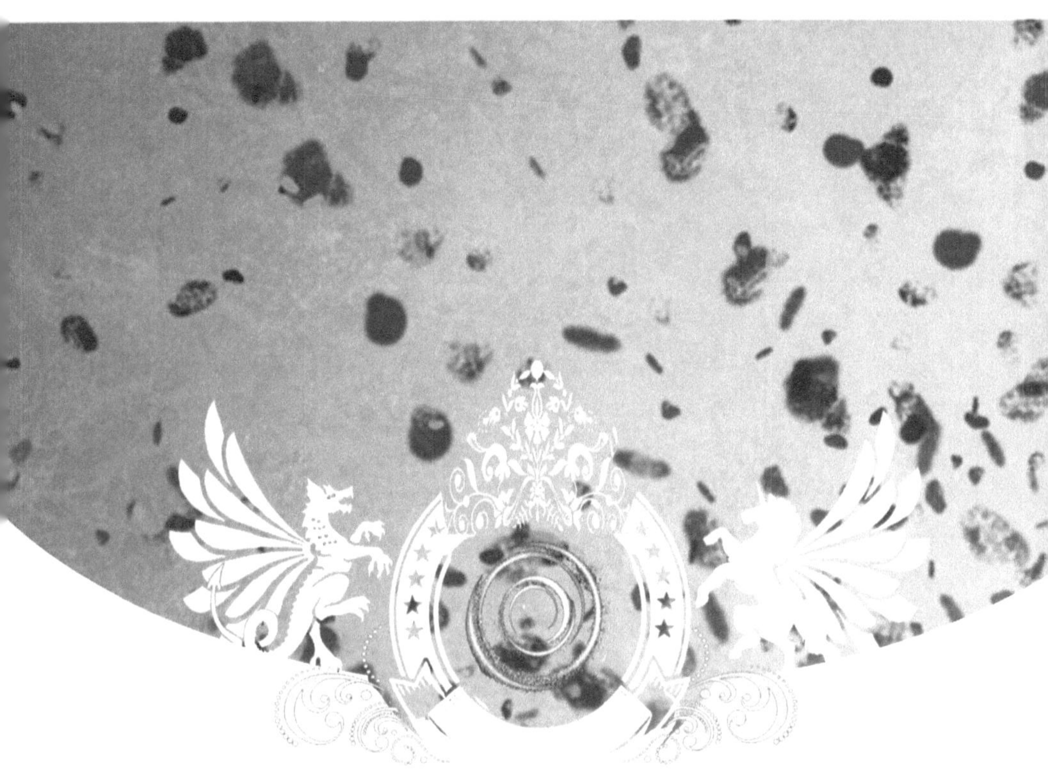

11TH MAY

I woke in a glorious haze the next morning and stretched my fingers and toes toward the headboard and footboard of my bed. I covered my face with my hands and shook my head, unable to suppress the grin that stretched over my features.

I was well rested, and for the first time in a while, I felt like I was living in a dream. The unicorns were back. I had a beautiful daughter, loving parents, and I lived in the most beautiful land anyone could ever dream of.

And—and here was why the grin continued to escape my hold—I had *Jay*.

Yesterday's memories swarmed me and I basked in their glow. Seeing him come through the forest, like a knight in tales of old. Talking with him. And then, even better, the best yet, in fact—getting to finally *kiss* him.

I hadn't realized how long I'd wanted to do that. How long I'd wondered what his lips would feel like pressed against mine. How his hands would feel if they tangled in my hair. I closed my eyes and relived the moment again. It was like a dream. Only I couldn't make it happen again by going back to sleep. For that, I'd need to get up and go find Jay.

I threw my bed covers aside with renewed energy and rushed to my mirror. First things first, I needed to get my hair in order. The past two days had blurred together and even though I'd washed the hours in the forest off me, my hair looked like it hadn't been touched. Hurriedly, I ran a brush through it, taming the worst of it and then my fingers deftly fashioned it into a braid. At least, I didn't look unkempt anymore.

But—I covered my smile with my hands—I knew that it wouldn't matter to Jay even if I *did.* He *loved* me. It was that simple for him. I wanted to look nice for him, but that was more for me than for him. I could be covered in mud with hair in tangles and vines and he would still love me. All he asked of me was that I be me. That was more than enough for him. And he was more than enough for me.

And as if he weren't wonderful enough, he loved my daughter as well.

My heartstrings tugged. I hadn't seen my beautiful little girl in more than a day. I wanted to see Jay too, but first I needed to hold her close and gather her in my arms once again.

If I wasn't a mother, I might then have thrown open my closet and tried on a dozen outfits, knowing that I'd see Jay later today. But I was a mother and I was in a hurry to hold my child again. I knew realistically that she was safe, having spent the night with *my* mother, who would sooner walk through fire than allow any harm to come to her grandchild. But it was different from seeing her with my own eyes and holding her in my own arms.

I dressed as quickly as I possibly could in the first article of clothing I could, a purple, off-the-shoulder day dress. With nearly inhuman speed, I did up the laces on the front of the dress and threw open the doors to my suite.

The guards outside jumped. I winced when I realized that the man and woman outside were most definitely not Avery and Williamson. My mother might need a little more time to cool down about that one, but I resolved that I would fix that soon. They shouldn't be punished for my manipulation. They'd followed the letter of their orders and only bowed to my pressure. And what were the chances that something like that would go so terribly wrong? They deserved another chance.

"Can we help you, Your Highness?" The female guard was shorter than I was, but she had a self-assuredness and confidence to her in her steely gaze that made me sure that she could subdue me, or any attacker who came her way.

I tilted my head in the direction of the hall's exit. "I'm just going to go visit my parents and retrieve Princess Fae. You're welcome to—"

She cut me off before I could finish my sentence. "We'd be happy to accompany you."

So it was that I set off toward my parents' rooms with my new guards in tow, following me like we were parts of the same body, like a snake's rattle winding behind it as it slithered its way around; a warning to all who saw it that it would not be wise to threaten it.

The same way that I hadn't recognized the guards outside my own door, I didn't recognize the guard outside my parents' rooms either. It wasn't Hardy. Come to think of it, he was probably still busy with the investigation hunting down Rumpelstiltskin.

I paused before I knocked. Gods, I had barely spared that devilish imp a thought in days. I'd been so caught up in first the drama with Jay and then—well, being trapped in a gods-cursed forest, and then the happy reunion with Jay and the return to the palace—that other priorities had quite distracted me from the plight of the imp who had vowed revenge on my family.

It wasn't that I wasn't worried about Rumpelstiltskin anymore. It would be foolish to think that just because I was happy now that he'd just give up. But at the same time, dwelling on it wouldn't do anyone any good either. We'd continue to pursue our leads, but we shouldn't let it prevent us from being happy either. We'd live. We'd love. We'd continue on. There were so many things for us to look forward to. A new relationship. The celebration of Fae's birth next week. And just living—watching my daughter and this life that I had created—blossom.

I raised a hand and knocked on the door, but no sooner than I had I finished my rhythmic tapping than the guard in front of the door was shaking his head. "They're not in there, Your Highness. They're down in the throne room."

I raised an eyebrow. "Both of them? This early?" That was unusual. Usually, my father spent a few hours in the throne room a day consulting with his advisors about the economy and trade. In a kingdom like ours, there wasn't much cause for more frequent meetings. And my mother usually only got pulled into things if foreign dignitaries were in town and she needed to play the part of an esteemed hostess.

But again, it was *early*. It was not normal for other royals to demand a meeting this early in the day.

And just that quickly, Rumpelstiltskin had my thoughts in his grip once again. "Is it Rumpelstiltskin?" I asked, half-hopeful, half-afraid of what the answer might be.

He shook his head. "No, Your Highness. I don't believe there is any news on that front."

I sagged in a strange mixture of feeling let down and relieved. No news was good news, I supposed. "Well, that's fine. I'll see them later, if they're attending to important matters. I just need to get inside and retrieve Princess Fae..." My voice trailed off as the guard again began to shake his head. "What do you mean?"

"Her Majesty the Queen took Her Highness Princess Fae with her to the meeting. There's no one inside."

"Ah." I gave him a deep nod, indicating that I understood. "Thank you. I'll meet with them there, then."

"My pleasure, Your Highness."

My brow furrowed deeply as my new guards and I set off for the throne room. I had a nagging feeling that something strange was going on. We reached the double doors of the room and, after greeting the guards outside of that room, I lifted the solid brass knocker and thumped it down on the door. "Princess Eliana for Princess Fae," I called out lightly. Just formal enough—just teasing enough to straddle the line of proper royalty and a daughter talking to her mother.

The murmur of voices inside the room halted. It felt like an eternity before my mother's voice came, resigned. "Come in, Eliana."

The guards pushed the doors inward and my

confusion didn't abate when I saw what was within the room.

My parents were indeed inside. And as the guard outside of their rooms had indicated, they were not alone. But the foreign royals that were inside weren't what I had expected.

For starters, they were all so *young*. My age, it looked like. And maybe I was just sheltered—well, I supposed that I *knew* that I was—but I had never been sent on a mission to another country, and I didn't think it was just because of my mother sheltering me. Often, if royals were sent to another country without being invited, it was because they needed something from the other country. So, usually the people who showed up were older, more experienced in the art of statesmanship.

I drew closer, and as the light glinted off the eyes of one of the visitors, I sucked in a quick breath.

It had glinted *gold*.

Gold like mine. Gold like the unicorns'.

One of them, another woman about my age with long, curly hair nodded decisively, as though she'd confirmed something upon seeing me.

"I knew it." She turned to others, who watched me uncertainly. "You see? I told you. She's one of us."

"One of you?" My eyes darted through the group, comprised of both men and women. They were a strange-looking bunch. The one that had spoken wore men's clothes that looked like they hadn't been washed in a week, but her face and hair were so feminine. On her shoulder sat a purple dragon. An actual purple dragon. In a belt around her waist was a sword with the hilt craved into the shape of a dragon. She was mesmerizingly beautiful, but looked battle-worn and tired despite the apparent excitement on her face. Beside her stood a girl who'd at least tried to make an effort with her appearance. Her strawberry-blonde hair was tied in a braid down her back and her blouse and trousers, while still tattered, were clean. The two men couldn't have looked more different from each other. Where one was tall and clean shaven, with the look of an academic despite his broad shoulders, the other, slightly shorter one was wiry and had a guarded expression. They were, quite frankly, the strangest looking bunch of folks I'd ever met—but their eyes! Their eyes were just like mine.

So I worried over what she might mean. Because their sudden appearance had the eerie pressure of fate to it.

"Eliana, right?" The young woman who had first spoken strode forward with a decisive stride, clomping down the stair of the dais where she and her companions had congregated around my parents.

"Ye-es?" I drew the word out into two syllables, making it a question. I darted a look at my mother, who watched wide-eyed. My father's face remained nearly impassive, but I caught how he tightened his grip upon the arms of his throne.

What had everyone in such a twist?

"I'm Azia." The curly-haired woman brushed a strand of hair out of her face with impatient fingers. "Azia, Princess of Draconis. And you—" She reached down and seized my hands in hers. "You're one of us," she repeated.

I looked back at my devoted parents and swallowed hard. What did she mean? I thought of the times I'd spoken to the unicorns and they'd spoken back to me. Was this what she was talking about? It seemed she knew more about me than I did. I dropped my voice so that they wouldn't overhear everything. "You're gods-touched too?" I whispered.

Her eyebrows flew to her hairline. "Gods-touched?" she repeated loudly. I yanked my hands free and made shushing motions, but to no avail. She said it again, this time with clear laughter in her voice. "Gods-*touched?*" She looked back at her companions, and it was clear that they were sharing a private joke that I wasn't in on. "Gods, you really have no idea. Eliana... you're not gods-touched." She reclaimed my hands and held my gaze steadily. "You're magic, though, right, Eliana? We all are."

My hands fell to my sides, fingers numb, as she turned to the others. "Meet the others... We think we are your brothers and sisters."

I nearly fainted. My vision blurred at the edges and I fell to my knees as someone went to fetch water. There was a strange buzzing in my ears and I could distantly hear Azia apologizing for the way she'd sprung the news on me.

I sipped at the water and gradually, my senses cleared. Not completely. But enough. It was like I was hearing and seeing everything through a haze of water.

My parents knelt before me, Mother smoothing my hair back with shaking hands, reassuring herself that I was still there, still safe. My eyes fixed on their familiar faces. So warm. So comforting.

And then I looked past my parents to the people behind them. The people who shared my eyes.

"Brothers and sisters?"

I knew I was adopted, and yes, I'd had idle thoughts about my real parents over the years, but I'd not once visualized siblings. "You came from Draconis to find me? Do you know my... our mother... our father?" I asked.

Azia shook her head slowly. "I wish that I could tell you that was the case. We'd love to be here just for a family reunion. But there's more. We have a duty to the kingdoms that we're here to fulfill. We aren't all from Draconis. Blaise is from Atlantice, Castiel from Elder, and Deon from Floris. It seems we were scattered around the kingdoms as newborns."

"So why are you here? What duty?"

She swallowed. "Magic is..." She turned her hands in a circle, as though trying to grab on to the right words. They fell open as she settled for words she seemed to find inadequate. "Magic is failing," she said simply. "In all of the kingdoms."

I stood up, Mother and Father scrambling to do the same. "Vale doesn't have a particular affinity for magic," I said slowly. "I'm not sure this really has anything to do with us."

Even as I said it, I felt the lie on my lips. I'd been talking to the unicorns for weeks and they'd been answering back

She gave me a half-smile. "None of us were eager to believe it. But if you're not prone to spells and the like, you do have magical creatures here. Has anything strange been happening there?"

I'd kept my secret so well, but it looked like I wasn't going to be able to keep it much longer.

She took my silence as a confirmation. "I thought as much. But we're going to fix it. You have to come with us, Eliana. We're stronger together."

"Her place is here," my mother croaked out, her voice choked with emotion.

Normally, I'd object to my mother speaking for me, but in this case, I couldn't help but agree. "She's right," I said. "And it's not that you're wrong, not entirely. There *are* issues plaguing our unicorns, but they've returned now and I can't..." I trailed off, thinking of what I had to lose.

My life was so perfect right now. Jay and I had embarked upon something new and wonderful. Mother and I had seemed to reach some sort of an understanding. And I fell a little more in love with Fae every day. And that was really what decided it.

Part of me, the old Eliana who longed for a world outside of Vale, a life without restrictions, would have jumped at the chance to go with them on some sort of fated quest if it meant I'd get to see the world. But I was a mother now. And that changed everything.

"I have a daughter," I said quietly. "Not even three weeks old. I can't leave her."

"Then bring her with you!" Azia said. Her brow furrowed with emotion. Frustration, maybe? I didn't know her well enough to read her completely yet. "I wouldn't ask if this wasn't serious. We didn't come here on a whim. There is something very wrong with the magic in our kingdoms. It's spreading and we need your help to stop it. My mother is sick... maybe dying. Same with Blaise's mother. Castiel's entire village is sick and all the crops in Floris are failing. It's bigger than me or us; this is affecting—or is going to affect—everyone. "

I laughed humorlessly. "I'm sorry, but I don't know what you think I can do to help. You haven't been around babies very much, have you? That's no place for her."

Azia's mouth opened, probably to voice another

argument, but I held up my hand. "I can see you've come a long way to meet with me, but I'm not taking a newborn on an adventure. I've made up my mind. I wish you all the luck in the world, and I truly hope to get to know you all at some point in the future. But as far as your mission goes..."

I pressed my lips together in a grim line.

"You're on your own."

GODDESS OF LOSS

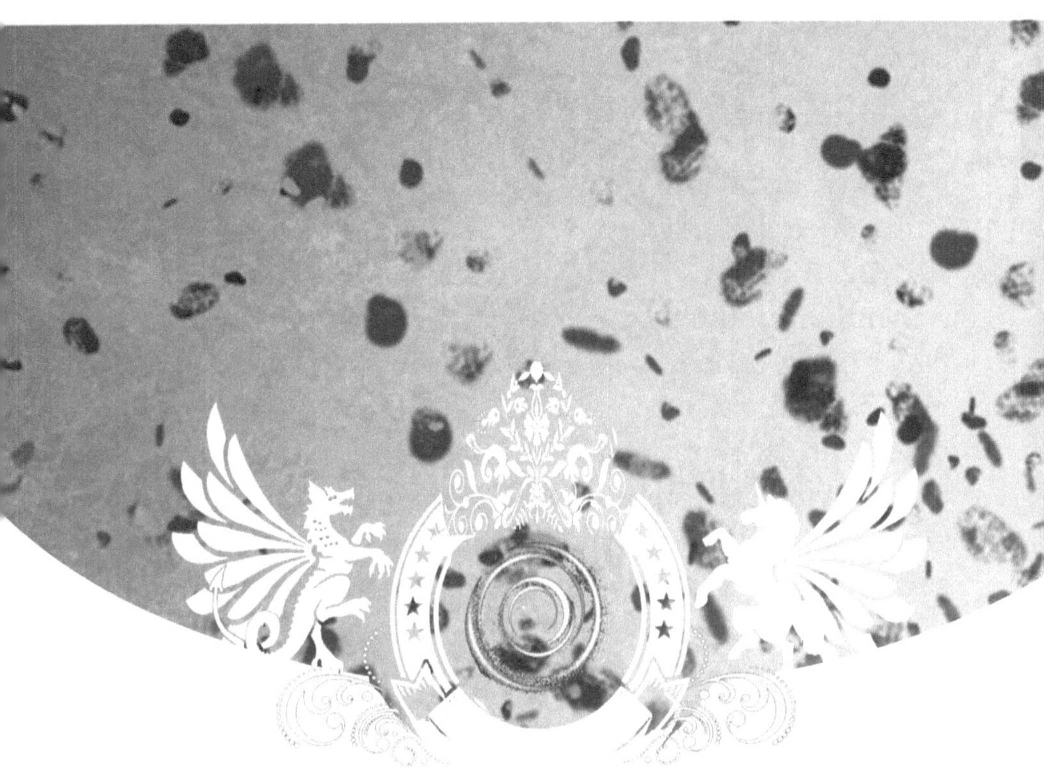

13TH MAY

Fae chose the most restless night I'd ever had to decide to sleep through for the first time. She was asleep by ten and softly breathing right through until just after six in the morning. Even if those strangers claiming to be related to me hadn't shown up so unexpectedly, I probably would have woken up, wondering if Fae had stopped breathing or any number of other things that could befall a baby, but as it was, the strangers had me tossing and turning most of the night. It meant I could check on Fae regularly. The sight of her little chest rising and falling, and the movement of her lips suckling in her dreams were the only things that kept me centered the whole night.

Just like any other only child, I'd dreamed of having brothers and sisters. Of course, with my mother's stance on having children of her own, that dream of mine had been scuttled when I was very young.

Never in all my childhood dreams of siblings had I imagined I'd have four. Four! Azia, Blaise, Castiel, and Deon. I mentally checked them off on my fingers, remembering their names. Alphabetical. I was number five, Eliana. Whoever had brought us to our prospective houses just after our birth had obviously given our new guardians our names. It would be too much of a coincidence otherwise. My mother had always told me she'd loved the name Eliana, but was that just another secret she was hiding? There'd been no mention of a baby whose name began with F or G, but did that mean they weren't out there? The strangers didn't really seem to know any more about their history than I did mine. And yet our stories were so similar. All of us brought to the leaders of a kingdom soon after our birth by an older woman and a younger woman who seemed to have disappeared soon after, never to be seen again. They'd told me that right after dropping the bomb on me that they needed me to accompany them on an adventure to save the world from some magic apocalypse and bring my sweet baby. I still wasn't sure which part of their story was the most insane.

If it wasn't for their eyes and the golden rings around their irises, I wouldn't have believed them. They probably wouldn't have gotten a meeting with my parents. The whole thing was very strange and had rattled me more than I liked to admit.

A small cry took me from my bed and over to Fae. When she saw me, she quieted down immediately.

"Good morning, beautiful," I whispered, picking her up from her bassinet. Her onesie was soaking wet due to her not having been changed since ten the previous night.

"As if I'd take you away from your home," I whispered soothingly to her as I peeled the onesie from her body. "Your granny would lynch me on the spot if I so much as tried it!"

A quick change later and she was ready for her morning feed. Less than a month ago, I'd been an only child with my only family being my mother and father, and now, I had so many new family members I was practically fighting them off.

"How things change," I whispered to Fae, who was busy suckling at my breast for real this time. As anticipated, she ignored me. The concerns of the mother were not the concerns of the daughter.

After a quick shower and change for me, I bundled Fae up and headed downstairs, taking the stone steps carefully with her in my arms. Avery and Williamson, who had reappeared this morning, walked, as always, two steps behind. With no particular agenda for the day, I headed to the breakfast room.

My mother was there, but, surprisingly, so were my father and Jay.

Jay jumped up when he saw me and gave me a kiss on the cheek before taking Fae from my arms and cooing softly to her. I noticed my father raise his eyebrow at the gesture, but my mother merely had a sly grin on her face. All she'd ever wanted for me was to see me settled, happy and safe, and she saw I could be all of those things with Jay by my side.

"Toast and jam?" she inquired as I sat down, pushing the toast rack toward me. I took a slice and slathered it in butter, then jam.

"This is cozy," I said, taking a bite.

"Your mother has had quite a bit to say this morning," my father commented. "I guess she thought it better if jam was involved."

"Everything's better with jam involved," Jay interjected. A quick look told me he was talking to Fae rather than the rest of the people at the table. Fae was gazing back at him with adoring eyes.

"I've told your father everything," my mother explained. "He knew most of it, but it was long overdue that he knew the whole story. After the strangers... your, er... possible siblings turned up, I couldn't keep any more secrets."

At the mention of the visitors, Jay finally dragged his eyes from Fae. "Do you really think they're your siblings?"

I guessed my father wasn't the only one who had been party to my mother's words.

I shrugged my shoulders and put my unfinished toast back on the plate. I had stayed up most of the night thinking about it. "I don't know how they can be. Quintuplets are very rare. I mean, have you ever heard of anyone in The Vale having five babies at once?"

I shuddered at the thought of it. Giving birth to Fae was hard enough; doing it another four times right after was a terrifying thought.

My father pointed the knife he'd been using at me. A glob of butter dropped onto the tablecloth. "I looked it up after they left. Not once in the history of The Vale has the royal family ever given out a gift to parents of quintuplets. We've had a few sets of triplets over the years, which is the lowest multiple birth we recognize to get a gift, and twice we've had quadruplets, but never more than four." He seemed to notice his butter was on the table, and he swiped it back onto his knife and went back to buttering his toast.

"We give gifts to parents of multiples?" I asked. I'd

never heard it before.

"It's a gesture. Must be hard to have that many babies at once. I gave one out myself in my first year of being king. They were a family from a poor village in the north. I didn't visit them myself, but the guards who made the journey told me they were very happy to receive such a gift. We sent them enough diapers and baby clothes to last for two years, along with a substantial monetary donation. There was another one in your great-grandfather's time. Of course, there could have been others that we were never made aware of."

I poured myself a cup of coffee and took a sip. It was already cold. "I don't think my birth parents were from The Vale," I replied, gesturing to one of the servants and handing him the coffee pot.

"What makes you think that?" Jay asked.

"The strangers weren't from The Vale. They were from all over. Azia and her dragon were from Draconis..."

At the sound of my mother's voice, Fae began to cry. My mother reached forward, and Jay handed Fae to her. She cuddled her close and swayed softly, humming so quietly I could barely hear it. It was working on Fae, though. She quieted down quickly. My mother passed her granddaughter back to Jay.

"Wait up," Jay interrupted. He leaned forward on his elbows. "There was a dragon here?"

"Only a little one," my mother said, shooing him back. "Carry on, Eliana."

Jay let out a low whistle. He would have been fascinated to meet a real dragon. I made a mental note to tell him all about the impish Nyre once we were out of earshot of my mother.

"Blaise was from Atlantice, Castiel was from Elder, and Deon was from..." I tried remembering where he'd told me he was from, but in all the information I'd been given, I'd clean forgot.

"Floris," my mother answered for me.

"Yes, Floris. My birth parents could have been from any of those places, or none of them. They could have been travelers. If they'd delivered five babies while on the road, maybe they thought it was kinder to give them away."

Jay looked deep in thought.

"What?" I asked him.

"Your mother told me she thought you were siblings because you were all brought to your new parents at around the same time."

"That's right. Very late in the year. We all estimated our birthdays to be around the winter festival."

Jay sat forward again, and this time my mother didn't shoo him back. "How did those mystery women manage to get to all the kingdoms at the same time? Elder couldn't be further away from Floris. Even at the fastest speeds, it would take many weeks to get to all the kingdoms."

He was right; it was impossible. How had I not thought of that last night?

"Maybe they came by train?"

"Train would take a week or more to get right across the kingdoms, and that's only if it did a straight run. Trains don't just go in a straight line from one kingdom to another, and even royal trains can't just drive around the others on the tracks. I don't see how it's possible to deliver five babies to five kingdoms within a week."

"Even the Urbis Express has a timetable," Father said. He munched down on his third helping of toast and looked pensive. "Of course, the airships of the Urbis Express aren't the only flying vehicles. There are others. Privately owned."

This was something I didn't know. "What vehicles?"

"I hear that The Forge is making headway with steam-powered flying machines. Nothing like the airships, but smaller vehicles that carry one or two people. I'm not sure they're completely ready yet, though. When I last talked to Alice Rowntree—she's the president of The Forge—she was kind enough to give me a tour of the guild there. I must say, the inventions those Forge people come up with are nothing short of extraordinary. Anyway, I did speak to a young man who was working on a flying machine."

I sighed. It was all well and good there being an almost flying machine, but that didn't help me figure out what had happened over eighteen years ago.

"There are the flying ships of Skyla too," he added. "Real ships like the ones that travel across the sea, except they fly. I expect it has something to do with the magic that makes their islands float. Of course, the only people I've heard of that use flying ships are pirates."

"You think I came from pirates?" I asked, amused by the thought of it. My mother, however, was not.

"Of course he doesn't mean that," she cut in, giving him a heap of side eye. "You aren't descended from pirates. The women that brought you looked very respectable. Besides, if there had been any sightings of flying ships over the Vale, we would have heard about it."

My father shrugged his shoulders. "They did come in the dark, my love, and Skyla is only a short distance over the sea."

"She's not a pirate, and that's the last I'll hear of it," my mother said, standing up and wiping her mouth with a napkin. "I'm sure there is a reasonable explanation, I just can't think what it is right now."

I caught a smirk on my father's face, though he remained silent. He loved winding my mother up. I expect he loved the idea of having a pirate as a daughter too.

"What are you two doing today, anyway?" my mother asked, looking to Jay and me.

"The ball is tomorrow. I was thinking of helping you get all the last-minute bits ready for it."

"Actually, I was hoping you'd come out with me today." Jay interjected, looking at me. "I was planning on going into town, and I was wondering if you'd like to join me? I need to buy supplies for the staviary."

"The party is in hand," my mother said, to my surprise, scooping Fae up from Jay's arms. "I think it would do the both of you a world of good to get out for a change. I'll look after my darling Fae." She rubbed noses with Fae, who let out a rather large burp. "Judith can help me."

I looked to Jay, who gazed back at me with expectation in his eyes. "Okay, I guess we're going into town."

After wolfing down breakfast, my mother practically shooed me out of the castle. Avery and Williamson ran on ahead to get their horses ready as Jay and I ambled slowly through the courtyard.

"You planned this, didn't you?" I asked.

"Maybe... but your mother was happy to let you go. Come on, how often does that happen?"

"Not for a long time," I conceded. I almost never ventured into the nearby town of Shipley. The last time I had spent any decent amount of time there was before I was married, when Luka and I were courting. Since he'd died, I hadn't had any reason to go back.

My stomach knotted into nerves as we jumped

up onto our horses. No matter how much I loved the unicorns and had an affinity for them, I much preferred riding an animal that kept its feet on the ground. Avery took the lead with Williamson following up in the rear.

Blue skies with fluffy white clouds and a slight breeze made the morning as perfect as it could be. With anyone else, this journey would have filled me with dread, knowing the memories of the many times I had made the exact journey with Luka would come rushing back, but I found with Jay, it wasn't happening.

I waited for a stabbing pain of loss to fill me like it had done a hundred times before, but as we trotted down the well-worn road to Shipley, that never came. Instead, I felt a sense of freedom that I was barely used to and an overriding feeling of wellbeing and happiness.

"What are you grinning at?" Jay asked, looking over his shoulder.

"Nothing. It's just a lovely day. The weather is perfect."

"It is," Jay agreed. He slowed down so we could ride side by side. For the first time, I didn't feel the shadow of Luka looking over my shoulder. He was there, all right, but safely in my heart where he belonged. A whisper of a breeze whistled past my ear, and I swear I could almost hear Luka giving me his blessing to be with Jay.

I could speak to unicorns, but I was under no illusion I'd really heard Luka's voice in the wind. Even so, I felt it. It was time to let him go. It was time to move on.

"Are we really going to buy supplies?" I asked once we were on the periphery of the town. I had a feeling my mother wouldn't let me out for something so inane as buying straw.

"Of course," Jay replied. "What else?" He trotted off ahead, almost passing Avery. I couldn't see it, but I knew there was a grin on his face. This wasn't merely a shopping trip. We were heading into town for another reason. A reason my mother had agreed to.

The mud road soon gave way to cobbled streets as we left behind the farmhouses that dotted the land around the castle. They were replaced by houses and, as we rode closer to the center of town, shops.

Luka's shop was still there, though it was now a grocery shop. Fresh fruits and vegetables had been meticulously piled up out front, a riot of color in the early morning sun. The sign Luka had carved himself had been covered over by a new sign, reading *Mr. Robinson's Fresh Produce.* Again, I waited for the pang of pain to hit. It came, but not as hard as I expected. Jay slowed down again and caught the shop I was looking at.

"You okay?"

I nodded my head. I was okay. I was better than okay.

"Luka would have liked that his shop was used for something," I said. "He'd have hated if it remained empty."

"I wasn't talking about what Luka would have wanted or not wanted. I was asking about you."

I looked him square in the eye. "I'm good. Very good... I'm happy, Jay, and that's the truth."

He reached forward and gave my hand a squeeze.

"Where to now?" I didn't know the town at all. I'd only ever come as far as Luka's shop and had never had any need or desire to venture further into the hustle and bustle.

"I told you. We're buying supplies." He cantered on ahead again, and this time, I kept up with him. Some of the people of the town recognized me and waved and bowed as we rode past. I waved back, enjoying the simple pleasure of smiling faces happy to see me.

Avery kept having to speed up and ride around us, but it was clear Jay hadn't told him where we were going, so he ended up doing this kind of shuffling dance where he was in front of us, then behind, then in front again. I almost felt sorry for him, but then I remembered that this was an outing for him too. It must have made a nice change from him standing outside my chambers all day.

Eventually, Jay pulled into a yard through some open wooden gates. A large sign hung over the gates that read *Horse and Stable Supplies.*

So Jay hadn't been putting me on after all. We really were here to buy things for the staviary. I knew that the castle staviary was the only one of its kind in the kingdom... in all the kingdoms, probably. There wasn't a dedicated shop for unicorns, but apart from their ability to fly and their amazing healing ability, they were much the same as horses.

A small man with a round stomach and ruddy cheeks walked out of a huge warehouse-style building when he heard the clip-clop of our horses' feet enter the yard.

When he saw me, he immediately dropped into a low bow, and when he stood back up, his already ruddy cheeks appeared even redder.

"Good morning, Your Highness," he said, running over to me. He looked a little unsure of himself, whether to hold out his hand to help me down or leave me to jump down myself. In the end, Jay saved him by jumping down from his own horse and extending a hand to me.

"Jay." The man nodded his head in recognition.

"Loftus, this is Eliana. Eliana, Mr. Loftus."

"Pleased to meet you, Mr. Loftus," I said, extending

my own hand. This time, he took it and did another bow while holding my hand.

"The... err... thing is ready," Loftus said to Jay, all the while darting curious eyes to me. I didn't meet the public very often, but when I did, there were two types. The first, who couldn't get enough and brought flowers and felt honored just to be breathing the same air as a princess, and the second, who were like Loftus. People who were unsure of protocol and scared to do the wrong thing. I was sure there were people who didn't give a unicorn poop about meeting royalty, but I was yet to come into contact with one of those.

"The things I ordered for the staviary, you mean?"

Loftus looked startled at this, and his cheeks colored further. "Yes... that's exactly it. Come with me and I'll show you."

We followed him into the warehouse. I'd expected a huge, open-plan building, but we'd ended up in a small office. It was neat enough, with nothing out of place, but it had an overwhelming smell of horse about it. It reminded me of Jay. Another door led to what I assumed to be the rest of the warehouse. Apart from the small desk with a couple of well-used pencils and a clipboard, and a filing cabinet, the only decoration was a hand-drawn picture of a horse.

Loftus picked up a clipboard and shouted out a couple of names. Within seconds, two young lads, aged about fifteen, came into the office from the second door.

"Tom, Jacob, I need you to get the order for Jay and pile it all up in the wagon to be delivered."

If it was being delivered to the palace, and we'd ordered it, why were we here? I didn't have time to ask because already Loftus was shouting out items, and the two boys were scurrying from the warehouse, through the office, and into the yard where I watched them pile up the wagon through a small window. The wagon was already full of hay, and another sat beside it, equally full. The boys had to climb up to put the items on top.

"Three new saddles," he bellowed, and Tom came rushing back. I watched with fascination as they piled the equipment higher and higher.

"Five new sets of bridles… a broom… a new bucket…" The list went on and on. After the first two wagons were full, Jacob drove another around from a different part of the yard. I stepped outside, eager to feel the sunshine on my face and get away from the overwhelming smell of horse.

"We aren't here to buy stuff for the staviary," Jay murmured, coming up behind me. "Well, not only that. There's something else too."

I turned to face him as he slipped his hand in mine. A thrill of electricity ran up my arm at his touch.

"What are we here for, then?" I whispered, scared at the sudden intensity of my feelings. Feelings I'd been pushing down for way too long.

He didn't speak. Instead, he led me back into the office. Loftus tipped his cap as we continued through the second door. This time, we were in the large warehouse. Tom ran past with an arm full of straps as we entered. At the far end of the warehouse was a huge pile of straw, bundled up and piled right to the roof. In the half where we stood, everything an equine enthusiast could ever want was stacked neatly on shelves or on the floor. Jay walked right past all this toward the straw. Light from an open skylight gave it the appearance of spun gold. It reminded me of my mother and how she'd been told to do just that—spin straw into gold. And she had with the help of Rumpelstiltskin. I pushed the thought away.

"What are we doing?" I asked as we got to the stack of straw bales.

He gave me the most beautiful smile, then pulled me around the corner of them. Where I'd thought there was nothing but hay, the bales I'd seen were actually a wall. Bales lined the end wall of the warehouse and the back wall too, but in the middle of the three straw bale walls was a floor of messy straw with another two bales with a tablecloth on it. On top of the cloth were a picnic meal and a bottle of wine.

"What's this?"

"I asked your mother if I could officially take you out on a date. She was more than happy for you to dine at one of the fine restaurants in town as long as Avery and Williamson joined us, but I don't know any fine restaurants in town," he admitted. He leaned forward and whispered in my ear. "And I didn't want Avery and Williamson to join us. This was the only compromise I could think of. Just pretend we're somewhere fancy."

I laughed. "I don't know any fine restaurants either," I said, sitting on a bale of straw that had been brought out as a seat. "I've never been to one. For all I know, this is the most exclusive restaurant in the whole of Shipley."

"Oh, but it is!" he said, pouring me a glass of champagne. "We are the only two customers there will ever be. I rode down here late last night and organized it with Loftus. He was happy to set it up for me. He even said he'd do it for free, but I wouldn't hear of such a thing. His only stipulation was that we don't have candlelight."

I looked at all the straw around us. "I can see why."

He handed me the champagne. I took a sip, enjoying the bubbles and the sweet taste. Jay bit his lip, waiting for me to do something... say something.

“This is a date, Lia. Not as friends. I wanted to bring you out on a real date before we go to the ball together tomorrow. I wanted you to be sure this is what you want.”

“You brought me here as a practice date?” I said, suddenly full of nerves. It was one thing eating a picnic with a friend, even a romantic one with wine. It was another thing entirely to call it a date.

“I guess you could call it that.” He seemed suddenly unsure of himself, as though he didn’t quite know what to say or do. I understood how he felt, completely. I felt the same. This was the line, and it was up to me to decide if I officially wanted to cross it. “I wanted to make sure you were okay with that before we do it so publicly. The newspapers have been invited to the ball, and everyone will be gossiping and...”

I put the glass back down on the straw bale and knelt down until I was level with him. I leaned forward and brushed his ear with my lips. “I accept.”

He shuddered lightly and whispered back. “Accept what?”

I pulled back slightly so we were looking at each other eye to eye. My heart was hammering so hard I could barely speak. “I accept your invitation to this date.”

I brushed my lips against his, and our date became real.

14TH MAY

"I knew we should have gone with the yellow," my mother said, fussing around me as three people tried squeezing me into the dress that had been made especially for me.

"I like the blue," I murmured under swathes of fabric. "I just wish I'd thought a bit harder about the style. New mothers shouldn't be expected to wear ball gowns mere weeks after birth."

"Don't be silly, Eliana," my mother shot back once my head had popped out of the dress. The three maids began the task of pulling it straight and making sure it was on correctly. I felt like a trussed-up leg of lamb. It didn't help that the corset they'd made me wear under the dress was practically stopping my lungs from expanding. "You can't go to a ball in loungewear and horsey clothes."

If only. I'd worn loose fitting and baggy clothes for so many months, I'd forgotten what it felt like to have a waist. I'd been under the delusion that mere days after giving birth to Fae, I'd be back in my regular clothes, but here I was, weeks later, and I was still rocking maternity chic. Or, at least, I had been before today.

My hair had been thoroughly washed and styled, and for the first time in forever, didn't have spit-up in it. I'd even gone so far as to let my mother bring a makeup artist in.

"You are right about the blue, though," she admitted, clapping her hands together and giving me an appreciative look. "I've never seen you more beautiful. Motherhood really suits you."

"I think a good night's sleep is what suits me. Thank you, by the way."

My mother had pretty much ordered Judith to look after Fae through the night, only bothering me when Fae needed to be fed. She dealt with the diaper changes and the general soothing that Fae usually needed when she woke in the night. My mother had brought a bed into my sitting room for her, so Fae was never too far away from me.

"That's what mothers are for," she said, ushering me to the full-length mirror. "Judith has agreed to do the same tonight so you can stay at the party as long as you like. And unlike last night, she will have formula."

I doubted Fae would like that, but I kept my mouth shut because I wanted to stay up late. I wanted to dance and eat and drink and be human. I wanted to enjoy being with Jay.

The kiss I'd shared with Jay the day before had been brief. Too brief. Any misgivings I'd had about the pair of us had melted away, but kissing him in a glorified shed was not where I wanted our relationship to begin. Jay was special. He'd always been special to me, and I wanted everything perfect. I wanted everything tonight. We'd kiss again, I was sure of it, but this time I'd be a true princess, and he'd be dressed fit for a prince. He'd told me he'd had my mother helping him out in that department too.

I'd never seen Jay in anything but scruffy work clothes. Seeing him in a suit would be a revelation. As I was imagining the pair of us dancing in each other's arms, my mother angled the mirror toward me.

My mouth dropped open at the sight of me. I'd looked like a princess once, but those days seemed a long time ago. I'd gotten used to stained shirts and baby dribble covering everything. I'd gotten used to the lack of shape my body had molded itself into...until now. I was back to me again, but somehow better. My waist was clearly defined thanks to the corset that heaved my breasts high, giving me a feminine look that I'd always lacked.

Tears sprang to my eyes as I gazed down at myself. My long, blonde hair had been pulled from its ponytail and curled into waves that swept my shoulders.

"You look beautiful," my mother whispered as she placed my tiara on my head.

I could barely tear my eyes from myself, but the part of getting ready I was most looking forward to was about to start. No matter how beautiful the makeup artist, hairdresser, and maids had made me, I wasn't the belle of the ball. Fae was.

I'd let my mother be in charge of my dress, but when it had come to picking Fae's, I'd been the one to make the final decision. I'd picked a dress with so many frills that she'd be lost in them. It was a pale blue to compliment the dark blue of my gown, and I topped it off with a ribbon around her head with a flower embroidered into it along with the initial L.

If anyone asked, I'd tell them it was for the shortened form of my name, Lia, but truly, it was for Fae's father, Luka. I was moving on with Jay, but Luka would always be a part of me and a part of Fae.

When she was dressed, I picked her up and moved back over to the mirror, pointing at her in it. She was completely unmoved by how beautiful she was, but I knew that was something she would grow into. I gave her a light kiss then wiped away the lipstick I'd left on her cheek with my thumb. The music in the grand hall had already begun, and we were in danger of being late to our own party.

Judith met us by the door to the main hall, waiting to take Fae from my arms.

"I'll introduce her to everyone, and then, when she gets tired, you can take her to bed," I said to her. No one was robbing me of formally introducing my daughter. "Feel free to enjoy the party before that. Make sure you get some food."

Judith nodded her head and walked down the corridor that would bring her to one of the side entrances to the grand hall. The main entrance where we were was reserved for royalty only. Normally, it wasn't used, but on nights like this, it was the best way of making a grand entrance.

My stomach was in knots as my father appeared. He kissed my cheek and Fae's, then took my mother's arm. I knew my nerves had nothing to do with Fae. The people would love her. What was there not to love? She was perfection in an overly frilly dress. I was nervous because Jay would be inside waiting for me, and I had to act like it was normal, that my insides didn't feel like

I'd swallowed a hundred snakes.

The master of the doors put his hand to the door handle. I took a deep breath as the guards inside signaled their fanfare. A hand on my arm had me spinning around.

Jay stood there, looking more handsome than I'd ever seen him. He'd had a haircut and a shave and didn't have the usual smudge of mud across his cheek.

I opened my mouth to say something, but his attention was already on Fae.

The doors opened and we walked in, already a couple. He'd planned it that way, knowing I'd be nervous. As the photographers jostled for the best position and the guests applauded our arrival, I clung to him, fearful that if I let go, he would disappear.

He clasped my hand tightly, and right then, I knew he'd always be there for me. From planning a practice date the day before to walking through the main doors with me, something he'd almost certainly asked permission from my father to do, he was always one step ahead, anticipating my needs before I even knew I had them.

I took a quick glance over at him. He had a flower in his hand. It was a gerbera daisy. They didn't grow in The Vale. I knew this because they were my favorite flowers. Bright, colorful, and yet simple. They were the flowers that Luka used to buy me when he could. Jay knew that, and he'd gone out of his way to make sure I was happy. At least, I'd thought that, but as I watched, he handed the flower to Fae. She grabbed the stem in her little fist, squashing it, breaking the stem so that it bent. She then let go, dropping the flower to the floor.

"She's going to be a feisty one when she grows up," Jay whispered to me, and I broke into a laugh.

Somewhere in front of me, another light went off as the photographers captured the special moment.

There was so much I wanted to say to Jay, but once the photographers had been given their turn to take photos, they were ushered out to keep the rest of the party private, and I was given the chance to introduce Fae. She was the star of the show, and having people cooing over her made it so much easier to be with Jay in an official capacity. No one was looking at us as I made a trip around the room, introducing Fae to as many people as possible. No one noticed his hand on my back, the whispers of encouragement in my ear, the looks we gave each other. They only noticed the baby. She was the perfect decoy. I even managed to get some food before she became cranky and began to wail. I didn't even need to look for Judith. She appeared out of the throng of people, ready to do her job. I gave Fae a quick cuddle and handed her to Judith. Jay bent over and kissed her forehead.

"You'd better go and let the king and queen say goodnight to her," I said, nodding toward my parents who were in deep conversation with a couple I didn't recognize.

I watched as Judith walked through the crowd with Fae, who was still wailing. My mother lit up when she saw her, even though she'd been with her less than half an hour earlier. She really did love us all. She doted on Fae, and I was pretty sure the only reason she didn't insist on accompanying Judith up to my room was that she'd miss out on the opportunity to gush about her new granddaughter to all her friends.

"She'll be all right, you know." Jay slipped his hand in mine as the music started to play. I turned to face him.

"Here, I have one for you too." He pulled out another gerbera daisy from a pocket. It was almost as bent as the one Fae had dropped on the floor earlier. I gave him a shy smile as I took the flower from him. With his free hand, he gestured to the dance floor. People were still eating and talking, and, as yet, no one had ventured out to dance. "Would you dance with me?"

My stomach squirmed again. I no longer had Fae as a shield. Dancing with Jay would tell the world that we were together, but as I looked into his eyes, I knew that I wanted it. I'd wanted it for so long, and it was way overdue that I acknowledged it.

"I'd be delighted."

All eyes were on us as Jay swept me out onto the dance floor. As he spun me around, I saw Judith slipping out with Fae. I closed my eyes, blocking the whole world out, and rested my head on Jay's shoulder. It was such an intimate moment, watched by hundreds. I didn't care. Being in Jay's arms felt so right. How could I have not known how perfect we were together? The signs had been there all along. He'd been my best friend my whole life. He was one of my earliest memories, and now, he was the man making my whole body sing. The music played faster and faster, and the evening flew by. By the time the orchestra was playing the slow songs, my feet were aching and my heart was full. No one had bothered us, and yet I'd seen with my own eyes the people watching us dance. I wondered briefly if this would cause a scandal in The Vale. After all, I'd not long since given birth to another man's baby. Then I found I didn't care. Those people, supposedly our greatest friends, although I'd never met half of them, didn't know what it was like to lose a husband and then months later give birth to his child.

"What are you thinking about?" Jay whispered in my ear as we swayed together, my head on his shoulder. "Are you thinking about Luka?"

I pulled back a little so I could look him in the eye. "Kind of. I was wondering about how this would be perceived in the papers tomorrow. People of The Vale are straight-laced. They might not like the fact I'm dancing with a man who isn't the new princess's father."

"And does that bother you?"

I shook my head and whispered back. "Not in the slightest." Leaning forward, I pressed my lips against his to show him I was telling the truth. All around us, I heard a collective gasp, but I drowned the sound out, preferring to listen only to the music and to fall into the kiss, among the first of many.

"Let's go outside." Jay took my hand, and together, we made our way through the crowds of people. Like most palaces of royalty, ours had a balcony where we would pose for royal photos on days when the public demanded it, such as royal occasions. What most people didn't know was that we had a private balcony at the back of the palace that overlooked the palace gardens.

It was lit by a beautiful combination of torches, stars, and fireflies that danced around us.

"I meant what I said inside. I really don't care what people think. It took me a long time to get here, but I'm here now. I love you, Jay."

I'd never seen his face so lit up or animated at my words. He'd been waiting a long time to hear them.

"I know that Luka will always be part of your life, I don't want to change that, I..."

I held a finger to his lips. "This night isn't about Luka. It's about us."

"Actually, it's about Fae, but..."

I silenced him with a kiss, moving my lips against his in a way that felt so natural that I wondered how I could ever have thought otherwise. I ran my fingers through his dark hair and inhaled his scent of fresh soap and a hint of the staviary that never really left him.

When I finally pulled away, I noticed some of the unicorns flying over the garden. One of them was Zacharina, followed by Epiphany. My stomach lurched, and for a second, I thought they were coming to tell me something was wrong, but then I saw they weren't just flying, they were parading in the air, almost a dance, giving the fireflies a run for their money.

"Jay?"

"Hmmm?"

"Did you happen to talk about the ball in front of the unicorns at all?"

Even in the torchlight, I saw his cheeks color.

"I might have been practicing the courage to ask you as my date in front of them."

I tried to hide the smirk on my face by turning away from him and looking out to the unicorns again.

Zacharina nodded then flew off into the night, followed by the other unicorns.

"I don't know. I sometimes get the feeling that they understand every word we say."

Jay held his hand out to me. I still hadn't told him that, as well as unicorns understanding us, I could understand them and speak to them, too. Even now, with no other secrets between us, I wasn't quite ready to give this part of me up. It felt too real. It would mean admitting that there was something weird about me. The strangers had all talked about magic, and I'd sat there silent on the subject. Maybe I should have told them. After all, magic wasn't something to be ashamed of, but they all had powers that made sense. Azia could control dragons. Blaise could swim underwater. Castiel could actually change into an animal. My ability wasn't really so different from theirs, but I couldn't control the unicorns, nor could I turn into one. I could only talk to them, both verbally and telepathically.

"There you are!"

I turned to find my mother walking out onto the balcony.

"Sorry to interrupt you love birds, but the orchestra is packing up and people are leaving."

She moved toward us and kissed first Jay, then me, on our cheeks. "You two were just beautiful out there. You'll be the talk of the town tomorrow. The editor of the Echo told me himself he's going to put you on the front page."

"That's what I'm worried about!"

My mother furrowed her brows. "Why?"

"She's worried that they'll think she's awful for dancing with a man that isn't Fae's father."

My mother tutted, then brought me into a hug. "Of all the silly things to worry about. Didn't you hear what everyone was saying?"

I shook my head. I'd seen a lot of them looking at Jay and I dancing and chattering to themselves, but I'd not heard the topic of their conversations.

She put one hand on my shoulder and another on Jay's shoulder and began to guide us back inside.

"After they'd finished up telling me how beautiful Fae was, they all remarked how nice it was to see you looking so happy. You know, I'd not noticed it before, but they were right. You looked radiant tonight, and it had nothing to do with the dress or the hair and makeup. It was the look of complete happiness as you danced with Jay. It's been too long since I saw you so happy."

In the hall, a couple of stragglers were still getting their coats on, but in the main part, the maids had taken over the room and were clearing everything away.

"I was wondering if you'd permit me to escort Eliana to her room," Jay asked, his face a picture of complete innocence. Inside I felt the heat rise in embarrassment. Shockingly, my mother answered him with a wink.

"By the gods, that was embarrassing," I said five minutes later as we walked up the stairs to my room.

"Worth it, though," he answered, backing me up to the door to my suite and kissing me so hard that I completely forgot why I was mad. And, oh, he was right. It was worth it. Williamson and Avery were nowhere in sight. It was just Jay and me.

His lips crushed mine and I kissed back with urgency. I caressed his head in my hands, pulling him closer, deeper to me. My body ignited, excitement coursing through every pore. It had been a long time since anyone had made me feel this way. A really long time.

"I want... you... in my room" I breathed heavily, speaking between kisses.

"For however much I want that, and believe me, I do really want that, tonight isn't the night. Fae and her nanny are asleep behind that door."

I laughed, mainly so I didn't cry.

"There will be time for that," he said, kissing my nose, this time much more chastely. "Tonight was only our first date, remember."

"Second," I pouted.

This time he laughed. Somewhere I heard the clock strike midnight.

"Goodnight, Lia." He kissed my hand and walked away.

15TH MAY

I tiptoed past Judith, who was sleeping soundly on the bed my mother had brought up for her and checked the bassinet. Fae was sleeping too, her little chest rising and falling with each breath. Judith had taken her out of her frilly dress and put her in a onesie to sleep in. Fae had managed to kick her covers off completely, so I picked them up and tucked her back in, careful not to wake her. A big part of me wanted to pick the bassinet up and carry it into my bedroom, but that would no doubt wake Fae, which in turn would wake Judith. It was kinder to walk to my room alone and let them both sleep.

I pulled my dress over my head, then struggled to get out of the corset I'd been squeezed into hours before. When it finally loosened, I took a deep breath, letting my lungs expand and my body return to its natural post-birth shape. With a long sigh, I fell into bed and went to sleep almost immediately.

My dreams were full of happiness, of dancing and kissing. When I woke up, much later than usual, the memory of a dream of dancing with Luka lingered. But it wasn't a sad dream. He'd given his blessing to Jay and I. As I had let him go, he was finally letting me go.

Fae wasn't in her bassinet when I walked through my sitting room to get to the bathroom, and Judith was also absent. Judging by the brightness coming through the windows, the day was already half over, so it was no surprise that Judith would be elsewhere in the castle.

As I padded across the room in my bare feet, a sudden feeling of panic engulfed me. The sight of the framed picture on my wall, the one that had been there as long as I could remember, reminded me that we were still in danger.

Rumpelstiltskin.

I'd not given much thought to him in the past couple of days. My dates with Jay had eclipsed everything, but suddenly his name struck terror in my heart. Had Judith been told to stay in the room with Fae until I woke up? Or had something happened to them? I opened the door to the corridor. Avery caught sight of me in only my nightgown and blushed.

"Can I help you, Your Highness?" he asked, not knowing where to put his eyes.

"Have you seen Judith this morning?" I asked, my heart pounding in fear.

"The lady took Fae down for breakfast with the queen. The queen's orders were not to wake you."

Feeling foolish, I headed back into my room. I walked over to the framed print of the word *Rumpelstiltskin* and yanked it off the wall. The paint behind it was much brighter and more vivid than the rest of the room. Not that I cared. I wanted the thing to be gone. It had plagued my life enough. It wasn't as though I was likely to forget his name now anyway. I opened the door again.

"Avery. When Williamson comes on shift, can you take this and dispose of it?" I handed him the picture that had become the bane of my life.

Avery raised an eyebrow. "Where would you like me to dispose of it?"

"I don't care. Destroy it. Smash the glass and rip the picture up into a thousand pieces. I just don't want to see it ever again."

"Very well, Your Highness."

I shut the door and went for the bath I'd set out for ten minutes earlier.

Now that I knew Fae was all right, I let my mind drift back to Jay. To the kiss we'd shared before I'd retreated to my room. It was no chaste goodnight kiss on the cheek. It was full of the passion we'd both repressed for so long. I'd forgotten how wonderful it was to be touched, how my body felt like it was on fire with each caress. Unfortunately, I hadn't forgotten that beyond the door I'd been pushed against, my baby daughter—not to mention her nanny—had been sleeping.

I'd said goodnight to Jay, but I hadn't wanted to. I hadn't wanted the night to end at my door, but it had. Just because Williamson and Avery had given us some space didn't mean they weren't just around the corner.

But Jay and I would have our chance to be together again. Last night was just a promise of things to come.

I washed and dressed quickly and headed downstairs. I found Fae in the grand hall in the arms of my mother who was overseeing the cleanup of the event from the night before. She gave me a knowing smile as she handed Fae over.

"Did you have a good night?" she inquired with a smirk. My mother never smirked. It just wasn't something she did.

"I did, as a matter of fact. I was thinking I'd grab some food and head out to the staviary to see Jay."

"He's not in today." She saw my look and quickly added "He's in town sorting out an order, that's all. Apparently, you two were so busy glancing lovingly into each other's eyes the other day that neither of you checked the order and some of it's wrong. I'm sure he'll be back later."

Disappointment flooded through me. "Thank you. Do you want help clearing up?"

"I think we have everything in hand. Most of it was done last night. It's just the decorations that need taking down. It's such a glorious day, why don't you take Fae out for a walk around the castle grounds? Avery and Williamson can go with you."

She waved her hand to dismiss me, so I did as she suggested and took Fae outside. We spent the afternoon in the shade of a tree, resting on the lawn.

As the sun began to lower in the sky, two unicorns soared down and landed on the grass next to us, beating their wings so hard my hair blew across my face. Zacharina and Epiphany.

I scrambled up to my knees. "How are the unicorns doing?" I asked, sitting up. Like last night, I felt a lurch of foreboding.

"We are doing very well." Zacharina lowered herself, folding her legs beneath her. Epiphany frolicked around Fae in an attempt to make her giggle. *"I saw you last night. I hope you don't mind that we interrupted your*

romantic evening."

"Not at all. I'm sorry that I've not been out to see you in a while. I've been busy with the party and other things."

"Yes, I saw what other things have kept you away from us. Jay is a wonderful human. Although I cannot speak to him the way I speak to you, I feel that he understands the unicorns too in his own way."

"I know. I just wish I could have figured it out sooner. I only saw him last night and I miss him already. Does that sound stupid?"

"Not at all, young one. It sounds like the first flush of love."

I felt the blush rising to my cheeks. "I've seen Jay practically every day of my life. I didn't even know it was possible to miss someone after having them there all the time."

"You'd be surprised what is possible. You speak to us. Most humans would say that's impossible, but here we are having a conversation."

"In our heads," I pointed out. Everything she said, I heard in my mind, rather than my ears.

"It doesn't make it any less valid."

Thinking about talking the way Zacharina and I talked made me think back to the strangers, and the foreboding feeling in the pit of my stomach returned. I hadn't had a chance to tell her about them yet.

"I had a visit the other day from a group of strangers. They thought they might be my brothers and sisters."

Zacharina tilted her head to the side, and I saw a look of interest on her face. *"What made them think that?"*

I absent-mindedly picked at the blades of grass between my fingers as I thought back to the conversation

I'd had with them. "You know I'm adopted. They told me that they were adopted as newborns too. Their story is remarkably like mine. They were all left on the doorstep of a ruler of a kingdom by two women. They all had golden rings around their irises like I have. I always thought that had something to do with the unicorns."

Zacharina shook her head. *"While it's true that some unicorns have gold-colored coats or golden horns and, yes, golden eyes, I've yet to see that in humans. You are the only one I've ever met with eyes quite like yours. I cannot deny the link between us, but your eyes are nothing to do with the unicorn world."*

"Do you think they mean I have magic?"

She seemed to contemplate this for a while. *"I don't know much about magic apart from the magic of unicorns. I know it exists. Ask yourself this. Before these people turned up claiming to be your siblings, had you met other people of magic?"*

I thought back to the balls my mother and father had held in the past. "I've met some. We've played host to a number of dignitaries from Enchantia. They are full of magic."

"And did they have the gold ring around their eyes?"

I shook my head. "Before the other day, I'd not seen anyone with the gold ring. Not even the mages of Enchantia."

"But you do have magic. You can talk to us."

I leaned forward and gave her a stroke behind her ear.

On the picnic blanket beside me, Fae waved her fat fists at Epiphany, although she was yet to giggle. She was still so young. Her eyes were just like her father's. The same shade. There was no golden ring.

"They asked me to go with them," I said, turning

back to Zacharina. "They thought that a great disaster was about to befall The Vale as it had in their kingdoms. They were on a mission to change things. Put them back the way they used to be."

Zacharina rose to her feet. *"And you did not go with them despite sharing your magic and perhaps your blood?"*

"There's nothing I want to change," I said, following suit. "My life is as perfect as it has ever been. I've had sadness in the past, but my future looks wonderful. My future is here in The Vale."

She rubbed her head against my side. *"In that case, I'm very happy for you, child."* In spite of her words, there was an edge to her tone—a hint of worry or doubt.

"Do you know if anything bad is going to happen?" I asked, stroking my fingers through her mane.

"I'm no seer. I only see what you do. If you want my advice, do what makes you happy."

With that, she took to the sky, Epiphany following close behind.

I folded the picnic blanket, picked Fae up and placed her in her bassinet, and headed back to the house. Williamson and Avery, who had been watching me from a distance and enjoying their afternoon of sun, got up and followed.

"Is Jay not back yet?" I yawned, handing the bassinet to Judith as I entered the dining room.

Judith took Fae for her nighttime bath and to get her ready for bed. I was so tired I'd probably join them both after dinner. Judith was only to stay with Fae until I took over. I'd been lucky to have her in the sitting room of my suite for two nights, but tonight I was back to looking after Fae on my own, and I was already exhausted after last night's ball.

"Not yet," my mother answered, passing me a plate. "He sent word about an hour ago that he'd be a while yet. He told me to tell you to go to bed, and he'll see you in the morning. He wanted to get all the stuff put away in the staviary when he gets back."

I yawned again and waited for the servant to put food on my plate. I was almost too tired to eat it. However disappointed I was at not seeing Jay, I was craving my bed more.

Fae was already snuggled up in her bassinet when I entered my room after dinner. I thanked Judith, dismissing her for the evening, then took the bassinet into the bedroom where I placed it next to the bed. Picking Fae up, I snuggled us both into bed for her nightly feed. I sang a soft lullaby as her eyes began to droop, and before long, she was completely asleep.

I held her close, inhaling her baby smell, and kissed her head before putting her in her bassinet and covering her with a thin blanket. Closing my eyes, I fell into a deep, dreamless slumber.

Something woke me with a start. I sat up in bed, my heart pounding. I couldn't see anything, but even in the dark, I knew something was wrong. I strained my ears to hear Fae breathing. When I couldn't, I felt down to her bassinet, but it was empty. In the turmoil of my mind, I tried to make sense of it. I'd been exhausted when I came to bed. Could I have given Fae to Judith again and not remembered? I scrambled out of bed, but before I got anywhere close to the door to the sitting room, I saw something in the moonlight that sent terror into my soul. There was someone there in my room. This person was much shorter than Judith. It was a small man. In his arms was a baby—my baby.

"Who are you?" I hissed in a panic, my heart rate

accelerating.

"You know who I am," he said in a creaky voice. "Come on now, Eliana. You're an intelligent girl."

I took a step closer, but he stepped back and waggled a finger at me.

"Ah, ah, ah, don't come closer. You wouldn't want anything to happen to the child, would you?"

Now that my eyes had adjusted to the faint light, I could see him more clearly. In his arms, Fae was beginning to stir.

"Just hand her back, and I won't call the guards." My eyes flickered to the door. How had he managed to get past Avery and Williamson?

"I don't think your guards will pose a threat to me." He hopped up and down as if with excitement.

"What do you want?" My heart pounded. "I'll give you anything. Gold, I have gold. My mother..."

He cut me off. "Your mother cheated me all those years ago, but now I'd say this little beauty is mine. It's about time she paid off her debt. I've been waiting a long time for this moment."

I jumped forward with the intention of snatching Fae from his arms, but he held his free arm out toward me. A blast of deep purple light shot out, hitting me and sending me flying back to the bed. When I tried to move, I found I couldn't. His magic was holding me down.

"This has been fun, but I think I'll be going now!" He did a little dance and gave an odd laugh that sent tremors up my spine.

"Rumpelstiltskin!" I screamed. "Rumpelstiltskin!" I screamed his name so hard that Williamson or Avery, whichever of them was currently on guard, must have heard me.

Rumpelstiltskin smiled a crooked smile as Fae began screaming in his arms.

"What is owed is owed. A debt is a debt, and a name is a name. It doesn't matter how loudly you scream it, it will only ever be a name."

He began to sing to himself or perhaps to soothe Fae, who was having none of it and was screaming louder than ever. I struggled against his magic, but he was too strong.

"You can't take her!" I shouted. "Your rules. You can only take something of mine if you had given me something in return. You've given me nothing, and there is nothing I want from you. You have to give her back. You can't expect me to settle my mother's score. She promised you her firstborn. She's never given birth."

He looked like he was considering it, and, for a second, I hoped I might have gotten around his warped logic. But then, his grin widened. His body began to change shape, The grotesque, hunched figure shot upward and slimmed down until he was almost six feet tall. Bile rose in my throat as I recognized him. It was the man by the river who'd helped us free the unicorns from the net. He looked so much like Luka I almost cried out, but his face was twisted and mean.

"I gave you a knife, remember? You told me I could have anything in return."

He swished his coat, and the magical bonds holding me evaporated. I stood up to rush over to him, but he'd gone, disappearing into thin air along with Fae. The room was completely silent.

A glow of purple light hurtled toward the window, smashing right through it and down into the front courtyard of the castle.

"No!" I screamed, falling to the floor.

Fae was gone, and so was Rumpelstiltskin.

16TH MAY

"He's taken Fae!" I screamed, running through the door to my suite. Avery stood to attention as I raced past him.

I didn't know what I was doing or how to save her, so I ran through the palace to the front doors, screaming Rumpelstiltskin's name to wake everyone up. The guard on the front door seemed surprised to see me rushing toward him, but he saw the urgency in my face and I didn't need to yell at him to open the door. He just did it. Behind me, footsteps pounded. Turning, I saw Avery and a number of other guards who'd come to see what was going on.

At the top of the stairs, my mother's face appeared. "Eliana. What is it?"

"Rumpelstiltskin. He's got Fae."

My mother's face lost all color, but I didn't have time to explain further. When the thick oak doors had been opened enough for me to slip through the gap, I ran out into the night, my nightdress flapping behind me. Up ahead, the purple light hovered, moving slowly toward the main gates.

"Stop it!" I shouted loudly enough for the guards at the gate to hear as I pelted toward them.

Some of the guards, who had been following behind, ran right past me, their swords aloft, chasing after the purple light. They probably didn't even know what it was.

"Don't hurt her," I screamed. "It's Fae."

The guards stopped and turned around as my mother caught up to me. She grabbed my hand and held it tightly.

"That purple light is Rumpelstiltskin. He has Fae," I explained between sobs.

My mother pulled herself to her full height and walked toward her guards with the swords.

"Put your weapons down. Whatever you do, don't lose sight of that ball of magic." She spoke with authority, and the guards did exactly as she asked. "It is imperative that no one harms it. That is my granddaughter. Do not let her be taken."

The men sheathed their swords and began to walk slowly toward Rumpelstiltskin. Ahead in the distance, the two guards at the gates readied themselves for when the ball moved again. The line of guards increased as more ran out of the castle and began to edge their way around Rumpelstiltskin and Fae, circling around the purple light.

"What's happening?" Jay said, appearing at my side.

He had bits of straw in his hair which told me he'd fallen asleep in the staviary where he sometimes slept.

I pointed to the magic light.

"It's Rumpelstiltskin. He says I owe him." I heaved a breath and tried to tell him everything, but all I could think of was Fae. I couldn't even see her, but I knew she was in that light somewhere. I could hear the faint squeals of her cries, even from this distance.

"I'll kill him!" Jay muttered, striding forward and pulling a sword from one of the guard's sheaths. Before I could stop him or explain that the light held Fae, he raced forward, the sword aloft and a war cry on his lips.

I screamed his name, but he didn't hear me, so intent he was on hurting Rumpelstiltskin. Over the sound of Fae's cries and Jay's screams, I heard the sick laugh and the little tune of Rumpelstiltskin singing his own name to himself.

I could only watch in horror as the ball of light transformed back into Rumpelstiltskin. With relief, I saw Fae, unhurt but wailing, in his arms. The pair of them glowed with purple light, almost like ghosts of themselves. He danced down the driveway, twirling and taking dainty steps. He was dancing so slowly, and Jay was running at top speed, but they never seemed to get closer to each other. Rumpelstiltskin waved his free arm in the general direction of Jay, who was having a hard time pushing against the Rumpelstiltskin's magic. The whole scene seemed odd, as if time itself was somehow warped, and above everything else, all I could hear were the cries of my daughter.

The pain in my heart reached a crescendo, and I pushed past the wall of guards and ran after Jay. I had to get to Fae before the unimaginable happened. Rumpelstiltskin was only holding her loosely with one hand as he danced in circles to his disgusting song with only one word.

Light still surrounded the pair of them, though as Rumpelstiltskin twirled, it peeled off him, floating into nothing. He was completely surrounded on all sides now. The guards formed a complete circle around us. On the outside of the circle, I could hear my mother shouting. No longer was she the voice of authority, but the voice of a grandmother about to lose her granddaughter. I was vaguely aware of my father's voice joining the chorus of noise.

Inside the circle stood me, Jay, and Rumpelstiltskin with Fae. I ran forward, managing to catch up with Jay, but then I felt the force that was driving him back. It was invisible, but it was there. While I couldn't push past it, Jay kept trying, his legs running swiftly but not moving him an inch.

I grabbed his hands. "Stop running. You can't get closer."

"I'm not running," he wheezed. "He's got control of my legs. He's doing this."

As the circle around us closed in, Rumpelstiltskin twirls got faster and faster, and along with them, Jay's legs were moving so quickly they were nothing more than a blur. Sweat poured down his face, but his look of determination never faltered. As the guards closed in, there was a flash of light. The bonds holding Jay and me were broken, catapulting him forward so quickly that he went flying, tripped over the cobbles, and rolled right into the guards opposite, knocking some of them over. Rumpelstiltskin turned back into the purple ball of light and drifted upwards slowly before disappearing with a faint pop.

I stood stock-still in shock, unable to move, barely

able to breathe. The night was now dark and eerily silent. Then, just like that, everyone began to shout at once. The guards were in chaos, though one of them was shouting orders to grab the palace horses and unicorns to start scouring the nearby countryside.

Behind me, my mother's wails filled the air, but all I could think about was the silence between the noise. The silence that should have been filled with Fae's cries.

She was gone. Completely gone. I already knew there was no point in scouring the nearby countryside. If Rumpelstiltskin had run away, then maybe we would have had hope, but he had evaporated using magic. We'd already spent so much time looking for him and found no trace. What chance did we have of finding him now?

The only other person silent in all of this was Jay. I looked to where he'd fallen to see him lying on the ground. Blood poured through one of his trouser legs, and the other leg was bent at an unnatural angle. It was all I needed to bring me out of my stupor.

"Call a medic!" I yelled, rushing toward Jay. His skin was ashen, and tears fell down his cheeks.

"I couldn't stop him, Lia. I couldn't stop him. I tried."

"I know you did," I soothed, wiping his forehead with my sleeve. It came away soaked. "You did your best."

My parents were at my side in seconds. "Go get the court physician," my mother barked at one of the guards. "Quick. He's going into shock." She turned to another. "Get blankets and supplies... and you—" she spoke to yet another "—get one of the horses and go into town as quickly as you can. The court physician won't be enough. We need a team of doctors. Bring the best. Wake them up if you have to. Tell them they will be paid handsomely."

All around me was a hive of activity. I couldn't call it chaos, because, thanks to my mother, everyone had a job to do. By the time the court physician appeared with his doctor's bag, my father was already heading out on his horse to look for Rumpelstiltskin and taking the guards with him. Above us, the sky was filled with unicorns. Only a few lived in the staviary. These were the wild ones we'd saved, ironically, with Rumpelstiltskin's help.

I saw Zacharina and shouted up at her, not caring anymore if people thought I was crazy. "Rumpelstiltskin took Fae."

She nodded, and in my head, I heard the words, *"We'll find her."*

As one, the unicorns bolted off into the sky.

The palace courtyard was now empty, but lights blazed in every window of the palace itself as the staff were awakened by the commotion.

All through everything, I cradled Jay's head as he slipped in and out of consciousness.

The court physician, a small, wispy, gray-haired man by the name of Smith pulled a vial out of his bag and injected the contents into Jay's arm.

"It will make him sleep," he explained as he began to cut the length of Jay's trousers to get a better look at his legs.

"He's broken both legs. I can see that. How badly, I don't know. He'll need to go to a hospital, that is certain."

"I've sent one of the guards to fetch the best medics in town," my mother said

"We'll need a stretcher and a way to transport him. I have a stretcher in my office."

My mother looked stunned, and for a second, she

lost her composure. “I sent all the horses out. There’s none left to pull the carriage.”

“We’ll worry about that when the time comes,” the physician said. “Maybe one of your guards will come back. For now, I need the stretcher.”

“Right!” Without bothering to ask one of the servants that had begun to gather in the courtyard, she ran back into the castle to bring the stretcher back herself.

“Will he be okay?” I asked, tears streaming down my face. He was completely asleep, which was the only mercy in this night of horrors.

“I’d not like to say too soon. This leg is fractured badly. The bone has ripped right through the skin. I’ve not looked at the other leg closely yet, but it’s bent at a funny angle. If he ever walks again, he’ll need months of physical therapy.”

I measured my breaths, concentrating on each inhale and exhale. It was the only way not to have a complete meltdown. Doing that would only take the physician’s attention from Jay.

My mother was quick to come back with the stretcher. She placed it on the floor next to Jay, but the physician had moved from stemming the blood flowing from Jay’s leg to feeling his wrist for his pulse. I looked up to the skies. The three of us moving Jay onto the stretcher would only hurt him more, I was sure of it. His legs were so mangled that I was afraid any movement would cause more injury. We’d have to wait for the town medics to arrive, but what then? We’d have to waste time hooking the horses up to the carriage. The only person that knew how to do that quickly was Jay.

I closed my eyes and called to Zacharina with my mind, hoping she was still in range enough to hear me.

“What is it, my child?”

"Will you come back to the palace? I need to hook a horse up to a carriage, but the horse isn't here yet. I need to get Jay to a hospital quickly. He's in a bad way."

"I'll fly him."

"No, I need you to pull a carriage. He'll be on a stretcher. I know you don't believe in unicorns working and hauling things for humans, but..."

"Hush, of course I'll pull the carriage. I'll be back as quickly as my wings will fly me."

"Who were you talking to?" my mother asked, eyeing me curiously. "You were moving your lips."

There was no point in denying the truth now. I didn't care if anyone thought I was crazy anymore. I felt more crazy now than I'd ever been.

"I was speaking to Zacharina, the unicorn, with my mind," I said flatly. "She's coming back to pull the carriage to take Jay to the hospital."

My mother raised her eyebrows in surprise, but she didn't question me. "Meet her at the staviary and get one of the servants to help you."

Leaving Jay almost broke my heart as much as losing Fae had, but getting him help was more important than staying by his side.

I jumped up and ran around the palace, almost bumping into Williamson, who was still in his nightclothes.

"I need help. I need to prepare a carriage. A unicorn will be here in a few minutes to pull it. Help me get everything ready."

It was a job I didn't have much experience with, but between Williamson, Zacharina, and I, we managed to get the carriage out into the courtyard. Epiphany was too small to help, so she cantered alongside her mother.

The medics showed up not much later, a whole

swarm of them. The guard must have knocked on every door in town to bring so many. Between them, they got Jay onto the stretcher and into the carriage. Williamson jumped up to drive and a couple of the physicians hopped up into the back of the carriage with Jay.

They held the door open, waiting for me to jump up. I hesitated. Even though Fae was gone, leaving the palace made it seem so final, like I was giving up on her.

"I'll be here," my mother said, wrapping her arms around me. "I won't leave until we've found her and brought her back."

I choked back the sobs and stepped up into the carriage.

I barely noticed the time going by as we rushed down the track to town. Both physicians, Smith and one I didn't know, were busy working on Jay, muttering to each other in hushed tones. I didn't care what they were saying. I just wanted him in the hospital where he could get help.

Pain churned inside me as I continued to wipe Jay's brow, stroking his hair. I whispered words into his ear in the hopes he knew I was with him. But all I could think about was Fae. My breasts ached, full of milk as they were. It was way past her feeding time. Would Rumpelstiltskin know what to feed her? Did he know anything about babies at all? What if his intent wasn't to look after her? The guy obviously didn't mind maiming innocent creatures. I felt the bile rise in my throat as I thought about Epiphany caught in a trap laid by him. Thinking of all the sadistic, horrible things he could do to Fae wasn't helping me stay calm, but it was all I could think of. Grotesque images floated in my mind. I leaned over and threw up on the carriage floor as we came to a stop outside the hospital.

Williamson jumped down from the front of the carriage and spoke through a window in the back.

"I'll go and get someone to help."

The stench of vomit filled the back of the carriage, making me feel even more nauseated. In the darkness of the carriage, I could barely see Jay at all, so I held his hand, willing the blood to keep pumping through it, circulating around his body. It didn't take a lot of light to see the patch of blood on his trousers growing. I'd moved past the stage of hoping he'd walk again and moved onto willing him to survive the night. The doctors didn't say anything to me, but I could tell by their concerned whispers that this was more serious than I'd first thought. Within minutes, a group of four doctors or nurses, I couldn't tell, ran out and began to pull Jay on his stretcher from the carriage. The two physicians that had traveled with us helped, leaving me alone in the carriage surrounded by the stink of my own stomach contents.

In all my years, I'd never been ignored. As a princess, people talked to me first, making sure I was happy above all others. Now, in the dark as the team hoisted Jay onto a gurney, I'd never felt more alone. I was paralyzed with fear, scared to even get out of the carriage.

"Come on. He'll need you when he wakes up." I looked up to see Williamson standing outside the carriage door with his hand out. I took it and felt the cool breeze and fresh air as I stepped down.

I followed the team in through the hospital doors from the darkness of the night to the burning lights of the hospital reception.

The team of people dashed down a corridor, and when I tried to follow, a woman held out her hand to stop me.

"I'm afraid you can't go down there, miss."

I looked at her through tearful eyes. A look of recognition dawned on her face, and she fell into a curtsy.

"I'm most awfully sorry, Your Highness, I didn't know..."

She didn't know. She couldn't. My daughter was gone, and Jay might not survive the night.

"It's okay," I said, even though it wasn't, because what else could I say? What else was there to say?

17TH MAY

At some point, the night had given way to day. At the hospital, the medics had rushed Jay into the operating room, and I had been shown to a private room for grieving families. The nurse assured me it was only because they didn't want the general public staring at me, but it felt appropriate. I was grieving. The loss of my daughter, the possible loss of Jay. No one would give me an idea of if he'd survive the surgery. All I could do was watch the sun come up through the window and sip on weak coffee that was brought to me every half hour or so.

The tears I'd cried so freely before had dried up. The pain was as acute as before, but the tears wouldn't come. Pressure built in my head, which I was only able to alleviate with the steady flow of coffee.

The manager of the hospital came to ask if I needed anything. I could tell she didn't quite know what to say to me. I wondered if she'd been told about Fae or if she thought I was only sad over Jay.

"Do you know if he's all right yet?"

She shook her head sadly. "Not yet. They are doing everything they can. We'll know more when he's out of surgery. I promise, he's got the best of the best looking after him."

Her words were meant to be a comfort, but they didn't pierce the wall of pain that surrounded me. "They are doing everything they can" meant nothing.

I paced the room for hours until the door opened, and a familiar face greeted me. It was Williamson. He'd gone home and changed and was now in a fresh uniform. Avery stood behind him.

"Any news?" I asked, but I already knew the answer was *no*. It was written on their faces. Before they even spoke, I fell into Williamson's arms and began to weep. The hours of pent-up emotion came pouring out of me in the form of tears.

Williamson and Avery had been my shadows for a long time. They'd gone everywhere I had, watching over me. I'd never thought of them as friends, but now as Williamson held me tight as I drenched his jacket and Avery rubbed my back, I was glad they were there with me.

I didn't notice when the door opened, but when Williamson pulled back, I saw that the hospital manager had once again entered the room. This time she had a smile on her face, and she beckoned me to follow her out of the room.

We walked down a corridor decorated with bright paintings. I hadn't noticed when I'd come in, but the hospital was an old stone building with beautiful moldings and a polished stone floor. We stopped at a door with the number *11* on a brass plate screwed to it.

"His doctor is in here with him. I'll make sure you aren't disturbed."

Jay was still asleep, both his legs splinted and bandaged. Next to him, his doctor was writing something in a chart.

The man walked around the bed to greet me. Instead of the usual bow, he held out his hand.

"I'm Dr. Coveney. I'm the surgeon who operated on your friend. He's a strong one. His left leg will be in a splint for at least three months, the right considerably longer. We'll have to take it month by month to see how he does."

"Will he walk again?"

"I don't want to give you false hope. There was a lot of damage, especially to his right leg. I believe he will regain movement, but how much, I wouldn't like to say right now. We've placed the bones back together. It was a nasty break, but the bone was in clean pieces rather than shattered completely. He'll need a lot of work to get any movement back. It's going to be a long journey, and there is a chance he might never walk again."

My insides hurt with all the pain. It was too much. "Thank you for everything you've done."

The doctor nodded his head. "I'm sorry I couldn't do more, but I promise he'll receive the best care. He's been given something for the pain. He'll be a little woozy when he wakes up."

The surgeon left as Jay began to murmur. I ran to his side and stroked his head as his eyes fluttered open.

"Fae?"

I shook my head, not trusting myself to speak.

Saying she was still missing would only make it more real, and I didn't want it to be more real than it already was.

I felt his body stiffen. His legs must have hurt with the movement, but his face showed no pain, only anger.

"I'm sorry, Lia. I'll find him. I'll find him and kill him with my own bare hands."

"Shh, you're not well. My father has half the kingdom out looking for Fae and for Rumpel... him. There's nothing more you can do right now. You need to rest."

He clenched his fists. "Rest? How can I rest knowing Fae is with that... that... creature. I don't even know what he is. He's not human."

"You have to rest because I need you. I need you, Jay."

My body trembled, but I held the tears back. He didn't need me to dissolve into a soggy mess on his hospital bed.

Jay finally took his eyes from the ceiling where he'd fixed them on some spot and turned them to me. "I'll bring her back. Once I'm healed, I'll go and look for her, and I won't stop until I find her." He took my hand in his. "I promise you, Lia. If it's the last thing I do, I'll bring her back safely to you."

My already broken heart shredded even further. "You can't. The doctors think you'll need months of recovery time."

He looked down at his legs, seeming to notice them for the first time since waking up. Both were covered by a sheet, but the shape of them made it clear they were heavily bandaged and splinted.

His voice cracked. "What exactly did the doctor say? Will my recovery time be sooner if I work hard at rehabilitation?"

I lowered my voice, trying to keep it as gentle as possible, as though a quiet voice could soften the blow I was about to give him.

"The doctor told me that it will be a long road, and there is a chance..."

"He told you that I'll never walk again, right?"

I shook my head. "He said there was a chance of that, but he also said that he expected you to regain some movement. I know you. You never let anything stop you when you put your mind to something. You're the guy who gave me a date in a warehouse full of straw just so we could be alone, remember?"

"This isn't a date, and I'm assuming this is no warehouse," he replied.

"No, but to give up hope is to give up everything, and I refuse to do that. I'm not giving up on Fae, and I won't give up on you."

The anger dropped from his face, but it was replaced by something much worse. He looked helpless and hopeless.

"I promised myself that I'd always protect you, and when Fae came along, I promised myself I'd protect her too. The last thing Luka said to me before he died was to look after you. I've failed on every level."

"You haven't failed me. You did everything you could." I squeezed his hand. "You have a decision to make right now. You can either succumb to self-pity, or you can take a deep breath and help me fight this. I don't know how, but if I know anything about you, you'll come up with something. I love you, Jay. It took me a long time to see it, but when it finally hit me, it punched me with such a force. You and I are in this together." I stood up. "I'm going to get you a drink. When I come back, I want no more self-pity, because if there is something I do know, it's that self-pity never solved any problem."

Out in the corridor, I practically bumped into the hospital manager, who seemed to be in deep conversation with Williamson and Avery. I was pleased to see they both had a cup of coffee in their hands.

"Please, can I have some water or juice for Jay?" I asked the manager.

"Of course. I spoke to the doctor. The best physiotherapists are being brought in by the hospital. I've also spoken to some friends in a clinic in Enchantia and they said they're available to come over and try some magical remedies for your friend. Of course, we don't usually practice magic here as a rule, but for the royal family, we'll make an exception. I'm led to believe that although magic doesn't work perfectly for all normal ailments and scrapes, it certainly can help when it's used along with proper medicine."

She left to fetch some juice. It was clear that Jay was only getting this treatment because of who I was. I wondered what would have happened if he was just some regular person off the street. Still, that wasn't my concern, and I had too much to worry about without wondering if everyone else in the hospital was getting weak coffee and promises of magical help.

"Let's look at this logically," Jay said as I nudged the door to his room open with my hip to get in with a jug of juice and two cups.

I noticed he'd managed to sit himself up a little by propping pillows behind his back. He looked a lot more animated than he had just moments before. The pain of losing Fae still gripped me, but his strength fortified my resolve to keep fighting.

"What do we know about Rumple?" he asked.

"I don't know," I said, pouring him a cup of the juice

and passing it to him. "He's a thief, he's magic, he's wicked, he's strange." I sat down in the chair next to the bed. "He likes to make unfair bargains."

"Exactly!" Jay said pointing his index finger at me. "Every person who has ever met him has made a bargain with him, and all of them have lost something huge for the price of something small. Your mother is a perfect example. She needed help because her father was being abusive. Rumple could have done anything to her father. He's magic, he could have made him disappear if he wanted, but, instead he spun gold for her, and in exchange, he asked for her firstborn. You were collateral damage. I guess he took Fae because your mother never gave birth."

"Actually, that's not quite true," I said, remembering what he'd told me in my room as he'd snatched Fae. "Remember the guy who helped us save the unicorns from the magical net in the river? That was him. He took Fae in exchange for that knife he lent me. Apparently, I told him I'd give him anything he wanted, and he took that statement literally."

Jay winced at my words, and the edges of his mouth began to fall. "The man, or whatever he is, is the worst form of pond scum."

"He is. I wondered why he looked so much like Luka. I guess it was his way of making him seem believable to me... trustworthy."

"That just proves my point, though. Rumpel only turns up when people are in dire need. When they're at their most desperate. That's when he can get what he wants out of them."

All the stories I'd heard about him certainly seemed to point in that direction. "My mother was in real need. I was only in need because of the unicorns drowning, although he was the one that threw that net down in the first place. It was hardly a fair trade."

"Going back to using you to get back to your mother," Jay said, leaning forward. "Maybe Rumple was the one who put the idea of your mother being able to spin straw into gold into her father's head in the first place. From what your mother said the other morning, the man was a drunk. He probably picked up the notion in a tavern or something."

"That might be true, but we'll never know. My grandfather died years ago. I don't know how this helps us anyway."

"It helps because we know Rumpelstiltskin turns up when he sees opportunity. He takes people and manipulates them. Usually, the people he manipulates are at the very end of their rope. What if we hire someone who pretends to be wealthy but down on their luck? Maybe a sick kid or something? We could have them sitting in a bar telling people that they'd give every penny they have to make their son well."

I mulled it over in my mind. There were so many taverns in the local area. Hundreds. The chances of him being in one at the same time as the person we hired were slim. Still, if this plan gave Jay some hope, maybe he'd recover quicker.

"I'll speak to Williamson and ask him to go to the castle," I said. "I doubt my father will be in, but my mother will. She can set this up."

"Great, but instead of hiring one person, tell her to hire as many as she can," Jay said. "Come up with many different reasons a person could be down on their luck. We need to mix the story up a bit, because we don't know what it is he wants now."

I asked Williamson to bring my mother to the

hospital rather than sending her a message. I knew her well enough to know that she'd want to speak to Jay and me about the plan.

Deep in my heart, I knew it was pointless. Rumple had what he wanted right now. In the future, he'd need something else to keep him occupied, but right now, he'd be keeping a low profile. He wasn't the kind of criminal that liked to flaunt his wins. Still, if this kept Jay and Mother occupied and gave them something to do, it would take their attention off me. I'd made a decision, and I knew that if either of them knew what I was about to do, they'd stop me. In Jay's case, he'd either try and talk me out of it or try and come with me despite two broken legs. My mother would be even more drastic and have guards watch my every move.

When she turned up, it was with a task force of palace advisors. Usually, she wouldn't travel without guards, but there were simply none left. With the exception of Williamson and Avery at the hospital, they all were out scouring The Vale for my baby girl.

"Williamson told me you had a plan," my mother said, taking the only other seat in the room. Behind her, the advisors stood in a semicircle, all of them with notepads in their hands ready to write things down.

"We know a bit about Rumpelstiltskin," Jay began. He was so much more animated than before. "We know he likes to barter, but he only does it when he knows the prize at stake is huge, and he can't lose. He has a strange sense of what's right. He could easily steal the things he covets, but he doesn't. He makes people swap them for his help..."

I stood up while Jay talked and filled my mother and the advisors in on his plan. He looked so much happier now that he had purpose. My mother, too, was absorbed in every word he said.

"I'm just going out to get some air," I said, opening the hospital door. Jay and my mother barely noticed.

"Tell Jay and my mother that I've gone out to look for Fae," I said to Avery. "Tell them I'll be taking the mother unicorn."

I waited for either Avery or Williamson, who was also listening, to try to stop me. They wouldn't be able to, of course, but they'd do their best. It was a mark of the seriousness of the situation that they didn't even try.

"I'll take you on horseback up to the castle," Avery said. "She'll probably be around there."

The journey to the castle was swift, and as predicted, Zacharina was standing in the meadow near the castle. Epiphany stood with her.

Jumping down from Avery's horse, I ran over to Zacharina.

"I have no good news to tell you, dear child. The unicorns have spread far and wide searching for her."

"I know. I'm grateful. I was hoping you'd let me search for her. I was hoping you'd take me."

"I'll take you anywhere you wish. You know that, but your fear of heights..."

"The fear of not finding my daughter is much greater."

She nodded, then bent her knees to allow me to climb onto her back. I knew before we even launched into the air that I wouldn't find Fae. If my father, all his guards, and all the unicorns couldn't, then I didn't stand a chance, but by not helping to look for her, I was dying inside. I'd given Jay a reason to feel hope by giving him a task to set his mind to. Flying around The Vale was my task. If it took away some of the pain in my heart and allowed me to breathe a little more easily, at least then I'd be able to think clearly.

The gust of wind that hit my face as we took to the air made me gasp. My stomach lurched as the ground got further and further away, but I kept my eyes on the ground, hunting for any clue as to Rumpelstiltskin's whereabouts. I didn't even know what I was looking for. He was hardly likely to be walking the streets with my daughter.

I instructed Zacharina to head away from Shipley. The town would be thoroughly searched by the castle guards. Instead, I was going to comb the countryside for small outbuildings or tiny cottages away from other people.

Epiphany flew beside us, pumping her wings frantically to keep up. We flew for hours, dipping to the ground every so often to knock on a door or peek through a window of an isolated cottage. As the sun began to set, I knew I'd done no better than the castle guards had. I'd knocked on the doors of scores of cottages, only to be looked upon with curiosity. I guessed it wasn't every day that the daughter of the king knocked on people's doors.

As the sun faded in the sky, I directed Zacharina to take me back to the hospital. I'd lost my last chance of looking for Fae. My mother would never let me leave her sight ever again after pulling a stunt like this. But as the houses became denser and the hospital building came into view, a thought crossed my mind. Maybe this wasn't my last chance, after all.

"Zacharina," I said, leaning down and speaking into her ear. "Take me to the inn. There's someone I need to find."

18TH MAY

It turned out that there was more than one inn in Shipley. I'd naively thought I could fly into town, walk into the nearest inn, and find the strangers who had come to see me at the palace. Instead, I walked the streets, trying to keep as inconspicuous as possible, which wasn't easy with two unicorns in tow. While The Vale was full of unicorns, they usually stuck to the forests and meadows. The streets were practically empty due to the lateness of the hour, but the few people we did see stared at us. I saw the light of recognition in some of them. Others were so taken with Zacharina and Epiphany that they didn't even notice the princess by their side.

After a couple of hours, I stumbled into a smaller inn on the edge of town. My feet hurt, and my stomach grumbled as I walked through the front door.

I'd almost lost hope, not even knowing if the strangers were traveling using their real names or if they were even still in Shipley. The inn on the edge of town was not one of the finer establishments and not anywhere I'd expect princes and princesses to stay, so I was surprised to see Deon in the reception area. His head was buried in a book, or so I thought, until I walked closer and saw that he was actually writing a letter and using the book to rest it on.

"Deon."

He looked up, a smile coming to his lips when he saw who had caught his attention.

"Eliana! You came to us. We were planning to leave first thing in the morning. I was just writing a letter to my wife to let her know where I am." His voice warmed a little on the words *my wife*. "There's not always a post office where we travel."

I nodded, unsure what to say.

He stood, tucked the writing paper between two pages of the book, and placed the pen in his top pocket.

"I'll get the others to come down. I'm sure they'll open the restaurant if we ask. We seem to pay an inordinate amount of money wherever we go. As a result, people trip over themselves to help us."

I nodded sheepishly. I still wasn't used to these strange people who proclaimed to be my siblings, but were so different from me. "I'd like to talk to you all. I have my unicorns outside. I'll go and let them know I found you."

Deon raised an eyebrow at the mention of unicorns, but made no comment.

Less than ten minutes later, the restaurant in the inn was open, and our orders were being taken. Both Azia and Blaise only ordered a drink. Deon ordered some weird kind of salad, so I was glad when Castiel requested a large steak. I couldn't remember the last time I'd eaten. I ordered a steak too, although more well done than Castiel's. Nyre, the pretty little dragon, found herself a place to sit on Castiel's shoulder, no doubt waiting to help him with his meal.

"I'm glad you decided to speak to us again," Deon said.

"We'd given up on you," Blaise added. Her red-blonde hair flowed around her shoulders, making her look every inch the princess she was.

"I guess you guys haven't heard the news," I said, playing with the edge of the tablecloth.

I had hoped they'd already heard. They would only have had to look at the cover of a newspaper to see what had happened. Wanted posters were already plastered all over town with a reward for Rumpelstiltskin's capture. But I got the feeling they didn't like to be seen.

"What happened?" Azia asked, sitting forward in her chair. "Fae?"

She was a perceptive one. The only one to notice I hadn't walked in with my baby.

"She's been kidnapped." My voice faltered on the word, but I pressed forward. "Rumpelstiltskin took her last night... or the night before. I don't even know what day it is anymore."

Blaise gasped and covered her mouth.

"I've been at the hospital all day with my boyfriend. He tried to stop him, but Rumpelstiltskin has magic and Jay does not. Jay's legs are broken. He's pretty messed up. I already told you about my magic. Talking to unicorns isn't much help when a dangerous imp is stealing your child."

I was babbling and couldn't seem to stop myself

until the waiter came to our table with drinks. No one spoke as our drinks were handed out, but Azia held her hand out and placed it on top of mine.

"We'll find her," she said when the waiter had left. "This is what we were talking about the other day when we met you. Something has brought the evil back. Did this Rumpels..."

"—stiltskin," I ended for her.

"Yes, did he ever do anything before like this, or is it out of the blue?"

"He told my mother that he'd take her firstborn in exchange for helping her. That's why I think she took a baby from a stranger, no questions asked, when I was brought to the castle as a newborn. She never wanted to give birth in case he came for her child." A lump formed in my throat, choking me. "He came for mine instead. My father has half the kingdom out looking for Fae. It's in all the newspapers, posted all over town. I even knocked on doors myself, but there is no trace."

"He won't be here," Azia said. "This situation is bigger than The Vale. Things like this are happening all over. Admittedly yours is the worst so far. We think it's something to do with Urbis."

"Urbis? You think that's where he's taken Fae?"

"I don't know for sure. A friend of mine thought it had something to do with the gods."

Castiel rolled his eyes at this, but remained silent. I could see that it was a bone of contention between the group.

"The gods?" I was a believer, but I had always figured they were too powerful to actually come to our world.

"I know it sounds odd. I didn't believe in the gods at all, but my friend thought that at least one of them had something to do with it. She believed that the Fae and the mages of Enchantia and other magical beings weren't powerful enough for what is going on. The only beings with this kind of power are the gods."

I noticed Castiel wasn't looking at her as she spoke.

"What do you think, Castiel?"

He shrugged. "I don't believe in gods. Where I come from, nature is god. The earth, the trees, the animals. We are all enmeshed together. I don't believe that magical beings sit on the clouds above us playing harps."

"I know at least one that frequents the night clubs of Urbis," Azia interjected.

A knot of embarrassment ran through me. I'd pondered this exact thing on the day in the meadow before Fae was born.

"I believe in the gods, but I believe them to be powerful in a good way. I saw Rumpelstiltskin. He looked more like an imp than a god, though he could shapeshift, and I think he might have been able to read minds, but I'm not sure. He turned into a weird facsimile of my dead husband. He could have seen his picture in the paper, though. I don't know."

At this, Blaise burst into tears. Azia passed her a tissue.

"You've gone through so much," Blaise said. "I'm so sorry for all this. This is awful."

"But this is what we are here for," Azia reminded her. "This is what we are doing. We're going to put an end to this, whatever *this* is." She turned to me. "You told us the other day that you didn't want to come with us. Am I correct in thinking you've changed your mind?"

"If you think you can help me find Fae, yes."

Everyone around the table nodded. "Of course. We're heading to Urbis, but the plan is to stop in Aboria along the way. We'll visit the royal palace there and see if they've experienced anything strange lately. I haven't seen anything yet, but I'm sure it's coming."

"I'm scared if I leave The Vale, and someone brings Fae back, I'll miss it."

"We are not asking you to abscond," Azia said gently. "Tell your parents you're coming with us. We try to travel incognito, most of the time going by foot or renting a carriage when we can do that without arousing suspicion, but we're going to cities. We're all keeping in contact with our families as best we can by mail. Tell your family our next destination is Mosa in Aboria and then on to Urbis. They can send letters to the main post offices there. Deon has been writing ten letters a week to his wife."

"Seven," Deon corrected. "We're newlyweds. I got married, and then this lot showed up."

"Congratulations."

"Thank you. So are you coming?"

"I have no choice. I need to find my daughter."

"We will find her," Azia said.

It was strange to see how four people—people I'd only met once—cared about what was happening to me and my daughter. There was a bond between us that I couldn't explain. They said they thought we were siblings. I wasn't so sure, but I could feel some kind of connection. I'd felt it the other day when they'd come to the castle to speak with me. It was more than their willingness to help me; there was a thread of energy that ran through us. I'd felt something building within me since the night I first heard Zacharina speak, but I'd been so caught up in everything else going on that hadn't really paid attention to it. These people had told me it was magic.

Well, magic sure beat crazy, but it scared me all the

same.

I associated magic with people from far off lands like Enchantia and people like Rumpelstiltskin, who used it to hurt people. Now I had some kind of magic, and I didn't know how to turn it to good.

The waiter appeared with our food, and my stomach grumbled again. Nyre hopped excitedly up and down on Castiel's shoulder as his steak was placed in front of him.

"Can you control your dragon?" Castiel grumbled, pulling his plate to him and trying to shoo the small purple dragon from his shoulder.

"Nyre, come here. I'll order you something if you like, but you've eaten already this evening."

Evidently, Nyre didn't care that she'd already eaten; she was still hungry. Azia asked the waiter to bring her a plate of whatever they had left in the kitchen. The waiter plastered on a fake smile and headed back to the kitchen.

I devoured my food quickly, grateful for the full feeling in my stomach and for the people around me. I'd forgotten what it felt like to talk to people that didn't live or work in the castle. My life had been so insular and secluded. Beneath the agony of losing my daughter, I felt a spark of something else—excitement and crippling nervousness. I was going to not only leave the castle where I'd spent most of my days, but also the Kingdom of the Vale. I'd never left the kingdom once in all my years. I had never wanted to before now, but as I thought about the trip ahead, I realized I was looking forward to seeing something new. Above all that, I'd be actively looking for my daughter rather than doing what I always did, passively sitting my tower letting everyone else do the work. This was my time.

The others bickered good-naturedly as we ate our fill, and I tried to get a good take on them. In some ways, they were remarkably alike. They all had spirit and energy, although that might have had something to do with the magic running through all of them. In other ways, they differed immensely. For a start, they looked nothing alike. The two girls both had blonde hair, although where Azia's was dark and curly, Blaise's strawberry-blonde hair flowed in waves around her shoulders. If someone had told me they were sisters, I wouldn't have thought anything about it. Castiel, however, had jet-black hair and dark eyes, which contrasted with the golden ring around the iris. Deon looked like someone's good-natured big brother. He was taller and built thicker than the wiry Castiel, with thick arms and a smile perpetually on his face. Of all of them, he was the one I trusted the most. There was something about him that made me feel comfortable. He seemed easygoing compared to the others, but he wasn't stupid; he just let the others have their say before jumping in with his own observations. Blaise talked the most, chattering about her life in Atlantice. I had a feeling that after a few hours in her company, I'd need a rest. Azia was obviously the leader of the group. I noticed that she kept the others motivated, while Castiel sulked a lot.

By the time I'd finished, I felt more energized than ever. Azia had made it very clear to me that they'd put looking for Fae at the top of their priority list.

"I have to go pack," I said, standing up from the table.

Azia stood too. "I'll walk you out."

I bade farewell to the others and walked back through the inn to the main entrance with Azia by my side. She slipped her arm in mine, and for the first time, I felt that maybe I did have a sister. I couldn't express how nice it felt.

"I just wanted to say how sorry I am about Fae," she said. "I know I said it in there, but I understand how painful this is for you. I almost lost my brother thanks to this... whatever it is. It was the worst feeling of my life. I can't even imagine what you are going through right now, but you know something? I can feel her."

"You can feel her?"

She looked to the side as we stood in the entranceway. "I didn't want to say anything in front of the others because I didn't want to upset you in case you thought I was being... weird... but there's an energy between us. Our magic binds us. I've felt it strengthen with each one of us I've met, but when I met you, I felt it doubly. I felt Fae's energy too. Don't you feel it?"

I thought about what she was saying. I had felt an energy, a connection between Fae and me, but I'd put it down to being her mother. I hadn't associated it with the energy I felt from the strangers.

The strangers... I was going to have to think of a different term for them. They would be strangers no more.

"You think she's magic?"

"Maybe not yet, but I think she has the potential to be. Whatever it is that marks us as different, she has it too."

"But her eyes. They don't have a gold ring like ours. They look like her father's more than mine."

"My mother once told me that the gold ring only appeared around my irises when I was two or three. Perhaps she'll get hers when she's older."

She pushed the inn door open, and we stepped outside. Zacharina immediately trotted over to us.

"You said you feel her. Do you..." I couldn't bring myself to say the final words.

"Yes. I think she's still alive. I know she is. Do me a favor. Close your eyes."

Normally, I would have thought it a strange request from someone I didn't really know, but Azia was different. I closed my eyes and Azia took both of my hands in hers. The energy ran through us like electricity through a closed circuit.

"You can feel my energy, right?"

I nodded. I could barely feel anything else.

"It's different from yours. Can you feel the difference?"

I paid close attention to the new feelings rushing through me. At first, it was just one massive, overwhelming rush running through my body, but as I concentrated, the energy became strands. Two different strands of the same energy.

"Keep going. You'll soon be able to feel Blaise, Castiel, and Deon. Their energy will be much weaker because they aren't touching us and they're inside, but they are there."

The magic pulsed through me, and the strands separated again. Three small strands peeled off, and then another—smaller, much faster, familiar.

"I feel Fae!" I said excitedly. "Does that mean she's close?"

I dropped my hands and opened my eyes. The energy dropped away.

"I wish I could say it does," Azia said. "I feel lots of strands. I feel them stronger when I'm close, but I also feel them stronger when their emotions are running high. It could be that you feel Fae's energy more than mine because you're her mother. I can still feel her, though. I feel that she is well, but I don't feel her close by. I told you before that I think this will end in Urbis. We are pretty sure it started there with our births. I'd bet the whole kingdom of Draconis on her being there."

My excitement faded. Urbis was a long, long way away.

19TH MAY

My stomach squeezed tightly as I stood at the front of the hospital, not quite daring to step up through the large front doors.

I'd committed the ultimate sin in my mother's eyes. I'd left without taking my guards, without telling her I was going. I was in no doubt that Avery and Williamson had told her that I'd gone looking for Fae with Zacharina, but when I'd set off, even I didn't really know where I was going to look or how long I'd be gone. I certainly hadn't expected to take all day. The clock had long since struck midnight, which brought me into day three without my daughter. Three days I'd gone without seeing her face, without feeling her little body next to mine.

Did Rumpelstiltskin know how to keep an infant as young as Fae alive? Was that even a concern of his? It was all well and good Azia telling me she could still feel Fae, but what did that mean?

When Azia had left me outside the inn, I had tried feeling Fae's energy again. Without Azia's help, it was lost to me. That was another reason I was prepared to fight with my mother to be allowed to go with the strangers... my siblings. I needed their magic. I needed to feel Fae, to know she was alive.

It was going to be the fight of my life. My mother had never intentionally let me out of her sight before, not without guards, at least, and even then I'd been permitted no further than Shipley or the meadows surrounding the castle. She was already going to be angry with me for leaving her today... yesterday.

I pulled my shoulders back and took in a deep breath as I climbed the stone steps to the hospital entrance. The reception area was quiet as I walked through. A woman at the desk desk looked up and smiled as I walked past, but let me go without comment. The only other person in the reception area was a man with his head in his hands. Judging by the ball of bloody tissues in his hands, he'd been in some sort of fight.

The corridor to Jay's room was empty and deathly silent. The lights were dimmed, and the usual hubbub of activity was absent due to the late hour. The nurses would be up soon checking the patients and delivering breakfasts, and then there'd be visitors. I preferred the quiet. It was the calm before the storm.

Most people would have assumed my mother would head back to the castle when she realized I wasn't coming back, but most people didn't know my mother like I did. She knew me well, too, and would expect me to come and visit Jay before even thinking of going up to the castle.

Outside Jay's door, I breathed in again, ready for the tirade that I knew was coming. Holding my hand up to his door, I was about to push when I felt a tap on my shoulder. I turned to find my mother. My eyebrows shot up at about the same time that she held her finger to her lips to shush me. Taking my hand, she walked me to the room I'd been in while Jay was having his surgery. Empty cups littered the table, and a blanket rested on the sofa next to a pillow.

"What happened?" I asked, panic filling me once again. "Is it Jay? Is he all right?"

"He's perfectly fine," my mother whispered. "I couldn't exactly sleep in there with him, so the hospital administrator offered me a room and a bed. When I told her I couldn't possibly take a bed from a patient, I was offered a blanket instead. I figured you'd come back here, eventually."

"I'm sorry, I..."

She took both my hands in hers. "Don't. Just don't. I don't want to hear any more apologies. You have nothing to apologize for. I've kept you locked up for far too long, and I wouldn't expect any less of you than to go out searching for your daughter. If it weren't for the fact that your father is out looking for Fae and there's no one but me to lead the kingdom at the moment, I'd be out on flying unicorns looking for her too."

She gave me a warm smile. It was so full of love that it brought tears to my eyes.

"I didn't find her. I didn't find any trace of her."

She put her arm around my shoulder and sat me down on the sofa, pushing the blanket to one side. "I know. You wouldn't have that look on your face if you did. You look exhausted. I think it's about time we both went home and had a good night's sleep. We'll get all the maps of the kingdom out and plan a strategy of where you can go looking. I'm guessing that you'll cover a lot of ground on a flying unicorn."

"You want me to go looking... alone?"

"You're so tired that you probably didn't notice Williamson and Avery's absence outside Jay's room. They're out looking for Fae too. They are needed far more out there than in here. Jay doesn't need them, and neither do we. So yes, I expect you to go out alone and bring our girl back."

If I had any tears left to cry, I'd have been bawling, but I was cried out. The few droplets that managed to escape fell down over my cheeks.

"What about Jay's plan to send people to all the bars in Shipley and pretend to be down on their luck to capture Rumpelstiltskin?"

"I think we both know it wasn't the best of plans. We don't have any people left to send out. They already are out; they're looking for Fae."

I knew it. I was just surprised that *she* knew it. She'd been humoring Jay, just like me.

I nodded. "I went to the strangers," I said as I stood back up.

"Who?"

"The people that claimed to be my siblings. I went to see them. They practically foretold this. They knew something was going to happen."

She sighed deeply, as though she knew this was coming. "You are going to tell me that you want to go with them, aren't you?"

She didn't seem upset. Weary maybe. She folded the blanket and laid it neatly on the sofa.

"They have magic," I said. "I felt Fae when I was with them. I think she's magic too, or at least will be when she grows up."

"They spoke of magic, but you aren't magic, Eliana."

I cast my eyes down to the ground. "I've been speaking to the unicorns... actually, speaking *with* them. They understand me. I can converse with them through my mind when they're not nearby too. I've been able to do it since the day Fae was born. I thought I was going mad, but now I'm not so sure."

My mother didn't even look surprised by this announcement. Maybe she was too tired to be surprised about anything anymore. "Come on. It looks like we have a lot of talking to do, but first, we both need sleep. You can visit Jay tomorrow. I'll leave a message telling him you're home safe."

I stifled a yawn. I'd never felt so exhausted in my whole life. The nights I'd stayed up feeding and cuddling Fae were nothing compared to this. I felt it in my bones, in my soul, like I could sleep for a thousand years and it wouldn't be enough. Outside the hospital, it became apparent that all the guards had left my mother to search for Fae. Zacharina was our only way of getting home. My mother hoisted up her skirts and jumped on Zacharina's back like a pro. I followed suit, and before long, we were in the air.

Once home, I fell asleep in my clothes, not even bothering to undress for bed. Sleep came more quickly than I imagined it would, though it was filled with nightmares of Rumpelstiltskin grinning at me and snatching Fae away again and again. I woke covered in sweat, my heart beating wildly. Outside my window, a songbird announced the dawn. My eyelids were still heavy, and my body ached, but I knew that I wouldn't get a real night of sleep until I held Fae in my arms again. I dragged myself out of bed and showered quickly before heading out of my room. It was strange to walk the corridors without guards watching my every move, especially Avery and Williamson, who had been at my side day in day out for so long. The castle was eerily quiet, reminiscent of the hospital the night before. Even the staff who cleaned and fetched and carried were going about their jobs in silence.

I found my mother in the breakfast room. The strangers were with her, all seated around the table eating.

"I didn't realize you meant to leave so soon," my mother said, passing me a plate. Tears were forming at the corner of her eyes. She'd spent her life waiting for the day her daughter would be snatched away from her, and here it was, just not in the way she'd expected. Because I was going freely. "Your, er... they knocked on the palace door about ten minutes ago. The least I could do was to offer them a warm meal before they left."

"I'll come back," I said quickly. "Once I've found Fae, I'll bring her straight home."

She nodded and dabbed her eyes with a handkerchief. "I know you will. I was just talking to your... siblings..."

"Possible siblings," Castiel corrected her. "We aren't a hundred percent sure what our connection is yet."

"Possible siblings. They agree that your magic together is stronger than when you're apart. I think that's encouraging. I can't say I know much about what is going on. I never took much stock in magic. My only dabbling in it led me into hot water, shall we say, and I've steered clear of it ever since. But I'd be foolish to think that you aren't all connected to this somehow."

"That's what we're trying to find out," Azia said, throwing a buttered bagel to Nyre, who was sitting on a seat of her own rather than someone's shoulder.

Nyre tossed her head back and opened her wide jaws to catch the bagel, swallowing it whole.

"If Eliana is part of... this—" my mother waved her hand around the gathered guests "—whatever it is, I'd at least like to know what you know and what your plans are."

Azia was the one to speak first. "Our magical powers seem to be coming in at different rates, starting after we all turned eighteen. Mine was the first. After me, Blaise found her powers. They're affecting the adopted sons and daughters of the leaders in order."

"What order?"

"Alphabetical, strangely enough. Whoever named us did it in alphabetical order, so I was the first to find my abilities, and I was the first whose kingdom was affected by the bad magic."

"Bad magic?" Deon said, raising an eyebrow.

"Whatever it is. We don't know yet. Each of us has had problems come back from our past. For you, it was Rumpelstiltskin, but each of us is battling a different foe. Around the time of our births, a whole load of witches, imps, faeries, whatever, were all defeated. Peace came to the kingdoms. We happened to turn up on everyone's doorsteps a bit later. That's our only connection."

"And the golden eyes," I reminded her.

"Yes. We can guess from the pattern which kingdom will experience a magical malady next."

"Prince Fallon of Aboria," Blaise added. "He is the son of the king and queen there. His name begins with F, and the photos we've seen of him show he has eyes like ours."

"Then Princess Gaia of Badalah, I assume?" my

mother said. “I met her once. She was very young then. I can’t say I noticed her golden eyes, but then, she did have them in a book the entire visit.”

“Actually, we’re mostly going to see Fallon because we have to pass through Aboria on the way to Urbis,” Azia said. “Urbis is our final destination. I’m sure of it.”

My mother regarded the information. “And you think Fae is there?”

“I don’t know for sure, but I believe so. I think Fae was taken because Rumpelstiltskin couldn’t get Eliana, or Eliana wasn’t interesting enough to him anymore now that he could take her baby. I wish I could tell you more, but we’re piecing the whole thing together as we go. I feel that this is moving so quickly that whatever is going on will come to a head before the year is out.”

“It’s only May,” I said, feeling bile rise in my throat. “Fae is only weeks old. The end of the year is over six months away.”

“I’m sorry. I hope I’m wrong,” Azia said, lowering her eyes. “We’ve been trying to cut this magic off before it hits, which is why we can’t waste any time getting to Aboria. Maybe if we can cut it off, it won’t get as far as Urbis.”

“You don’t believe that, though, do you?” I said.

She shook her head. “I think we were born in Urbis, and I think that this whole thing had to do with our birth somehow. It’s ridiculous to think that there are twelve siblings, but...”

“Twelve?” My mother sat forward in her chair.

“There are twelve kingdoms. We’ve been researching as best we can on the road and pooling our information. Some kingdoms have presidents or other rulers, but this is what we know. If we discount the five of us here, you next have Prince Fallon in Aboria then, as you said,

Princess Gaia in Badalah. There is no prince or princess whose name begins with H as far as we can tell, but President Alice of The Forge has twin daughters. One is called Pearl, and one is called Ivy which gives us our letter I."

"Twins? How does that work if we're siblings?" I asked. "Unless Pearl was renamed at some point and originally was called Helen or Heather or something. But why would the two women drop two babies there?"

Azia shrugged. "I don't know. The leader of Oz had a number of children, but we haven't managed to find out too much about them."

"There's a princess Kelis in Enchantia. I've met her," Blaise interrupted. "We don't know if she's adopted, though. She might not know herself. I didn't know I was adopted before this all started."

"What about Skyla?" my mother asked. "It's the one kingdom you've not mentioned. Do they have someone there who fits in this?"

"No," Azia replied, batting Nyre away from her plate where she was trying to steal a jam tart. "Skyla is a weird kingdom. Half of it is comprised of islands in the sea and the other half is islands that float in the air, but there's no royal family as such."

"We aren't going to Skyla!" I said quickly, turning my eyes to Azia. "It's the opposite direction to Urbis. You said you thought Fae was in Urbis."

Azia shrugged. "Our plans aren't set in stone. We're taking everything one day at a time."

"Even so, we should be going!" Castiel huffed, throwing his napkin down on his empty plate.

"Now?" my mother asked. I saw the fear in her eyes. This was the moment she'd been dreading her entire life.

"Not yet." I wasn't trying to put off our goodbyes, but I hadn't packed. I hadn't said farewell to Jay. "I need to pack... I need to..."

"I'll ask the staff to pack you a bag," my mother said. "Judging by what the rest of you are carrying, you'll be traveling light. I'll have a servant bring it to the hospital so you can say your goodbyes to Jay. Can I offer you some assistance? I can't lend you a horse and carriage because all our horses are out with guards looking for Fae, but. I could contact the Urbis Express and ask for an airship."

"Thank you," Deon said. "Unfortunately, we need to lie low. We usually travel by night, but just outside of Shipley, we've found a route that doesn't pass through any major towns or cities. We can walk through the day when it's light and camp at night."

"Camp?" My mother slid her eyes to me. She knew that I'd not spent a night away from my own bed in my whole life.

"I can camp," I said.

"Of course you can."

She put her arm around my shoulder as the others stood up from the table. Azia, Blaise, and Deon walked out, with Castiel following behind after stuffing his bag with the leftover bagels. Nyre flew over his head and landed on Azia's shoulder.

"I have to say goodbye to someone," I told them. I can't go without seeing him."

Azia put a hand on my shoulder. "We all had someone we said goodbye to. How about you meet us at the inn in an hour?"

They left me there in the entrance hall to the castle with only my mother. The few servants that weren't out searching for Fae were nowhere to be seen. My insides were as empty as the castle. I'd never felt more bereft in my life.

"I'm sorry I'm leaving," I said, finally breaking down.

Mother pulled me into a hug. "I'm only sorry your father isn't here to say goodbye to you too."

"I hate leaving you."

"For the longest time I've kept you here. I won't do it anymore. You're a grown woman, and for that matter, so am I. I've always been so scared of losing you." She pushed a lock of hair from my face and swiped it behind my ear. "But now that you're going, I'm proud. Proud how you've turned out, proud of the daughter I brought up. Once you find Fae, I'll never try and force you to stay here with me again. I won't make you travel with guards, and I'll never ever tell you how to live your life."

I kissed her cheeks, tasting the salt from her tears.

"When I find Fae, I'll be bringing her back here. This is her home. It's my home. I hope it will always be our home."

She held me tight, almost squeezing the breath out of me.

Saying goodbye to my mother was one thing, but I knew saying goodbye to Jay was going to be infinitely harder.

Zacharina flew me to Shipley, over the heads of my maybe-siblings as they walked down the road from the castle.

Jay was sitting up in bed, eating breakfast when I entered. When he saw me, his eyes lit up, but then I saw the light flicker and die when he saw Fae wasn't with me. He put his breakfast tray to the side.

"I hoped you'd come back with her," he said plainly.

I sat on the bed next to him, careful not to knock his legs. "I hoped that too. There is still no word."

He took my hand in his. His face was a picture of anguish. He really loved that little girl, almost as much as I did.

"I have something to tell you," I began, not sure how to finish the sentence.

"About Fae?"

I stroked the back of his hand with my finger as my heart ached. He was already feeling the worst he'd ever felt, and here I was, about to add to his pain.

"Kind of. I went to see the strangers, my siblings, last night."

Jay nodded at my words.

"Their magic... my magic... I felt Fae."

He sat up straighter. "Felt her? How?"

"I don't understand it. I guess my mother will fill you in."

"Why don't you tell me now?"

"Jay... I'm leaving. I'm going with them."

I held my breath as I watched the expression on his face. It didn't crumble as expected, but there was a weariness to it, as though he had expected something like this to happen.

"Lay with me," I said when he didn't speak.

He flinched as he moved back on the bed, giving me just enough space to lie next to him.

He kissed me in such a way that brought sorrow into my very soul. I closed my eyes so I couldn't see, but I could feel the wetness of tears, taste the salt on our lips. I didn't even know who was crying. Perhaps it was both of us. As he held me close, I had a flicker of what might have been. We shouldn't be like this, squeezed onto a hospital bed, my daughter missing, with me about to leave the kingdom, my family, and the man I loved. I wasn't ready for this adventure. I wanted nothing more than to sink into Jay's arms and stay in that bed forever, blocking the whole world and all of its problems out.

But I couldn't. If it wasn't for Fae, I might have... I probably would have. But Fae was everything. My whole body ached to have her beside me. My breasts, full of milk, pained me, and beneath them, my heart was squeezed vice-like in the most pain I'd ever known.

"I have to go," I said, my voice so choked up it was barely audible. But Jay didn't need to hear my words. He knew what I was saying.

"I wish I could come with you."

I waited for him to tell me how much he hated being stuck here in the hospital while I searched for Fae without him, but Jay wasn't about to indulge in any more self-pity.

"Go and talk to Loftus before you go. He'll give you supplies. Tell him you need a weapon."

I sat up in the bed, startled. "A weapon?" I'd never had a fight in my life, much less one that involved swords or bows and arrows.

"Lia, this isn't the time to be scared. You need to protect yourself. I'm not asking you to take a full suit of armor and a sword, but you saw the others. Azia carried a sword, Castiel had a knife. Loftus will give you something, even if it's just a small knife. He'll also give you horses."

"I'll go to Loftus, but I won't be needing horses. I've been thinking about it, and I'm going to take Zacharina with me."

Jay's eyes widened. "You think she'll come? She has a baby of her own!"

"She'll come."

I knew because I'd already asked her.

"Then I'll take care of her baby while you go out and find our baby," Jay promised.

Saying goodbye to him fractured my already broken heart further. The pain was immense, but he let me go, without fuss, without complaint.

"Lia," he said as I got to the door.

"Yes."

"Come home. When this is all over, come home."

"There's nowhere in any of the kingdoms I'd rather be," I said, blowing him a final kiss as I left.

My baby girl was out there somewhere, her tiny thread of energy calling to me.

I would find her.

And I would take my daughter back.

FALLON

SON OF BEAUTY AND THE BEAST

GRAB THE NEXT BOXSET IN THE KINGDOM OF FAIRYTALES SERIES

MEET THE TEAM

The Kingdom of Fairytales Series was a team effort. Below are the people that made it possible:

EQP Management: Rhi Parkes & J.A. Armitage

Our authors: J.A. Armitage, Audrey Rich, B. Kristin McMichael, Emma Savant, Jennifer Ellision, Scarlett Kol, Rose Castro, Margo Ryerkerk, Zara Quentin, Laura Greenwood and Anne Stryker.

Our Editor
Rose Lipscomb

Our Beta Team
Nadine Peterse-Vrijhof
Diane Major
Kalli Bunch
Stephanie Woodwood

Our Proof Reader
Tina Merritt

And to all the wonderful people who loved the world we created and reviewed our stories.
Thank you

READING ORDER

SEASON ONE
SLEEPING BEAUTY
Queen of Dragons
Heiress of Embers
Throne of Fury
Goddess of Flames

SEASON TWO
LITTLE MERMAID
Queen of Mermaids
Heiress of the Sea
Throne of Change
Goddess of Water

SEASON THREE
RED RIDING HOOD
King of Wolves
Heir of the Curse
Throne of Night
God of Shifters

SEASON FOUR
RAPUNZEL
King of Devotion
Heir of Thorns
Throne of Enchantment
God of Loyalty

SEASON FIVE
RUMPELSTILTSKIN
Queen of Unicorns
Heiress of Gold
Throne of Sacrifice
Goddess of Loss

SEASON SIX
BEAUTY AND THE BEAST
King of Beasts
Heir of Beauty
Throne of Betrayal
God of Illusion

SEASON SEVEN
ALADDIN
Queen of the Sun
Heiress of Shadows
Throne of the Phoenix
Goddess of Fire

SEASON EIGHT
CINDERELLA
Queen of Song
Heiress of Melody
Throne of Symphony
Goddess of Harmony

SEASON NINE
ALICE IN WONDERLAND
Queen of Clockwork
Heiress of Delusion
Throne of Cards
Goddess of Hearts

SEASON TEN
WIZARD OF OZ
King of Traitors
Heir of Fugitives
Throne of Emeralds
God of Storms

SEASON ELEVEN
SNOW WHITE
Queen of Reflections
Heiress of Mirrors
Throne of Wands
Goddess of Magic

SEASON TWELVE
PETER PAN
Queen of Skies
Heiress of Stars
Throne of Feathers
Goddess of Air

FALLON

SON OF BEAUTY AND THE BEAST

GRAB THE NEXT BOXSET IN THE KINGDOM OF FAIRYTALES SERIES

www.ingramcontent.com/pod-product-compliance
Lightning Source LLC
Chambersburg PA
CBHW020247030826
48979CB00030B/2649/J

* 9 7 8 1 9 8 9 9 9 7 4 9 9 *